## THE AUTHOR

Edward Montague Compton [Mackenzie was born in] Hartlepool in 1883, the eld[est son of the actor] Edward Compton and the [actress Virginia] Bateman. He went on from S[t Paul's School to Magdalen] College, Oxford, graduating in History in 1904. In his twenties, like his sister Fay Compton, he went on the stage, but found his true vocation with the publication of *The Passionate Elopement* in 1908. He gained enormous popular and critical success with *Carnival* (1912) and *Sinister Street* (1913); also in 1913, he went to live in Capri, haunt of writers and artists and the scene of *Vestal Fire* (1927) and *Extraordinary Women* (1928), both published by The Hogarth Press. He was received into the Roman Catholic Church in 1914.

During the First World War, Mackenzie was a Secret Service agent in the Aegean, but afterwards returned to writing – over a hundred books on everything from cats, tobacco and Bonnie Prince Charlie, to spying, music and country houses; from panoramic novel cycles like *The Four Winds of Love* (1937-45) to farcical entertainments such as *Monarch of the Glen* (1941) and *Whisky Galore* (1947). Even in his eighties he was finishing his ten-volume autobiography *My Life and Times*.

In 1929 he co-founded the Scottish National Party, and still managed to find time to get involved in a spy trial in 1932, to become a popular broadcaster, wage constant battle with the Inland Revenue and to move his vast library from island to island to island. One of the century's most extraordinary characters, he was married three times and died in Edinburgh in 1972, aged eighty-nine.

# EXTRAORDINARY WOMEN

*Theme and Variations*

# Compton Mackenzie

*spirat adhuc amor*
*vivuntque commissi calores*
*Aeoliae fidibus puellae.*
HORACE

*New Introduction by*
*Andro Linklater*

THE HOGARTH PRESS
LONDON

Published in 1986 by
The Hogarth Press
Chatto & Windus Ltd
40 William IV Street, London WC2N 4DF

First published in the Great Britain by Martin Secker 1928
Hogarth edition offset from original British edition
Copyright Macdonald Publishers
Introduction copyright © Andro Linklater 1986

All rights reserved. No part of this publication may be reproduced, stored in a retrieval system, or transmitted in any form, or by any means, electronic, mechanical, photocopying, recording or otherwise, without the prior permission of the publishers.

British Library Cataloguing in Publication Data

Mackenzie, Compton
Extraordinary women: theme and variations
I. Title
823'.912[F]    PR6025.A2526

ISBN 0 7012 1017 6

Printed in Great Britain by
Cox & Wyman Ltd
Reading, Berkshire

# INTRODUCTION

If ever a novel required rescue from the circumstances of its publication it was *Extraordinary Women*. Its subject is the lesbian society which assembled on the island of Capri in the years after the First World War, and its theme is the absurdity and pathos of sexual desire. In 1928 the subject was sufficiently scandalous for Compton Mackenzie's publisher, Cassell's, to refuse to accept the book, and as a result it was brought out by Martin Secker in a limited edition of 2000 copies at a guinea each. Yet, having avoided the fate of Radclyffe Hall's *The Well of Loneliness*, which was published one month earlier – in August – only to be withdrawn under threat of prosecution, *Extraordinary Women* was condemned by liberal opinion for being facetious about a subject requiring sensitive and serious treatment. After almost sixty years and a revolution in sexual attitudes, the sensationalism has long since vanished, but so too should the need to write of lesbian relationships as though they demand a deliberately kid-gloved approach. In Compton Mackenzie's novel, to fall victim to sexual passion, no matter what its nature, is to become a figure of fun. It was an outlook inherent in his personality and central to the events from which *Extraordinary Women* sprang.

When Mackenzie first came to Capri with his wife Faith in the spring of 1913, he was thirty years old, the author of an immensely successful second novel, *Carnival*, and blessed with an almost indecent profusion of gifts. Men and women alike found him attractive, as much for his contagious high spirits as for his dramatically good looks. He had an eye for the ridiculous which transformed all he saw into the stuff of comedy, and his conversation glittered with stories, mimicry and jokes. His manner was theatrical as befitted one whose mother was a Bateman and father a Compton – families which occupied as many column inches in *The Playgoer's Companion* as an Elizabethan earldom in Burke's *Peerage*.

Early in 1914, after the first volume of his masterpiece, *Sinister Street*, was published, Henry James wrote to express his admiration, not only of the book but of the way he had escaped from the family tradition: 'you are so rare a case of the kind of reaction from the theatre – and from so *much* theatre – and the reaction in itself is rare – as seldom taking place . . . But your pushing straight through the door into literature and then closing it so tight behind you and putting the key in your pocket as it were, – that strikes me as unusual and brilliant!'

Yet it was not a complete escape. Almost his first memories had been of his father rehearsing the Compton Comedy Company in its staple fare of eighteenth-century comedy, and the influence of a childhood immersed in Sheridan and Goldsmith, alternating with London plays and pantomimes, can be detected in most of his comedies, not least *Extraordinary Women*. Of his writing he once declared, 'The theatre is in my blood, and I ask nothing better than to succeed as an entertainer.' It is not surprising, therefore, to find that his characters are created largely through dialogue and that the development of the story proceeds like a play through a series of scenes. He visualised these settings with great exactness, and to make the most of them he demanded of his readers 'a sense of dramatic expression'.

The influence of the theatre was not confined to his writing. 'He dramatised everything,' his friend Frank Swinnerton remarked, 'from the last person he met on the street to Compton Mackenzie.' His dress was flamboyant – he had a weakness for white suits, lemon ties and black capes – and his temperament he described as 'Protean', taking on the characteristics of his surroundings and the company he was in. To such a man Capri offered an unusually congenial background.

Among its society of cosmopolitan expatriates, self-dramatisation was an asset as valuable as any other and more practised than most. In his clifftop home of San Michele, Dr Axel Munthe wove himself an heroic past as the man who halted a cholera epidemic in Naples single-handed. In the Villa Lysis, the opium-addicted Count Adelswaerd-Fersen created the persona of a gallant French gentleman, and in Morgano's café a dozen novelists, poets and translators magnified their various works to the proportions of masterpieces. Such embroidery was admired rather than frowned upon, and if people did not supply their own legend, gossip made good the deficiency. The need to earn a living, which in other communities occupied so much time and energy, hardly existed for the foreigners on Capri – food and lodging were cheap and the incomes of most of them came from dividends, remittances and allowances. Elsewhere conversations might turn on the state of the land, of trade or of industry, but in Capri they revolved around people (followed by lavatories and the view from one's villa) and since there was so much time for talk, it was no more than thoughtfulness to marinade the raw facts of one's history in the juices of invention.

This habit was clearly of long duration, for gossip and invention had coloured the reputations of Capri's incomers at least since Suetonius composed his exotic tales of the Emperor Tiberius's perversions while staying on the island. Its reputation as a lotusland had never quite disappeared, but it received a powerful stimulus in the late-nineteenth century when German tourists discovered there a toleration of homosexuality which Bismarck no longer permitted in their own country. They were joined by refugees from similar hostility in Britain following Oscar Wilde's trial and imprisonment in 1895, and Norman Douglas, who arrived there in 1898, described them as a colony of 'lovable freaks'. In the early years of the twentieth century the island also became a refuge for political and artistic, as well as sexual, outsiders. Lenin and Gorki discussed revolution among the *rentiers* and remittance-men; Somerset Maugham and E.F. Benson shared a villa; American painters, Scandinavian writers and the intelligentsia of half a dozen countries came to live or holiday there. Among them was one of the women whose portraits appear in *Extraordinary Women*, Romaine Goddard, then a struggling art student. Although she was homosexual, she appears not to have acknowledged it at the time, and in her uncertainty went so far as to marry – a union which gave immoderate pleasure to Capri gossip because her husband was John Ellingham Brooks, a companion of Somerset Maugham, and unmistakably homosexual himself. Realising her mistake, she soon left and did not return for almost twenty years.

The first person to bring this society to wider notice was Norman Douglas, who celebrated the strange blossomings of northern sensuality beneath a Mediterranean sun in *Siren Land*, published in 1912. It was this book and some enjoyable dinners with the author which led Compton Mackenzie to choose Capri as his home after a severe attack of sciatica convinced his doctors that he should live in a warm climate. The debt was acknowledged in his dedication of *Extraordinary Women* to Douglas. From the moment that he stepped from the funicular which carried visitors from the ferry to the Piazza, the atmosphere of bright clothes and colours and lifted voices suited him. Despite the lure of parties and talk at Morgano's, he managed to write part of *Sinister Street* and all of its successor, *Guy and Pauline*, on the island, and his reputation reached its peak during the first two years that he lived there. When he left to join the Gallipoli Expeditionary Force in May 1915, the *Manchester Guardian* declared that 'the future of the English novel lies very largely in his hands', and its opinion was endorsed by the Master of the English Novel, Henry James, who described him as 'very much the greatest talent of his generation'.

He ended his service working for MI6 in Greece, and was sent home in November 1917 before being invalided out. The Capri he returned to had changed, and its pre-war atmosphere had given way to a wilder appetite for pleasure. They listened to jazz instead of ragtime, drank cocktails instead of wine, sniffed cocaine and ether rather than smoking opium, and in place of the discreet exchange of lovers among three sexes there was an open grasping for partners, with the pace set by the fourth sex.

Mackenzie was changed too. His wartime career as a secret agent had been dangerous and dramatic, and he had come home in a state of exhaustion to find that Faith had been having an affair with a boy scarcely half her age. He forbade her to see him again, and a fortnight later her lover died from pneumonia contracted while waiting to catch a glimpse of her. Their marriage continued to exist in external appearance, but it never recovered from this double blow. Although by no means a faithful husband, Mackenzie had depended deeply on his wife's love for him, and her infidelity removed a central prop of his existence. Its effect was to bring to the fore a sense of life's absurdity, which had never been entirely absent from his habit of self-dramatisation but now became a central tenet of his philosophy. In his work this outlook was a significant factor – although not the only one – in turning him from the high moral tone of four of his first five novels towards comedy. A more immediate consequence was the relief from his own troubles which he found in the dramas being played out around him.

Faith's reaction to the loss of her lover and her husband was to seek the company of other women, and in the charged months following the catastrophe she made friends with the three women who are the main characters in *Extraordinary Women* – Renata Borgatti (here portrayed as Cleo Gazay), Mimi Franchetti (Rosalba Donsante) and Romaine Brooks (Olimpia Leigh). Herself a pianist of considerable ability, she recognised in the piano concerts which Renata gave during and after the war an exceptional talent and a powerful technique. Mimi's attraction was simply that of a light-hearted amoral hedonist, and Faith invited her as she had invited Renata to dinner and musical evenings in Casa Solitaria, the Mackenzies' cliffside house in Capri. Romaine's was a more powerful personality than either of the others. She was in her forties when she returned to Capri in 1918, for the first time since her ill-advised marriage to John Brooks. In the intervening years, she had discovered her true nature, established a reputation as a painter and inherited a fortune from a Pennsylvania coal mine. Self-assured and self-sufficient, she was, in Faith's words, 'a woman complete in herself, isolated mentally and psychically from the rest of her kind, independent in her judgement, accepting or rejecting as she pleased movements, ideas and people.'

Warm-hearted and unprejudiced, Faith enjoyed the company of homosexuals of both sexes – she was, for example, Norman Douglas's favourite woman companion, and the loyalist of John Brooks's friends – and her husband was in consequence given a privileged position from which to view the seductions, liaisons, conspiracies and betrayals of the lesbians who came to Capri between 1918 and 1920. Like all Capri's games of sexual snakes and ladders, they became the stuff of gossip, a reality to be pointed up so that absurdity stood out sufficiently to amuse a dinner-table.

This attitude is the starting-point of *Extraordinary Women* and it accounts for much of the irritation which the book caused amongst those expecting a serious story of female homosexuality. More recently some feminist critics have detected a note of masculine superiority in the mockery, but the novel is even-handed in its approach. Heterosexuals and male homosexuals fare no better than lesbians – all are figures caught up in the comedy of sexual desire – and in treating the sexes alike, *Extraordinary Women* adopts the attitude that lesbian relationships are normal, or at least no less bizarre than those of other sexes. Mackenzie's outlook was almost precisely that of Madame Anastasia Sarbécoff, the one character whom he treats with consistent sympathy: 'She had achieved that perfect tolerance which the unsophisticated enthusiasts of a democratic civilization call cynicism. She had in fact a sense of humour which compelled her to admit that she and all the world were equally ridiculous. This made her love the world, and she hoped it made the world love her.'

With the exception of Rory Freemantle, the characters and events in *Extraordinary Women* are all based upon real people and actual incidents. 'In two books – *Vestal Fire* and *Extraordinary Women* – I painted portraits of one after another of the Capri characters I knew,' he wrote in his autobiography, 'and almost without exception they looked and behaved exactly as I made them look and behave.' Among them is an outsider; although Radclyffe Hall did not come to Capri at the time, Mackenzie probably could not resist introducing her in spirit at least. Even an absurd occurrence, such as the burglary of Rory Freemantle's villa, is based upon a real burglary of Casa Solitaria. Other than some jewellery, only a cheese and a bottle of absinthe – gifts from Mimi Franchetti to Faith – were missing, but the thief had also turned a framed photograph of Faith upside down and, although nothing could be proved, the general assumption was that Renata Borgatti had committed the crime out of jealousy, fancying that Faith's friendship with Mimi was an affair. In the book the upside-down photograph becomes an upside-down chamber-pot and Rory finds her portrait decorated with horns, but it is a matter of exaggeration rather than invention.

Although incidents such as this lean towards farce, the general pattern of the comedy belongs to a different genre – the harlequinade – that highly stylized clowning which formed part of the nineteenth-century pantomime on which Mackenzie was raised. There were many ingredients, but they always included the innocent love of Pierrot and Pierrette, the touching passion of Columbine for the heartless, mischievous Harlequin, and the clod-hopping Policeman's efforts to control the knockabout anarchy of Clown and Pantaloon. *Theme and Variations* was the sub-title Mackenzie gave to his novel, and the theme of the harlequinade recurs throughout, from the opening pages in which the Pierrette figure of Lulu de Randan is pursued by her governess vainly trying to prevent an assignation with her Pierrot, the handsome Carmine.

The promiscuous, high-spirited Rosalba is Harlequin, and her Columbine is the grotesque, square-chinned, monocle-wearing, one-time boxing promoter, Rory Freemantle, who despite her masculine name and attributes is female. These two roles remain constant, but others change for, as ever in love, a Pierrette can become a Pantaloon at the slip of a banana skin.

There is no pretence of realism, and to underline the point, Mackenzie returned to an eighteenth-century technique he had employed in his first book, *The Passionate Elopement*, of introducing the author's voice to comment on the action of the characters. Thus of Rosalba Donsante, he observes, 'It seems absurd after the way she had been behaving in the last chapter to find the headwaiter of the Hotel Augusto bursting his braces in the pleasure that her arrival gives him. One feels that he ought to know better . . . Our own varicose veins throb with indignation at the homage she receives because we know that her beauty is only skin-deep.'

It is Rory Freemantle's misfortune to fall in love with this will o' the wisp, and the central strand of the novel is her unceasing attempt to transform the dancing light of Rosalba's sex appeal to the glow of domesticity. The arrival of Olimpia Leigh, a composer with the reputation of a modern Sappho, brings on to the stage a powerful wizard-like figure who is immune to Rosalba's blandishments. Olimpia is an apostle of homosexuality as evolution's answer to the heterosexual licence of post-war society. Culled from Mackenzie's extensive, if slightly confused, reading of Jung and Freud, this philosophy is the nearest that the novel comes to seriousness, and it rests a little heavily amidst the polished comedy. Nevertheless, it serves to convey the weight of Olimpia's personality since she is, with the possible exception of Madame Sarbécoff, the only person who is able to rise above the human comedy and to understand that behind it lies another reality.

By the time he came to write *Extraordinary Women*, Mackenzie's star had fallen from the high position assigned it by Henry James. Forced by financial troubles to write at high speed a steady stream of novels, reviews and journalism, he produced work which was often uneven, both in quality and subject matter, until his return to *Sinister Street*'s Olympian scale with *The Four Winds of Love*, begun in 1935. All this goes some way to explain the critical exasperation which his work provoked. But something more is needed to account for the hostility aroused by his two novels about Capri – *Vestal Fire* (1927) and *Extraordinary Women* (1928). Both are stylish, mannered and as immensely entertaining as eighteenth-century comedy, yet each in turn was shot out of the water by the two most influential London critics of the day, Cyril Connolly and Raymond Mortimer. The former damned *Vestal Fire* as 'a witty and unpleasant chronicle of clique life', and on the appearance of *Extraordinary Women*, Raymond Mortimer declared, 'Mr Mackenzie is undoubtedly neither uneducated nor inexperienced. Having had the enterprise to deal with a subject unexplored by English novelists he might have produced an interesting book. But all I can see in *Extraordinary Women* is an expression of male pique and wounded vanity.'

To have missed the point so completely is explicable not as the reaction to a single novel but as the dislike of that entire body of pre-war literature in which Mackenzie had held such a prominent position. He stood for a style which was the antithesis of the plain, journalistic prose espoused by post-war critics. Indeed, Mortimer had already satirised the luxuriant language of *Sinister Street*, and in *The Enemies of Promise* it was a passage from *The Passionate Elopement* which Connolly picked out to illustrate his dislike of the old Mandarin style. Caught up in this campaign, the virtues of *Extraordinary Women* – its stylized structure and polished humour – became vices to be condemned, and unjust though it was, the critical reputation of its author sank still further.

Despite his later work and the affection in which he was held in old age, Mackenzie's standing never fully recovered. Yet he was never less than a superb craftsman. His ear for dialogue was exact and his creation of setting extremely precise. To a sympathetic reader, prepared to catch the clues he offers, the humour has a teasing delicacy which is addictive.

Today it is journalistic prose which is synonymous with cliché and careless language. *Extraordinary Women*, by contrast, has improved with age. Once the misconceptions aroused by its subject matter and by literary fashion have been stripped away, its merits are plain. It is a well-made and witty book, preaching no moral and offering no profound insights into the human condition other than the single truth, that love makes fools of us all.

*Andro Linklater, Ullapool 1985*

*My dear Norman Douglas :*

*Your delightful commentary on the birds and beasts of the Greek Anthology took no account of the peculiar Æolian fauna whose life I have ventured to observe in this book. Nor can I recall that you, the most erudite of living Sirenians, have ever turned your naturalist's eye to study the migration of these Ægean creatures into Tyrrhenian waters. So I offer you this little treatise on what can hardly without a smile be called natural history as a kind of footnote to your own enchanting volumes; for it was you who sent me to Sirene by the magic of your conversation so dearly enjoyed among the fogs of London fifteen years ago.*

*Why we are not both there now I cannot think; but under a vine-wreathed bower conjured by fancy I drink to our long friendship in the wine of the country.*

*Yours ever,*
*Compton Mackenzie.*

*Isle of Jethou,*
*November 3, 1927.*

## CHAPTER ONE

Γλύκηα μᾶτερ, οὔ τοι δύναμαι κρέκην τὸν 'ίστον
πόθῳ δάμεισα παῖδος βραδίνῳ δι' 'Αφροδίταν.
SAPPHO.

*I really cannot be sewing, dear mother; Aphrodite has overwhelmed me with desire for a slim youth.*

ABOUT four o'clock of an exquisite April afternoon little Miss Chimbley emerged from an aromatic tangle of lentisk and rosemary upon a stretch of level green (cleared by the local baker to provide his ovens with fuel) half way up one of the foothills that lead on to the great amphitheatre of limestone heights towering behind Stabia in the Bay of Naples. She sat down in the fresh grass plumed with rosy orchises and tried to recover her breath after the ascent. Her puffing mingled with the murmur of the placid sea far below, with the etherealized shrieks of children at play in the white-roofed town, with the bourdon of the wild bees at their honeying, and the flute of a mountain-thrush flashing up to greet the outflung shadows of the highest crags. At last with an effort Miss Chimbley picked herself up and, turning toward the bosky slopes beyond, she quavered:

" Are you there, Lulu ? "

Her tremulous voice was too faint to provoke even the mockery of an echo. A silence made up of the myriad infinitely minute sounds of nature was the only response. Miss Chimbley expended in a long sigh the small amount of breath she had recovered. For ten years now, ever since she came as governess to Lulu de Randan, then a child of six, she had had to hurry after her charge. In early days the rush had usually been to prevent her falling over the cliff that bounded the garden of the Villa Castalia. Even then it had never been too easy to catch Lulu, and with every year that passed it had grown more difficult. How many times she had turned a corner in Stabia to find Lulu vanished, how many times she had breathlessly appealed to one of the loiterers in the Piazza for news of her! The Contessina had passed this way a minute ago or that way a minute ago, but by whatever way she had passed it had always been a minute ago, and whenever at last she had found her it had always been in the company of boys. Common boys, too. And what had often been so painful was the way they had called after Lulu when she was being led off, not only that but the way Lulu had looked back over her shoulder and called after them. In dialect, too, of which her governess had not understood a word. It might have been *any*thing. It probably had been. And now here was Lulu at sixteen hurrying away from her faster than ever, turning corners with incredible rapidity, quite three corners for her one.

This afternoon they had set off along the orange-scented alleys of Stabia for a walk, which as usual had developed into a chase. Lulu must have taken this direction. She had caught a last glimpse of her striding up the paved zigzag through the olive groves that ended in the woodman's track up which she had been toiling. And this track was rather steeper and a little farther than she cared to walk nowadays, even at the slowest pace. Should she be neglecting her duty if she sat down again and read the casualty list in the *Weekly Times* which Mrs Benson still sent her from England? So kind of Mrs. Benson. For ten years without missing a single week, though Celia, her pupil, was married now. People *were* very kind. Lulu had not the slightest intention of being unkind when she hurried on ahead like this. It was only youthful thoughtlessness. The little governess eyed the newspaper that a grateful mother still sent her. The casualty lists! Ever since somebody had told Miss Chimbley that her name must be a corruption of Cholmondely she had felt herself a more important unit of the British Empire. A romantic Vere de Vere emotion warmed her fading womanhood. Miss Chimbley's pride was Norman when in the casualties of some famous regiment she read the name of a dead or wounded officer who might be considered a very remote kinsman of her own. *Cassis tutissima virtus.* How nice to have such a family motto! *Virtue is the safest helmet.* She had never been false to that sentiment. Chimbley or Cholmondely, as the little governess led her company over the top, she was, the deplorable externals of modern life momentarily thrust on one side, as brave and as pure as Joan of Arc . . . The casualty lists? Miss Chimbley overcame the temptation to feed her pride and regretfully rolled up the *Weekly Times.*

" Lulu," she quavered once more. " Are you there ? "

A green-flushed lizard sitting with upreared head and palpitating throat upon a boulder of limestone was the only being that paid the least attention to her feeble tremolo.

"Oh well, it must be excelsior, I suppose," Miss Chimbley murmured courageously. She planted her coffee-coloured *en-tout-cas* like an alpenstock before her in the narrow track winding up through the odorous thickets of the hillside, and pressed on in the hope of overtaking that errant pupil.

Now, Lulu had miscalculated Miss Chimbley's ability to climb even so high as the grassy clearing on the plateau below. She had made a tryst with Carmine Bruno, the youngest son of the local chemist, whom she loved with all the desperation of sixteen. While her governess was drawing nearer, Lulu was sitting beneath the sun-spangled bough of an Aleppo pine, locked in Carmine's arms.

"*Dimmi, Lulu,*" breathed the youth, who was like two or three million others in Italy, but not less attractive for that. "*Mi vuoi bene?*"

"*Ti voglio bene assai,*" Lulu responded fervidly and, as once more their lips met, she tied her two pigtails of golden-brown round his sunburnt neck and clasped him to her more closely.

"*Ah, Lulu,*" he murmured, "*sei bella come . . . io non so . . . .*" He broke off to rack imagination for a simile worthy of his sweetheart. "*Sei bella . . .*" his eyes lighted with poetic fire . . . "*Sei bella come una bellissima bambola.*"

"Darling," Lulu breathed, quite as well pleased to

be called a beautiful doll by her Carmine as the angel of his heart.

"*Mi piace,*" the boy said pensively, "*quando tu mi chiami 'darlink'. Non so . . . è carino. Darlink,*" he repeated with relish, and we must turn his Italian into English. "Strange that people like the English who do not know how to make love and who are in every way antipathetic should have a word as pretty as darlink."

"All the English are not antipathetic," Lulu told him. "Miss is very sympathetic."

"But ugly enough," he objected. "She is truly a horror."

And at that moment between a myrtle and a myrtle Miss Chimbley appeared. Carmine, whose Latin appreciation of obvious beauty had been much tried by the homely little governess, was overlong in disengaging his own sunburnt beauty from Lulu's plaits; and though he fled as fast as he could he was not fast enough to escape being recognized as a son of the chemist, in spite of Miss Chimbley's moral and physical distress.

"Oh, Lulu dear," she quavered in dismay. "He had his arms right round you."

The girl's lovely face was on fire with what Miss, who was a great deal more innocent than her pupil, hoped might be the roses of shame.

"What will the Countess say?" she wailed.

"You're not going to tell Mamma?"

"But, Lulu, what else can I do?" she asked trembling. "And oh dear, please dust your frock.

It's covered with twigs and grass, and there's a small pine-cone in your hair. Anybody might think that you'd been lying down."

"You're not going to tell Mamma?" Lulu pressed.

"But, Lulu, I must. I should be as guilty as you if I held my tongue about *this*."

"One must fall madly in love some time," Lulu declared in a matter of fact voice, looking down to see if the bows of her two plaits were once again tied in a perfect match.

"Not necessarily madly in love ever, Lulu," the governess gently corrected. "In love, yes, when you get married. That's as it should be. But there can be no question of marriage at present."

"Why not?"

"Why not?" Miss gasped. "Why, because you aren't big enough yet, for one thing."

"Not big enough?" Lulu repeated. "Thank you, I don't want to grow any bigger."

Indeed she was already twice as big as her little governess, and she seemed standing there like one of those large and expensive china dolls who stare down from wide open blue eyes at some shiny-faced Dutch doll beside them in the toyshop window. Not that there was any of the lifelessness of a doll about Lulu.

Miss Chimbley substituted age for size.

"Quite old enough," Lulu retorted firmly, as smiling to herself she pulled the pine-cone out of her hair.

They argued all the way back to the Villa Castalia about the necessity of telling the Countess. But Miss was adamant, if such an epithet may be applied to that tremulous little woman. It was the notion of being made love to by a chemist's son which gave her the courage to withstand her beloved Lulu's appeals. It was not so much the moral as the social impropriety which steeled her heart to a benevolent cruelty.

What between the climb up and the slither down, the shock of Lulu's behaviour and the loss of the *Weekly Times*, which had dropped from her nerveless hands into a myrtle bush at the sight of Lulu's lips pressed to Carmine's, Miss Chimbley was physically and emotionally blurred when she left her pupil to study the second volume of Macaulay's *History of England* as a punishment and tottered nervously along the wide path between red and yellow tulips toward the columned terrace at the cliff's edge where Madame de Randan was talking intimately to her friend Madame Sarbécoff.

Hermina de Randan was the daughter of a wealthy Polish nobleman, who in the excitement of her first season in Paris had married a Frenchman of equally ancient but less wealthy family. When Lulu was four years old, her mother was compelled to quit France in order to avoid meeting her husband's mistresses at dinner, which owing to the Count's dislike of committing adultery beneath him had become nearly impossible. She bought the Villa Castalia in the bay of Naples; and a year or two later the Count died, leaving her a rich widow. True, the wealth was her own, since all she inherited from her husband was freedom from the strain of having to pay his gambling debts. Yet that was a not inconsiderable legacy, to which many people would have added the rosaceous beauty of their daughter, for in Lulu's extravagant dolliness no trace as yet was superficially apparent of her mother's finely cut profile, the slight hardness of which was accentuated by her dark complexion and sharp arrogant eyes. Nevertheless, a sculptor habituated to seeing through the flesh to the bone behind might have prophesied that Lulu would ultimately add the fineness of her mother's profile to her father's colouring, that she would indeed reverse the way of roses and grow from the full bloom to the slim creamy bud.

Madame de Randan had long ago decided that the behaviour of her husband entitled her to display openly the animosity and scorn she had always felt for the male. The mere contour of a man affected her mind as unpleasantly as the contour of a mountain affected the old Roman mind. She was convinced that no Phaon would ever trouble her dreams, and she looked back at her marriage as one looks back at a painful little operation of youth, like slitting the tear-duct. Madame de Randan was accustomed to speak of herself as an exile from the world ; but in spite of the implication life had moved pleasantly by at the Villa Castalia during these twelve years. The gold of the sun and the gold of the earth in abundance ; emotional friendships that could at any moment be turned into dramas on which the leading character was able to ring down the curtain at her own caprice ; hobbies like spiritualism and gardening and collecting old furniture—all these led the Countess to wonder how it was that other people so often made a muddle of existence. Even her hobbies sometimes provided more than idle diversion; as when the trumpets and tambourines of Eudoxia, the Greek medium, had to be rescued from the aspersions of male investigators, or Mrs Rabjohn's ectoplasm defended against attempted man-handling by the Society of Psychical Research. To be sure, the war for the first few months had interfered a little financially with the amenity of the villa's life; but too much of the Countess's money was invested in France to make her unduly anxious, and should the worst happen to Poland she should not be greatly incommoded.

Her friend Anastasia Sarbécoff was less happily situated, for what little was left of her property as the widow of a Russian diplomat had been swallowed up in the Revolution. Though her future loomed dark, Madame Sarbécoff did not allow the prospect to vex her debonair spirit. She stepped out as dauntlessly toward an old age of penury as the French nobility stepped forward to the guillotine. Not once since she had been staying with her greatly loved Hermina had she alluded to her own outlook, for it would have seemed to Madame Sarbécoff ill-bred and inconsiderate to cloud even for a moment by a suggestion of her own malaise the atmosphere of well-being that imparadised the Villa Castalia. Had her friend ever alluded to that obscure prospect, Madame Sarbécoff would have made light of it; but, although Madame de Randan had no words to express the depth of her distress over poor Anastasia's past, she said not a word abour her future. To have been a rich man's wife at fifteen seemed to Madame de Randan a much greater calamity than to be a penurious widow at forty, and in any case experience had taught her never to commit herself far ahead. Madame Sarbécoff, who had the exquisite tact of Mozart's music and who was as much as Mozart one of the fine flowers of a now derided world, always took the trouble to gratify Hermina by shuddering over that premature sacrifice of hers to man. There were plenty of people to call Madame Sarbécoff insincere. So often is an April day; but an hour of April may be worth all August's honesty. It must not be supposed that Madame Sarbécoff at this date appeared upon the verge of a decline. She still had a little jewellery; and her manners were so naturally courteous that none of the servants at the Villa Castalia ever dreamed of ascribing such courtesy to any diffidence about her position. "*Una buonissima signora*," they all agreed, and they were glad to see her walking up and down the alleys of the Castalia garden, where her presence seemed as appropriate as the motion of a swan upon the placid surface of a lake.

Madame Sarbécoff, whatever might have been her experience of matrimony, was not the enemy of men her hostess was. If they did not greatly trouble her passions any longer, they were by no means displeasing to her intelligence. She lacked any missionary zeal. She would have considered the red cross of the crusader and the blue ribbon of the teetotaller equally blatant. She had no desire to impose her own opinions;

and she found it easy to agree with the various opinions of other people, because to her they all seemed so deliciously futile. She had achieved that perfect tolerance which the unsophisticated enthusiasts of a democratic civilization call cynicism. She had in fact a sense of humour, which compelled her to admit that she and the world were equally ridiculous. This made her love the world, and she hoped it made the world love her, for Madame Sarbécoff had grasped another truth taught her by humour, which was that love was no more and no less than a recognition of a vitality outside oneself. Thus, her goodwill was rooted in humanity and her laughter rose from the heart. Madame de Randan on the other hand was so deficient in humour herself that she supposed her friend's humour was the expression of a deep inward seriousness.

"Anastasia is the only friend on whose sympathy I can always depend," she would often declare. "She is perhaps the only being who really understands me." Which was perfectly true.

Not that Madame Sarbécoff refused to allow herself illusions. She was at one with her crony the world in many a pastime of the fancy. She always liked to believe that other people were in love. She would have found a passion for a lobster credible rather than believe that a human being was passionless. And perhaps her own apparent freedom from any desire for man was due to a fear of shattering this illusion of other people in love. She was at once too wise and too sentimental to take the risk; but she was also too much of a voluptuary to remain entirely cold. So to herself she permitted sensation, but not emotion. To others she permitted anything. The real link with Hermina was that she too esteemed sensation above emotion, though in her case it was not a conscious choice. Madame de Randan, indeed, had no idea that there was any difference between the two.

When Miss Chimbley divulged the dreadful pastoral of which she had been a witness that afternoon, Madame Sarbécoff had to summon all her tact to appear suitably horrified.

"Oh dear, I am so sorry to hear of that, Miss," she sighed.

And though her red lips were pursed in sympathy, her big bright blue eyes were dancing like the obstinate flame of a lamp that refuses to be puffed out.

"I cannot understand how you allowed yourself to let her out of your sight, Miss," said the Countess, fixing Miss Chimbley with a cold monocle.

"He is such a handsome fellow," Madame Sarbécoff murmured. "I have seen him in his father's shop. I am sure he is very much in love with Lulu. It is terrible—terrible!" she added in a hasty effort to look as much dismayed as poor quavering little Miss Chimbley.

"I hope you have already punished her very severely," the Countess went on.

"I've set her to read Macaulay's *History of England*," Miss Chimbley answered like a pitiful executioner.

Madame Sarbécoff shuddered.

"Poor child! I am so sorry for her. She must be suffering so much."

"I'm quite sure she didn't realize what she was doing, Countess," Miss Chimbley said more hopefully, for the impression made on Madame Sarbécoff by her choice of a punishment for Lulu encouraged the little governess to suppose that at last she had her pupil well in hand.

"*Ah, par exemple,*" the Countess exclaimed, "that is not very consoling, for it is certain that the young man understands very well what he is doing. It would not be a pretty thing to find myself a grandmother."

"She was not out of my sight ten minutes," Miss Chimbley gulped through a surging blush.

The Countess shook her head.

"It is long enough," she decided.

"Youth is so beautiful," Madame Sarbécoff sighed to the golden afternoon. "*Comme j'adore la jeunesse!*"

"What must I do with Lulu?" her mother demanded. "April is not a month in which to take such bad risks."

"Perhaps if you spoke to her yourself," Miss Chimbley suggested. "I'm sure she'd promise never to do such a thing again."

"Oh yes, I am also sure that she would promise anything," the Countess agreed. "*Les paroles sont femelles, mais les faits sont mâles.*" And then, feeling perhaps that the proverb reflected upon femininity, she added illogically, "Lulu is as weak as her father."

"Perhaps if you forbade her to walk up hill . . ." Miss began.

"Ah yes, it is so tiring to walk up hill," Madame Sarbécoff agreed. "She would be almost so sure to repose herself at the first occasion. Poor child, I am so sorry for her, and I find your sympathy so charming, Miss."

The little governess flushed with pleasure.

" Miss has been too much sympathizing with Lulu," said the mother. " If she was whipping her sometimes it would be much better."

" Oh, Countess ! " the little governess gasped, a gladiatorial vision dimming her eyes.

" Well, something must be done," the Countess insisted.

" You are always so right, Hermina. Indeed I find something must be done," Madame Sarbécoff agreed.

" Yes, it must," Miss Chimbley quavered. " It really must."

And at this moment as if to invite an immediate solution of the problem the culprit herself appeared upon the scene.

" Lulu," said her governess reproachfully, " I told you to read your history."

" I know. I did read it."

" But I told you to read till I came back."

" I know. But you didn't come back." Lulu turned to her mother. " Mamma, I want some money."

" I gave you money yesterday."

" I know. I spent it."

" Why are you wanting more money ? "

" There's a new hat at Barbato's."

" Lulu, you shall not have a new hat," said her mother fretfully. " I have heard all the abominable story of your behaviour. *C'est navrant !* "

"Well, I want to marry Carmine."

"Lulu, I think you are entirely mad," the Countess replied angrily. "First you ask me for a new hat, and when I say 'no' you tell me you wish to marry, as if hats and husbands were the same. Your behaviour is quite atrocious."

"Yes, but it wouldn't be if I was married, Mamma."

"But you cannot marry the son of a pharmacist. Do not talk so ridiculously."

"But I love him, Mamma."

"*Ah non, tu es méchante, Lulu.* Make me the kindness not to talk like an imbecile. It does not flatter me as a mother, I must tell you."

"Carmine is the only man I have ever loved and he is the only man I ever shall love," Lulu continued firmly.

"I am quite revolted to hear you talk like this in front of Madame Sarbécoff. *C'est honteux!*"

"Well, Madame Sarbécoff was married when she was younger than I am. So, she can't be so very much disgusted," Lulu insisted.

"I will not listen to these insignificant arguments, Lulu. Your behaviour is abominable. If I were sure that the Germans would not be there presently, I would send you to Paris. You are impossible any longer in Stabia. To-day it is the son of a pharmacist. To-morrow it is perhaps the son of a butcher."

"I have told you I would never love anybody else, so you needn't worry yourself about to-morrow, Mamma."

"*Écoute*, Lulu. I will not permit that you speak like a vulgar *cocotte*."

"Oh, I say, don't exaggerate too much, Mamma!"

"I do not exaggerate. It is you who exaggerate when you say you are in love with the son of a pharmacist."

"I *am* in love with him."

"You cannot be in love with anybody who is underneath you."

"Well, may I have that hat before I forget about it?"

"You may have nothing at all. You are a very naughty girl, and you may have nothing. Now go away, please, and do your lessons with Miss, for I cannot at all endure you."

Madame de Randan spent the rest of that day and most of the next one in bewailing the number of places to which she could not banish Lulu on account of the war.

"*C'est affreux!*" she avowed to Madame Sarbécoff.

It would not be fair to say that the Countess had never realized until this domestic crisis that a stupendous war had been in progress for nearly four years; but the catastrophe had certainly never touched her so inconveniently as now, and she became more bitter than ever against the male sex.

"And this detestable boy is so young, my dear friend," the Countess lamented, "that there is no chance of the horrid little creature being called to fight till next year, when of course the war will come to an end just when it might have been so useful. If I could get a German governess for Lulu instead of Miss! But no, it is not possible at such a moment."

Lulu firmly refused to ignore the existence of the chemist's son, and after she had escaped on three successive afternoons from her governess—the third time for two whole hours whilst Miss was running about the Piazza like a lost Yorkshire terrier—her mother gave orders that she was not to go outside the gates of the Villa Castalia.

"And you must occupy her mind, Miss," said the Countess. "Her studies must be more profound. For example it would be admirable if she were to begin the philosophy of Bergson."

"Ah yes, Hermina," Madame Sarbécoff applauded. "I find Bergson so charming. He has such wonderful ideas, and they are so beautifully expressed. You will be quite enchanted by Bergson, Miss. There is nothing so delicious as to fall asleep over a volume of Bergson. One wakes so refreshed. It is like sleeping in mountain air."

So Lulu and Miss studied Bergson together, and Lulu certainly did fall asleep over him; but whether it was the effect of the philosopher's thought or the effect of climbing out of her bedroom window every night and wandering through the orange-scented moonlight with Carmine is not so certain.

If the servants at the Villa Castalia were aware of the Contessina's escapades, none of them betrayed her; and if Carmine himself had not taken to falling asleep over his father's pestle Lulu might have contrived to spend white nights for the rest of that spring and summer. But he did; and the old chemist went into the question of his youngest son's leisure. He soon found out what Carmine was about and, being a strong Radical, a despiser of rank, and the only trustworthy chemist in Stabia, he wrote and invited the Countess to take steps to prevent her daughter's leading his son astray.

The fancy of Lulu's moonlit pastoral was so exquisite to Madame Sarbécoff that she had acute difficulty in stifling her enthusiasm with sighs.

"Oh, it is dreadful! It is dreadful! But I think they must be very much in love, and Lulu is so beautiful. She must appear so sweet in the moonlight. I am only so sorry for *you*, my dear."

"What must I do, Anastasia? I receive an atrocious letter from this abominable pharmacist. What must I do? Lulu must in future sleep with Miss; that is evident. And I will certainly buy no more aspirin from this detestable Bruno. '*Vostra figlia*,' he calls Lulu. I have never suffered such insolence."

Madame de Randan was sitting on the columned terrace at the cliff's edge, and suddenly she pointed to where fifteen miles across the milky sea the island of Sirene pale as a great chalcedony dreamed in the morning haze. "I shall send Lulu and Miss to Sirene for the whole summer," she proclaimed.

"What a wonnderful idea, Hermina," her friend agreed. "You are always so brilliant. At moments when everything appears so dark you have such a genius for lighting it up. You are so profound, my dear."

"I suppose that in spite of everything I am always a mother," the Countess allowed herself to admit.

"I would never have thought of such a wonnderful idea myself," Madame Sarbécoff went on. "And I'm sure that is because I have never been a mother."

The amount of maternal wisdom one would have attributed to Madame de Randan's choice of a place of exile for her daughter might have depended on one's point of view about Sirene. Its reputation as a decomposer of character was classic. However, there was this to be said in its favour—Lulu received the proposal with an agreeable equanimity. She was of course extremely distressed at the prospect of being separated from Carmine; but her distress was mitigated by the memory of Sirene's rugged contours. There was hardly half a mile of level road on the whole island; and she looked forward with some excitement to several months of being always at least an hour ahead of Miss. Then the pleasure of staying in a big hotel like the Augusto where there might be dancing every night was not to be scoffed at. It was, looked at from every point of view, the nearest approach to perfect freedom that she had yet known.

"My dear, how beautiful you are to-day!" Madame Sarbécoff exclaimed. "Your eyes are shining. I have never seen you so beautiful."

Lulu bent her head and blushed. She could hold her own against the most adverse criticism with the aplomb of a woman of thirty; but a compliment always turned her back into a girl with two long plaits of golden-brown hair.

The parting with Carmine was full of the warm South. The Countess would have packed her daughter off without allowing a word of farewell; but Madame Sarbécoff pleaded for the parting as a child might plead to finish a book, and finally Lulu was allowed to say good-bye to Carmine on condition that Miss was present. So she was as the crow flies; but her restraining influence as a chaperone was spoilt by the disappearance of Lulu and Carmine into the middle of a dense carob-tree in the leafy privacy of which they could be as oblivious of Miss below as a couple of caterpillars.

Carmine played up passionately to the occasion. He vowed that life without his Lulu would be intolerable, and the varieties of suicide he threatened, which varied from leaping headlong into the crater of Vesuvius to hurling himself single-handed against the Austrian hordes, thrilled Lulu's young heart. There was too his jealousy of a thousand potential rivals in Sirene, which enabled him to threaten assassination before he made away with himself. If Lulu had not had to hold on to the branch of the tree, she might have hugged him to death in the ecstasy of her appreciation.

"*L' amore è la morte*," cried Carmine, unaware that the poignant assonance had probably been noticed as long ago as the reign of Romulus. "No sooner will you be gone than I shall inevitably die. It is destiny."

"*Ah no, caro!*"

"*Ah sì, mia Lulu! Parola d' onore!*"

"I will write to you every day. I will tell you everything I do," she vowed.

"Not to my father's house," he interposed. "You

can write to me at the Albergo Pollio. Address the envelope to Federigo Stingo. He is the waiter there, and he is my greatest friend. But remember," he added fiercely. " If you miss one day, you will write to a corpse."

Lulu shuddered ecstatically.

" *Sei un amore !* " she breathed.

" *Sono pazzo di te*," he vowed. " *Anima mia !* "

" *Ed io sono pazza di te. Baciami in bocca.*"

"Are you there, Lulu?" Miss quavered from earth as up there among the leaves their lips met.

## CHAPTER TWO

Ἄστερες μὲν ἀμφὶ κάλαν σελάνναν
ἂψ ἀπυκρύπτοισι φάεννον εἶδος.
SAPPHO.

*The lovely moon dims the brightness of stars round about her.*

IT is recorded by one of the Roman historians that, when the Deified Augustus set foot for the first time on the island of Sirene, a withered ilex came abruptly to life and put out new leaves in token of a civic welcome. The Emperor, touched by the flattery of this politic tree, immediately took steps to make Sirene his own property by exchanging for it his own island of Nepenthe with the city of Neapolis; but revivification since that first imperial visit has been more conspicuous among the visiting fauna than the native flora, and it was never more conspicuous than in the old age of the Emperor's successor.

We need not look beyond the sublime extravagance of the natural scene to account for the quickened pulses of Sirenians. When sun and moon enter into an alliance with earth and sky and sea to put mortals beside themselves, it is surely unnecessary to attribute the exciting quality of the air to rich deposits of radium. The many ordinary people of divers nationalities who let themselves go on that air as they might let themselves go on champagne were the wisest. *Aria di Sirene* does not demand artistic expression. The poets who tried to mix it with their own afflatus were not so wise. The painters who sat under large umbrellas and tried to mix it with their colours were positively foolish. Nokes might outdare Stokes in azure feats; but just as rocks in the neighbourhood of the most famous belvederes were dabbled with blobs of wasted cobalt and ultramarine, so, alas, were the canvases and more wastefully, because while the blue on the rocks did not spoil the view the blue on the canvases did.

In the April when Lulu de Randan arrived with her little governess to cure herself of a precocious attachment, Sirene lay under a heavy mental cloud cast by the war, and it happened that on the day she landed there was also a cloud of *scirocco*, which was sitting upon the island like a great grey goose. The customs officials dressed as Tyrolese sportsmen declared everything they touched to be contraband. Beccafico the *guardia* sweated vinously. The harbourmaster pricked by red-hot needles blasphemed. The boatmen that rowed the passengers ashore and the weather-beaten caryatides that heaped the luggage upon their heads swore angrily and corrugated their faces with mutual defiance and contempt. The military force protecting the island against German invasion consigned the southern half of Italy to hell (a pleonasm on such a day) and sighed for the raw fogs of Torino, the icy river blasts of Firenze, the infernal whirlwinds of Genova, even for the sound of the Austrian guns among the snow.

" *Che paese di bestie,*" groaned one.

"*È una porcheria, quest' isola*," grumbled another.

And then in a bright orange and purple boat gliding over the thick blue water came Lulu, her shiny luggage heaped high in the prow, the rowers singing for pleasure in their fair freight.

The young lieutenant in charge of the military force began to hum the latest fox-trot and clank his sword. The harbour-master forgot his pains and started to order away the boats that might crowd the landing steps. The customs officials clustered round to wave all that shiny luggage through without a question. Beccafico the *guardia* loosed a tremendous hiccup of importance, and routed with his stick among the ragamuffins of the quayside.

"I should like to know who this lovely doll is," said the lieutenant as he flipped the beads of damp from his moustache.

Beccafico approached, beaming.

"*È la figlia della Contessa Rannadanna*," he fruitily proclaimed. "*Scusi, signor tenente*," he added with a most deferential salute in case he had trespassed upon the young officer's dignity.

"*Ha-ha! non c' è male*," the young lieutenant murmured.

"*Sì, sì, signor tenente. Bella ragazza! Molto bella!*" Beccafico agreed.

And raising his hand to his mouth he belched appreciatively.

"*Benarrivata, signorina*," he gulped on the dying fall as Lulu stepped ashore.

Beccafico got an impression from Lulu's beauty that

the war was nearly over. This vivid girl was the right kind of creature to step ashore on Sirene. If he had been a withered ilex instead of the *guardia civile* he would have put forth new leaves.

And as Lulu pulled Miss after her into the carriage of the funicular the wind shifted out of the south, so that by the time they emerged on the busy terrace and turned into the Piazza the sky was a dreamy blue and the loiterers were buzzing like bees in the sunshine. Lulu immediately escaped from her governess to post a letter she had been writing on the boat. It was a passionate letter, proclaiming in four pages of tender superlatives the desolation of parting from her adored Carmine. Several tears dropped upon the notepaper had made the ink of her fountain pen even more indefinite than usual. She had enclosed her signature in a frame of symbolical crosses, and in the top right-hand corner what looked like a dirty thumbmark was stated to be the imprint of her lips. It thrilled her to fancy Carmine's red mouth pressed rapturously to that romantic smudge. She kissed the back of the envelope and scrawled in pencil *Un altro bacio qui.*

" *Mon dieu,*" she said to herself, when the letter had flapped down into the post-box like a released dove, " I forgot it was addressed to his friend." How stupid of her ! She hoped that Carmine would not be jealous of Federigo Stingo and suspect him of taking advantage of that kiss on the outside.

" *Comme je suis bête,*" Lulu murmured. But she forgot about her anxiety in the sight of Miss on her trail. She hurried away and dived into the tobacconist's under the archway leading out of the Piazza. There she bought a box of cigarettes; and when ten minutes later Miss, very hot and agitated, came tottering into the entrance hall of the Hotel Augusto Lulu was smoking in one of the big wicker chairs and reading a copy of *La Vie Parisienne*.

"Lulu, where *have* you been?" the little governess panted.

"I've been waiting for *you*," said Lulu reproachfully.

"And where *did* you get that dreadful paper?" Miss Chimbley gasped.

"An English officer left it in this chair."

Miss Chimbley quavered between patriotism and propriety.

"Don't you think you'd better let me give it to the porter?" she suggested.

"It's very dull this week," said Lulu indifferently; and she handed her governess the paper, on the outside of which was a picture of a young woman with nothing on but a scarlet cap of liberty and a bunch of cherries. Miss Chimbley coughed and turned the paper over. She coughed again, put it down in a chair, and covered the back page by sitting on it.

Meanwhile, Lulu had lit another cigarette and strolled across to the framed card with the names of the occupants of the various rooms.

"The hotel's very empty," she said resentfully.

And so it was. Even the convalescent English officer was leaving that afternoon, and he was the only man in the place except a bunch of Milanese profiteers who had just bought out the old management and were spending the whole of their time arguing about estimates for redecoration.

"I suppose they dance every night?" Lulu asked the headporter hopefully.

"Who is there to dance, *mademoiselle?*" he sighed with a despondent shrug. "*La guerre, vous savez.*"

Lulu, sitting cigarette in mouth by the open windows of her bedroom that night and gazing mournfully down on the great moon-blanched terrace abandoned to the courtship of two sandy cats, began to realize what war meant. She had expected to be dancing at this hour.

*Carmine mine*, she wrote desperately in Italian, *I am dying for love of you. This separation is a thousand times worse than I dreamed it would be. It is now ten o'clock and I am quite alone dreaming of you. Do not be jealous of me. I hate everybody in this hotel. It is you I want. You and you only. Everybody else in the world has no importance. Eternally thy Lulu.*

It was so dull on Sirene during the first month of Lulu's banishment that the poor child took up the study of botany quite seriously. She and Miss Chimbley used to wander over the fragrant hills and gather quantities of flowers, which they would bring back to the hotel and press between blotting-paper by heaping upon them the out-of-date literature of pre-war travel. The only occasions that Lulu found it necessary to run away from her governess were when she had to go to the post-office to get Carmine's letters. Poor Lulu, she even took to playing bézique with Miss Chimbley, so long were the unoccupied hours—bézique with its wearisome marriages of convenience and rows of cunning complacent knaves and kings, its cross hungry queens.

The situation in Europe becomes graver. The allied press has just announced for the fifteenth time that this really is the darkest hour before the dawn. It is dark enough. Big Bertha is crashing shells into Paris from nobody knows how many leagues away. German offensives rush madly from weak point to weak point of the allied line. Frantic reunions take place between soldiers and politicians. The world begins to look damned dangerous for democracy, as the tooth-comb of conscription goes over it once more. The tuberculous, the pathic, the neurasthenic, even the middle-aged father of a family with his suspensory bandage, are all held up to the light, judged to be alive, placed on the anvil of the great war for civilization, and cracked with a hammer borrowed from Donner.

And on Sirene sits Lulu like a solitary discredited swallow belying summer. She hears that Carmine's class has been called up. She hugs the pillow to her breast in an ecstasy of amorous despair. Miss quavers by the bedside with her only imaginable anodyne—eau de Cologne. Lulu's legs beat the air in a paroxysm of cheated youth. Miss is joined by Maddalena the chambermaid, who prescribes orange-flower water as an infallible sedative. Maddalena recounts the numbers of passionate despairers whom with orange-flower water she has lulled back from love's poetic agonies to face the prose of life again. Lulu rejects the flask of orange-flower water and cries out for salts of lemon.

And then in the hotel corridor outside Lulu's bedroom sounded a rumour of cheerful porters carrying a quantity of heavy luggage, a quick feminine voice, the laughter with which willing slaves responded, and most authentically the sense of a sudden change from dullness and depression in the Hotel Augusto to gaiety and hope.

"What's that?" Lulu asked, releasing the pillow abruptly and looking, as she sat up on her bed, like a rose after a heavy shower of rain.

"*Sarebbe la signorina Rosalba*," cried Maddalena, hurrying to the door and peeping excitably into the corridor. "*Sì! sì!*" she confirmed. "*È arrivata! Come sono contenta! Dio, che bella cosa!*"

Time may be a fairly reliable physician for human grief, but the finest surgeon is curiosity. A minute later Lulu was powdering her face. She had been granted a conviction that life was worth living after all.

## CHAPTER THREE

οὔδιαν δοκίμωμι προσίδοισαν φάος ἀλίω
ἔσσεσθαι σοφίᾳ πάρθενον εἰς οὐδενά ποι χρόνον
τοιαύταν.   SAPPHO.

*I fancy no maiden under the sun will ever rival you in your accomplishment.*

ROSALBA DONSANTE had reached Sirene from Lucerne, travelling with as much speed and comfort as anybody ever travelled in Europe during that last year of the war. Rosalba pacing slowly beside her grandmother under the avenues of lime-trees along the lake had suddenly decided that this was the last year of the war, the shadow of which had lain darkly and coldly upon life as over the lake all through the winter had lain the shadow of Mount Pilatus.

" I must at last begin to live, grandmother. I will not suffer to lose my youth no more. *Vous savez, j'ai déjà vingt-quatre ans. Vingt-quatre, vingt-quatre, vous savez!*"

Rosalba would venture most things, but she never ventured to address her grandmother in the second person singular.

Old Baroness Zaccardi eyed the young woman with a kindly contempt.

" Here we sit for a little," she said, indicating a bench whose painted wood looked shabby but inviting in the sunlight of mid May.

" It is quite idiotic for me to be without a life of myself. Mamma has now divorced her fourth husband and is married again," Rosalba went on.

The old lady nodded.

"And the only time I see my daughter for a minute is when she comes to Switzerland to make herself a new divorce," she chuckled to herself.

They were talking mostly in English. At any moment they might be talking mostly in French or German or Italian. The Baroness who belonged to the great cosmopolitan banking house of the Glaubers spoke several languages equally well, but each of them with the accent of another. Her only daughter Emilia had married first a Frenchman, then an Austrian, then the Italian painter Donsante, by whom she was the mother of Rosalba, then a Spaniard, and she was now married to a handsome Sicilian fifteen years younger than herself who was already expecting to be taken across the Swiss frontier and divorced as soon as his wife would not be kept waiting all day for her passport. Rosalba was the only fruit of these five marriages, and even she was a windfall. '*Un' accidente però non troppo prospero*,' Madame Cantini always declared. We shall not meet Emilia Cantini: let it be recorded here that none of her five husbands and none of her fifty lovers ever tired of her; and all of them were still alive to maintain that she was the only woman in Europe who would never cease to trouble their memories with the thought of what she had once been to them.

Emilia Cantini was careful not to imperil that easy supremacy by hampering it with the company of a grown-up daughter. Twenty years ago she had left Rosalba to the care of her grandmother, and it was generally understood she would inherit the old lady's fortune, which, when people remembered that she was a Glauber, was estimated to be large enough.

When Rosalba, walking with her grandmother under the lime-trees of Lucerne, announced that she must begin to live, the old lady did not argue with her, because she was a little tired of Rosalba's restless companionship which had now been hers for nearly three consecutive months. She felt perfectly willing for Rosalba to begin to live provided she was not disturbed by her activity, so willing indeed that she omitted to remind her that she might be considered to have been living expansively and expensively for several years already.

"You have been in Lucerne quite long enough to remind me that you expect to have all my money when I die," she told her granddaughter. "And I am quite glad for you to go back to Sirene with this English friend of yours you have met in Paris last autumn. I think she is quite an ill-bred elephant of a woman, but as she is your friend, my dear Rosalba, we need not argue about that."

Rosalba had no intention of arguing about Aurora Freemantle. She was always too much occupied with making her own impression upon her friends to bother what kind of impression they made upon the world.

"But there is one thing I find a little curious about you," the old lady went on, passing from English to French in the way that one instinctively does to approach a delicate subject. "*En effet, chérie, je te trouve un peu trop beau garçon.*"

"*Garçon?*" Rosalba repeated with obvious satisfaction as she lit a cigarette stuck in a long holder of white jade.

"*Tu t'habilles en garçon. Tu te comportes en garçon.*"

"That is because there is plenty of room in Europe for young men in these days," said Rosalba. "When the war is over you will find that women will be entirely different from what you have known. It is very much in the air, I can assure you, this change."

The old lady grunted contemptuously.

"Women will always be what they instinctively suppose men want them to be. And if men want them to be boys, I am sorry for what men will be."

"I am not at all interested in men," said Rosalba. "They have let themselves be enslaved too easily by this war. I have lost my respect for men. I assure you that I could not like Mamma choose five husbands among such obedient creatures."

"You might choose one," suggested the old Baroness.

"Ah, you are so deliciously *ancien régime*," her granddaughter laughed. Then in her husky Florentine accent she fell into Italian to discuss her journey South. "They will be so glad when I come back to Sirene," she declared. "Last year when I was staying there with Giulia Monforte everybody has said that it was the only amusing event since the war began."

"If you find the flattery of Southern Italians already so precious," the old lady growled, "I shall begin to think that you are already an old maid."

"*Zitella?* Ah, thank you, you are very polite."

" And apropos of your friend the Contessa Monforte. You will, I hope, take her with you again to Sirene," said the old lady.

" Why ? "

" Because I do not wish to be tired out with her rhapsodies over you. I find it quite tiresome to be told by her that what you lack *est la refuge de l'étreinte maternelle*."

" Giulia is in Rome. I am quite tired of her myself."

" On the contrary, my dear, the wretched woman arrived in Lucerne this morning. Françoise gave me her card."

The old lady fumbled in her reticule and produced it for Rosalba, who stared at it in disgust.

" *Che seccatura !* " she exclaimed.

" But much more of a bore for me than for you," the old lady insisted. " So, I am quite decided that you will take this poor creature away from Lucerne when you shall go yourself. She has for me the effect of a stove that is too hot. *C'est très désagréable*. And now, run away, please, because I wish to sit here alone in the sunlight."

The Swiss are probably better used to the eccentricity of human attire than any other nation ; but the sight of Rosalba walking about Lucerne attracted the eye of the native as much as the scenery of his country attracted the eye of the tourist. The splendour of women in the war had not hitherto been remarked by the Swiss preoccupied as they were with a prosperous neutrality. They did not recognize in Rosalba a purely decorative expression of the instinct that led other young women to drive lorries in France. They merely stared at her because they thought it odd that such a pretty young woman should be trying to dress and behave as much like a handsome young man as she could.

Yet Rosalba was a portent.

What did those Minoan crinolines signify? What sophisticated feminine emotions surged in those bared Cretan breasts? Did that Ægean culture die of feminine domination? Or was feminine domination merely a visible symptom of the decay within? Anyway, they were certainly not boy-girls. And their successors in Hellas? But the maidens of Lacedemon are dust; the Lesbian flutes are silent; Atalanta's course is run; and we do not know what those boy-girls signified any more than their apparently ultra feminine predecessors of Cnossos.

Of what *is* Rosalba the portent? What signifies this boy-girl at whom all the clumsy Swiss are staring on this fine May morning? What signifies she in the curve of a civilization?

Her profile was Greek, or at any rate that was the effect it made, which is not to say that the line of her nose and forehead was one. Her profile was Greek in the way that Virgil's hexameters are Greek. Every feature was in proportion and every feature was clear cut. Her mouth curved up at the corners like the mouths Leonardo da Vinci loved to paint; and like Leonardo's saints and sinners her face was heart-shaped, so that her mouth broke into flower above a slim and pointed chin. Her brown eyes were deep and brilliant beneath eyebrows which on a pale complexion might have seemed too thick, but whose glinting bronze under that rich weight of rippling hair was perfectly displayed. On that fine May morning in the last year of the war her short accordion-pleated skirt made the long-skirted bourgeoises of Lucerne shudder and crick their necks to stare after her rifle-green jacket and waistcoat, her double collar and her black satin tie with the coral pin, her long jade cigarette holder and slim ebony stick, and that rippling hair lustrous and hatless. Rosalba was often pleasantly aware of the attention she drew from passers-by, but this morning since her grandmother's announcement of Giulia Monforte's arrival she was too much puzzled by the problem of fitting in Giulia Monforte with Aurora Freemantle to bother about her own effect. Not that she was annoyed by Giulia's arrival. Her own power of intrigue was too dearly cherished to let herself be vexed by Giulia. She would know how to flatter Rory by giving her to suppose that Giulia's presence was odious; and at the same time she would know how to use poor Giulia to quell that faint inclination of Rory to fancy that she belonged to her, which had been tiresomely noticeable in her new friend's attitude lately. And at that moment the Contessa Monforte melted into Rosalba's arms.

"*Eh, eh, mon cher!*" Rosalba protested, disengaging herself from the Countess and smiling at her, more like a mischevious *gamin* than a *beau garçon*. It was Rosalba's habit to call her victims '*mon cher*' without regard to the appropriateness of the gender. Nothing more softly feminine than the Countess was imaginable. She was indeed almost flabby. Tears of emotion furrowed chalky rivulets down her rice-powdered cheeks. Her skirt gathered up the dust. She dropped her handkerchief. She dropped her parasol. Between tears and the perspiration caused by hurrying all over Lucerne in search of Rosalba she looked as if she had just been dragged out of the lake itself.

" Oh, I have been so desolate without you, *carissima*," she moaned.

" Well, here I am," said Rosalba practically, " so please control yourself and do not make a figure of me in this dirty little place, which I find altogether disgusting."

" You hadn't written to me for ten days," sighed the Countess reproachfully. " *Il y a dix jours que je n'ai pas vu la chère enveloppe bleue m'attendant à midi.*"

" There are times when I cannot write at all."

" Not even to me ? " the Countess appealed, her soft lips trembling. " *Je ne vis vraiment que lorsque je lis tes chères phrases.*"

" There are moments when I become entirely shut up inside myself," Rosalba declared sternly. " And Rory is here also. She would be very jealous indeed if I was always writing to you."

" You love her more than me," the Countess challenged. " *Pour moi tu n'as qu'une affection banale, parfois indifférente.*"

" *Ah, mais écoute, mon cher*, please do not let us make

comparisons in the public street. More or less love is not a thing to be discussed with a lot of people turning round to look at us."

"You know I don't mean to annoy you," the Countess apologized meekly.

There was a touch of the swashbuckler in the way Rosalba was carrying herself, something of the rapier in that long cigarette-holder.

"I cannot understand why you must cry like this when you have found me," she grumbled. "We have had all rain for so long now, and I am quite tired of it." She ejected the butt of her cigarette with a vicious puff. "Now I must go to meet my friend Rory because it is twelve o'clock and you must go to buy something in the shops, because I think we shall be leaving Lucerne to-morrow and you will want all the time to have your passport visé."

"Where are we going?"

"We are going to Sirene."

"You and I?"

"And Rory whom you will like very much. She is very, very original."

The rapturous sigh of the Countess on hearing of Rosalba's plan turned to tears again as wind brings rain.

"More original than I?" she choked.

"Ah, *par exemple*, my dear Giulia, you are not at all original."

"You said I was very original last summer when we were sitting on the rocks at Sirene. I thought it was my originality that appealed to you so much."

"Ah, *dio*, I cannot tolerate people who live in the past," Rosalba cried. "Live in the present, *mon cher*, if you wish to please me."

"You know I wish to please you. You know it's the only thing on earth I want to do. *Je ne peux pas être pour toi un objet de repulsion. Ce que je ressens de chaud, de tendre, d'unique pour toi—choses tellement intimes, tellement douces, tellement . . .*"

"*Tu sais, Giulia*," Rosalba interrupted coldly. "There are moments when I am really very sorry for men, because it is evident that women can be quite impossible. Now please go and do your shopping, because all the cuckoo-clocks in Lucerne have struck twelve and Rory is waiting for me."

"What shall I buy for you, Rosalba?" the older woman asked miserably.

"You can buy a cuckoo-clock for yourself."

The Countess collapsed wretchedly on a seat.

"I believe you hate me," she groaned.

"No, no, but I am not in a mood for these tears," Rosalba answered, as lightly she turned away from her melting friend toward Miss Freemantle's hotel.

Aurora Freemantle was so masculine as almost to convey the uncomfortable impression that she really was a man dressed up in female attire. But she was without doubt an Englishwoman who had lived for over twenty-five years in Paris, where under the pseudonym of Demonassa she had contributed poems to various advanced reviews and under her own name pence to support them. She had begun as a symbolist and was at present an imagist; but through all the mutable fashions of literature she had remained faithful to the breeding of French bulldogs. She was not beautiful, having herself a considerable likeness to the bulldogs she loved. Her prominent chin was as hispid as the leaves of borage. She was indeed, if one may use a botanical family to classify a human being, a boraginacious woman combining in herself the sentimentality of the forget-me-not with the defiance of the bugloss. Like the Demonassa whose name she had borrowed from Lucian she was rich, and like her she could fairly be called a Corinthian inasmuch as she had done more than anybody to promote the sport of boxing among women. She had derived as much pleasure from the protection of likely young feminine feather-weights as in the bewhiskered prime of the Victorian era elderly gentlemen derived from the protection of ballet-dancers. In early days she had had some bitter experiences in the way of empirical love-making; but for many years now, until Rosalba Donsante entered her life, she had always been able to feel that she was the protector with perpetual freedom to dismiss the protected. At present, however, Rosalba eluded her. And to the enslavement of Rosalba Rory set that massive and hispid jaw. One of her practical reasons for coming to Sirene (romantically she could not bear the thought of even the briefest separation) was the hope that she might cut Rosalba off from relying too much upon her grandmother's financial help, which was one of the chief bars to the indisputable protection that she had craved ever since she met

Rosalba at a friend's house in Paris last October. Under the pseudonym of Demonassa Rory had expressed very frankly her feminine ideal, and there is no doubt that Rosalba came nearer than anybody so far to realizing it. Poems of hers written before Rosalba came into this world foreshadowed her. She might have met her unborn shade and cried ' *Tu Marcellus eris.*' There was published privately in the early 'nineties a slim volume of verse bound in sea-green vellum called *Cydro*, which is still met with in second-hand book catalogues under the heading ' Curious.' Rory Freemantle had not yet assumed the name Demonassa at this period, and the only indication of authorship was a portrait of her at the beginning which in spite of being reproduced from a silver-point, with all the advantages that such an ethereal style of sketching provides, showed a determined young woman quite alien from the Cydro whose beauty and fascination the poems celebrated. This Cydro became in turn Gyrinno, Anactoria, Atthis, Megara, Telesippa, Leaena, Megilla, Gongyla, Ismenodora, or Mnesidice ; and she was sometimes a slim anonymous flute-player of Pyrrha or Methymna flitting through the verses of Demonassa as her prototype may have flitted through the olive groves of Mytilene. But whatever her name or occupation she certainly might always have been Rosalba with her upcurving faun's mouth, Rosalba with her long legs and weight of glinting hair. And now when that poetic ideal was incarnate in Rosalba's Greek beauty verse was not sufficient. Rory must take to painting and paint her. She was rich enough to experiment with another art in approaching middle-age, and the fashion of the moment was kind to her lack of technique. She was rich enough to be credited with a freshness of vision, and the portraits she made of Rosalba that first winter had a vogue in her Parisian côterie. They made one feel, her friends assured her, that the war would at last come to an end. Whereupon the Germans nearly broke through again, and the côterie was dispersed. Rory did not allow Rosalba to be dispersed. She had not found the incarnation of her feminine ideal after searching twenty-five years to lose her a few months later. She left her bulldogs and feather-weight female boxers and followed her ideal to Lucerne. Here it was that owing to the restrictions of war-time which made Mytilene a difficult island to reach they planned to spend the late spring and summer in Sirene.

When Rory was presented to the Contessa Monforte and informed that she was to make a third on Sirene, she decided that she could afford to show her jealousy. There were likely to be rivals in the future much more powerful than this soft over-powdered creature, when it might have to be concealed in order not to lose Rosalba. She knew Rosalba would be flattered by a display of jealousy, and she saw quite clearly Rosalba would by no means relish being left alone with the Countess. So she cancelled the tickets and announced she would return to Paris.

"Go," Rosalba invited. "It is quite all the same to me, *mon cher*."

"And I hope you'll enjoy the company of that

idiotic woman who is trailing after you," said Rory, pacing the room with an almost nautical roll.

" She has at least good manners, *mon cher*."

To Giulia Monforte Rosalba confided that she could no longer put up with Rory's ugliness.

" *Avec sa figure de bouledogue*," she complained. " Let her go. I am sick of her *prepotenza*. You and I will go alone together to Sirene."

" *Oh, cara, sarebbe un sogno*," the Countess sighed.

So Rosalba went to her grandmother to provide herself with the extra amount of ready money Rory's defection made advisable.

" You have had too much money from me this year," said the Baroness unexpectedly. " I think you will be wise to learn a little prudence."

Rosalba frowned. The Countess was not rich. The prospect of a straitened visit to Sirene was by no means to her taste. Perhaps she should be wise not to quarrel with Rory. In spite of her possessive airs she was a more useful companion *en voyage* than poor Giulia.

" I think you are absurd, *mon cher*, to be jealous of Giulia," she told Rory.

" I cannot stand a flabby creature like that daring to follow you about all over Europe."

" But she is so harmless."

" That is precisely what I dislike about her. It's no recommendation of an earthworm to call it harmless."

" Then I suppose I must send her away."

Rory hesitated, turning her bright prominent eyes intently upon Rosalba. She was trying to make up her mind whether this easy victory was worth while. It was clear Rosalba had no interest in the poor Monforte. This was probably a favourable occasion to surrender.

"Oh, let her come, let her come," she said impatiently. "But if she has a headache all the time, my dear, don't expect me to hold her hand."

Rosalba's only way of getting even with Rory was to share her compartment in the wagon-lits with Giulia; but, having done that, she spent half the night in strolling along the corridor, wrapt in a brown and amber kimono, her hair flowing down her back in a torrent of bronze, to enquire how Rory was getting on, and by these repeated visits much perturbing a Frenchwoman who was on her way south to share her husband's leave from Salonica, and who asked every time Rosalba entered the compartment and switched on the light if there had been a railway accident. There was too something in the nature of a scene at Rome, because Giulia had found the kimono-clad solicitude of Rosalba for Rory's comfort so painful that she was inclined to abandon the journey and return home to her husband the Count, who in spite of the tax he laid upon her sensitive nature was, she vowed, all in all less cruel than Rosalba. However, as soon as the Countess divined she might carry too far the scene in Rome station she walked across to the Naples platform in meek attendance.

The arrival on Sirene was a triumph. It was not merely that Rosalba on her previous visit had spent more money on the island than anybody since the war began to make itself sadly felt. Rosalba did possess the gift of imparting to the fifty-lira notes of which she was so prodigal some of her own vitality. The waiter who found one of these notes pressed into his hand did not feel that he was being coldly bribed to neglect the guests at the next table in her favour, but that in accepting the note he and the Signorina Rosalba—she was always the Signorina Rosalba, never the Signorina Donsante—were entering into a compact to get by hook or by crook the best out of life. She gave the note with such an air that the recipient would not have been astonished to find it being pinned to his breast like a decoration instead of being pressed into his hand. And his acceptation of it conferred upon him the right to do everything he could to please her. Her enemies might say she bought this popularity with her friends' money. It was to some extent a justifiable sneer. Still, it was not merely her friends' money that made all the coachmen waiting off the Piazza for fares crack their whips and jangle their reins and wave their hats and cry '*Benarrivata, signorina!*' Notwithstanding the number of stout little cobs which had been commandeered for war service, there were still a dozen or so more regular coachmen plying for hire, and few fares they earned in these lean days. However often the Signorina Rosalba might drive up to Anasirene or down to the two Marinas they would not be able to loosen overmuch their own belts or the girths of their cobs. But when with her grey skirt and grey flannel coat and waistcoat, when with her soft double collar and grey silk tie and cat's-eye pin and weight of rippling bronze hair, she emerged from the funicular and stood swinging her slim cane of harewood and puffing at her long cigarette-holder of mother o' pearl, there was nobody on the Piazza who did not look up to smile a genuine pleasure at seeing Rosalba in Sirene again. Such kissing there was of her hand by bare-legged old market-women and shrill welcoming children! Such shaking there was of it by the familiar loiterers of the Piazza who, peaked and hunched though they all were by four years of war, forgot those years for a moment in the grasp of that sunburnt boyish hand.

The enthusiastic confusion of her welcome did not make Rosalba forget anybody. She hurried into the shop under the archway to greet the cripple girl who sat working at her lace all day in the shadow. She hurried into the post-office and even extorted smiles of welcome from the bilious and neurotic family whose members one and all handed out stamps as if they wished the gum on the backs were mixed with arsenic. She hurried into Zampone's Café to embrace Donna Maria; and it was Persephone embracing Demeter; it was in spite of her boyishness the Koré, for Rosalba had the quality of touching with timelessness the least significant scene in which she played a part, so that one remembered her in a series of beautiful moments made immortal as one remembers great sculpture. Fat Ferdinando, Donna Maria's son, came forward from the darkness in which he worked at his ledgers to greet her with little black eyes twinkling in his great firmament of a face. She was already full of a scheme to celebrate her arrival with a marvellous picnic on the summit of Monte Ventoso, and Ferdinando whose experience of visitors' excursions had made him a profound cynic was discussing the details like a schoolboy.

So, all the way along to the Hotel Augusto Rosalba went in and out of shops, greeted old acquaintances, and swung her harewood cane. And the sound of her debonair progress along the cobbled street would have warned the staff of the hotel to be waiting for her, even if they had not been looking out ever since an excited pageboy had leapt into the entrance-lobby with the news of her arrival.

"*Benarrivata, signorina*," said the head porter bowing like a seneschal. Since the death of Don Cesare Rocca, the old proprietor, the spirit of the hotel abode in him. The Milanese profiteers who owned it nowadays had less individuality than the bluebottles buzzing in and out of its sunny windows. The head waiter came into the hall to say there were prawns for lunch. The barman came up to say he had managed to get some good gin again after a long drought. The new manager came forward to assure the Signorina she would find the Augusto as anxious to serve her under his direction as in the days of the lamented Don Cesare.

When the luggage arrived more quickly than luggage had ever reached the hotel before, because the weather-beaten females who carried it on their heads had swung along with it as if it were the fruits of the vintage and the muscle-bound male porters had run all the way with the biggest trunks, shouting, it seemed, for glee at their burdens. And what was even more astonishing in the history of the island, they all went away contented with their remuneration, went away without even arguing over the division of the tips.

"There will be music to-night at dinner?" Rosalba turned at the foot of the stairs to ask the head porter.

He shook his head dolefully.

"The war, signorina. . . ."

"Ah, but I must certainly have music to-night," Rosalba declared.

"It can probably be arranged. There has been a great deal of misery among the musicians lately."

"But Bozzo is still here?"

"*Sissignorina.*"

"He will play to-night," she commanded. "And afterwards we will have him in the ballroom."

Then the hotel staff escorted Rosalba, her two friends, and their luggage to the rooms reserved for them.

It was not surprising that Lulu de Randan sitting up in bed like a rose after a heavy shower of rain should have divined that life was worth living after all. Rosalba Donsante was perhaps the only person since the Deified Augustus whom Sirene recognized as capable of giving as well as of taking vitality.

## CHAPTER FOUR

> ἦ τίν' ἄλλον
> μᾶλλον ἀνθρώπων ἔμεθεν φίλησθα;
> SAPPHO.
>
> *Whom in the world do you love more than me?*

RORY FREEMANTLE did not allow evening to interfere with her masculine style. She came down to dinner at the Augusto in a good imitation of a dinner-jacket, though without the stiff-fronted shirt which she would have liked to affect every night, but which owing to the inconsiderate femininity of her bust caused her so much discomfort that she could only affect it on the grandest occasions. Rosalba on the other hand in her dress after sunset was always frankly feminine. As for poor Giulia Monforte she might have been anything after sunset. Nobody cared.

This first evening Rosalba wore a frock of dead white crêpe de Chine with round her waist a galloon of silver and round her left forearm a silver bracelet so heavy as almost to seem like a fetter. Her shoes were vivid scarlet, and it was upon these shoes that the eyes of the dull people scattered sparsely about the dining-room were fixed in disapproval. The old maids peered round the half-consumed bottles of white wine left over from other meals at these shoes as if they were scarlet tanagers escaped from an aviary, and when they were hidden under the table they stared censoriously at Rosalba's face. In fact they thought the whole party at that new table most extraordinary, and the way the little orchestra was so obviously playing for them most conspicuous. And it looked, yes, it looked very much as if they were going to have a special dinner and probably a better one than the other guests. Oh, and they were drinking champagne. Profiteers evidently. One of the old maids beckoned to the head waiter who limped away from Rosalba's table like an unwilling rook to attend her. But before there was time to ask him who and what Rosalba was Rosalba had beckoned him to her table again. He cawed a hasty excuse and fluttered back to the Signorina's side, waiting there with wise obsequious head to know what the Signorina wanted. Another condiment or another tune? Anything, anything.

"Who is the signorina with the fair hair sitting with the tiny little woman at the table in the corner?"

The head waiter smiled.

"*La contessina de Randan. Molto simpatica.*"

"The daughter of the Countess de Randan who lives at Stabia?"

"*Si, si, signorina,*" he replied eagerly. "*Proprio lei.*"

Rosalba raised her glass of champagne and drank across the dining-room to Lulu, who blushed deeply and seemed on the point of dissolving over the table in rosy petals.

"What's the matter, Lulu?" Miss Chimbley quavered anxiously. "Have you swallowed a fish-bone, dear?"

Indeed Lulu was crimson enough to give cause for apprehension.

For the rest of the meal, while the orchestra devoted all its music to Rosalba, Rosalba herself laughed, talked, ate, and drank with an eye on Lulu.

"I tell to you, Rory, that there is a very charming girl behind you."

Rory put up her monocle, thrust out her chin, and turned round to stare at Lulu.

"Where is there a charming girl, Rosalba?" Giulia Monforte asked fretfully.

"But, *mon cher*, you are not quite blind, I suppose," Rosalba commented with such cold impatience in her voice that poor Giulia nearly burst into tears. She had only meant to imply that no girl was worth looking at when Rosalba was in the room. A lump of self-pity came into her throat for the way her little compliment had miscarried.

"You are right," said Rory, dropping her monocle with the air of a satisfied connoisseur of Dresden china. "I have met her mother in Paris. A tiresome conceited woman. You would not have your usual success with her. She dislikes anybody under thirty."

Rosalba frowned. She did not consider herself anybody under thirty, and she made a mental note of Hermina de Randan's prejudice as a climber might hear of a difficult mountain and resolve to conquer it next time he was in the neighbourhood. But Rory did not see, or at any rate she pretended not to see that Rosalba had taken her last remark as a challenge. Without the least appearance of malice she began to tell scandalous tales of Hermina de Randan's absurdities, offering each one as lightly and casually as salted almonds or pickled gherkins. And then she thrust abruptly at poor Giulia Monforte a chili.

"She would take a great fancy to *you*. *You* are her type."

And since most of the tales had been about women with more emotion than brains and more years than discretion, Giulia could not pretend that the chili had not burnt her.

"She may be the most stupid woman in Europe," Rosalba declared. "But her daughter is awfully beautiful."

Giulia Monforte who had produced nothing but a thin-legged little boy of ten with lank ebony hair did not find this opinion welcome. When she had met Rosalba last year at Sirene and fallen a victim to her charm, Giulia had supposed that the intimate friendship into which she had plunged was something that perhaps had not happened to any other woman before. She had disliked her husband for fifteen years and she had never had a lover. She had reached the point of supposing that the life of a woman was after marriage an inevitable tedium. She suffered from all the inhibitions and suppressions that were presently to become as familiar to the housewife as the complaints in a book of home remedies. But she was still ignorant of her mental state and instead of consulting a psychoanalyst she sought to cure the discomfort life caused her by taking baths and drinking waters. Weakened by the strenuous methods of an Italian spa she had gone to Sirene to postpone the dreaded return to conjugal existence. Here Rosalba at a loose end for a month had passed the time in binding her with a spell. She had found this friendship strangely exciting, and she had announced to Rosalba as a wonderful discovery that, as she had always supposed in her heart despite all she had read to the contrary, the truest love was utterly untouched by passion.

"*Il ne peut pas exister d'equivoque entre nous. Nous sommes tellement au dessus de ce sombre abîme*," she had avowed.

Rosalba had laughed.

"And I wish henceforth to live entirely in you."

And then Rosalba had laughed again, shaking her bronze hair out to catch the sea-breeze.

"Why do you laugh, Rosalba?"

"*Mon cher*, I was thinking what strange ambitions women have."

"But you do realize, don't you, that my nature has been completely changed by our friendship? Why, I feel twenty years younger for one thing. You seem to understand me better than I understand myself."

And Giulia Monforte had gone back to her quiet Roman house and to that dim secluded life so many well-bred Latin women lead, which is in essentials hardly distinguishable from the life of the zenana. But the thought of Rosalba in Paris had tormented her throughout the winter. She had felt all the while as if in her quiet Roman house she were being stifled beneath black velvet. The *madre addolorata* whose pale tear-gemmed face had comforted so many heartaches could console her no more. She lived only to receive Rosalba's hasty scrawls in answer to sheets of notepaper covered with her own thin sloping handwriting. She wrote the same vague outpourings of emotion now in Italian, now in French, now in English, for each time she changed the language she supposed she was saying something new. Finally she had been able to stand the separation no longer and had arrived in Lucerne. And now she was in Sirene, feeling miserably insecure and always slightly shocked by the conversation of Rosalba and Aurora Freemantle, as on board ship one may feel slightly sick for days at a stretch, yet never sick enough to retire below.

After dinner, Bozzo the consumptive little violinist, whose temperature must have risen several points from the excitement of earning a few liras again, took his orchestra of mandolin and piano down to the ballroom, where the french-windows opened on a big terrace, the pale-blue porcelain tiles of which shimmered in the warm moonlight like water. This terrace was enclosed on three sides by the lofty fabric of the hotel; but in front, beyond a row of white columns, there stretched a dim wilderness of perfumed shrubberies, and a date-palm stood up tall and black against the moon-drenched southern sky. The old maids, though they had disapproved of Rosalba's scarlet shoes, followed the orchestra downstairs, and sat round the ballroom with their knitting. They were inclined to think that Rosalba intended to dance; and they were right, for as soon as her coffee was finished she walked over to where Lulu was blooming in a corner and invited her to be her partner.

"*La Bambola Infranta?*" little Bozzo asked eagerly.

Rosalba nodded. *The Broken Doll* was a fox-trot which had reached Italy the year before and had been a great favourite of the Signorina. In those days the fox-trot was still a dance with a regular step—a two-step touched faintly by the spirit of the mazurka. Lulu overcome by self-consciousness stumbled round the ballroom in a confusion of blushes and lack of rhythm.

"Steady, *ma gosse*," Rosalba murmured. "You are quite able to dance if you are careful. *Bien! Bien! Ça va mieux! Piano! Piano! Le zitelle ti guardano.* Follow me, my dear. Don't please let these ridiculous people suppose that you cannot fox-trot."

But Lulu was too much overcome by the audience in the ballroom to dance with the least assurance, and she tumbled over her feet in a way that would certainly have prevented Rory Freemantle's investing any money in her as a female boxer. The exhibition she was making of herself gave a good deal of pleasure to Giulia Monforte, who perked up wonderfully. *La Bambola Infranta.* It was an appropriate tune, for Lulu did look in Rosalba's arms not unlike a large and broken doll.

"My dear, why are you so shy?" she was asked in a thrilling whisper.

"There is nobody else dancing."

"Perhaps you do not think that I make a very good boy for you?"

"Oh, it's my fault entirely," Lulu assured her so serenely confident partner. " I don't know why I am being so stupid."

The next time they passed the orchestra, Rosalba called to the leader :

" We shall dance outside. Do not wait for me to come back before you begin to play again."

Little Bozzo acknowledged her command by sweeping the bow across his violin in a deep affirmative, and Rosalba guided Lulu through the nearest frenchwindow out on to the empty shimmering terrace.

Here undisturbed by any eye except the moon's Lulu at once began to dance more easily.

" Better ! Better ! " Rosalba cried. " I knew that you could dance if you would try. I was looking at you all through dinner." And then she repeated the compliment in French for the sake of using the second person singular.

" *Tu n'es pas gênée parce que je te tutoye ?* " she asked softly.

Lulu shook her head and, blushing, stumbled wildly in her step.

" Steady, *chérie*," Rosalba whispered. " You know, you are awfully beautiful. I wish I had golden hair like you. *Quel beau toison d'or !* "

" Oh, but you have much more beautiful hair than I," Lulu demurred. " And it's only golden-brown."

" Mine is not too bad," Rosalba agreed. " But I wish it was gold. You know, I love gold so much. But hark, the music is stopped for a minute. Let us take a little walk under the trees. *Tu veux ?* "

Rosalba put an arm in Lulu's and drew her away from the terrace along the gravel walk that faded into the darkness of the shrubbery. The air was sweet with roses and mimosa and various other plants of which people do not want to know the names, caring only that they are very sweet. Soon Rosalba had heard the whole of Lulu's brief passionate history.

"I think such a love of Romeo and Giulietta is awfully beautiful," she said solemnly. "Ah, how tired I am of ordinary people! You have seen my friends who I am with here. I will tell to you now something about them. They are quite entirely awfully boring. And so ugly! I do not believe that I could have endured them another moment if I had not found you to be my great friend on Sirene. One cannot walk about this lovely place with two such ugly women, I think. *Dis, Lulu, tu seras contente être ma petite amie sirénienne? Ah, qu'il fait bon ici! E la luna, cara! Che sguardo simpatico!* Don't you think the moon is very sweet, my dear?"

We have seen not so many pages ago a completely self-possessed Lulu handling her mother and her governess with a tranquil conviction that it was her natural right to be having a love-affair with the son of the local chemist. Can this bashful mumbling Lulu be the same creature?

That was the effect of Rosalba. She put older and wiser people than Lulu beside themselves. Rosalba was a harlequin.

It would not be true to say that Lulu had already forgotten all about Carmine's kisses; but while she wandered through this perfumed shrubbery and stood darkling beside this ghost-white harlequin the call to arms sounded like a faint echo and the kisses were become like the flowers from which she and Miss Chimbley had pressed out the life beneath a pile of old time-tables. Despite Rosalba's praise of Romeo and Juliet, Lulu was beginning to wonder if all her moonlit adventures with Carmine could equal this one. She was like a girl who has hitherto had to decorate herself with a cluster of little diamonds and is suddenly presented with a great solitary brilliant. Lulu had enough worldly wisdom, which she had picked up like rich scraps of cake from her mother's tea-tables, to apprehend to what in the eyes of the world she was committing herself by a surrender to Rosalba's magic ; but like so many young people she fancied her wilful credulity to be the cynicism and scepticism she had heard imputed to her generation. Yet, though she felt perfectly secure mentally, she did resent that shy and clumsy youthfulness which would presently envelope her again. Only so long as she and Rosalba kept walking arm in arm about the dimness of this perfumed shrubbery should she be able to feel as old as her new friend. The closeness and earthiness of it were kind to whispers. Burnt she with never so fierce a crimson, the darkness would hide her blushes. But presently they would emerge into the naked moonlight and somehow she must overcome her self-consciousness; for they would be standing together cut off from the rest of humanity and with nothing before them but the sea, and behind them the hotel chequered with golden windows as impersonal and unregardful as the stars, and behind the hotel the huddled houses of the town with their white domes and more impersonal unregardful windows, and beyond them the hills of Sirene rising black and grey against the sapphire sky sown thick with those impersonal unregardful stars. They would be so completely apart from the world in that blaze of searching moonlight that, if then she were to stumble and mumble and whisper bashfully, Rosalba might despise her youth and not realize how much she knew already about life, how deeply she appreciated the equality of emotion she was being offered. A year or two ago Lulu had had her tonsils removed and in the white blaze of the operating-room at the Naples clinic she had felt the same kind of desperate desire to be brave as now she felt with the moonlight blazing beyond this scented and earthy shrubbery; and not merely to be brave, but to preserve all the dignity of herself when the anæsthetist would in another moment reduce her to the equivalent of the mattress on which she lay.

A few more steps, and the two girls were standing in that moonlight Lulu had been imagining so fiercely.

"*Rosalba*," she murmured, flinging her arms round her. "*Rosalba, ti adoro! Sei incantevole.*"

"*Lo so*," Rosalba agreed coolly. "*E tu, piccina, sei stata incantata.*"

Poets have often played with the fancy of a statue coming to life, of a figure stepping from the cold enlacements of an urn into this green world. The notion is an obvious exercise of the poetic faculty. Lulu was not a poet, and she had never played with such a fancy; yet now in the moonlight, as she pressed her sweet warm lips to Rosalba's cool upcurving mouth, she was reminded of an afternoon when she had run away from Miss in the museum at Naples and discovered in a remote room a young faun whose marble lips she had climbed up to kiss. Her behaviour had caused a sensation, for she had been only twelve years old at the time and the museum attendants led by the distracted governess had arrived at the moment when her arms were clasped round the statue's dimpled back. Lulu had never for an instant fancied her kisses could give life to the slim and disdainful faun. The impulse had been nothing more than a surrender to a childish delight in that debonair nudity —a display of premature sensuality perhaps in acknowledgement of the beauty which had roused it without her knowing why. She had caught hold of the faun's tail when the museum attendants led by Miss had burst in, and she had held fast as long as she could to this tail while she was being forcibly removed from the pedestal. There was nobody to break into this moonshine to-night and drag her down from the pedestal; but she clung very close to Rosalba nevertheless, and it was just as necessary for Rosalba to steady her out here as it had been to guide her stumbling footsteps through the fox-trot under the censorious and inquisitive eyes of the old maids in the ballroom. Lulu longed for an eloquence that would startle her new friend with the profundity and experience of her emotion. She thought sadly of the wonderful similes that must have been showered upon Rosalba, and of the burning epithets to which by now she must be so accustomed. One might as well try to surprise a prima donna with the flowers of a bouquet.

"I'm afraid you will think me awfully dull," was what at last she managed to gulp out.

"Why must I find you so dull?"

"Well, I mean after all the people you must have known."

"I can assure you that they were nearly all of them terribly dull."

"But you're so critical."

"That is just why I find you so charming, my dear."

Sixteen was not proof against this devastating compliment from twenty-four.

"If I could only believe that you really meant it," youth sighed.

"Why should I be standing here with you unless I am meaning it?" age and experience countered.

And so remote did Lulu feel herself to be out here in the moonlight with Rosalba, so far did they seem to have voyaged together from ordinary existence, that she began to wonder if perhaps Rosalba might not be in earnest after all, because it would have been such a long way to come merely to make fun. And then as if to rebuke her fancy of an immense silver distance severing them from the world the sound of fiddle and piano and mandolin reached them from the ballroom, the music seeming loaded with an extra sweetness from the dim earthy airs of the shrubbery through which it had to pass.

"I think you will dance much better now," Rosalba decided coolly.

She was right; and for another hour their frocks of rose and white swayed backward and forward across that big empty terrace on which the pale-blue porcelain tiles shimmered in the moonlight like water. And when they came back inside the ballroom the old maids had taken their knitting and retired to bed. There was nobody left downstairs except Giulia Monforte, who was cutting a French novel in the way people bite their nails, and an elderly gentleman with a white moustache who like a conjurer's audience was watching Rory Freemantle smoke a long black cigar.

"Where is Miss?" asked Lulu, who had danced away most of her self-consciousness.

"Here I am, Lulu," the little governess quavered, just managing to show herself behind the pianist. "I was turning over the pages of the music for Madame."

Madame, who was a tall feverish Russian refugee in folds of tarnished black silk, flashed such a smile at Miss Chimbley as almost to give the impression that the lid of another piano had been opened.

"If you want to go to bed, Lulu, *I'm* quite ready," Miss Chimbley suggested.

"Bed?" Rosalba echoed indignantly. "But it is only a little piece after ten. This is now the time when we shall drink stingers."

"Drink stingers?" Miss quavered.

Rosalba led the way to the bar which opened on

one end of the terrace. The rest of them followed her:
Miss like a child who is going to see another child do
something desperate with a doorbell, and the elderly
gentleman like one of those toy fish which are drawn
across a bath by a magnet—the magnet being Rory
Freemantle's cigar. Giulia Monforte dallied on reaching the door of the ballroom in the hope that Rosalba
would turn back and coax her into enjoying herself.
But Rosalba did not notice she had been left behind
until the first round of 'stingers' was ready, and when
she did ask where Giulia was Rory told her she must
have gone to the cloak-room to powder her nose, so
that when poor Giulia made a gloomy re-appearance
nobody exclaimed as she hoped somebody might, 'Oh,
here you are!' because naturally everybody supposed
she would prefer not to be conspicuous.

A 'stinger' consists of half a wine-glass of brandy
filled up with crême de menthe and as much ice as
will give the mixture a frosted look. The elderly
gentleman, who had perched himself on one of the
high chairs in a corner of the bar, ordered a stinger
for himself, and the effect of it may be gauged by his
asking Rory Freemantle, the moment the last drop
had gone down his throat, if she had visited the Purple
Grotto yet.

"No, I haven't," she snapped.

"Well, when you do," the elderly gentleman
earnestly advised, "be jolly careful to keep well down
in the boat as they row into it. Otherwise you'll
bump your nose."

Rosalba called for another round of stingers, and

the elderly gentleman ordered a second glass for himself, on the strength of which he asked Miss Chimbley if she had been up to the top of Vesuvius yet.

"Not yet," Miss Chimbley nodded.

"Nor have I," said the elderly gentleman. "But I think I shall go up to-morrow."

"You'll have to cross to Naples first," Miss reminded him, shaking all over with the benevolence of her local knowledge.

"Ah, ça va sans dire," said the elderly gentleman, stroking his moustache as one strokes an old dog in whom it has been discovered there is life yet. "Sans dire," he repeated, and beckoned to himself another stinger.

"Lulu," Miss Chimbley quavered. "Lulu! Lulu! Not another, dear, please!"

"This is quite a calm little drink, Miss," said Rosalba, who had ordered a third round.

"But Lulu isn't used to drinking *any*thing," her governess protested.

"Oh yes, I am, Miss," Lulu contradicted, tossing off the third glass; and before her governess could take any steps to deal with her she hurried away to dance again with Rosalba on the terrace.

The elderly gentleman ordered himself a fourth stinger, after drinking which he invited Miss Chimbley to dance with him.

"Not that I claim to be a Purple Emperor because I've seen the Purple Grotto, but well, nous verrons, yes, exactly, nous verrons. Voulez-vous, madame?"

Miss Chimbley declined his invitation nervously.

"Will you honour me, madame?" he asked, turning to Rory.

"I don't dance," she said curtly and lighted up another cigar.

"Will you, madame?" This to Giulia Monforte, who shrank from him with a shudder.

"Give me another of these green-eyed monsters," said the elderly gentleman, pushing his glass toward the barman. When he had swallowed it he passed out into the moonlight and danced by himself a slow waltz to the wild one-step that the orchestra was playing.

"Loathsome old brute," Rory ejaculated. "I hope he won't make himself objectionable to those two girls out there."

"We would be prudent to call to them to come in," Giulia suggested anxiously.

"I'll go and fetch Lulu at once," Miss Chimbley volunteered; but as the little woman crossed the pale-blue porcelain tiles in pursuit of her charge one had the impression that she, like the elderly gentleman with the white moustache, was dancing a *pas seul*.

"I cannot think what Rosalba sees so interesting in that girl," Giulia observed peevishly to Rory.

"Ah, you don't know her as well as I do," responded Rory, puffing hard at her cigar.

"Why you say that? I was knowing her before you."

"There are degrees of knowing, my dear woman."

"There are no degrees in love," said Giulia. "*On aime ou on n'aime pas.*"

"Precisely," Rory jeered with a rich puff.

"Ah, pah! This smoke of your cigars is excessively disgusting. I find it so very unsympathetic to smoke cigars. I cannot see that there is any beauty to become like a man."

"You'd better tell Rosalba that," Rory suggested.

"Rosalba is beautiful. It matters not at all what she makes of maleness."

"You grumble at me for smoking. But at least I *can* carry my cigars. . . ."

"What you are saying?" interrupted Giulia fretfully. "When you speak gobble-gobble-gobble *comme ça, je ne comprends pas un mot.*"

"But if you take my advice, Giulia," Rory went on, "you'll give up drinking, for you certainly can't carry your liquor."

"You mean I'm drinking too much! *Oh, mais c'est abominable.* . . ."

"Precisely. That's what I am trying to tell you. And if I were you I should toddle off to bed as soon as possible. The room's going round you now, and if you aren't careful in another minute or two you'll be going round the room."

In an access of indignation Giulia Monforte started to cut more pages of her novel; but, as she was holding it upside down, the paper-knife met with no resistance and shooting out of her hand, struck the third button of the barman's white jacket. Rory Freemantle laughed loudly, and Giulia was on the point of flinging the book at her when Miss Chimbley came wambling back.

"I must say good-night, I'm afraid," she quavered. "Lulu has gone for a drive with Signorina Donsante, and I must get another carriage as quickly as possible. You see, she's in my charge here."

The little governess hurried away, uttering a faint scream as the old gentleman returning from his solitary dance bowed very low to her in the entrance to the bar, because somehow it did not look quite like a bow, but more like an attempt to catch hold of her ankles and trip her up.

It cheered the belated loiterers in the Piazza when Rosalba and Lulu arrived to take one of the carriages that were still waiting in hope of a fare up to Anasirene. The war really could not go on much longer, they felt, when the girls jumped in and the driver with a tremendous cracking of his whip urged his stout little Abruzzi cob at a gallop over the rough pavement of the Strada Nuova.

"*Dove andare?*" he turned round on his box to enquire.

"*Alla luna,*" Rosalba commanded.

"*Sissignorina,*" he cried enthusiastically, urging his cob to greater speed.

Now, in Littlehampton or Bognor or even in Brighton you could not tell the driver of a hackney-coach to take you to the moon; but in Sirene the drivers have a less literal notion of direction. Moreover, owing to the recent extortion alleged against the island *cochieri*, the *municipio* at the instigation of the Milanese profiteers had nailed a table of legitimate fares to the little baroque clock-tower in the corner of the Piazza. English tourists who alighted after being driven up from the Grande Marina would consult this table, which presented itself to them with the authority of Leviticus or Deuteronomy. And after a careful scrutiny the tourist could turn to his driver with an air of austere omniscience and present him with the just fare supplemented with a pourboire calculated at ten per cent of the authorized charge. The fare to the moon, however, was not recorded. The mean temperature of the water at midday was recorded, but not the mean temperature of foreign visitors at midnight. Had that been recorded, the *municipio* might have fixed a legal fare to the moon.

At the first loop of the road which climbs up to Anasirene and coils itself at last round a twelve-hundred-foot precipice sheer to the sea, Marianno, the driver, turned round and waved his whip to the moon whither he was bound.

"*Bella nottata*," he exclaimed, his eyes glittering with exultation in his journey. He was a young man, and he was a very cheerful young man, because through some error he had not been called up as he ought to have been. He had presented himself to be shot by the Austrians, but the military authorities had rejected his offer. He laughed and sang all day when he got back to Sirene, because by the time the mistake was discovered with any luck the war would be over.

"*Bella! Bella!*" he sighed, and up they went more slowly now. The *macchia* was dewy and sweet, not yet dusted over by summer traffic. The dark gorges of Monte Ventoso loomed up to left of the road, and far below on the right the sleek sea was preening itself in the moonshine. Rosalba and Lulu may not have been charioted by Bacchus and his pards, but Marianno and his little Abruzzi cob were by no means a negligible substitute.

The carriage climbed and climbed, reached the last loop of the road, and galloped on again along the level until it pulled up with a ceremonious jerk in moon-parched silent Anasirene, where Rosalba and Lulu left it to wait while they wandered even yet a little nearer to the moon through cherry-orchards and groves of oaks and plantations of lisping poplars, both of them rapt in the folly of the moment.

Miss Chimbley arrived in the Piazza of Sirene five minutes after the truants had started. She beckoned the next carriage on the rank to pursue them with her chaperonage. A certain hesitation in coming forward was perceptible. The low living caused by the war had reduced the amorous energy of the Sirene coachmen to its minimum, and none of them supposed anything but that little Miss Chimbley desired to be driven up to Anasirene for an ulterior motive. Each one indicated with a whip his neighbour as more suitable than himself to make the best of midnight and moonshine. However, Miss Chimbley managed at last to convince a driver that all she wanted was to follow the *signorine*, and was accepted as a fare. Close on her heels came Rory Freemantle and Giulia Monforte in another carriage. The shock of the elopement had steadied Giulia's nerves. By this time it was decided that some kind of *festa* was proceeding at

Anasirene, and when the elderly gentleman with a white moustache arrived there was nearly a fight between the last two drivers over his body. The driver who won the argument shouted with triumph as he whipped up his cob, and the elderly gentleman who had taken a strong brandy and soda on top of the stingers shouted back. He was feeling that for the first time in sixty-five years he was grappling with the problem of enjoying life to the full. From shouting he turned to singing as much as he could remember of the comic songs of his youth, and when he could not remember any more songs he recited fragments of old verses from Mrs Hemans or Adelaide Proctor and finally *How do the waters come down at Lodore?*

In the Piazza of Anasirene the pursuing carriages pulled up. There was no sign of Rosalba or Lulu. There was the barking of a hundred dogs disturbed by the unusual traffic. There was the dome of the church flashing its sea-green tiles at the moon. There were the flat white roofs candescent-seeming. There were the olive-woods sloping dimly to the sea. There was the line of Monte Ventoso written in a flowing hand across the tender southern sky. But no Rosalba and no Lulu.

And it was four o'clock in the morning before Rosalba and Lulu drove down to Sirene to meet the lilac dawn coming over from Paestum across the Salernian gulf like Aurora herself in her fabled drapery. But not at all like Aurora Freemantle.

## CHAPTER FIVE

οὐ γὰρ θέμις ἐν μοισοπόλῳ οἰκίᾳ
θρῆνον θέμεν.
                              SAPPHO.

*Sorrow is forbidden in any house dedicated to the Muses.*

THE strain of watching the intimacy between Rosalba and Lulu wax in fervour all through that summer was too much for Giulia Monforte; she retreated to brave the rigours of a cure at some cathartic spa. Rory Freemantle, however, held her ground. Rory had within the limitations of her temperament lived hard. She was convinced she had long ago outgrown the illusions of first love in which Giulia had been indulging herself. In fact she derived from the contemplation of Rosalba and Lulu a certain amount of pleasure. Nevertheless, the obvious anxiety of Rosalba to be always in the company of Lulu and her equally obvious impatience of a third person did disturb a little the sentimentality of the older woman, who in spite of her bulldogs and female boxers and big cigars did partake, it must be remembered, as much of the forget-me-not as of the bugloss. One aspiration, in the possibility of fulfilling which she quite definitely believed, was a final and permanent friendship with another woman. So far, the only woman who had presented herself as the complete solution of ultimate loneliness was Rosalba. She did make pictures in the smoke of her cigars of that life with Rosalba—of the house they would live in, of the garden they would plan, of the view Rosalba's window would frame, and of the uniform of their maids. This preoccupation with Lulu did not worry Rory at all seriously until she decided that here in Sirene she had found the ideal house for that future, and only then because she knew how tactless it would be to propose her plan at a time when Rosalba's attention was concentrated upon the present, not at all upon the future. As a matter of fact Rosalba's mind never did engage itself with the future. In her sense of time, or rather in her lack of any sense of time, she was more genuinely an old Greek than in her form. Few people had such a feeling for the present moment as Rosalba, and half the troubles in which she involved herself and other people were due to that. You never heard her talk about the past or the future. You never heard her say 'last year we did this' or 'when I was a little girl I thought that.' She could no more have pledged that rainbow future to the unbroken monotone of a friendship with Rory Freemantle than have planned a series of picnics in Elysium. Lots of people will assure you they are true Bohemians or complete pagans, and you may always be sure they are neither. Lots of people will thank heaven in your hearing for their sense of humour, and you will wonder why they are wasting their gratitude. Rosalba never said she was a pagan. But she was a pagan. And she never thanked heaven for a sense of humour. Which was just as well, for with all her charm she had no humour, and not even the slightest appreciation of the ridiculous.

That at any rate was in Rory Freemantle's favour. She would not have to fight that in Rosalba. Could she but find the right moment to propose a perpetual partnership, the absurdity of her position, should she accept, would never strike the younger woman.

Rory did debate for a time the advisableness of leaving Sirene herself after Giulia left. She felt pretty sure Rosalba would soon grow tired of educating Lulu and follow her to Paris. She had known how to give Rosalba a very amusing time in Paris notwithstanding the difficulties of war-time.

And then Rory found that villa. She had tired of painting Rosalba and Lulu in secluded coves to which they used to be rowed every day for their bathing. Away from the flattery of her Parisian côterie she found the technique which there had seemed so modern merely unskilful. She could not pretend to herself in the clarity of these southern airs that she was anything but an incompetent dilettante with the brush. She even surrendered so far to failure as to buy a kodak and esteem its capture of the sunlit pose above the passionate endeavour of her own hands. Nor did she feel the least inclination to write any more verse, now that she had found the perfect lyric in Rosalba herself. Her muse, who for so many years had been her confidante, was dismissed like an old servant grown stiff and presumptuous. They had been so long used to gossiping together about Rory's dreams that she had come to allow her confidante an excess of freedom. This was no longer tolerable in the presence of reality. Besides, her muse was the same age as herself, and who wanted a middle-aged muse?

Having dismissed her muse, Rory discovered that to sit and watch two beautiful young women chatting about the moment was to feel marooned. She did not relish the conversation of Miss Chimbley, to which she was restricted while Lulu and Rosalba dived and swum and splashed about in the blue water. Rory felt like a nurse eating dry biscuits out of a paper-bag shared with another nurse. 'Stale biscuits,' she said to herself, travelling back in fancy to the beach at Hastings in the 'eighties, to the feel of the shingle under her diminutive bustle, and the smell of the dry seaweed, and the expression of her nurse's face chewing away at the biscuits. 'Rory has been having some very nasty spots on her shoulders lately,' her nurse was saying to another nurse. And now 'Lulu was very sick last night when she came up to her room,' Miss Chimbley was telling her. It was that attempt by the little governess to involve her in the domestic secrets of a beautiful girl which drove Rory into taking long walks by herself. She detected a desire to talk about Rosalba with the vicarious maternity of a nurse or a governess, and she fled from the humiliating impulse, abandoning Miss Chimbley to be marooned not only in conversation, but more actually on remote rocks while Lulu and Rosalba lay on the sun-baked shingle, discussing matters Miss Chimbley was much too old to hear discussed without being shocked. They even shut her up in a bathing-cabin once and rowed away to swim over the ruins of the sea-palace of Tiberius buried now five fathoms. Lulu in her pink bathing-dress looked like one of the voluptuous nymphs one sees on a painted Italian ceiling; Rosalba's dark green silk suggested the patina of a bronze. Rory cannot be blamed for refusing to discuss what was and what was not suitable medicine for such a pair.

The road from Sirene up to Anasirene did not demand the moon for beauty's heightening. Nor could an excess of white dust spoil it. The spread of beauty from headland to headland of the Tyrrhenian was invincible. There was no point at which one could say on the way up ' Now we are in Anasirene,' or on the way down ' Now we are in Sirene.' On that road one was always as much suspended between Sirene and Anasirene as on a vaster journey one might have been suspended between sky and sea.

The traveller who comes straight from Greece to the Bay of Naples finds the atmosphere in contrast as softly and luminously blue as in a landscape of Perugino or Mantegna. He cannot believe he once fancied Southern Italy dazzling. He begins to understand the slumbrous luxury of Magna Græcia. Sybaris is no longer a mere name. So when the tourist passes from Sirene to Anasirene a fine veil is dropped over his vision, and he beholds the landscape as it might appear in a dream; but when he passes back to Sirene he re-enters a world of sharp contours and vivid light which never fails to impress him with the sensation of having abruptly woken up. And of the thousand charms of the island this passage from eternal afternoon in Anasirene to eternal morning in

Sirene, or the other way round, within half-an-hour is not the least delicious. From the green and gold of Anasirene to the blue and silver of Sirene seems in the imagination trying to recapture the road between them as far even as from the Hebrides to the Cyclades.

This road was Rory Freemantle's favourite walk, not so much for its beauty as for the opportunity it gave her to step out. Nobody stepped out in the narrow cobbled streets of Sirene, nor along the paved *viali* that wound among its terraced hills, even in rope-soled shoes. The impulse to step out was prompted as much by her own loneliness as by the chance she had to reduce some of the fat which had been encroaching since her friendship with Rosalba. Exercising bull-dogs, training female boxers, and writing verse in Paris had between them kept her tolerably thin.

One afternoon Rory stepped out with such vigour that when she rounded the edge of the mountain and saw the level dusty road running in a blaze of sunshine toward the flat white roofs of Anasirene she felt it really was too hot to go any farther. She sank down on the seat to which a notice-board fixed to the lime-stone a few yards back had directed the wayfarer's attention with a pointing finger. Here a tourist could dawdle, with nothing between him and the Bay of Naples except a low crumbling parapet, and watch through water of hyaline clearness the dolphins plunge lazily down to the enamelled floor of the deep. Unfortunately the seat was in the full glare of the hot afternoon sun and being situated in a shallow bend of the road, just where the carriages returning from

Anasirene came round the corner to meet other carriages on the way up, it was also noisy with cracking whips, warning yells, and the incessant mutual abuse of coachmen for breaches of etiquette. Besides the discomfort of this row there was the dust of the traffic, and as culminating nuisance there was a half-witted mendicant permanently twisted into an Early Egyptian attitude who came and gibbered for alms, which he usually obtained not out of compassion for his infirmity, but because tourists were afraid he would push them over the parapet if they refused him.

Just beyond the belvedere on the right of the road was a grove of cypresses planted as thickly as in a Turkish cemetery, behind which portions of an ugly square house were visible. A marble tablet by the gate proclaimed this to be the Proprietà Beer, and above the marble a wooden notice-board was painted with the legend familiar enough in those days toward the end of the war SI VENDE. Rory had noticed every time she passed this way that the Villa Beer was for sale; but the unromantic name and the dusty cypresses and the glimpse of what seemed a dull ugly house had not attracted her curiosity. This afternoon, however, she decided she must somehow obtain a little shade and a little peace without walking any farther. Every time she had felt sure that at last she had managed to identify Rosalba among those bright specks which were people bathing all those hundreds of feet below the half-witted mendicant had thrust a distorted hand into her face. Rory could bear it no longer. She bade him be gone in English, in French, and in what she fancied was Italian, and at last she turned aside through the gate of the Villa Beer to escape. She could pretend to the caretaker that she was a prospective buyer, and perhaps there would be a shady corner in which to sit and rest awhile.

The house itself when she came into full view of it was as ugly as the glimpse of it from the road had led her to suppose it would be—a great square barrack with gaunt windows and a wide wooden verandah running round three sides of it in the style of a sanatorium. But the garden was another matter. There was a large flagged terrace with as good a view as that from the seat, but shaded from the sun by the cypresses and completely hidden from the road by a thick shrubbery of evergreens. This is not the moment in the age of the world to inflict another description of the Bay of Naples. Here it was in perfection; and, though Rory had been for many years under the impression that she despised a beauty which was too evident and in her mind had always classed the view of the Bay of Naples with Mendelssohn's Spring Song, she now surrendered with a gasp to this beauty.

"The Villa Leucadia," she murmured, and by thus naming it she realized with another gasp that she contemplated making the Villa Beer her own. Turning inward to herself she asked why she had called it the Villa Leucadia, and as she looked down into the hyaline water that washed the base of this promontory she knew that she was wondering whether she should have the courage to fling herself from it, should Rosalba refuse to spend the rest of her life up here with her.

From where she stood there was only one other villa in Sirene visible. That was the Villa Hylas on such another cliff as this two miles away. She had had letters of introduction to Count Marsac, the owner of it; but he was away in Naples. She thought of what she had heard of his unfortunate history, and wondered if Sirene would be kinder to her. A pity he was away. She should have liked to meet him. They had many friends and many tastes in common. There was something ominous about the Villa Hylas, seeming now almost deathly white on its high cliff at the other end of the island. Rory turned away from the contemplation of that deserted beauty in the thought of how foolish she should be to risk the malice of fortune like Count Marsac.

"If one is abnormal," she said to herself, "one ought to avoid high promontories."

Then she wandered on into the garden, which followed the cliff's slowly diminishing height to lose itself at last in the sweep of olive-woods flowing down in a gentle monotone almost, it seemed from here, to the water's very edge. This olive-thick slope was the body of the crouching sphinx to which the island seen crossing from Naples had so often been compared.

At the bottom of the garden Rory found a kind of amphitheatre round which were set up marble statues much larger than life-size of gods and nymphs and emperors with three or four marble sarcophagi and cinerary urns. It looked as if somebody had emptied one of the rooms of a museum into this quiet hollow. Spring was dead; but high summer was not yet come, so that there was no sound of twittering birds, nor rasping of cicalas. The silence was acute ; and these viewless gods and nymphs and emperors made it seem tremendous.

Rory was accustomed to find every interesting place a wonderful setting for Rosalba. It was only another way of saying she always missed her. But this amphitheatre with its marble population did seem made for her. Rory did not humbug herself with the fancy that these statues were anything but the coarse and blatant work of journeymen Roman sculptors. She did not suppose they were lost masterpieces of the best period. Still, with all their faults of taste, they did produce in such surroundings an effect. And Rory could not resist the picture of Rosalba lightly clothed, perhaps in the dappled skin of a lynx—though probably while this damned war went on lynxes were as difficult to get hold of as butter and sugar—or perhaps in a chlamys, a saffron chlamys stencilled with the key pattern in gold, or perhaps in nothing at all. Yes, here was surely the place to wear nothing at all—yes, the picture of Rosalba in nothing at all against the robust legs of that Diana was irresistible. Bronze and marble. Bronze! That's all Rosalba was. A well-cast bronze. The other women who had surrendered to her charm had supposed her to be a complicated piece of ultra-modern humanity. They had expected so much from Rosalba. They had embarked upon a friendship with her in the way they might have embarked upon a novel by Henry James. She was to provide them with a finespun web of emotion in which they might run hither and thither like distraught spiders. And Rosalba did spin her web, but in the old simple way for flies. Yet no doubt those other women had derived more pleasure from being a fly in Rosalba's web than in trying to spin webs for themselves, only to find them slashed to pieces by a man's walking-stick. Yes, a bronze to be housed and tended and always admired. That was Rosalba. "And I," thought Rory, "I am just one of those great clumsy marbles fit to be leant against eternally." She moved away from the hollow and the olives which cast their light shade upon the lupins and the yellowing corn beneath to retrace her steps up the garden and find out from the caretaker some details about this property that was for sale.

Somebody not so long ago must have planted many young trees on the terraces—cypresses and pines, acacias and almonds and casuarinas. But there had been no attempt at grouping. They looked like a nurseryman's stock in trade put in by the dozen. The land was probably an abandoned vineyard. No doubt formerly there had been olives all the way up, and then some avid peasant must have cut them down, dreaming of a richer return from vines. The west wind would soon have taught him his mistake, and he would have been glad to sell—to whom? The Villa Beer. Who could have called his house by such a name and set up those gods and nymphs and emperors in marble?

Ah, there was evidently the caretaker waiting on the topmost terrace—a depressed-looking woman with three small children dragging at her skirts and gradually destroying any shape she had left after bearing them. The caretaker was unable to give Rory the least information about the history of the villa and referred her for all details to Ferdinando Zampone. However, she was glad to show Rory through the house, which was as dull inside as out, consisting of two long rows of rooms on either side of a corridor with ceilings too high for them. Rory, however, in her mind knocked them all about, put windows where there were none, took out windows that were the wrong shape or looked in the wrong direction, built a studio at one corner and a tower at another, transformed the sanatorium balcony into a loggia with five white domes, and finally constructed a marble stairway from the terrace in front of the house as far as the hollow where the statues stood. What a stairway it would be, tumbling down in a frozen cascade to that quiet amphitheatre and the olive-groves beyond. She became so enthusiastic over it that she tried to explain her scheme to the caretaker, who smiled and said ' *Molto bello* ' without a vestige of a notion what was likely to be beautiful, but who was firmly convinced that no caretaker ever earned a smaller tip by withholding flattery. Yet even her optimism was staggered by the three ten-lira notes she received from Rory and the five-lira note offered on top of that to her youngest child, so much staggered indeed that she was barely in time to prevent the infant's swallowing it. She kissed Rory's hand and hailed her as ' excellency.' Then, as soon as her benefactress had vanished round the corner on the way back to Sirene she locked the children in one of the empty rooms and hurried along the hot road to proclaim in the Piazza of Anasirene that a female millionaire had arrived on the island and was going to buy the Villa Beer immediately. She added that she was mad, but very sympathetic.

"How was she dressed?" somebody asked.

"Like you or me. There was no gold or jewellery on her. I remained stupefied when she regaled me with thirty-five liras."

Rory stepped out as never before down the winding road back to Sirene, where in Zampone's Café Ferdinando was pleasantly full of information. It seemed the property had originally belonged to a German called Beer who had run the place for some years as a restaurant without much success. Then a week or two before the war a Pole had appeared in Sirene one morning, walked up to Anasirene in the afternoon, and bought the place from Beer the same evening. Three days later the sale was completed, and the statues and sarcophagi arrived from Naples, the memory of whose transport made the sweat stand out on Ferdinando's brow. The Pole had stayed long enough to have them set up at the bottom of the garden.

"Where I sink zey will be for always," Ferdinando added.

After the statues were set up the Pole had given orders to plant the garden with trees, had gone over to Naples again and sent across twenty-five wicker chairs, since when he had not been heard of until two months ago when his lawyers had written from Poland to say that he had been killed early in the war and that the property was to be sold for 120,000 liras.

"Offer a hundred thousand," said Rory.

Whatever Ferdinando did ultimately offer, that was the price Rory paid.

## CHAPTER SIX

εὔκαμπτον γὰρ ἀεὶ τὸ θῆλυ
αἴ κέ τις κούφως τὸ πάρον νοήσῃ.
      SAPPHO.

*For woman is ever easily swayed when she disdains her own surroundings.*

LULU'S infatuation with Rosalba had been warmly encouraged by her mother. She felt it had struck as hard at the whole male sex as it had at one presumptuous youth. She read aloud to Madame Sarbécoff Lulu's enthusiastic letters with all the pride of a mother whose son was as they used to say ' doing well in the war.'

" I am quite delighted, Anastasia," she avowed.

" I am sure you are, my dear Hermina, and I am so glad for you. And I am so glad for her, dear child. I think that life can be so beautiful sometimes," Madame Sarbécoff agreed.

" *La vie*," the Countess sighed pensively.

" *Ah, la vie!* "

And for a moment the cloud of that impoverished future darkened Madame Sarbécoff's vivid blue eyes; only for a moment, however, because she fancied that Hermina was going to propose something, and she was anxious to return her hospitality by agreeing enthusiastically with the delightfulness of the most unexpected plan.

"I think that *we* will go to Sirene," the Countess announced.

"Oh yes, indeed, that will be quite charming," Madame Sarbécoff agreed.

"I think it is not very prudent to leave Lulu to herself."

"You are always so right, Hermina."

"And I think poor Miss is very innocent," the Countess added, with a sigh and a shake of her neat head.

"I am sure she is very innocent indeed. I do not believe she has ever known what love is."

The two women on the columned terrace gazed out across the pale blue waters of the Bay that were sheened at this hour with evening's delicate gold.

"I think perhaps we will take the boat to-morrow," said the Countess.

"Oh, I quite feel that you are so right not to lose any time," Madame Sarbécoff agreed.

So, on an August morning the Countess de Randan, monocle in eye, with her friend and her maid, threaded her way through the noisy crowd of Neapolitans who since the outbreak of war had discovered that Sirene was as good a place for a summer holiday as any other more remote.

Rosalba measured that icy peak with a critical glance.

Two days later she had climbed it.

Outwardly the party of five and a half women (Miss could hardly be counted as an integer) who sat round the head waiter's favourite table at the Hotel Augusto was a happy and united one ; but like a political party it only achieved this effect by the contemptuous face it presented toward the rest of the world. Within disruption was perpetually imminent. That it did not break up sooner was due perhaps to the lack of a sufficiently credible tale-bearer with no other object than to make mischief. Rosalba herself was a *pasticcio* maker of the first order, but she was not in the least anxious to break up this party. It amused her to let Hermina de Randan suppose that she cared for nothing except the prospect of a *solitude à deux* with her ; but inasmuch as Hermina bored her to death she had no intention whatever of finding herself committed to it. Besides, she liked to see Lulu's jealous and mortified beauty when she came back from a long *tête-à-tête* with her mother in the Augusto garden. She was gratified by the set of Rory's hispid chin when she talked of spending the autumn in Stabia with Hermina de Randan ; but she always knew the right moment to make that chin relax by begging Rory to drive up with her to Anasirene so that she could see how the new window in her bedroom at the Villa Leucadia was shaping and how fast the walls of the studio were rising. She enjoyed waving a brief farewell to Hermina when she jumped into the carriage and took her seat beside Rory. And if she remembered that the Countess had been reputed not to care for women under thirty, she always remembered at the same time that it had been Rory who had told her so ; wherefore all the way up to Anasirene she would talk about Hermina's delicious cynicism and noble origin, praising her wealth and wit and worldliness until Rory's chin was as firmly set again as ever.

"Supino assures me that all the alterations will be finished by next March," said Rory, looking at the masons who, white as millers from the dust of lime, were working with intense deliberation to make the Villa Leucadia a shrine fit for Rosalba to hallow for the rest of her life.

Rosalba seemed doubtful.

"How glorious next summer will be," Rory added with a sigh.

Rosalba still seemed doubtful.

"I don't know what to make of you," exclaimed Rory, turning away fretfully. There would presently be nothing for her but writing poetry again if Rosalba remained in this difficult mood. Rory was indeed beginning to feel a little shaken in her confidence. She was confronted by the failures of her youth, by the old snubs and heartaches she had been fancying long outlived. Had it not been for Rosalba's extravagance, she might have despaired altogether. But the thought of that revived her hope, and with the return of optimism she began to tell herself it was only natural Rosalba should enjoy playing off Hermina against herself. And after all it had been she who had cited Hermina as a difficult conquest. Dear Rosalba, of course she could not have stood that. Dear, dear Rosalba, with what an enchanting grace she had strolled across the terrace to survey the classic scene outspread below. If the Winged Victory of Samothrace had kept her head she might have smoked a cigarette in a long jade holder just as Rosalba was smoking one now. The sight of the girl poised on that terrace in the lucid air reassured Rory. She seemed there as perdurable as stone itself.

"There was never so lovely a figure in the foreground of so lovely a scene," she fondly cried.

Rosalba looked back over her shoulder to smile an acknowledgment of so just a compliment; and Rory joined her on the terrace, gazing down beside her at the dolphins casting their shadows on the enamelled floor of the Bay twelve hundred feet below.

"I wonder if we could make a swimming-pool up here," said Rory. "You'd like one, wouldn't you, dearest?"

Rosalba said she would. She always liked things that would be expensive and difficult. And when Rory told her on the way down to Sirene that Supino had said a swimming-pool was perhaps feasible, but that it would cost at least forty thousand francs, Rosalba was convinced it would be impossible to live at the Villa Leucadia without one.

"Then you shall have one, dearest," her adorer promised.

And the enthusiasm with which Rosalba was willing to discuss existence at the Villa Leucadia for the rest of that drive down seemed to Rory more than worth the sum she should have to spend.

"Ah, there is Anastasia," Rosalba exclaimed irritably. "You know, I cannot at all stand that conceited creature, *mon cher*."

This was uttered sincerely. Madame Sarbécoff afforded Rosalba no pleasure at all, not even the pleasure of feeling she had quite cured Hermina of that incomprehensible infatuation for her, because the more earnestly Hermina showed her desire for Rosalba's company the more gracefully did Madame Sarbécoff retire from the friendship. Rosalba knew from Hermina herself that Anastasia was without any prospect in the future except of an ever deepening poverty, and she could not help being annoyed by such indifference. She did not expect her to aspire to a passionate friendship with herself. That would have been a little presumptuous; but it could only be a most ridiculous affectation of indifference that prevented her appearing at least piqued by the way she had been supplanted.

There had been one or two occasions when Rosalba had felt that Madame Sarbécoff was actually laughing at her, and in her position to dare to laugh at a younger and more fortunate woman did seem to betray an almost morbid lack of humour. There were moments when the twinkle in Madame Sarbécoff's bright blue eyes was definitely offensive, moments when Rosalba felt much inclined to pick up her glass of champagne and throw it in Madame Sarbécoff's aristocratic face. The high bridge of that finely chiselled nose appeared susceptible only to assault. After the mess Russians had made of their own and European affairs the least any individual Russian could do in these days was to abstain from giving an impression that she was daring to laugh at other people. There had been that wife of a dead Russian general who with only one torn frock to her back had arrived in Sirene with an Italian waiter as her protector. She had not laughed when Rosalba, moved by the wretchedness of her situation, had made a levy on her friends' clothes and presented the poor creature with armfuls of them, so that she had been able to sever the connection with the waiter and retire to a tiny cottage in the most remote corner of Anasirene and there ward off starvation by selling *batik*. She had not known how to express her gratitude for all that Rosalba had done for her. And what had Anastasia Sarbécoff done? Nothing. And what had she said? 'You know, my dear Rosalba, I am afraid that poor woman is quite *hystérique*.'

"*Eh bien, ma chère,*"—the feminine gender was the mark of Rosalba's ultimate disdain for another woman —"you would perhaps be *hystérique* if you must sleep with a greasy waiter, *ma chère*."

"She could have killed herself very easily. It does not cost at all a great deal to kill oneself."

"Oh, you other Russians are so much alike," Rosalba had exclaimed. "You kill yourselves instead of taking a little piece of medicine."

"It is not easy to argue with you, my dear Rosalba, because you are quite too young and quite too beautiful for arguments. To see a beautiful young woman argue is not at all æsthetic. It awakes too much her sexual emotions, and I find it so ugly when the argument stops and the poor girl is quite unsatisfied. For me youth must always be beautiful," she had murmured after a pause. "And of course always right."

Few women could have withdrawn themselves with such tact from a difficult situation as Madame Sarbécoff. The success with which she did so was generally attributed to her diplomatic experience, both her father and her husband having been in the service. The Countess, who liked to bring all her friendships to an end with a strong last act, spoke about this diplomacy with resentment. One had the impression that Anastasia had been practising its perfection as she might have practised sleight of hand. For the Countess, who had always been deeply and devotedly an admirer of spiritualism, her friend's withdrawal savoured of a medium's dishonesty. She could not get over the idea that there had been some kind of trick about it. On Monday Anastasia in the guise of a guest, though actually a dependent, had been one of the party of women sitting round the head waiter's favourite table in the Hotel Augusto. On Tuesday she had retreated to a tiny villa at the other end of the island. And on Wednesday she had actually invited them all to dinner with her! If Madame de Randan had not burned with an almost vindictive curiosity to see in what state her friend was proposing to live independently, she might have declined that dinner-party. And if she could have been sure that by writing a cold refusal Anastasia would have descended from the slopes of Timberio to beg her friend to tell her why she had allowed Rosalba to come between them, Hermina certainly would have refused to dine with her. She had never been so indignant in her life. She was as indignant as an actress whose curtain has been spoilt by the unwillingness of another actress to play up. She knew that Anastasia was wounded to the quick by her treatment of her, but how was she to demonstrate to the world the wound she had made? No, Anastasia had not played fairly. She had really behaved rather like a man.

So, on Wednesday evening the Countess and Lulu and Rory and Rosalba walked for miles, it seemed, along the narrow paved *viali* that led toward the gigantic ruins of the imperial villa. And when they arrived, there was Anastasia mixing cocktails for them. There was a lovely little red-haired girl of fifteen who must have been milking goats yesterday, yet who already called her mistress ' *madame* ' like a French maid of lifelong career. It was true the villa was small. But the view from the belvedere at the end of the small garden might be said to include the civilized world. A Roman would have said so, anyway. French novels splashed the walls with a vivid, almost an ostentatious yellow. Anastasia was, so long as her jewellery lasted, at home. And the Countess looking for something to criticize could find nothing except the absence of electric light. But on so calm an evening that did not greatly matter, because the candles burned truly in their glass shades. It would be idle to remind Anastasia they would not burn like this on windy nights, as idle as to remind her she could not exist for ever on the sale of her diamond rings. She would have agreed with too much composure to make the warnings worth while. Anastasia always agreed with everybody and everything, her old friend thought fretfully. She even agreed with being abruptly dropped in favour of Rosalba.

And walking back by moonlight from Anastasia's little house after dinner the Countess had a further mortification, because Rosalba, feeling that somehow Anastasia had deprived her of a triumph by this calm withdrawal from the centre of the emotional storm in which only did she breathe with freedom, took it out of Hermina by exalting that secluded life in a garden with a wonderful view of the bay of Naples and by chattering all the way back to the Augusto of the secluded life she and Rory were going to live in a garden whence the view of the bay of Naples was even more wonderful, and possessing the additional advantages of electric light and a carriage road passing the front gate. The Countess in her spleen was driven into a petulant comparison between the charm of Sirene and Stabia, which of course can never be seriously debated by people who have visited both. It ended as any such argument must end in allowing that the oranges of Stabia were larger and sweeter than those of Sirene, but that in all other respects Sirene was superior.

There are few things more trying to the temper of women than walking downhill in high heels and arguing along a rough and cobbled road. When Madame Sarbécoff's guests arrived back at the hotel they were all in a very bad temper, all except Rory Freemantle; but then she was wearing Sirene shoes with rope-soles, and Rosalba had clung to her arm all the way. Nor perhaps is it fair to

say that Lulu was in a bad temper, for though her
heels were higher than anybody's she had had the
satisfaction of observing her mother's irritation. It
had been a habit of the Countess to eat the greater
part of any box of chocolates presented to Lulu,
although chocolates gave her indigestion. She had
taken Rosalba away from Lulu just as she used to
take her chocolates, and here she was once more
suffering quite obviously from severe heartburn. Lulu
wished she could withdraw like Madame Sarbécoff
with plenty of French novels and a little red-haired
maid. Not that Lulu cared particularly for reading
or for red hair ; but she did like digging into French
novels as she liked to dig into pâté de fois gras for the
truffles. Lulu's education had consisted of a quantity
of extra thick bread and butter cut by Miss and all
the truffles she had been able to steal. And really
that was quite as nutritious an education as most
girls get.

In the end Lulu allowed herself to make eyes back
at a young Neapolitan neither more nor less good-
looking than innumerable other young Neapolitans
who were screaming at one another all over the island
night and day to the perpetual astonishment of elderly
Englishmen who could not understand why they were
not in the trenches. This particular young Neapolitan
had waited every morning to take the same car as
Lulu on the funicular when she went down to bathe ;
but until now Lulu had avoided his glances and thought
about Rosalba, as pious folk curb their passions when
tempted with the picture of a saint. It was no use

thinking about Rosalba any longer, and Lulu allowed herself to make eyes back. That evening she danced with him at the Augusto, which by now was full of Neapolitans providing a brief illusion that the war was over. The next evening she returned his kisses, and within a week Miss was asking all the people she met if they had seen Lulu anywhere. Life had resumed both for her and for her pupil its normal course.

This left Rosalba with rather more than she wanted of Lulu's mother, who soon began to bore her extremely because they only had two tastes in common. One of these was an entire lack of humour, which is a fragile link to hold two people together. Nor, it may be added, is the other taste a very strong link, because such a passion is sterile, and women's emotions do not thrive on sterile passions. It is difficult to find any woman who has not become dissatisfied at some time or another with the course a normal love pursues. But when women fall in love with each other the passion always seems to begin at the point when normal lovers know in their hearts it will soon come to an end. It is hard for a woman in the most favourable circumstances of a normal love-affair to be content ultimately with friendship, because what a woman really means by friendship with a man is being able to depend on him to look out trains for her in Bradshaw, which is not what a man understands by it. What a man understands by friendship with a woman with whom he has been in love is a complete relief from all responsibility either for her emotions or her trains. It is doubly hard for two women to pass from a highly emotional relationship to a humdrum talking-about-clothes friendship, because though a woman may forgive a man for a failure of emotion at last, since that is what she has been perpetually expecting, she is not going to forgive another woman. Her physical responsibility is so slight compared with a man's that there is simply no room for excuses.

Yet somehow Rosalba and Hermina did manage to become friends (perhaps because either of them was a match for the other in denying depth of emotion) with at last nothing in common except an equal lack of humour. However, it was one of those friendships in which the principals avoid being left alone together for a single moment. Perhaps it was hardly so much a friendship as a respect for each other's style of dressing.

When Madame de Randan went back to Stabia early in October, she did not remember her plan that Rosalba should spend the winter with her, or if she did, it was only to congratulate herself on her coldness. She was always proud of that, since it never struck her that the shallower the water the more easily it freezes.

"I have been excessively frivolous all this summer, Miss," she said to the little governess when the steamboat turned the corner and the honeycombed cliffs of Stabia appeared. "I think this winter we shall make a lot of spiritualism. One feels a great need of the deeper things of life at such a time. I am terribly shocked by this war. It is sad how much a failure Christianity has been."

With this sentiment Madame de Randan retired into winter quarters at the Villa Castalia, where presently she had the pleasure of entertaining Mrs Jammett, an American medium who had lately crossed the Atlantic to put her psychic talents at the disposal of the peace movement. The French who were in no mood at this date to tolerate even defeatist spirits had expelled her from France for attempting to extract from the spirit of Bismarck an opinion on President Wilson's fourteen points. Under Mrs Jammett's influence the Villa Castalia became a *salon* of ghostly celebrities, and the Countess was not as much disappointed by their ambiguous raps and jejune communications as she might have been if she had not already met so many of them in the flesh.

Lulu spent the winter playing poker with some of the young people of Stabia until the arrival of a Dalmatian baroness whose suspiciously fluent Neapolitan gave rise to a rumour that before she became a Dalmatian baroness she had been a Neapolitan dancer and of course during the war a spy. She was a handsome young woman of about thirty with a hard mouth, coarse hands, and bright bitter eyes which always seemed to be looking as if she had been given the correct change. The Countess decided Drenka Vidakovitch would be a suitable friend for her daughter, because the health of Miss had broken down under the strain of teaching and chaperoning for so many years. Those last weeks of poker had been just too much for the little woman. Lulu had not meant to be unkind, but it had been necessary several times to shut Miss in a cupboard when the young people had felt inclined to rest from poker and drink cocktails or make love; and there is no doubt that the sound of glasses and kisses, rarefied though it was by the stout cupboard door, had wrought upon the little woman's nerves. Miss had never managed to reach a clear understanding of precisely what seduction did consist, but she did know that it was the sort of thing to which no well brought up girl should be exposed, and whenever she was locked up in that cupboard she always used to torment herself with the idea that it might be taking place. The Countess did not want to lose the services of Miss Chimbley, because besides teaching and looking after Lulu she had always had an exceptional grasp of the linen at the Villa Castalia. The number of towels and sheets and table-cloths that Miss Chimbley had saved her employer was inestimable, and when she came to proffer her resignation on account of bad health the Countess was genuinely distressed. Miss must have a long holiday. That was essential. But who would keep Lulu out of mischief meanwhile? The problem was solved by the arrival of Drenka Vidakovitch. Miss went home to England for a long holiday; and in February when Lulu asked her mother if she and Drenka could not go to Sirene and take a *casetta* together for the spring and summer the Countess at once assented. She wanted to visit Paris upon business. It was most convenient.

"Lulu will learn something of the world from the Baroness," she confided in Mrs Jammett. And Mrs Jammett, who for a woman so much occupied with the other world knew a great deal about this one, agreed. She had just obtained permission to return to France, and she hoped for some valuable introductions to Parisian society from her patroness, possibly even for her fare as well.

Neither Rory Freemantle nor Rosalba went to Paris during that first winter after the armistice. Rory did her best to persuade Rosalba to stay with her in Sirene, where she felt she must remain to superintend the building of the Villa Leucadia. But Rosalba did not think it would amuse her.

"I adore the perfect thing, *mon cher*," she told her friend. "I will come back in April to find everything quite perfect for me *chez nous*."

"But I should have liked your advice to be getatable," Rory complained.

"*Ah oui, je sais*, so that you could have the pleasure to tell me that I was entirely wrong."

So Rosalba went away to Rome, and Rory stayed behind in Sirene, quelling that tendency toward corpulence by walking up to the Villa Leucadia in all weathers and abstaining from lunch.

There are few more soothing spectacles for jaded nerves than the deliberate motions of Southern Italian workmen, perhaps none except the contemplation of fish in an aquarium. It is not the exasperating slowness of the British workman who works slowly for the sake of a political-economic theory. You feel a Southern Italian workman has inherited a long tradition of leisure from sunshine, and that he is working slowly with a kind of savour, not as a protest against industrialism. The work itself must be surrounded with all the luxury he can give it, because work is genuinely the most important factor in his existence.

When the Greeks wished to personify extreme restlessness they usually gave it a female exterior. The Furies and the Harpies come at once to the mind. Rory Freemantle like most women was inclined at first to hustle her workmen unreasonably; but little by little she succumbed to the charm of their deliberate motions, and the sentimental side of her derived great satisfaction from the attention given to every single stone that went to build the arch of Rosalba's new window. While the mason chipped it and turned it over in his hand and laid it gently in place and removed it as gently to pare away some small protuberance, she felt that each of the stones was being carved to the shape of Rosalba as lovingly as though the grave-eyed workman were a Phidias. She enshrined too her own thoughts like unwritten sonnets in every block of limestone. She was not a geologist to know that limestone was the product of a swarming primeval life, and in her fancy she ascribed to it a virginity it did not deserve, supposing it to have been belched forth from the molten core of earth to serve ultimately æons afterwards as the protection of Rosalba from wind and rain and sun. Hence the one poem she did write awarded to fire the credit that belonged to water. However, since she had the poem built into the fabric of the wall as soon as it was written, she could afford to be inaccurate.

At first, Rory had been depressed by Rosalba's desertion of her that winter; but as every day the villa grew more beautiful she began to hope that Rosalba would not return a day before it was complete. She wanted on some supremely exquisite morning of spring to drive up with Rosalba and set her, a willing captive, to dwell in the Villa Leucadia for ever. The winter became a protracted dream. Her servants in Paris wrote urgently about the quantities of bulldog puppies whose arrival was making a nightmare of the house for them. She did not answer. Friends wrote to say they had discovered really promising young female boxers. She did not answer. And not until like a miniature and very rickety tower of Babel her unanswered cosmopolitan correspondence trembled every time she sat down at the table to write to Rosalba in Rome did she finally send a postcard to her solicitor, bidding him sell up her establishment in Paris and pay the money into the Credito Italiano. Her friends in Paris prophesied disaster; but then everybody who has lived more than a few months in Paris comes to think of it as the centre of the world and cannot help supposing that a final severance from it is a doom akin to death.

Rosalba on her side had an exciting winter in Rome, and perhaps she might never have returned to Sirene again if her grandmother had not shown less and less desire to supply her with all the ready money she needed.

"For once when I am a little free and amusing myself it is so annoying that my grandmother must be so stingy," she complained to Giulia Monforte, who was suffering torments of jealousy for this freedom and who in despair of not having the wherewithal herself to give Rosalba what she needed and imprison her in a cage of her own was plunged into a profound melancholy and talked of suicide for all a blue and white morning in the Borghese gardens, walking with Rosalba under the pines. Then her husband fell ill. Convention was too strong for Giulia. She nursed him devotedly, found consolation in the regular practice of her religion, and passes from this tale, no doubt as much to the relief of the reader as to Rosalba, who was too busily engaged in the problem of affections nearer her own age to waste a sigh for poor Giulia Monforte's thwarted and velvet-muffled womanhood.

## CHAPTER SEVEN

"Άγε δῖα χέλυννά μοι
φωνάεσσά τε γίγνεο.
SAPPHO.

*Come, divine shell of mine, and speak thy music.*

SOME stress has been laid in this narrative on the Greekness of Rosalba, and the enthusiasm of one who remembers her grace and gaiety and charm, her everlasting ability to be decorative even at times when she was making the biggest fool of herself, must be his excuse if he has conveyed to the reader an impression that Rosalba had anything of the age of Pericles about her. She had not. She was as deceptive as one of those flowers of the Greek Anthology whose perfume of Arcadia seems so authentic that it comes as a shock to find it was composed far on into the Christian era.

But Cléo Gazay really was outwardly Greek of the age of Pericles. She really did resemble, not merely convey an impression of numerous statues of antiquity. There is a marble copy in the Vatican Museum of the Apoxymenos of Lysippus. The youth stands with outstretched arms combing from his limbs with a strigil the dust of the palæstra, and it was in such an attitude that Cléo Gazay seemed to play the piano, not standing, of course, but combing the music from the black and white notes. Cléo came from the Midi, and the fancy that she inherited her outward form from far-off Greek ancestors who had settled on its seaboard was not too extravagant. So long as she played the music of Bach she remained this tranquil and marmoreal youth; but when she played the operas of Wagner in the wild way she did, groaning forth the melody in a husky tenor above the crash of the accompaniment, she was a valkyrie writhing to be free from the marble in which she was confined; and this manifestation of a gothic soul was a little disconcerting.

Picture her then, with straight nose and the jutting brows that hold music within them, with a finely carved chin out-thrust less for a sign of obstinacy than for some austere determination of her mind. Her feet are large like a man's, and her clothes are flung round her without any regard to the fashion of the moment. They are not really so much clothes as curtains hung up to exclude the night or let in the day as desired. The fancy of the young athlete fades into an evocation of the Cumean Sibyl. The Sibyl turns to the Aphrodite of Melos. The Aphrodite of Melos kilts up her draperies to imitate the garb of some early Artemis. The early Artemis becomes a terra-cotta figurine of pre-Mycenean queen or goddess, half-throne, half-woman. We have lost that power of assimilative perception; had we still the child's eyes of those earliest artists, we should recognize that the queen is a queen because she is seated on a throne and that simultaneously the throne is what it is because a queen is seated thereon. Realities become dim as the world grows old. We can no longer incorporate the person in the thing or attribute to the thing the life of the person. But that was the way to look at Cléo and her piano. Not that such assimilation produced a perfect result. She was masculine enough to play well, yet not masculine enough to be one of the world's genuinely great pianists. Her playing was never judged as a woman's, but as the performance of a man of undisciplined genius. Critics declared she did not practise enough. It was true she was lazy; but that was not the reason for her failure. Although unceasing practice might have kept those fingers not so careless of wrong notes, listeners would have continued to judge her as a man and still found something lacking. Her femininity dragged her back just as her petticoats always seemed to drag her back, for nobody can go about wearing curtains without appearing hampered by them. She had not enough awareness of herself in relation to the rest of the world to affect deliberately a masculine style of attire. She merely reached as far as despising her feminine clothes and being indifferent to dowdiness.

At this date Cléo was twenty-five years old, and her friends were beginning to say it was time she took her art seriously. As a matter of fact in spite of her laziness she did take it very seriously indeed; though nobody was allowed to know this so that, should she never reach the top, she might always have it said of her that she might have reached it if she wished. Her parents were dead. She had enough private means to keep her from dependency, but not enough to free her from the necessity of supplementing her income by giving public concerts. She had suffered, as women of her temperament are condemned to suffer, from passions which were not returned, which could not be returned, because the masculine side of her was so dominant that she sought women as she found them without waiting for those who were temperamentally akin to herself. If ever she made a vice of necessity, she hated herself accordingly. Indeed, her grey eyes were half the time clouded with the preoccupation of why she had been made as she was. Then those clouded eyes would lighten, and her laughter would be as loud as Pantagruel's. She was enjoying the masculine side of herself, revelling in that privilege of coarse humour and intellectual ribaldry which even yet is mostly denied to women. She became a man with men and avoided the company of women, despising them as every healthy-minded boy at some period of his development does despise them. And then she would go and fall in love again with some utterly unsuitable person.

Cléo had fallen in love like this with Olga Linati, who might have returned her love if she had not been trying to sell a house for a friend and who might have been able to sell the house and earn the commission if she had not had to design twenty dresses the following week for another friend and who might have had one of the best dressmaker's businesses in Rome if she had not been occupied with one plan after another, each of which took up so many hours of voluble conversation during the day that she had to work half the night to achieve the few tasks she had not talked about. The warmth of Olga's heart made her always obliging, though some of this desire to help other people may have been due to a constitutional deediness. Cléo soon discovered that the love she was prepared to lavish was mixed up in Olga's mind with a hundred other tasks she had on hand, and that any reciprocation of it would have to be squeezed in between finding somebody an inexpensive flat and somebody else a becoming hat.

"But, my dear, I have no time for love," Olga protested when Cléo reproached her with superficiality of emotion.

Cléo's brows loured.

"It is really no use for you to look angry," Olga continued. "I have known what it is to love. I was unlucky, because he killed himself for another woman's sake. I read about it in the papers like that. They both killed themselves. And all I was able to do was to arrange for him to be buried beside her decently. It was my duty. That is ten years ago when I was a girl of eighteen. Now I have so much business that I cannot interrupt it with love. He was the best lover you could imagine. I find all other men horribly dull after him."

"Then you don't understand a love like mine," Cléo muttered scornfully.

"Oh, I understand it. I understand everything," Olga babbled on. "But it is not for me. I am very fond of you, Cléo. I like you better than any woman I know, and I wish you would practise more. You are terribly lazy. If you give this concert next month, I hope to sell all your tickets. I have been to everybody in Rome. And they have all promised to take tickets. Now, if you count without the tax that we sell two hundred seats at . . ."

"Don't go jabbering on about how much money I shall make," Cléo commanded fiercely.

"No, indeed I must not. At half-past four I have an appointment with the Duca di Aspromonte who hopes to let his castle in Sicily to some English people for the season. I am to have fifteen per cent commission if I let it for him, and I feel sure there are so many English people longing to go to Sicily now that the beastly war is over."

But at five o'clock Olga had come back to say that the Duke had let his castle without her help.

"For three thousand liras a month, my dear. Imagine what I would have made. Eighteen hundred liras at least. That would have paid for the material I want for nearly twenty dresses. I would have sold each dress for quite five hundred liras and I would have made eight thousand liras profit. But now a friend of mine is starting a big production of honey, and he has promised me the agency. I must see him at six o'clock."

Olga's dauntless optimism in the face of one disappointment after another outweighed in Cléo's heart her restlessness under the least display of emotion. She became an ordinary friend of Olga; and she promised after the concerts were over to spend the summer at her home in Sirene.

Olga was the daughter of an Italian father and a Russian mother. It was no doubt from her mother that she inherited the bad luck that pursued her as it pursues all Russians. At least it appears to be bad luck, though it may be a temperamental inability to finish anything off. The Italian in Olga carried her headlong to the verge of success; the Russian in her pulled her up short every time. She worked in Sirene: she worked in Paris: she worked in Rome, tearing feverishly from one job to another to earn the money to keep her family; and in spite of her rebuffs, in spite of being made use of by cynical friends, she kept much longer than most women her trim girlish appearance, her debonair enthusiasm, her fresh complexion, and her voluble charm. And Cléo found in her bubbling self-confidence an antidote to her own doubts about herself whether as an artist or as a woman.

Rosalba could hardly have been expected not to intervene in this friendship. It was not so much that she wanted to separate people. She was like a schoolboy with a penknife, for ever testing its sharpness. She only wanted to be sure that she could separate people. For some time, as a schoolboy might debate which of two trees should be inscribed with his name, she hesitated between Olga and Cléo. Which should she take from the other? In the end she decided to take Cléo from Olga.

All went well at first. There were grave walks with

Cléo along the Appian Way while Rosalba shed tears for the perfect love that was supposed to have been perpetually eluding her. She was still the schoolboy, shedding tears of exasperation for a rare butterfly his net has failed to capture. Rosalba's perfect love had apparently been dancing away from her like a Camberwell Beauty all her life. One could almost see it dancing away from her across the flickering Campagna on these blue mornings when the March sun felt like May. There were long discussions about life on the terrace of the Pincio while Cléo sat smoking cigarette after cigarette, all huddled up like a Rodin statue now, one of those mighty blocks of marble half hewn and seemingly abandoned as if the sculptor had found the modern world beyond his shaping. There were motor drives out of Rome to dine at Tivoli or Frascati and drink so many glasses of the sunset-coloured Romagna wine that Cléo used to start playing cup and ball with a world that was henceforth to be her toy. There were motor-drives back from Tivoli or Frascati where the waiters had learnt to mix stingers so well that Cléo would be singing like Tristan or Siegfried all the way home along the grey road glimmering in the powdered starlight. Once, at a curve of this road where a dozen arches of the great aquaduct shed from their bricks the stored sunlight of the day upon the chilly March night, the car broke down. Lying back on the cushions, while the chauffeur tinkered and cursed underneath, Cléo hummed in her hoarse voice first Siegfried's forging song and then the hammering of the Niebelungen at the beginning of the

Rhinegold until in a surge of excitement she began the entry of the Gods, snatched a big spanner from the chauffeur, and caught the tool-box a terrific clump to mark Donner's blow upon the anvil as he dispersed the clouds enfolding the rainbow bridge. But the chauffeur did not enjoy Wagner any better than most Latins, and the way Cléo bashed his tool-box made him jump to his feet to curse such madness. But his language did not worry Cléo. She emptied upon the road a tin of petrol—this too at a time when petrol was worth almost as much as Rhine gold—and set light to it so that she might summon Logi and encircle Brunnhilde with his guardian flames. When the infuriated chauffeur at last got his car going again, it became the ship bearing Tristan and Isolde from Ireland to Cornwall. *Frisch weht der Wind der Heimath zu*, sang Cléo, and never tossed so wildly the fatal ship as when she was being steered by that Roman chauffeur, who was convinced by now that he had a couple of lunatics on board.

Since Olga had no more leisure to be jealous than she had to be in love, Rosalba did not derive as much enjoyment over her conquest of Cléo as she had expected. In the first flush of compunction for stealing Cléo she had commissioned Olga to make her two evening frocks, not apprehending that this order would completely occupy the small amount of spare time Olga had left in which to be jealous.

"Poor girl, I want so much to be kind to her," she explained to Cléo, who had given a great guffaw and advised Rosalba not to waste her patronage on Olga.

Rosalba's vanity was piqued. She had expected to be congratulated on her generosity. She did not mind Cléo's being barbaric after two bottles of Frascati wine and several stingers; but she deplored such bad manners after morning coffee. It was the most ordinary kind of rudeness to laugh like this at her impulse to compensate Olga for a broken heart.

"Poor Cléo is a genius," she confided to Olga. "*Ma maleducata, cara, maleducata.*"

However, she decided that being French Cléo could not help it. The quaint delusion of the English that the French are polite is not shared by Italians.

"Do you really love me?" Cléo demanded of Rosalba after they had spent all their time together for a month.

"Of course I love you," Rosalba avowed with such an accomplished kiss that Cléo frowned at her suspiciously. She had been thinking for some time now that Rosalba used her kisses as skeleton keys that would open any lock.

"But do I love you?" Cléo asked with a scowl.

Rosalba flashed her eyes. This was going beyond bad manners. This was very near to insolence.

"*Oui, je t'aime. Oui, c'est vrai que je t'aime,*" Cléo growled, and caught Rosalba to her arms. She had seen that heart-shaped face so sharpen with anger that for a moment all its beauty had vanished. She was sorry for what she had said, because she revered beauty, and it seemed to her wrong for the sake of a mood to tease even for an instant a beautiful thing out of its beauty.

"But I demand a love beyond kisses," she declared in tones of sombre mystery.

"*E va bene, va bene,*" Rosalba responded petulantly. "But it is quite too hot this morning, *mon cher*, for philosophy."

"Have you ever heard Busoni play?" Cléo asked.

Rosalba shook her head, tossing the sunbeams from her bronze hair.

"That is how I would like to play," Cléo muttered to herself, for she was worrying about her concert now. "And if you loved me as I dream of love, that is the way I could play."

"I shall be in the front row, *mon cher*, so I am sure you will play *à merveille*."

And Rosalba was in the front row with disastrous results, for throughout Schumann's Toccata she talked to Principessa Flavia Buonagrazia until Olga Linati who was sitting on her other side dragged herself out of a thicket of financial calculations and nudged her to observe how she was affecting the player by her behaviour. Rosalba looked at Cléo's face and did manage to remain silent during some Preludes of Chopin, in spite of turning with relief as each one finished to speak to the Princess and turning away again with growing disgust each time another one began. She watched contemptuously the expression on Olga's face. What frauds people made of themselves at concerts! She knew that Olga was not listening to the music any more profoundly than herself. Those blue eyes that seemed to be melting with emotion were really melting with addition and subtraction. Oh, why did Cléo choose such long pieces and why had she herself chosen to sit in the front row? The Preludes came to an end, and Rosalba had hardly time to turn to reply to the Princess's last question before Cléo was off on Brahms' Variations on a Theme by Paganini. Five minutes. Ten minutes. ' *Buon Dio, la ragazza non finirà mai!* ' A quarter of an hour. ' *Basta! basta!* ' Rosalba muttered viciously inside herself, looking at the clock as big as the moon which hung on the white wall above Cléo, a great silent clock that was enough to drive the audience mad with its slowness. The composer's ingenuity was exhausted at last. The Variations came to an end, and the player leaping up from her stool lit a cigarette and prowled like a tiger up and down the end of the room while the applause of the audience died away into chatter.

The hands of the clock retarded by the music seemed to leap wantonly forward during the interval, and before Rosalba had nearly finished what she wanted to say to the Princess, Cléo was seated at the piano again and beginning one of the later sonatas of Beethoven. Now, Rosalba had heard it said that Cléo did not play Beethoven well, and in her resentment against the briefness of the interval she could not help whispering to the Princess what a pity she thought it was that Cléo should have chosen to play Beethoven this afternoon. A smashing chord made her jump. She thought for an instant it was addressed to herself. But no, Cléo, although her eyebrows were meeting over a chasmy frown, was still presumably playing what the composer had written. Yet something was wrong, and hearing a low 'tut-tut' behind her Rosalba looked round to see a man with long black hair clicking his tongue in pained surprise at the performance. Suddenly Cléo brought both hands down on the notes in a couple of crashing discords that would have restored Beethoven's reputation in the most advanced côteries. The Sonata was apparently finished, and the player was rubbing her forehead in a dazed way; but the applause which followed was the compassionate applause for an amateur reciter who has forgotten her words, when the throats of the audience tighten in sympathy. Cléo hunched her shoulders and broke into some dance of Albeniz or Granados from an instinct to help her patrons out of their embarrassment. At the end of it she jumped up from her stool and called fiercely to Rosalba and Olga, whom she drew aside with her to the farthest corner of the room.

"If you stay here," she said to Rosalba, "I will play not one more note this afternoon. You are not what you pretend to be. I am sure of that now. I regret that I have made myself a fool for you. *Tu es une cocotte manquée, ma petite Rosalba. Donc, cherche quelque gigolo. Tu n'as aucun besoin de moi.*"

"A lie! A lie!" Rosalba exclaimed. "I find you insufferably arrogant, *ma chère chère Cléo*. I do not admit that a complete lack of *chic* gives you the right to criticize my sincerity. I am quite as abnormal as you are."

"You are not. You are not. You are as normal

as a *petite bourgeoise*," Cléo declared. " You would be much happier to find a man to protect you."

" I hate men. How dare you say that I don't ! " Rosalba cried wrathfully.

The interval at a concert in the *salone* of a Roman palace before a fashionable and artistic audience hardly makes the most suitable time and place to discuss one of the major problems of psychopathy. Olga begged the antagonists to be silent. She who was unfortunately so much more normal than either of them was able to see the point of view of both a little more clearly perhaps than they could. If they talked so loudly about their temperaments it must cause a scandal. Could not the discussion be postponed ? They knew how busy she was, but she was so fond of them both that somehow she would find the time to reconcile them. But Cléo waved aside her intervention. *Cette femme*—and the contempt was more for the noun than the demonstrative pronoun in front of it—*cette femme* must leave the *salle* before she could ever bring herself to offer the fashionable part of the audience the piece of musical sugar with which she intended to bring her concert to a close.

" It is better that you go, my dear," Olga took Rosalba aside to whisper. " Cléo is in a state of mind when one cannot argue with her. But as soon as the concert is over and she is at home I am quite sure she will send you a word how sorry she is."

" *Elle est tellement femme soi-même*," Rosalba declared bitterly, " that to call me *femme* I find altogether ridiculous. I am quite disgusted by her behaviour.

*Dis, Olga, n'est-ce pas vrai qu'elle est beaucoup plus femme que moi ? Moi, je n'ai jamais fait l'amour avec un homme, je te jure; mais Cléo l'a fait deux fois. Elle m'a dit. Une fois, oui, on peut dire peut-être une curieuse; mais deux fois, non, ça veut dire une devergondée."*

" *No, ma senti, Rosalba,*" the intermediary begged. "*Parla più piano, ti prego. La gente ti ascolterà.*"

"*Che la gente mi ascolti ! Non mi importa.*"

With this declaration Rosalba went back and took her seat by the Princess, defying Cléo not to go on with the concert. Apparently Olga's entreaties to avoid a public scene had been successful, for Cléo came back to the piano and began the familiar Chopin waltzes that were intended to give her less musical listeners an opportunity of tapping their well-shod feet in time and rocking their lustrous eyes on the bosom of the lilting melody.

At the conclusion of the concert Rosalba was mortified to see Janet Royle go up to Cléo and congratulate her affectionately on her success. She had for some time been under the impression that Janet Royle might possibly provide Cléo with the profound passion she had been seeking so stormily all over Europe ; and she frowned jealously not because she admired Janet Royle herself, but because it seemed absurd for Janet Royle to overlook her and accord this public attention to Cléo. For a month now she had been aware that Cléo had been always finding excuses not to introduce her to Janet Royle and her mother, which, even if they had not had the best apartment in Rome and known all the people best worth knowing, would have been reason enough for Rosalba to desire their acquaintance.

Mrs Royle was a rich American widow who had lived in Europe ever since her daughter was born in Paris twenty-eight years ago. There are a number of English and American widows on the Continent who one can only imagine were fertilized like Semele by a shower of gold in the mythical past. It is impossible to fancy that they were not always as old and as ugly as they are now. Nobody ever hears a word of their dead husbands, and their children are often so good-looking that one must attribute a supernatural origin in the male line. Here for instance was Janet Royle, tall and slim and olivine, with graceful mind and body, and gentle melodious voice, fastidious and intellectual, the product of a long civilization, it seemed, with a mother who looked like a squat cracked little gilded bonze. Nobody could remember when Mrs Royle was not as much chipped as she was now. Not the oldest gadabout in Rome could claim to have known her when she was young or beautiful. The only explanation of her daughter and her wealth is that on a dateless night she was fertilized by a shower of gold. This may seem contrary to reason, but it is less contrary to reason than Mrs Royle and many women like her.

Mrs Royle was exclusive, for, as she said, what was the use of having money if you couldn't use it to create your own circle of friends? She had lived too long in Europe not to have learned what a mix up society was over here compared with home.

"Though indeed why I call it home I don't know, because I've not been back in twenty years. They tell me I would hardly recognize New York. Still, I keep some of my New England prejudices and I just don't care to know everybody. Dear Prince Frangipani said to me last week—you know the Prince, Mrs Huxtable? Such a handsome man and a great great aristocrat, a member of one of the oldest families in Rome. Yes, Prince Frangipani said to me that he liked my Thursday evenings better than anything in society because my apartment was the only one where he could be certain he would not meet any of his creditors. Now, when you've lived over here a little longer, Mrs Huxtable, you'll understand that's a very great compliment. I want you to meet Prince Frangipani."

The other American matron had tried not to look greedy as she expressed her gratitude.

"Oh, I like to have my real friends meet one another," Mrs Royle had assured her. "And Prince Frangipani is so very simpatiker as we say in Italy. Of course, he's poor; but you can forgive a man for being poor when his ancestors were ruined by the Crusades. Oh, you must certainly meet the Prince and if you'll give me the pleasure of your company next Thursday evening you will meet him. You'll have a real intellectual treat, Mrs Huxtable, because the Prince speaks English just as well as you or me."

Janet had suggested to her mother that she should ask Cléo Gazay's new friend to one of these Thursdays; but Mrs Royle had been firm.

"No, Janet, I don't at all care for that young woman. Not at all. I've heard some queer stories about her. Some very queer stories. I'm glad to do all I can for poor Cleeo herself, but I'm not prepared to keep open house for Cleeo's peculiar friends."

Janet had not bothered to try to change her mother's mind. For one thing she was too indolent and fastidious to argue with her and for another she did not feel sufficiently interested in Rosalba. Her duty toward Cléo's friends had been done, she felt, by ordering two frocks from Olga Linati. Moreover, the friendship between her and Cléo had reached the delicious state of tremulous equipoise that the intrusion of a third person would have disturbed. Whichever way the scales fell, Janet wanted them to fall from the weight of inward emotion gathering in either tray. Was she or was she not going to allow herself to fall in love with Cléo? That was the question for ever pleasantly at the back of Janet's mind while she was talking about taste with junior members of the diplomatic corps who came to tea with her and told her what was going to happen at Versailles or laughed with her over Lloyd George's latest geographical *gaffe* and the Tiger's last mordant and profane epigram at President Wilson's expense. She felt so securely wrapped up in the secrets of high politics that she had at present no inclination to answer the question about herself and Cléo. Like so many people who have never had to earn their living Janet was as cautious of her emotions as of her purse. It was not so much that she was mean with either as that she did not know the value of either. What she appreciated most was comfort, and the long contest she had had with a tendency to anæmia led her to imagine that it was always a struggle for her to achieve that comfort. She used to lie down every afternoon after lunch with a kind of wistfulness for the pleasures of the world that she must deny herself to go on living at all. Ever since she could remember she had heard her mother telling people with pride that her daughter was very delicate; and Janet never had the least suspicion that she was not very delicate, nor the faintest idea that to be delicate was not necessarily to be distinguished. The way all her young friends sent her carnations and roses with such tender enquiries after her health and came so often to consult her on questions of taste confirmed the high regard she had for her own delicate and artistic personality. Her tendency toward anæmia and her talent for music seemed to her equally valuable; and each seemed to excuse the other, for if she were not so delicate she might have played the violin much better, and if she did not insist on playing the violin so passionately she might be less delicate. In justice to Janet it may be admitted that she did play the violin well. She and Cléo used to play Brahms and Beethoven sonatas together, the pair of them wondering all the time about love, Cléo saying to herself that there might be many moods ahead of her when she should not be able to tolerate those faded lily airs and Janet thinking there was much to be said for not wantonly disturbing emotions which at present she could arrange as artistically as the carnations and roses her friends used to send her with such tender enquiries. Cléo had discussed with Janet her affair with Rosalba ; and the fastidious Janet had been slightly shocked, but certainly not in the least jealous.

"I think you allowed yourself to be rather easily fascinated, my dear," she said to Cléo, gently reproachful, when Rosalba's bad behaviour at the concert was related to her.

"She might fascinate you," Cléo growled.

Janet smiled and shook her head.

"But, my dear, Rosalba Donsante is not in the least my type."

Janet had always found how much it added to the comfort of life to have types. Otherwise she would have had too unwieldy a waiting-list, because her cautiousness and, it may be added, her consciousness of superiority prevented her allowing even her types to make any headway for a long time. As with her friendships so with her artistic tastes. She would think to herself that next year she would be tired of Schumann and interested in Brahms, and it always happened as she planned. Flowers and music and pictures and friends, they were always well arranged ; and if Janet's life seems a little bloodless it must be remembered that she had a tendency toward anæmia and that every afternoon of her life she rested on her back for at least two hours.

Rosalba did not relish the notion of retreating to Sirene to win the devoted championing by Rory of her side in the quarrel without making an effort to upset Cléo's affair with Janet Royle. She tried as a second-best revenge to break up the friendship between Olga and Cléo, not this time by obtruding upon it her own spell; but in the old-fashioned way. Rosalba could not recall any occasion when she had not been able to make one friend criticize another, and she decided that Olga was profoundly stupid. In fact she went about Rome telling everybody that poor Olga Linati would never succeed at anything she took up on account of a fundamental absence of brain. This of course was repeated to Olga, who wept bitterly over Rosalba's hardness and hurried off red-eyed to sell a Venetian palace to an English profiteer who had just built himself a palace on the banks of the Thames. Poor Olga was anxious to effect a reconciliation between Rosalba and Cléo on her own account, because so much of her fully occupied time was being taken up in carrying messages of defiance and contumely from one to the other. Olga foresaw that it would end in having to quarrel herself with one of them; and she hated quarrelling with people, not because of the damage to her own benevolence, but because everybody she knew represented to Olga a possible channel to the calm lake of financial security of which she dreamed.

In the end Cléo who was too lazy to go on quarrelling agreed to as much of a reconciliation as would allow Rosalba and herself to be on speaking terms when later she came to spend the summer with Olga in the Villa Rosamarina on Sirene. Olga turned feverishly to the cutting out of the frocks she had neglected for this running to and fro between Rosalba and Cléo. Rosalba at once sat down and wrote to Rory that she was altogether tired of the *pettigolezze* of Rome and that her one ambition was to retire from the evil tongue of scandal to the Villa Leucadia. ' *Ose-je dire la mienne?* ' she had asked roguishly. She was longing to bathe again and had bought a white silk costume which would stupefy Sirene.

A telegram from Rory arrived the next day :

*Viens chez toi*
*Rory*

## CHAPTER EIGHT

σκιδναμένας ἐν στήθεσιν ὄργας
γλῶσσαν μαψυλάκαν πεφύλαχθε.
                              SAPPHO.

*When anger spreads through the breast curb the yapping tongue.*

ROSALBA'S return to Sirene was as usual a triumph. If that part of the population which lived on visitors was always ready to believe the worst about a person, it was equally ready to recognize the best; and whatever else Rosalba might do she did infallibly cheer things up. In her own intimate circle she might be a dangerous drug, but for the rest of the world she was a tempting and efficacious *apéritif*. We have noted her lack of humour, her capacity for intrigue, her childish vanity, her egoism, and her insincerity. Indeed, they have been so much insisted upon that her personal charm may by now have been forgotten. It seems absurd after the way she has been behaving in the last chapter to finding the head waiter of the Hotel Augusto bursting his braces in the pleasure that her arrival gives him. One feels that he ought to know better. He really ought not to be making such an ass of himself. He ought to be looking at her down his nose like the pasty-faced American spinsters and the English matrons whose cheeks resemble so much a cheap pink blotting-paper. Our own varicose veins swell with indignation at the homage she receives, because we know that beauty is only skin deep. We apprehend too well the unscrupulousness of that crimson faun's mouth. We do not mean to be stifled by that flood of bronze hair. We do not suppose that in spanning that little waist we should be spanning the globe. Still, we must try to sympathize with the point of view of a head waiter whose life is spent not merely in the presence of more or less ugly people, but in watching them eat.

If the Sirens had returned to their former haunt, if Ligeia and Leucosia and Parthenope had taken up their old position on the rocks of the Piccola Marina, and by so doing added an attractive feature to island life, the Sirenesi themselves would never have tried to chase them away. The consumption of a few tourists would not have been grudged, for the Sirenesi supposed that tourists were meant to be consumed. They regarded quails and tourists as manna. But if the Sirens by coming home to roost had frightened one visitor out of landing, a decree of expulsion would have been signed at once by the local prefect. All the Sirenesi knew that the morals of Rosalba and her associates were deplorable; but since the days of Tiberius they had been accustomed to the odd behaviour of immigrants. Such behaviour was to be attributed either to a lack of morals among all people who did not live on the island or to the rejuvenating effect of the insular air. In either case the natives felt they could congratulate themselves. They expected foreigners to show signs of moral sunburn within a few days of arriving; and when, as occasionally happened, foreigners visited the island and complained of the way other foreigners behaved the Sirenesi only suspected the critics of worse vices than those they criticized. Several worthy Englishmen and Americans had had to leave the island because the Sirenesi had accused them of appalling secret depravities to explain their censoriousness of others. It is not recorded that any missionary has ever visited Sirene, but if one should be inspired by this chronicle to do so the legend of his private life will mark a new epoch in sexual psychopathy. It will make Freud blush, Adler blench, Jung lower his eyes, and Dr Ernest Jones write his next book in Latin.

Rosalba cheered things up. That was her justification in the eyes of the Sirenesi. Accustomed for years to the spectacle of ladylike men they were not capable of being shocked by gentlemanly women. They ascribed the phenomenon of Rosalba and her friends to the war. 'Poor women,' they said, 'there is a scarcity of men.' Rosalba was beautiful, and the Sirenesi living as they did in the Bay of Naples disliked ugliness.

'*Povera donnina*,' they said. '*Peccato che non abbia un bel uomo.*' They were genuinely sorry for Rosalba. When they saw Rory hanging affectionately on to her arm, they remembered what they had suffered during the war themselves from substitutes for bread. Moreover, the signature of peace was not bringing the crowd of visitors they had expected, and to invite them to criticize, ugly though she seemed to them, a woman like Rory Freemantle who had been paying out money the way she had all through the winter was not reasonable. And now here was the Signorina Rosalba again, her skirts a little shorter, her cigarette-holders a little longer, the Signorina Rosalba with a smile on her red lips that turned into an order for a dinner or a set of coral studs or an amber bracelet and with a handclasp that so often left a ten-lira note behind it. To criticize her was to criticize Spring.

" My darling ! " Rory cried, when Rosalba came down the companion way of the little steamer into the orange and scarlet boat waiting alongside, there to be clasped in Rory's arms. " My darling, how wonderful to have you here at last ! It's tragic the workmen aren't yet out of the Leucadia and the bathing pool not yet begun ; but never mind, you're here, and they have your old room for you at the Augusto."

" Ah, but I think it is much better so," said Rosalba. " We can always go up to the Leucadia later on."

Rory tried not to feel hurt at this answer, and still harder not to show she was hurt. She knew how fatal it was to let Rosalba see her power, and she sighed for that Parisian manner of hers, that manner which had been so successful with female boxers and French bulldogs, and which she had even used with great success on Rosalba herself in the first months of their friendship. Was she going to be melted away in the alembic of Rosalba's personality ? Worse, was she on the verge of being transmuted into a Giulia Monforte ?

They rowed on toward the quay across water which

was so thick a blue that one was astonished to perceive the oars emerge from it unstained. Everybody on the *banchino* rushed forward to welcome Rosalba, and in the general excitement Rory felt with relief she was not making herself too conspicuous by the expression of her own joy.

"I didn't know if you'd rather drive up in a carrozza or go up by the funicular, darling," she said. "But I ordered three carriages in case you'd rather drive."

"Three carriages?" laughed Rosalba complacently, as she turned to shake hands with Beccafico the *guardia*, who having cleared a space with his stick for the ceremony saluted her like a full red moon rising.

"Well, there was such an argument between Marianno, Carlino, and Costanzo which was to drive down and meet you that I told all three to come at last. We can ride in one, and the others can bring the luggage."

"The *facchine* can drive up too," Rosalba decided. And she packed the four weatherbeaten caryatides into the nearest vehicle after shaking hands with the three coachmen.

The porteresses of Sirene are not used to being driven up to the Piazza in carriages. At first they were slightly embarrassed; but presently the novelty of the trip tickled them. Before the procession had turned the first loop of the road that winds up in long dusty diagonals from the harbour to the Piazza the four weatherbeaten caryatides were shouting witticisms at all the people they passed on the road, who themselves shouted back such witticisms in dialect as made the caryatides yell with laughter, added to which was the screaming of the children who at every bend ambushed the carriages and ran beside them flinging bunches of faded weeds into the laps of the passengers. Rosalba scattered a largesse of *soldi* to right and left of her. The drivers cracked their whips and urged their horses. The trappings jingled. The pheasants' plumes and little metal horns warded off the evil eye. An elderly cripple was hurriedly woken from his fly-haunted siesta and assisted into a position of prominent misery by the roadside to earn him a five-lira note from Rosalba who alighted from the carriage to press it into his swollen fingers. He kissed her slim boyish hand, which was rather like being licked by a walrus when bathing, and gabbled benedictions in her wake until she was out of earshot. The carriages went on past the wistaria-bowered old Albergo Odisseo, past the old Schweizerhof whose neutral name had been patriotically obliterated in a burst of anti-Teutonic sentiment and changed to the Albergo Vittorio Emmanuele III, past the Villa Amabile with its turrets and minarets and white domes, past the rose-hung gate of the cemetery, past lush young vines and lemon groves and geraniums sprawling over crumbled grey walls, up and up till the saddle of the island was reached and the famous view of the two bays. Here southward beyond the olive-coloured slopes of the Piccola Marina the Salernian gulf glittered in a sheen of silver as far as the empty horizon. Here northward beyond the

Grande Marina dreamed the bay of Naples and Vesuvius and the long line of the Parthenopean shore. But the carriage did not pause. Before them stretched the cobbled Strada Nuova which ran between houses and stables for about three hundred yards to the Piazza. It was the only approach to a *corso* that the island had, the only place where a carriage could drive with real danger both to those inside and those outside it. The drivers mustered breath—how heaven knows—for even louder yells. The caryatides volleyed their chaff faster than ever. Dogs leapt out of dark interiors to bark wildly at the carriages and leapt back again into shelter with howls of dismay. The carriages clattered on. A troop of children ran shrieking behind. A mule team with a tun of wine backed into the smithy. The Piazza was reached. The carriages stopped. The loiterers in the sun crowded round to greet Rosalba. All the way down to the Augusto she was being welcomed by old friends. The head porter was standing apparently upside down with respect on the steps of the hotel. The head waiter, who had accumulated prawns for lunch, was waving the menu like a flag.

We may disapprove of Rosalba's behaviour among her friends; but when Sirene can somehow seem more fit for mirth and pleasure, even perhaps more beautiful for a young woman's arrival, while we may, while indeed we should continue to disapprove of her, we must be careful not to despise her.

Rosalba could not help letting Rory see her admiration for the reconstructed Villa Leucadia. It was now as much more beautiful and at the same time more comfortable than the original house as its new name was more beautiful than (if perhaps not quite so convenient as) the original Proprietà Beer. Gone was the sanatorium look; and, if the alterations had not succeeded in getting completely rid of that long central corridor between rows of doors, the elimination of sky blue paint and magenta fanlights, the blocking up here and there of a door when a couple of rooms had been thrown into one, and the cementing into the wall, wherever a space presented itself, of famous bas reliefs reproduced in plaster gave a different character to that interior; if it recalled a little an expensive seminary for young ladies that was nothing in its disfavour in the eyes of the owner. The bedrooms of Rory and Rosalba had been built at right angles to the original house, and instead of the old sanatorium balcony there was a snowy loggia between the two paved with old maiolica tiles on which was portrayed a baroc seascape of nymphs riding over the waves in a yellow chariot escorted by conch-blowing tritons and drawn by mettlesome dolphins. From the middle of this loggia a short flight of marble steps led down to the topmost terrace of the many terraces which ended in that green silent amphitheatre by the edge of the olive groves. This terrace had been planted on either side with a quadruple row of stone-pines which, when Rory and Rosalba had both been mouldering in the grave some years, would begin to give the effect they were intended to give. However, the disappointment of mortality over the trees might be endured with equanimity so long as the romanesque arches of the loggia framed that view, a view such as the heart which has Italy graved inside of it aches for, desiring that lucid air threaded with the scent of how many aromatic grey herbs, desiring those crystalline deeps, those classic mountains and history-haunted shores, and most of all that timeless azurous peace swung between sea and sky.

In Rosalba's white room empty as yet of furniture, but finished, the two friends stood by the long casement that framed the same view as the arches of the loggia.

" You'll be happy here, my dearest ? " Rory asked in a choked anxious voice that was not even the diminished echo of her own, but seemed to belong to a shy child.

For answer Rosalba stripped herself of her white clothes and stood in the empty room naked except for the petals of a rose which had fallen from her waistband and stippled with red her foot.

" You see, I am already quite at home," she laughed.

The vivid light outside by some trick of refraction gave the walls of the big white room a kind of semitralucency like moonstone, a strange noontide ghostliness in which Rosalba's body glowed with such a warmth of life as almost to seem lighted from within like a paper lantern, as if indeed its shadow might faintly incarnadine the floor.

" Dear, I can almost see your heart," Rory whispered, in awe of an effect that was so immeasurably beyond the technique of her own ridiculous painting.

Then as she walked round Rosalba the light refracting from another angle seemed to solidify that body to flesh again, entrancing flesh, but flesh, flesh. On an impulse she looked over her shoulder to beware that none of the workmen was passing by, so conscious was she now of a challenge in Rosalba's attitude which would make her nudity a scandal even here in this cloud-cuckoo palace swung between sea and sky. And as Rory looked out of the window she saw walking along the clustered cypresses the two white peacocks she had bought to symbolize herself and Rosalba. The quality of their plumage gave to them from whatever angle the sun caught it a lightness that humanity could not keep. Their tails trailed along the ground like smoke—no, hardly so opaque as smoke, but like a creeping mist. The crests upon their delicate and contemptuous heads glistened like thistledown. They seemed indeed all plumed with thistledown, those vain imponderable birds, those wraiths stepping so delicately and contemptuously beside the cypress-trees darkly clustering.

"Ah, look," Rory cried. "Look, dearest, there are the white peacocks that will walk here always like our two ghosts, when perhaps sometimes we are not together here."

Rosalba jumped back from the window and made the sign to protect herself from the evil eye.

"*Pavoni! Pavoni!*" she cried. "*Sei pazza?* Oh, I think you are quite mad to bring those horrible birds here."

And as if in her nakedness she were somehow more

dangerously exposed to their influence she began to fling on her clothes hurriedly.

At that moment one of the birds stopped and throwing up its head screamed. The scream was answered by its companion. Then both birds screamed together, screamed and screamed, until when they were silent the lucid air for miles around seemed full of screams echoing in the gorges of Monte Ventoso, echoing down terrace after terrace to be hushed at last by the olives, echoing down the twelve-hundred feet cliff to be lost in the waters of the bay, echoing up to be withered at last in the rays of the sun.

*And here of your courtesy let the chronicler lay down his pen a moment and, after closing his own fist, project his own little finger and his own forefinger to ward off the omen of evil influence, because he is, to tell the truth, as much afraid of peacocks as Rosalba.*

" Why, Rosalba darling, how can you be so superstitious ? " Rory protested.

" I tell to you I cannot suffer to see *pavoni*. They are entirely bad for me."

" But, my dear, these are white peacocks."

" It is all the same for me. I cannot suffer to see them."

" But, my beloved, I haven't bought them just for fun. They're meant to be the symbol of you and me."

" What is that ? *Non posso capire*. Those dam birds are putting all of English out of my head."

" Darling, of course I would never have got them if I'd known you felt like that about them. But I thought they seemed to express so perfectly what you and I are in this world."

"*Pavone? Io un pavone? Ma che*, Rory? Thank you so much. You are quite full of compliments."

"Well, don't be angry with me, darling. I meant it for the best. Of course, if you don't like them, I'll send them away."

"It is already too late, *mon cher*. *Dio, sei pazza, sei pazza!*" Rosalba grumbled.

"Darling, I beg you not to be angry with me. I really can't bear our first day up here to be spoilt. I thought you'd have felt the way I did about the poor peacocks. And they only scream occasionally. Like us really."

"When I scream?" Rosalba demanded indignantly.

"Perhaps I ought to have said like me," Rory apologized hastily. "For of course I *do* scream. Dearest, I'm afraid I scream for you when you are not with me."

"*Pavoni! Pavoni!*" Rosalba ejaculated again. "For me it is quite impossible to understand that a woman of the world like you must be such an awful duffer and buy *pavoni*. For me that is beyond the folly of the biggest imbecile I can imagine."

"Well, really I think you've said enough now. I'm sorry. I can't do more than say I'm sorry. I'll send the peacocks away. Now, darling, do let's forget about them."

"Please do not be proud with me, *mon cher*. It is for me to be proud with you. You have done a dam silly thing, I tell to you."

"All right! All right! But do let's talk of something else."

"I am not at all in a mood for talking. I am quite disgusted for to-day. *Pavoni! Pavoni!*"

"They're white peacocks."

"*Bianchi, rossi*, what does it matter when one has been as stupid as a pig?"

"Well, I'll buy two white pigs instead," said Rory with a smile.

"It is not anything for laughing," Rosalba snapped.

"Oh well, don't say any more, or I'll go out and wring the wretched birds' necks."

"*Pavoni!*" muttered Rosalba hopelessly.

In the carriage on the way down to Sirene, while Rosalba sulked, the owner of the peacocks was wondering what she should do with them. Superstition apart, one could not send a friend a couple of peacocks in the way one might send a brace of partridges in some autumnal mood of pensive and affectionate remembrance. She tried to think of any friend who would not so much be grateful for them, but at least not unduly annoyed; but none of the friends who might have accepted such a gift had a proper place to keep them. You couldn't have them walking about an apartment in Paris like Pekinese spaniels. People who owned Pekinese spaniels cherished a perpetual delusion that every time they infringed the sanitary code it was an exception for which either the maid's carelessness or an unexpected visitor's face was to be blamed. Actually in the sum total of sanitary indiscretions committed in the course of a year there would probably be little to choose between a couple of Pekinese spaniels and a couple of white peacocks. But what owner of Pekinese—and who among her Parisian friends did not own at least one?—would admit that her pets were any more liable to corporeal claims than cherubs? Whereas peacocks! The very name was a threat. For that matter, so was Pekinese. Still the verbal association was not quite so obvious. And then that screaming. It was supposed to herald rain, which if true would mean that in Paris they would be screaming most of the time, and that would be unendurable in an apartment. She might try to resell them to the bird-fancier at Nice from whom she had bought them, but having once got rid of them, would he be likely to re-purchase them? Better wring their necks. But that would be such a farmyard end for two aristocrats like them. It would be kinder to cut their slim throats as if they were being sacrificed to Hera. Yet why sacrifice such beauty to Hera, to that dull exponent of the female mind and morality at its dead normal most female level? Such a sacrifice would be a satire on the whole of her life. Besides, it would seem a silly piece of neo-paganism and would put her on a level with the foolish young men who played at being Greeks in order to justify in a theatrical way behaviour and impulses that needed no justification. Why kill the poor birds at all? Rosalba would only despise such weakness. There was a danger of allowing herself to be dominated too completely by Rosalba.

Rory fixed her monocle and pulled tight the sailor's

knot round her stiff collar. She had been weak. Henceforth she would be strong. She must recover somehow her old attitude, her old manner. The peacocks should be removed from the garden of the Leucadia. So far she would surrender to Rosalba's nervous apprehension. But they should not be killed. They should be boarded out. A large aviary should be built for them on the land of some peasant who was not superstitious and who for so much a week would look after the birds. She had bought them to be the image of a rare love. To have them killed or to give them away might indeed bring misfortune upon that love. That the birds should be imprisoned in a cage was appropriate, for were not she and Rosalba imprisoned by their temperaments in an uncomprehending world? But she must be firm with Rosalba. She must not let her fancy she could tyrannize over her. Rory pulled the sailor's knot still tighter, so tight indeed that in addition to being a prisoner in an uncomprehending world she was now a prisoner in her own collar.

"I cannot at all understand why you have not yet learnt to tie yourself properly," Rosalba observed in a tone of irritable criticism when Rory had been fidgeting for some moments to get free from the constriction in which she had involved herself.

"Damn it, Rosalba, I'm not going to stand any more of your bad temper to-day," Rory snapped. Uncomfortable though her collar was, it was serving her purpose. Had her neck been free she might have been tempted to lean over and try to appease Rosalba with a display of affection; but it is impossible to be affectionate or sentimental in a collar pulled too tight. She had to hold up her head high and console herself with the reflection that Rosalba had come back to her after six months in Rome. That showed how much Rosalba must really have been depending on her all the time. That was sufficient compensation for any lack of superficial fidelity. She need never be jealous of that provided she could always feel sure of Rosalba's dependency. That was where a love like theirs was so far superior to a normal love founded upon the will to procreate.

"Creation not procreation," she murmured, pleased with the phrase she had discovered to express the superiority of her way of love.

"You will quite choke yourself, *mon cher*, in another minute," said Rosalba in tones of scornful impatience. She was under the impression that Rory's murmured apophthegm had been a gasp of physical distress.

"If my collar worries you so much," Rory retorted sarcastically, "why don't you loosen it for me?"

"And give you so much pleasure?" Rosalba countered. "Thank you so much. I am not in a mood to give you any pleasure after your disgusting carelessness of those peacocks."

"Peacocks, darling. Not peas-cocks."

"*Assez de ton darling!*" Rosalba exclaimed angrily. "*Si mon anglais te tracasse, je ne le parlerai plus. Heureusement tu n'es pas ma gouvernante.*"

Rory could refreshingly have wept for Rosalba's

unkindness on this day to which she had been looking forward all the winter; but her collar saved her from such weakness.

"If you're going to look as disagreeable as you do now," she spluttered, "you can talk Hebrew for all I care."

"*Ça veut dire que je suis Juive?*" Rosalba demanded hotly.

"Oh, damn it, it says whatever you choose. I'm sick of your filthy temper."

"I do not allow impudence to any person if they have all the money in the world," said Rosalba pompously. "Please do not think that you can buy me as you have been buying your beastly *boxeuses*."

"I've never tried to buy anybody in my life."

"That is excessively fortunate for you, because I do not at all think that you would be very successful."

"I thought you weren't going to talk English any more."

"I talk English because I find you are quite so stupid that I am afraid you will not understand nothing else."

"What a silly schoolgirl retort!"

"Continue, my dear, continue. First I am *lâche*, then I am *illettrée*, then I am *Juive*, and now I am a schoolagirl. Perhaps you would like to say I am also a *cocotte*?"

"You behave like one sometimes. Oh, look here, Rosalba, I'm sick of wrangling like this. I'm going to get out and walk."

Rory prodded the driver in the back and told him to pull up.

"Sul mio conta," she said, as she alighted.

"*Sissignorina.*"

"No, no," Rosalba commanded. "*Pagherò io.*"

"No, no, sul mio conta," Rory protested. "I insist on its being put down to me."

"*Pagherò io,*" Rosalba repeated haughtily. "*Avanti!*"

The driver whipped up his horse. As the simplest way out of the argument he had decided to gratify both ladies.

No sooner had Rory seen the carriage clatter on ahead than she sat down on the dusty grass by the roadside and undid her tie. The relief, though pleasant, made her feel weakly tolerant of Rosalba's bad manners. She began immediately to reproach herself with having been too hard upon the child. It was foolish to treat Rosalba as if she were an ordinary person. Everybody had some kind of superstition. Poor dear, she had been genuinely horrified by the sight of the peacocks. It had not been done to create an effect. She should have been more sympathetic instead of thinking first, as undoubtedly she had, how much she had paid for the birds. It was a lesson not to let materialism take hold of one. And why not have passed over Rosalba's little slip in English? What did it matter if she did call them 'peacocks'? There was nothing so galling as being corrected over a trifling slip in grammar. The correction might be well intended; but, however tactfully offered, it always implied a superiority. Was she not herself always irritated when one of her French genders was corrected by a friend? And she had not corrected Rosalba tactfully. Poor little Rosalba who had come back from Rome so full of wanting to enjoy Sirene, so glad to be quit of the complicated jealousies over her of half a dozen women. She had been so obviously delighted with the villa until those wretched peacocks had appeared. She would never have taken off her clothes like that unless she had been wanting to express her joy at being back. 'At home,' she had said. Tears came into Rory's eyes. At home! The darling! And she had repaid that exquisite gesture of intimacy by correcting her over one miserable 's', one insignificant 's' which had wormed itself into the middle of a word. And peacocks evidently *were* unlucky. Rosalba had been right. First of all, by being there they had upset the whole day, and then by having only one 's' instead of two they had completed the ruin they had begun. They evidently were *very* unlucky. And she owed an apology to Rosalba. She owed it to her. Rosalba had been right all the time. There would be no feebleness in apologizing and begging her forgiveness. Thank heaven, women of her temperament had a sense of justice denied to the cowardly slaves of men's desires. They knew when they were in the wrong and could admit it. The contemptible instinct to protect themselves against the male prevented ordinary women from ever doing that, prevented them from ever rising above the mentality of the criminal in the dock. No doubt Rosalba would not forgive her at once. No doubt she would punish her. She had wounded her too deeply to expect anything else. Why, she had actually told her that sometimes she behaved like a cocotte. No wonder Rosalba had insisted on paying the driver. Her pride had been wounded to the quick. 'Pagherò io!' Poor darling child, she had driven off feeling she could never accept anything from her Rory again, her clumsy tactless old Rory, who had been granted the most marvellous love any woman had ever known and had not shown any more appreciation of it than a man. Why, Rosalba might have thought she was sneering at her for taking off her clothes. That beautiful frank gesture which had placed Rosalba on a pedestal beside the noblest monuments of plastic genius had been flung in her teeth by the one being on earth who was capable of appreciating its beauty. Poor child! Could she ever atone to her for such brutal insensibility? She might never be forgiven. She might for the sake of one silly and vulgar retort have spoilt her whole life irremediably. She had allowed vanity and egotism to take possession of her like unclean spirits. What did it matter if Rosalba did dominate her? What liberty should one not permit to the incarnation of one's ideal? Why should Rosalba be tamed? Such a process would reduce their sublime love to the level of a suburban marriage. 'Pagherò io.' Poor tortured darling! She must have been on the rack when she uttered those two words. 'I will pay.' It was not the mere proclamation of an intention to pay the few miserable liras that the driver would ask. It possessed a wider, a profoundly symbolical significance. It was the expression in two words of all that her Rory had made her suffer.

Tormenting herself thus with self-reproach, Rory reached the Augusto, where the head porter handed her a note.

*I have gone to stay with Lulu and her friend in Villino Krank. Please do not to come near me. I am in such a rage that I cannot suffer to see you.*
*Rosalba Donsante.*

The surname was the last straw for Rory. She felt that she could not face her misery alone. She almost became an ordinary woman. She yearned for a confidante. She set out on the long walk to where Madame Sarbécoff lived in wise seclusion, pastoral and remote.

## CHAPTER NINE

"Ἄτθι, σοὶ δ' ἔμεθεν μὲν ἀπήχθετο
φροντίσδην, ἐπὶ δ' Ἀνδρομέδαν πότῃ.
                              SAPPHO.

*But, Atthis, you have come to hate me now, and are flying in the wake of Andromeda instead.*

WHEN Rosalba left the hotel she turned into what used to be officially called the Via Kaiser Wilhelm. This road skirted on its right the rocky lower slopes of the Torrione, one of Sirene's four fantastic hills, and on its left looked down across a vineyard over the abandoned Certosa, whose empty quadrangles and cloisters in the sunlight and grey sea of roofs had the air of an Oxford college in the middle of the long vacation. When the Kaiser became a European nuisance, the municipality called this road the Via Garibaldi; but on the President's arrival in Europe they changed the name again to the Via Woodrow Wilson, and when American popularity sank to the Via Fiume. At the present moment its official title is Via Mussolini. The inhabitants of Sirene still call it, as they always have and probably always will, Via Certosa.

The Via Certosa apparently came to an end in a public garden on the edge of the cliff, which had been laid out by Krank, the great German maker of arms, and presented to the island. Despite his social disgrace before the war, despite the use the Germans had made of his weapons, the Sirenesi still called it the

Giardino Krank, and never by its latest title the Giardino Vittoria Veneto. Between the slopes of the Krank garden and the slopes of the Torrione the Via Certosa narrowed to a dark gully, from which it emerged to descend a perpendicular limestone cliff in a series of dizzy loops. This road had been constructed at great expense by Herr Krank for the good of the island he loved, and the municipality having exhausted the Italian victories won during the war let it remain the Via Krank, but took it out of the road itself by allowing it to fall into so ruinous a condition that some wit had suggested it ought to be called the Via Caporetto, such a landslide had it become with the winter rains of seven years.

About half-way down this road Rosalba stopped before an archway built against the cliff, in which was a door marked *Proprietà Privata*. On this she knocked, wondering in the sun-dyed silence if Drenka Vidakovitch and Lulu were at home. Presently she heard what sounded like a consultation behind the door, which at last was opened just far enough to see who the intruder was.

"*C'est moi! C'est Rosalba!*" she cried.

The door was flung open, and Lulu welcomed her with that warmth which somehow no one who had not seen Rosalba for a long time could ever manage to deny her, whatever the coolness of the last parting.

The cottage in which Drenka and Lulu had passed the early spring had been the simple retreat of Herr Krank when he fled from the noise of his hammers to Sirene. The studio, bedroom, and kitchen of its only floor were built against the face of the cliff. From a small courtyard in front steps led up to a semi-circular terrace surrounded by columns. Terra-cotta pots of agaves and aloes stood along the parapet of the narrow little garden beyond which followed the contours of the cliff's projection. The crevices of sparse soil were blazing with orange and magenta mesembrianthemums; great olive-jars, such as hid the forty thieves, were filled with earth from which roses and geraniums clambered up everywhere in a mad tangle of blossom. It seemed the quietest garden under the sun, with nothing to break its silence except the murmur of the sea far below, the scuffle of lizards through the fast-drying herbage, and the long hum of bees. The columns of the terrace weathered to a fair grey by the sea wind had an air of ancient magic holiness as if Poseidon had once been worshipped here. The little crumbled garden was still haunted by deities who had dignified these vivid flowers from America and Africa, these agaves and scarlet aloe-spikes and starry mesembrianthemums, so that they had lost their modern foreign air and grew here as naturally as the cistus and the rosemary. Seated on that columned terrace one no longer noticed the Via Krank. Its ruined zigzags had vanished into the cliff from which they had been carved. In the foreground the marine face of the Torrione gashed by an immense cavern rose sheer a thousand feet from the road that was like a narrow white beach. Beyond were the olive-covered slopes flowing down to the cluster of buildings that marked the Piccola Marina, and beyond these towered the precipices of Monte Ventoso. And everywhere—beyond—around—below—the sea.

"You know, I think it is very pretty where you have made yourselves your nest," said Rosalba. "I shall tell to Rory that you have found a place much better than she has found."

She lit a cigarette and nodded her head at the view.

"*Vous savez, mes chers, c'est épatant.* You know, I would awfully like to stay here for a little while with you. I can have a bed for myself in the studio."

Lulu glanced at her friend. The Baroness setting tighter her tight mouth frowned. She had heard a great deal about Rosalba's prowess, and she did not intend to offer herself as a target. The job of teaching Lulu worldly wisdom during this spring had been from her point of view a most convenient economy. She had not the least desire to return to that castle in Dalmatia of which she had talked so proudly at first and which now only served her as an example of domestic discomfort.

Rosalba had noticed the frown and the way Lulu had turned to her friend for the answer to her proposal.

"I am afraid," she said in Italian, "that you think I would be a big nuisance."

"Oh no, no," the Baroness replied after a momentary hesitation. "Not at all. But we are living up here in so simple a style. . . ."

"How well you speak Italian," Rosalba put in.

The compliment was not intended to convey a hidden sting. It was only Rosalba's favourite method of attack by flattery. But the Baroness flushed. She supposed that another doubt was being thrown upon the genuineness of her nationality. Nor did Rosalba improve matters by adding :

"How much I would like to dance with you! I'm sure you are a marvellous dancer."

The Baroness glared at Rosalba angrily.

"Why do you think I am such a marvellous dancer?" she demanded, flushing at the implication of her professional origin.

"Because you have the most beautiful figure I have ever seen," Rosalba replied at once. "And because all your movements are so full of grace. You move, *mon cher*, like a marvellous cat."

Perhaps it was the masculine form of address which set the mind of the Baroness at ease. Or perhaps it was the apparently complete sincerity of Rosalba's admiration which reassured her. Anyway, she understood from that moment what it was that people meant when they praised Rosalba's charm.

Lulu recognized the signs of succumbing to Rosalba. The most remotely occupied nurse after having assisted at a few operations can appreciate the technique of the fashionable anæsthetist. It was now Lulu's turn to look doubtful over Rosalba's proposal to stay here. She was by no means anxious to have the nest disturbed by a cuckoo.

"Why do you look so sad, Lulu, my dear?" Rosalba asked. "Don't you want me to be here?"

How Lulu longed to be able to say that she could not bear the idea of Rosalba's being there! But youth's uncertainty when faced with a situation from which it requires finesse to escape was too much for Lulu. She did not know how to express her dread of Rosalba's company without making herself look ridiculous. It was not that Lulu was jealous of the fancy that Drenka might fall in love with Rosalba. She was much too normal a young woman to suffer any pangs over that. But she was jealous of being out of it in the company of two women so much more worldly wise than herself. She dreaded allusions in the conversation which she would be unable to understand, and which indeed she might never understand because she would always have to pretend that she had understood them. The idea that Drenka and Rosalba might insist on assuming an immoral superiority to herself was extremely wounding to her vanity. Lulu had just reached the age when youth obstinately lingers like a cold May that keeps the flower-buds closed. She was dreadfully tired of being young, and she was supposing that the next seventeen years of her life would be as long as and immensely more exciting than the first seventeen. She did not realize any better than other young people that life was a gathering snowball with a wider circumference every year, nor that ultimately a fatal year was reached when it began to melt, so that however assiduously it might be rolled along it grew less and less until at last it melted utterly away. Readings of Horace were not included in the worldly lessons of Drenka Vidakovitch, and if they had been Lulu would have yawned over them.

"Don't be so silly, Rosalba," she said. "Naturally I want you to be here, if you can be comfortable."

Lulu was old enough to know that nothing would make Rosalba stay on more indefinitely than a consciousness that her stay was making somebody suffer acutely. And perhaps, she thought hopefully, Drenka would be a match for her.

And while Rosalba was gradually charming Drenka to the point of preferring to throw herself from the cliff rather than Rosalba should not send word to the hotel to have the contents of her dressing-table, the spoils of how many similar triumphs over feminine prejudice, sent down to the Villino Krank, Rory Freemantle, her out-thrust chin seeming more than usually hispid on account of the drops of perspiration that clustered on the fine hairs like dew on the leaves of any boraginacious plant, was marching up the narrow *viali* of the hill of Timberio. She had been to visit Anastasia Sarbécoff several times during the last six months, and she had never come away without feeling convinced that, should the worst come to the worst and Rosalba abandon her, it was possible to preserve one's dignity in solitude, and present at any rate to the world a spectacle of serenity. Indeed she was never quite sure that Anastasia was not truly serene, miraculous though such a state of mind would be when it was remembered that she had to face poverty as well as solitude. Rory had noticed last time she visited Casetta Bianca that another of Anastasia's diamond rings was gone, and she wondered with how much fortitude she herself would bear the sight of the little heap of diamonds gradually ebbing from her fingers, until not one rippling gem was left and she was stranded. Rory did not think that she in such circumstances could continue to wear her rings. She should hide them away in a drawer, and when the time came for one to be sacrificed she should take it out from the case at random in the dark. Deliberately to remove, one after another, the rings from one's fingers for ever must hurt as much as cutting off the fingers themselves. Yes, Anastasia's serenity was astonishing, Rory thought, as she turned aside from the *viali* to cross a small vineyard half overshadowed by a stone-pine, one of those great parasols of darkest green that Italy puts up against the sun. It was this tree which had persuaded her to plant the pines round the terrace at the Villa Leucadia, for Rory had some of a man's patience and was not depressed by the prospect of waiting for anything that took longer than nine months. From the vineyard a path led through a sloping orchard of almonds and peaches, and figs with snaky ashen boughs, to the small white house where Anastasia Sarbécoff had retired from emotional competition. It was a tranquil spot enclosed by greenery; but if a wider view was desired one could descend the slope and walk under olive-trees along the level edge of the high cliff between rows of purple flags now in their prime blooming as far as a belvedere whence one could look down on the busy Grande Marina, or watch the sun dip behind Monte Ventoso, or ponder the island of Nepenthe twenty miles away amarantine in this afternoon light, but in the morning a clouded blue as of chalcedony.

Casetta Bianca was not more pretentious than its

name. It was indeed nothing except a small white house with four square rooms and two white domes. There was neither loggia nor terrace. There was only a small flagged courtyard with the round parapet of the cistern-well in one corner and in the other a pomegranate-tree, and for the tenant a chair of sun-bleached chestnut wood in which she could sit and read her French novels, sheltered from the sun by a frayed and faded linen awning, while the little red-haired maid chinked away at her work within.

"Oh, I am so glad to see you, my dear Rory," said Madame Sarbécoff, rising to greet her visitor. "And I am so sure you would like to have some tea at once. It is already so hot that I could not imagine it is only April. We seem to be already quite in the middle of summer."

She led the way into her little sitting-room furnished with odds and ends of furniture which had probably always been unhappily surrounded by grander companions, but which now that they were gathered together on an equality had so much more distinction than the grand companions they had left behind. A tarnished Venetian mirror framed in pink and blue posies of blown glass, two rickety chairs deliciously painted on a dull chrome ground with shepherds' horns and shepherdesses' hats swinging from ribbons and wreaths of daisies or forget-me-nots, a spindle-legged papier mâché table in whose landscape a pair of scored cranes dipped their beaks into a lake of mother o' pearl, an old house-tile of the Immaculate Conception, a chipped and cracked honey-jar of maiolica for an umbrella-stand—nothing of any great value, nothing of any particular beauty, but combining to say that one was in Italy with something however humble of Italy's past to civilize one's interior.

"And see what I have found yesterday, my dear Rory," Madame Sarbécoff exclaimed, showing her friend an iridescent Roman lachrymatory.

"Do you mean you dug it up?"

"No, no, I wish I could have! No, I saw it in a little shop behind the Duomo. I find it is so beautiful. It is so wonderfully coloured. It is more beautiful in the sun than a diamond, I find."

Rory flashed the slim phial to and fro.

"Do you think they ever did fill these things with tears?" she asked doubtfully.

"Oh yes, I am so sure they would."

"I don't know of anybody who will ever manage to fill one for me," Rory sighed.

"But I am sure you will, my dear. When one is first dead one can ask quite a lot from people. It is really the only time one can. And now here is Assunta with the tea. She is so charming and so good."

The little red-haired maid, her brows meeting in an anxious frown over the responsibility of her task, set out the table.

"*La signora è servita*," she proclaimed at last and turned in the doorway to look back over her shoulder to see that the ceremonious announcement did not belie her.

"Well, Anastasia, I've quarrelled with Rosalba," Rory announced abruptly when they were alone.

"Oh, I am so sorry to hear that. But it is not an important quarrel, I think."

Rory related the episode of the peacocks and showed Madame Sarbécoff the note she had found waiting for her at the hotel.

"But she will be quite all right at dinner-time, I think. This is just a little letter one writes on a hot afternoon."

"She's never written me such a letter before," said Rory gloomily. "Suppose she stays for the rest of the summer with Lulu and this damnation Baroness of hers?"

Madame Sarbécoff smiled courteously at the poor petulant joke.

"Hermina is coming back next week," she murmured.

"But she may go and stay with her."

"No, excuse me, I do not think so. Hermina cannot now be dominated by Rosalba, and Rosalba cannot be dominated by her. Between them love was always a chemical experiment; but there was no explosion, which made it so dull; and the experiment was quite a failure."

"They might try the experiment again."

"And if they do it will be the same failure. Excuse me, I have known Hermina for many years, and in me perhaps she may find what she has not herself. But in Rosalba she will always find too much of herself. For one thing they are both . . ."

Madame Sarbécoff hesitated.

"Both what?" Rory pressed.

"You must not think that I am malicious if I say they are both so stupid, because it is not for me a criticism. I think stupidity is so beautiful; so restful. It is the beautiful stupidity of all the Greek statues which is making them so dear to us. Why I am always finding men so tiresome as lovers is because they must make love with their brains, so that I become quite exhausted myself to watch them. I find it such a pity that when a man has made love he should be so tired and sad. Poor fellow, I am always so sorry for him."

"I've never been made love to by a man," Rory admitted. "It must be horrible."

"*Non, non, il y a des moments très très agréables, je vous assure. Ça vaut la peine de les éprouver.*"

"Not for me," said Rory firmly. "I've outlived the age for experiments."

"But is not Rosalba a little bit like an experiment?"

"On the contrary she is the end of a life's experience," Rory proclaimed. "Outside Rosalba I am interested in nothing. And it is because she knows it that she treats me like this."

"But excuse me, Rosalba has not yet had her life's experience, I think."

"My dear Anastasia, I don't expect her to be faithful to me. Let me make that perfectly clear. She is free. But she has not taken herself off now to gratify a whim of curiosity. She has taken herself off with the deliberate intention of making me wretched. What else can this note mean? You see, she signs herself 'Rosalba Donsante.' She puts her surname."

"But that is only a little piece of girlish *suffisance*."

"It's all too spontaneous," Rory argued. "She

isn't trying to wound me. She's just expressing what she feels. She actually feels she is no longer my Rosalba, but just Rosalba Donsante. It's the thought that she can feel herself Rosalba Donsante when writing that frightens me. Oh, I know you've never been able to understand Rosalba's charm. But still you've enough imagination to realize that if one does find her charming one finds her maddeningly charming."

"Excuse me, I can perfectly understand Rosalba's charm," said Madame Sarbécoff gently. "But I regard it from a great distance, because it would be very imprudent for me to come too close, since I could never expect that she would find as much charm in me."

"It was Napoleon, wasn't it, who said the only way to win a victory over love was to run away from it? You're lucky to have the necessary self-control."

"No, I have not so much self-control," said Madame Sarbécoff. "It is for me quite an instinct as when I close my eyes against a thump. Besides, I am too much a fatalist. That is where I am quite altogether Slav."

"But, Anastasia, tell me. You were hurt by the way Hermina treated you last autumn?" Rory pressed.

"No, I am really too intelligent to be hurt. One cannot ever be hurt, I think, by what one understands. That is one of the reasons why I prefer women. It is not that they are better than men, but it is that they are always comprehensible. Woman is quite without mystery, I find."

"You're lucky. I find Rosalba a pretty deep mystery."

Before replying to this Madame Sarbécoff paused to take stock of her visitor.

"I wish I could dare to be quite sincere with you," she said at last.

"You can," Rory assured her. "After that note from Rosalba I can stand anything."

"Well then, you must excuse me if I am too impertinent to say that the only mystery of Rosalba for you is to wonder how much she loves you."

"Well, I suppose that may be true. I don't think *that* is very impertinent."

"Ah, but now I must be very impertinent. Excuse me, but I think you are always being quite so surprised why she can love you. Voltaire has said that no man could ever at all imagine why any woman could wish *coucher* with anybody except him; but I think he could have said also that after a certain age no man can ever be quite sure that the woman *qui couche avec lui veut coucher avec lui*. But from the first moment that a woman *couche avec un homme* she is always thinking that he is wanting *coucher avec une autre femme*. And I find you are so much both a man and a woman, my friend, and so for you the mystery is quite a terrible one."

"And what do you think about Rosalba?"

"I think that Rosalba wishes to be always amusing herself, and I think that perhaps she is able to be amusing herself more in your companionship than with other women."

"In other words that she's making use of me?"

"Yes, but she would say that you were making use of her quite as much."

"In fact, you don't believe love exists?"

"I will be so sincere with you. I do not believe that equal love exists. It is quite a stale thing to say that there is always one who kisses and one who is kissed."

"But that is why I have always hated the idea of love between men and women," Rory declared. "That love always is unequal and it always must be. No man knows what a woman really feels, and no woman knows what a man really feels even at the moment of their supreme intimacy. And if passion cannot make them mutually comprehend each other, what will? I maintain that my love for Rosalba is something beyond ordinary love."

"But that is what everybody in love has thought since the beginning of love," Madame Sarbécoff interposed with a smile.

"I don't mean my particular love for Rosalba. I mean the kind of love one woman can give another. Why, if I thought my love was nothing but a perverted vice I should fling myself off a cliff. It is because I believe my love is something beyond ordinary love, being creation not procreation, that I regard myself as privileged to be constituted as I am. I regard myself as the evidence of progress, not as a freak. I maintain that in the future all love will be homosexual."

"It would be one way of bringing the world to an end," Madame Sarbécoff whispered to herself. "Which of course is not entirely a displeasing notion."

"Oh, by that time humanity will have found a better way of procreation," said Rory optimistically.

"I find all talks about the future so soothing," Madame Sarbécoff murmured. "Because it is quite impossible for one person to contradict another person."

"But if you don't agree with me about the evolution of love, why are you homosexual yourself, may I ask?"

"But I am not," said Madame Sarbécoff. "I am only just so very tired of men."

"You know, you rather shock me by saying that," Rory declared, fixing her monocle and eyeing her hostess earnestly.

"I am so sorry, my friend, that I must shock you; but I find it is always a little shocking to speak the truth."

"Well, I won't bore you any longer with my dreams," said Rory with a note of bitterness in her voice.

"No, please, I find everything you say so interesting. I find dreams so beautiful. People always laugh at me because they say I am a great pretender, but I assure you that I have spent so many delightful hours listening to dreams. People are always so truthful about their dreams. I do not find that anybody takes the trouble to invent a dream. I think the only time I am quite sure that people are telling me truth is when they tell me what has happened to them in their dreams. Have you ever known a person invent a dream? I do not believe it would be at all worth while. But that would be the most perfect egoist, *n'est-ce pas*, the man who went about all day relating to people dreams that he never had at all?"

"Go on. Go on. I don't mind being laughed at," Rory declared from a cloud of cigar smoke.

"No, please, but I am not laughing at you."

"You've every right to, for I suppose my feeling for Rosalba must sound to you exactly like a stupid dream."

"It need not be a stupid dream," said Madame Sarbécoff gently. "It may be a beautiful dream. And I am so sure that one day she will be able to dream with you."

"Meanwhile, I suppose I am making a fool of myself?"

"No, I do not think to be in love is to make a fool of oneself. I find all my pleasure nowadays to see other people in love."

"But I thought you said you didn't believe in equal love?"

"I did not say it was my pleasure to be in love myself."

"Then you get your pleasure by laughing at other people who are deluding themselves?"

"I do not laugh at people. I do not laugh at you, my friend, because you are in love with Rosalba. If I laugh, it is because I think you permit yourself to be alarmed about nothing. You have sometimes met the Baroness Drenka Vidakovitch?"

"Yes, I have."

"And she is just quite a little vulgar thing. She is not more than that."

Rory got up to take her leave. There was something so consoling in that brief description of the Dalmatian baroness that she did not want to have it spoilt by any qualifications. It cheered her up so much that although she had intended to invite Anastasia to come and dine with her at the hotel she did not do so, because she was beginning to feel that Rosalba would have returned by now in a mood of forgiveness; and she did not want to run the risk of spoiling the exquisite intimacy of a reconciliation by the presence of a third person. But when she reached the Augusto and found Rosalba's dressing-table stripped of everything except an empty looking-glass she wished she had not been so optimistic.

The chambermaid came in to ask if the Signorina Rosalba really intended to pass the night elsewhere, because, though she had sent word to have the contents of her dressing-table carried down to the Villino Krank, she had not said a word about sending any *camicia di notte*. Rory looked across to the bed on which was lying a suit of powder-blue silk pyjamas. A sudden access of jealous rage seized her.

"The Signorina Rosalba will want all her things to-night," she spluttered. "You had better pack everything she has and ask the facchinos to take the trunks down to the Villino Krank."

It is a pity that Rory cannot be given the credit for having thought of an excellent joke; but to be honest it never entered her head that Rosalba's eight trunks might make the inside of the Villino Krank rather uncomfortable. She let them go without a chuckle.

## CHAPTER TEN

ἔγω δὲ μόνα κατεύδω.
                    SAPPHO.

*But I couch alone.*

ROSALBA had so little sense of the ridiculous that the arrival of trunk after trunk throughout the evening never suggested to her that Rory might have sent them to the Villino Krank for the express purpose of making her appear foolish. She did not even suppose that their arrival signified the exasperation of jealousy. She merely thought Rory had been afraid she might want something.

"Poor Rory," she said to her hostesses. "I am so much amused. She is quite frightened that I may not be comfortable *chez vous*."

The obstruction the eight trunks created in the studio was slightly mitigated by the exposition their contents afforded of the *plus dernier chic*.

Women possess an astonishing and patient interest in the wardrobes of other women. Jealousy may exist; but if it does, it is admirably subordinated to other emotions like curiosity. They become for a moment almost as polite as men. Schoolboys examining one another's stamp collections are not more amicable. When the clothes are put on it may be another matter; though even then, if they are put on while the wardrobe is open, are worn under a flag of truce.

The examination of Rosalba's trunks did nothing to imperil the peace of the Villino Krank. So long as that was prolonged her visit was not displeasing even to Lulu. But when the clothes had all been looked at and the trunks lay about the place like boulders, not all Rosalba's charm could keep Lulu and her Dalmatian baroness from wishing her and her luggage back in the Hotel Augusto. For one thing they wanted to go and dance there after dinner themselves, and it was a bore not to be able to go because Rosalba objected to remitting as much of her sentence on Rory as even to show herself.

"You will both oblige me so much by not going to the Augusto," she said. "I will not allow that woman to triumph over me. I am quite determined to give her a terrible lesson. She must learn that she cannot insult me with her *prepotenza*. Ah, my dears, I will tell to you that I am nobody's slave. I have for myself a certain importance."

Neither Lulu nor her baroness was prepared to contest that.

"It is not that I am unwilling to live another person's life," Rosalba went on. "But the other person must also live mine. I am so content with you, my dears, because you understand me so well. I feel perhaps for the first moment in my life a real freedom. Let us make a little society *contro il mondo*. We are quite sufficient for ourselves. Why must we annoy ourselves with other people?"

Lulu mentioned that her mother was expected in Sirene next week.

"I am fond of your mother," Rosalba continued meditatively. "But it is strange ; I find always something lacking in her. She has such a coldness. I could tell to you some things about her that would make you laugh, Lulu. But I will not do so. *Je suis toujours très gentleman.*"

Lulu pouted. She was remembering her own desertion by Rosalba last year when the sudden and violent intimacy with her mother began. She longed to get an opportunity of consulting Drenka about the situation. Were Rosalba's trunks going to stand about in their little studio for the rest of the spring and summer?

And when at last poor Lulu did find herself alone with Drenka it was only to be accused of caring more for Rosalba than her.

"As if I did not know that this is a plot between you and La Donsante," the Baroness declared angrily.

"What nonsense, Drenka ! Why, I showed perfectly plainly that I never wanted Rosalba here. It was you who encouraged her to stay. I don't want her here. If you accuse me of making a plot with her I shall begin to think you are in love with her yourself."

"*Quelle blague! Quelle blague!* I would have locked you up if I had known she was combining this plot to take you away from me."

"Well, why don't you tell her so yourself?" Lulu challenged. "It's no good abusing me. I'm not to blame. Tell her you won't have her here."

"If I tell that woman anything it will be told with a knife," the Baroness vowed.

Although a stranger might have feared from her vicious expression she would carry out her threat, Lulu was not alarmed.

"Yes, you say that now when Rosalba's out of the room. But you're polite enough when she's there."

"I cannot make a barbarian of myself when I am responsible for you to your mother."

"Thanks, I'm quite old enough to be responsible for myself."

"*Tu es une jeune fille*," the Baroness taunted.

"*Je ne suis pas une jeune fille.*"

"*Tu es une jeune fille*," the Baroness repeated.

"*Je ne suis pas, je ne suis pas, je ne suis pas!* It is insulting to call me *jeune fille* when you know I have nothing in me at all of the *jeune fille*. You will perhaps be telling me now that I am quite innocent."

"*Tu es fourbe, mais au fond tu es innocente*," the Baroness declared with a scowl.

Lulu burst into tears not because the Baroness had called her crafty, but under the disgraceful accusation of innocence.

If Rosalba had stayed much longer at the Villino Krank, there is no doubt the little nest would have been scattered. Lulu and her baroness could not have stood it much longer. They would have fled to the haunts of men and abandoned their sun-dyed corner to the lizards. The garden would have returned to its task of slowly crumbling away in the sea wind and the sun. There would have been no sound within that enclosure except the moaning of the Æolian harp not even yet rusted quite away which

Herr Krank had fixed in the boughs of a twisted Aleppo pine. Luckily, however, for the appropriate human population (Lulu was just the rosy nymph any wandering deity might expect to find in such a spot, even if the Dalmatian baroness did seem to have strayed thither from the high road to Corinth) Rosalba received a letter from Olga Linati in Rome to say that she and Cléo were arriving next week and adding in a postscript that Mrs Royle and her daughter were coming about the same time to stay at the Augusto.

Now, Rosalba had never intended that Cléo should administer a defeat to her over the Royles, and she knew this visit to Sirene was a direct challenge to herself. It had obviously been planned to demonstrate her fallibility. The Royles were being imported for the express purpose of snubbing her. Rosalba braced herself for the fray. She must obviously be back at the Augusto. There was no longer any point in keeping up the quarrel with Rory. She sat down and wrote a letter :

*I find that I must pardon you after all. Forget everything that we have both said. Tell the facchini to call for my luggage this afternoon and tell to Enrico that I must have prawns for dinner to-night. Lulu and Drenka will both be with us. All my best kisses.*

*Rosalba.*

Half an hour after this note reached the hotel Rory was accosting every fisherman she met to find out if he had any prawns, for after all the head waiter might fail to procure them, and a dearth of prawns must not be allowed to mar the perfection of Rosalba's return.

Nobody would have suspected from the behaviour of the four women at dinner that they had just been involved in a complicated emotional intrigue. They were, as one of the old lady guests in the hotel put it, quite hilarious. Rosalba kept beckoning to little Bozzo and ordering all Rory's favourite tunes to reward her for the care with which she had ordered all Rosalba's favourite dishes. The deep husky laugh of Drenka Vidakovitch was continually heard. Lulu behaved in a way that would have made little Miss Chimbley quiver like a plucked string, had her nervous breakdown allowed her to be present this evening. And if in Drenka's eyes there was sometimes a hostile glow, even that vanished when Rosalba danced with her incessantly after dinner and assured her all the while in a thrilling whisper that she was the most wonderful dancer she had ever known. Two rounds of stingers brought the evening to a close.

When Rosalba stood by the gates of the Augusto in the moonlight to wave Lulu and her baroness on their road, her gesture lacked all provocation and might indeed have been the farewell of a sister to her sisters, with Rory standing in the background like a benevolent aunt.

"Darling," Rory vowed, when she saw with moist eyes the blond tortoiseshell again set out on Rosalba's dressing-table and on her bed the pyjamas of dove-grey scrabbled with her scarlet monogram in such an amusing place to choose. "Darling, we'll never let peacocks come between us again. I was entirely to blame. The horrible birds have been sent away.

You have forgiven me, haven't you, for my want of imagination? I've gone through hell this week on account of my stupidity."

"Poor old Rory, I shall not reproach you no more."

"Oh, my dear, how wonderful you are!"

"Yes, I suppose there is something in me which is making me quite different from all the world."

"Oh yes, yes!" Rory agreed eagerly. "Utterly different!"

"I wonder why I am so different. There are so often times when I say to myself 'Why are you so different?' It is for me always a great perplexity."

"Well, I think it is because you're the only person in the world whose temperament can keep pace with her beauty."

"Yes, perhaps that is the reason," Rosalba allowed complacently. "*En effet, je suis hors concours, c'est vrai?*"

"Oh, oui, oui! Quite! Quite! Je t'adore, Rosalba," Rory declared excitedably.

"*Et je suis moi, n'est-ce pas?*"

"Oh yes, yes, you are you. You are so tremendously you. There is about you such a youness."

"*Oui, ça je comprends.* It is what I feel myself."

"Of course you do, darling! Anybody as sensitive as you must feel it. You wouldn't *be* you if you didn't."

"That is so true," Rosalba agreed solemnly. "You know, Rory *mio*, I find that you understand me quite very splendidly."

"My precious! It's the only thing I care about in

life. I don't really want to do anything else. But, of course, I failed over the peacocks. Oh yes, you're too generous. I failed there. Oh, I failed miserably."

"*N'en pense plus.*"

"I won't, but I do want *you* to realize that I do *know* how completely I failed you."

"It can occur to anybody."

"Ah, but it ought not to have happened to me. Oh, I failed; I realize that. But you've been so wonderful about it that I don't believe I *shall* fail next time. In fact I'm glad this has happened. Yes, I am. I've gone through hell over it, but I'm glad. I feel that those beastly peacocks have brought us nearer each other." She broke off with a gasp of sentimental despair. "Darling, your hot water is quite tepid. I'll go and see if I can't get hold of somebody."

"It does not matter," Rosalba sighed ascetically.

"But it does matter. It matters very much. Darling, I couldn't bear that you should come back and find your hot water tepid."

Cléo and Olga arrived from Rome a day after this reconciliation. Rosalba, delighted to have an opportunity of showing her house (as much to Rory's satisfaction she called the Villa Leucadia) to people who had not yet seen it and who would probably envy it, took up the attitude that a girl intending to enter a nunnery might take up. Over her lightest remark there trembled an air of wistful charity. Retreating as she presently was from the vexations of the world, she seemed to convey, she wished to leave behind her nothing but gentle thoughts in the memory of her friends. There was no longer the least wanton challenge in her brown eyes.

"I have the intention to do such a lot of reading when I come to live up here," she announced with something of the solemn awe-struck pride of a child telling people it would soon make its first communion.

It was natural that Olga should express the most voluble admiration of the rebuilt villa. For one thing she could not help fancying to herself that in the future she might be entrusted with the task of letting it for an enormous rent to some nice family that wanted to spend a few months on Sirene. Yet in her own mind a contrast with the Villa Rosamarina was inevitable. Not that the Villa Rosamarina tucked away on the lowest slopes of the Monte San Giorgio was to be despised. Even that, the way rents on Sirene were rising, might presently be considered a letable proposition, that is if Olga could think of some way of bestowing the globular bald-headed *cavaliere*, her father, her Russian mother who had the romantic look of a Siberian exile, and most problematically of all her Russian grandmother who was reputed to be nearly a hundred and who sat all day in front of a German earthenware stove with her hands crossed on her lap. It was uncanny to see Olga herself in both those older women. There were the same myopic blue eyes, the same slightly underhung chin, the same fresh complexion. She might easily live to a hundred like her grandmother; and who would then work hard to keep her? One's heart was chilled by the fancy of Olga's far future, when her voluble voice was cracked, when her busy hands were cramped with rheumatism, and when the German earthenware stove was full of ashes.

There was indeed a menace in the atmosphere of the Villa Rosamarina, a sense of a cold enclosing destiny gathering round Olga, for all her debonair courage in the present. Perhaps it was a mere trick of contrast between the white Italian exterior with the geraniums and glittering green palms all round it and the dark, over-draped, over-upholstered Russian interior. One apprehended that when the *cavaliere* had returned home from his official job he had furnished the villa with the contents of his house in Russia. What there might have been warm and cosy was here, with all the shabbiness that the years had brought and that the sun displayed, gloomy and over-powering. And the *cavalière* himself, though he still kept his old consular ceremoniousness and the jaunty air of a man who in his day was a great lady-killer, had deteriorated like the furniture. For many years he had indulged himself in the *dolce far niente* of an exiled official who returns to the sunny promenades of his youth; but since the war money, which had never been plentiful in the Linati household, had become much scarcer. The family decided the *cavalière* must have something more profitable to do than drinking vermouth in Zampone's and gossiping with his cronies over cards. He was made agent of a Neapolitan wine-merchant, and he was to be seen sitting all day at the door of the shop, not easily distinguishable at first sight from the barrel on the other side which stood as an advertisement of the wine on order within. Whatever he earned (and it could only have been a paltry sum) was appropriated for the family expenses, in return for which he was allowed three *soldi* a day to buy himself a cup of coffee, over which when the shop was closed he would sit for hours in Zampone's, watching the games of cards in which he was no longer able to take a hand. His wife, a woman of outstanding intelligence and great nobility of character, still worked as hard as her failing eyes would allow her at characteristic products of domestic Russia; but it was Olga who really kept the household together: always busy, always trim and debonair, always talking incessantly in four languages about some marvellous piece of business of inextricable complexity that was going to put her affairs on an entirely new and prosperous basis—a sanguine and courageous figure always ready to tell other people how they should manage this or that, and on a fine morning of spring a radiant and almost a beautiful figure in her orange tam-o'-shanter and high white kid boots and emerald green jumper and neat navy blue skirt. One was glad to see that Cléo Gazay had come to spend a few months in the Villa Rosamarina, telling oneself what a useful addition Cléo's board would be to its economy. The smallest piece of material good fortune that happened to Olga always cheered one up, because nobody was ever so much elated by so little as she was. And if, when Rosalba showed her the luxuries and the beauties of the Villa Leucadia, she could not praise them quite so fluently in French and English and Italian as she was wont to praise her friends' possessions, perhaps it was because she was saying to herself in Russian that half the money Rory had spent on Rosalba's new room would have kept the Villa Rosamarina going for three years. And then luckily for her, because she did not want Rosalba to see that she was a little envious, the plan of letting it for Rory next year or the year after occurred to her, and she became her sanguine voluble self again.

Cléo openly expressed her envy of the villa. It seemed to her that in such surroundings she really might be able to settle down and practise. A year of seclusion up here alone, completely alone, and she might return to earth a pianist indeed. Rory would never have admitted it; but there was no doubt the villa did provide Cléo with a background so completely right for her personality as to make the others appear out of place. She strode up and down that green amphitheatre at the end of the garden like a statue which had descended from its pedestal. Her affinity with those great marble gods and nymphs and emperors was immediately obvious. They ceased somehow to be stolid spectators and became her companions. Not that she admired them. On the contrary she thought them all ugly enough, pretentious and quite out of place. But then Cléo never admired herself a great deal. Her body was for herself a perpetual resentment. She attributed to its clumsiness all her failures to find the perfect love she sought.

She had no delight in being compared to a famous piece of old sculpture. It seemed to put her in the dusty shadows of a museum corridor. It made her feel she had no means of contact with the present world. It gave her a sensation of being already treated as old, or what was worse as unreal. This affected her playing, because she was for ever conscious that she was being judged monumentally as it were. So, she was contemptuous of the statues and scowled when the others told her what a setting they made for her. But she did envy the villa itself, and most of all that snowy loggia. She felt, sitting back there in a chair and staring out across the azure, as if she were swinging free of the inappropriate world in which she lived. She felt that beauty was at last her own and that with beauty for a prize passion might be forgone. She sat dreaming; and the others drew aside to watch her, because in her eyes for the first time they saw an expression that matched the lovely severity of her face.

Even Rosalba was aware of Cléo's heightened quality in these surroundings, and when later in the day Rory commented on the picture she had made sitting in their loggia Rosalba felt jealous.

"You would be better to invite her to live with you, instead of me, *mon cher*."

"Now, Rosalba, don't talk so foolishly. It doesn't mean I want to live with Cléo because I admire the effect she created on our loggia. I simply admired her quite impersonally as I might admire a well-placed tree in a landscape. It just happened that her pose was exactly right. You admired her yourself."

"I was admiring her pose, *mon cher, parce qu'en effet Cléo est une grande poseuse*. For me somebody is much more beautiful who is not always having to be *en pose*. I think that all real beauty in people is to be beautiful apart from their surroundings."

"Darling, I don't think it's a question of beauty, and certainly not of comparative beauty. What we admired was the appropriateness of the background."

"I am not saying that Cléo is not beautiful," Rosalba continued. "So please do not accuse me to other people of saying such a thing."

"Dearest, should I ever be likely to accuse you of anything to other people?" Rory protested in a hurt voice.

"I am always admiring Cléo," Rosalba maintained. "But what I wish to say is that I admire more the person who makes her *ambiente* beautiful than a person who is made beautiful by her *ambiente*."

"Like you for example," Rory agreed fondly.

"I do not choose myself for an illustration, because I am not so much conceited as that, but I must insist to say that Cléo is not always beautiful. I have seen her sometimes sitting in a room when she is quite a lump of nothing, so heavy and so clumsy that I have wanted to push her quite away into a corner. I find it a little curious, *mon cher*, that you should be so mad for Cléo when she has treated me quite abominably, just because I would not fall down to worship at her feet. *Ah non*, I will not worship anywhere."

"Why should you, darling? You have too many worshippers of your own. But do let me remind you that it wasn't I who suggested taking Cléo to see the villa. Had it been left to me, I wouldn't have had anything to do with Cléo after the way you told me she treated you at her concert."

"That is a piece of smallness for which I must laugh, *mon cher*. Please do not be supposing that I wish to make a great history of that. And if you are mad to be in love with Cléo it is for me nothing. But I regret to tell to you that you will find her excessively vulgar. With her air to be *la grande Minerve, au fond elle est cabotine. C'est un classicisme du theâtre.* Bébé Buonagrazia has spoken to me once a very spiritual thing about her. ' *Quel beau type de Racine!* ' somebody was saying, ' *Déraciné serait plus juste,*' Bébé Buonagrazia has whispered to me. *Mais Bébé est tellement spirituelle!* I quite adore her. You know who I am talking about? She is the Principessa Flavia Buonagrazia, who . . ."

"Yes, yes, I know who she is," Rory interrupted impatiently. She was prepared to hear about the morals and looks of Rosalba's friends, but even her infatuation could not tolerate their pedigrees.

"And one day," Rosalba went on, "perhaps I shall be hearing somebody say for Cléo ' *Quel beau type de Corneille!* ' And do you know what I shall be responding? ' *Lequel voulez-vous dire? L'homme ou l'oiseau?* ' And I am quite sure that Bébé Buonagrazia would not imagine anything more spiritual than that."

"How naughty you are, darling!" Rory said,

shaking her finger at Rosalba for walking about like this with an unexploded *mot* in her pocket. And since to feel importantly naughty was one of the chief pleasures of Rosalba's mind there was peace between them over the effect Cléo had made in the loggia of the Villa Leucadia. Besides, the Royles were coming in a day or two, and Rosalba was interested in proving to Cléo that if she determined otherwise Cléo could not prevent her burgling even the friendships she kept most carefully under lock and key. She was not at all afraid of Cléo's influence over Rory; but to keep what she had was not enough for Rosalba. She wanted to acquire what other people had as well. The only thing to be said for her is that she did not make her desert and call it the pursuit of an ideal. Indeed, Rosalba never did talk about ideals. Perhaps so many people had claimed her as their ideal that she would have been jealous of admitting there were any other ideals obtainable, even her own.

CHAPTER ELEVEN

καὶ γὰρ αἰ φεύγει, ταχέως διώξει,
αἰ δὲ δῶρα μὴ δέκετ', ἀλλὰ δώσει,
αἰ δὲ μὴ φίλει, ταχέως φιλήσει
κωὐκ ἐθέλοισα.

SAPPHO.

*For even if she flees you, she shall soon pursue; if she will not accept your gifts, she shall yet be giving; and if she does not love you, she shall soon love you, unwilling though she may be.*

THE Royles looked like being a difficult fortress to take. Had they been anywhere else except in the Hotel Augusto, Rosalba would have made a frontal attack and risked a repulse. But she could not afford that here. Her supremacy would be imperilled by going up to Janet Royle after dinner, asking her to dance, and being obviously refused. Nor did she dare tell the head waiter to take one of the special dishes he had ordered for her to Mrs Royle's table and beg her with compliments to partake of it.

So, for three days with an elaborate incuriosity Rosalba sat through meals at the Augusto without seeming aware of the Royles' presence at a table not so far from her own but that she could hear the equally elaborate incuriosity of the conversation between Janet and her mother. What made the situation more difficult was that Rosalba never confided in Rory anything of her set-back in Rome over the Royles. She would have died rather than admit to Rory that her acquaintance had ever been rejected by anybody.

Of her quarrels she could always speak freely, because in a quarrel the other side was always in the wrong ; but in a cold incurious rejection, although the other side might be equally in the wrong, the fact of the rejection remained. She would have felt like a conjurer who had been betrayed by his apparatus.

"Who *are* these Royles Cléo is always talking about?" Rory asked.

"Oh, they are such boring American people who I quite refused to know. She has wanted to make us friends in Rome, but I have said I will not."

That afternoon Cléo and Olga were having tea with Mrs Royle and Janet, and the conversation, as it always had ever since they arrived, soon went round to Rosalba.

"Well, I said in Rome I couldn't understand what anybody professed to see in that young woman," Mrs Royle declared. "And I'm quite convinced since I came here how right I was not to receive her. Miss Donsante may be very clever and amusing, but she's not at all the young woman *I* care to have in my house."

"I do agree with mother," Janet continued. "Cléo dear, I wonder what you ever saw in her?"

"But, my dear Mrs Royle," Olga burbled in. "I can tell you that she is most fascinating. I cannot say that I like her so very much, and I would not at all trust her ; but oh yes, she is awfully fascinating."

"Well, far be it from me to criticize anybody's friends," said Mrs Royle, who spent quite half her time in doing so. "But from what we hear of Miss

Donsante I feel perfectly sure neither Janet nor I would wish to know her. People may call us particular; I daresay we are. But we've gathered our own little circle around us and speaking for myself I don't mind at all if I never meet anybody new ever again."

" And I'm sure I don't," said Janet languidly. " You say the Englishwoman living with Miss Donsante is rich ? "

Olga jumped in her chair.

" Oh, she must be very rich indeed. She has really made a splendid place of the old Villa Beer."

" The old Villa *what?* " Mrs Royle asked, disgust adding even yet a few more wrinkles to her ravelled countenance.

" It is now called the Villa Leucadia. Miss Freemantle must have spent quite one hundred and fifty thousand pounds upon it. Perhaps more."

The old lady grunted.

" She seems quite a well-meaning person. I might have suggested your bringing her in to tea one afternoon, had she not been staying with Miss Donsante."

At this moment following an heraldic tap on the door one of the hotel waiters entered with a large bouquet of crimson carnations.

" *La signorina Royle,*" he announced, placing the flowers on the table and retiring.

" Well, who can this be from ? " said Mrs Royle, raising her eyebrows and smiling complacently. " Why, I expect one of the dear boys from the Embassy has come to Sirene. Janet, look and see who it's from. Isn't that charming, Miss Linati ? I often say that wherever we go the flowers seem to follow us." The old lady puffed with self-importance. One had an impression that she fancied her breath was balmy and fecund as the breath of Zephyr himself.

"*Hommage à Miss Royle
 Rosalba Donsante*"

Janet read out from the card attached to the bouquet.

Cléo, who had been silently kicking the leg of the table during most of the conversation, burst into a loud laugh.

"*Tu sais, Olga, elle est vraiment impayable. Quel type!*"

"Well, this is really too much," Mrs Royle gasped. "Miss Linati, will you be kind enough to ring the bell for the waiter and I'll have him take these flowers right back to Miss Donsante. Before we know where we are she'll be introducing herself to us."

The waiter returned, and the bouquet of crimson carnations was sent away.

That evening after dinner, when Mrs Royle and her daughter went up to their sitting-room, they found an even larger bouquet of white carnations addressed as before to Janet; and, though this was sent away like the first, when the chambermaid came in to call Janet next morning she brought with her a bouquet of pink roses.

"Really, it's almost laughable," Mrs Royle said to Olga, who before Cléo was out of bed had come bustling round in the middle of the morning to see if she could do anything for her friends. "I declare if I wasn't so angry I would almost feel inclined to laugh.

What does the silly girl expect to gain by such vulgar persistence ? Really, Miss Linati, the kindest thing you can do for Miss Donsante is to tell her from me that Miss Royle is not in the habit of accepting gifts from complete strangers. I'm sure I don't like to snub the poor young woman too hardly, but we cannot be deluged in this way. In fact you might add ' Mrs Royle says she's not accustomed to being deluged in such a pushing way !' "

"Yes, I will tell her," Olga promised. Even the bearing of a message filled Olga with as much suppressed excitement and importance as many women might not derive from the bearing of a child.

As soon as Olga found Rosalba she explained to her what a nuisance she was making of herself with her flowery oblations.

"If I wish to offer flowers," said Rosalba loftily, "it is for me all the same. I am offering them. If they are not desired they can be thrown away. It is for me all the same. I send them to please myself, because I find this Janet Royle is quite beautiful. If Cléo is afraid because I am sending these flowers I will send no more, because I do not wish at all to take her away from Cléo."

"Cléo doesn't mind what you do," said Olga, bubbling indignantly. "She has wanted to introduce you from the moment they arrived in Sirene. But it is Mrs Royle who does not wish it."

That evening a bunch of cattleyas arrived for the old lady, who realizing that they must have cost at least a hundred francs and probably more could not quite bring herself to stigmatize the present as laughable. She considered rank of more importance than wealth in these days; but money still stood high in her esteem. She was obviously shaken by the cattleyas.

"It's a very great pity that this Rosalba Donsante's reputation is what it is," she remarked to her daughter. "For really I can't help feeling a little sorry for the poor young woman. I suppose she hopes to climb into society on our backs. But I cannot allow that. It wouldn't be fair on our other friends. We must consider them."

"Of course," Janet agreed perhaps with a shade of uncertainty in her agreement. Then she coughed slightly. "My throat is a little sore to-night."

"Oh, my dear child, why didn't you tell me so before?"

"I didn't think it was going to be anything," said Janet with sweet resignation in her voice. "But it really is quite sore now." And she coughed again.

The possession of a delicate daughter had always seemed to Mrs Royle as interesting and important as the possession of a rare piece of porcelain. Her ministrations now conveyed the impression that she was dusting an article of virtu.

"We must have the doctor in at once," she declared.

So Dr Squillace was sent for, and looked very grave, because the graver he looked the more he felt he could charge. When he visited poor patients, he only looked irritable, unless they were on the point of death and unlikely to trouble him much longer.

"You think it's serious, doctor?" Mrs Royle asked.

Dr Squillace shook his head. It was serious, yes. Any affection of the throat must be considered serious. But, with the great care and the devoted medical attention he intended to supply, there was no reason to say it was dangerous. He should send round a gargle to-night, and to-morrow morning he would call again to see how the patient was. He should be better able to make a diagnosis then; but already he was sure of one thing and that was how lucky it was she happened to be in Sirene. The air of Sirene was peculiarly beneficial to weak throats. Even already he was tempted to prescribe a very long stay in Sirene as the best treatment he could suggest. A course of injections was indicated. Not immediately, but as soon as the superficial cure was effected. Yes, a course of injections extending over say a period of two months. And meanwhile, he would send round the gargle.

"What a fortunate thing to find such an excellent doctor here," Mrs Royle gratefully sighed. She felt as if a connoisseur had just told her what a rare and valuable piece of china her daughter was.

Janet did not feel well enough to go down to dinner, and in the business of ordering it to be served up in the sitting-room Mrs Royle forgot to send back the cattleyas. After dinner the head waiter came to express his condolences and his hope that the dinner he had served was what the Signorina liked. He added that the Signorina Donsante had sent enquiries and was most anxious to know how the Signorina Royle was feeling.

Now, Mrs Royle had never been able to resist telling

anybody how her daughter was feeling. She accorded the confidence as generously as a royal bulletin, so that before she thought what she was doing she had told the head waiter that Miss Royle was perhaps a little easier, but that it was too soon yet to say she was anything so definite as better.

"Dr Squillace is a very good doctor," said the head waiter.

"Yes, I have very great trust in him," Mrs Royle agreed.

"When I was wounded," said the head waiter, "he has kept me from the front. Otherwise perhaps I could not be here now."

"Dear me, that is indeed a real testimonial. He must be a very remarkable man."

And though Dr Squillace did not actually say that the head waiter was a very good head waiter he strongly recommended Mrs Royle not to be in any hurry to take her meals in the public dining-room, which was as much to the advantage of the head waiter's pocket as his own. Even before Fascismo there was always in Italy an admirable solidarity among the professional classes.

A large bunch of purple tulips arrived for Janet late in the day accompanied by a bottle of medicine.

"It's really almost laughable," said Mrs Royle. "What does that peculiar young woman expect to gain by sending us medicine? She surely doesn't think Janet will take it?"

Olga who was present declared that there were no limits to Rosalba's eccentricity.

"She is surely quite mad," Olga declared.

" She must be," Mrs Royle agreed. " Medicine ! Why, I've never heard of anybody sending medicine to perfect strangers."

" Shall I take it to her and say not to be so rude ? " Olga suggested.

" Well, I really don't know if I can quite call it rude to send medicine." The old lady looked at the bottle. " She has evidently heard that Janet is suffering with her throat, and she has sent this medicine for it. It's a gargle, I see. No, I don't think I can quite call it rude to send a gargle, though I must admit she's put us in a very difficult position."

Olga had to hurry off to keep some appointment in the Piazza, and Mrs Royle went into her daughter's room to consult her.

Janet who was lying down handed her mother a note:

*Dear Miss Royle,*

*I am so sorry to hear that you are so ill with your throat. I sympathize so much with you. When I was being ill with my throat last year the doctor has given me a splendid medicine and I must beg you to be trying it to your throat. Please to forgive my courage, because I am with much consideration,*

*Your sincere admirer*
*Rosalba Donsante.*

" It's a perfectly modest unassuming letter," said Mrs Royle.

" Perhaps the stories we've heard about her are exaggerated," Janet suggested.

" Well, it's quite possible," her mother replied,

opening wide her fishy eyes. " This letter doesn't sound at all like the kind of young person we have always heard she was. This is the kind of letter you or I might write, Janet, without of course the little mistakes due to her being an Italian."

" Did you send the medicine back, mother ? "

" No, my dear, I didn't. Will I bring it in for you to look at ? "

Janet nodded languidly; and for several moments she and her mother contemplated the bottle of medicine standing on her dressing-table. There was something human about it standing there. It was like a neat little messenger from Rosalba asking for the approbation of two important people. The parchment cap all goffred like a nun's wimple gave it a kind of virginal demureness. It seemed such an innocent and unassuming little bottle, and yet somehow so efficient and so earnest. One really could not have the heart to snub such a well-behaved little bottle as that.

" I really begin to think we shall *have* to ask her to tea," said Mrs Royle.

Janet, who had been wanting to find an invincible reason for asking Rosalba to tea ever since she had first seen her in Rome, sighed for the way this acquaintance had been forced upon them, but agreed that there was nothing else to be done.

So, Rosalba succeeded in breaking through the Royle exclusiveness; and, having done so, she did all she could to foster it, even going so far as to tell Rory she did not think it wise at present to suggest introducing her.

"They are quite awfully difficult people to know," she confided importantly.

"*I* don't want to know them," said Rory in some indignation. "I may make a fool of myself over you; but I've not yet reached the stage of making myself look ridiculous over a couple of snobbish Americans."

"But I think I will be able to manage so that you come with me one afternoon for meeting them."

"I don't *want* to meet them. If I do I'll ask Cléo or Olga to introduce me. They're not too exclusive to know *them*."

"Ah, but they do not really know poor Olga," Rosalba explained confidentially. "They are only kind to her. She could not introduce you to them. And Cléo will not. Oh, my dear, I tell to you she is quite furiated because I am now a friend of Janet."

"Well, don't go on talking about these Royles, or they'll turn into another pair of white peacocks," Rory warned her.

Rosalba was prepared to enjoy being exclusive until Sirene became more amusing. The protracted discussions at Versailles were still inflicting on the world all the lesser discomforts of war, so that visitors, though more frequent than last year, were not nearly as frequent as the Sirenesi had expected. The island was not yet itself again. Everybody was now hoping for a good summer season to compensate for this indifferent spring.

The Royles were flattered by Rosalba's comprehension of their social attitude. Her diffidence over introducing Rory Freemantle and her positive unwillingness to introduce either Lulu or her Dalmatian baroness were a sign that she appreciated the exception they had made in her favour. Moreover, the way she threw herself on their social protection was very appealing. She admitted frankly how many mistakes she had made. Her impulsive temperament had continually betrayed her. She knew that people told malicious stories about her behaviour, and her dear Mrs Royle must believe her when she said that those stories were entirely due to her lack of discrimination. Could she have had someone to advise her like Mrs Royle and someone whom she could admire like Janet, there would have been none of these tales going round Europe. She had a mother, yes; but her mother had always hated her.

Mrs Royle shook her head at this.

"Ah, my dear Mrs Royle, it is true. She is jealous of me because I am younger than she. She cannot suffer to see me. *Elle devient tout à fait folle quand elle me voit. C'est terrible! Ça me fait une grande peine, vous savez.* And so I must always be with my greatmother who is very sweet to me and will give me all her money when she is dead."

"Will that be a great deal?" Mrs Royle enquired cautiously.

"Oh yes, I will be very rich one day."

"What an immense comfort that must be to you, my dear!" the old lady sighed in a tone of relief.

"Yes, I am very happy for that," Rosalba admitted, a far-away look in her bright eyes.

With Janet Rosalba made no secret of her temperamental inclinations; but she always assumed that Janet would forgive her not as a woman of similar tastes, but as one whose superior intellect gave her a right to survey morals from an altitude of her own.

"It is always so sad for me," she said, "that Cléo pretends to be like me, because with her it is just to be *vicieuse*. I am made quite differently to other women. And I must be forgiven, therefore. I must indeed be pitied. You must imagine what I am feeling when I tell to you how terribly I am in love with you, because I know that you will be quite disgusted against me."

"In what way are you . . ." Janet began, and then checked her curiosity. "No, I am not at all disgusted," she said. "I think I'm too broadminded to be anything but interested."

"*Tu as des idées tellement larges*," Rosalba burst out, and then in sudden embarrassment put up that slim boyish hand to her lips. "*Oh, pardon! Je t'ai tutoyé.*"

"*Anzi mi piace, Rosalba*," Janet murmured remotely.

"*Grazie infinite*," Rosalba whispered.

"And so you think that Cléo isn't really . . . ?"

Janet allowed a cough to imply the rest of the question. She had been born and brought up in Latin Europe; but she had preserved an Anglo-Saxon prudery about the word. Words were to her as to so many of her race more shocking than deeds.

"Not at all! Not at all!" Rosalba declared vehemently. "I am so fond of Cléo, though I must tell to you that she treated me so badly. But it is terrible for me to see what a *posatrice* she must always be. She is really quite fond of men. But men do not care at all for her. And therefore she is a lover of women, because she cannot be a lover of men."

"You know, Rosalba, she said almost the same thing about you in different words."

"She is a terrible *menteuse*," Rosalba murmured compassionately. "I am so fond of her, but I must confess she is the most terribly false woman who I know. She cannot say the truth. Even poor Olga who cannot say the truth herself must always complain for the lies that Cléo says. *Oh, dio!*"

Rosalba broke off and pressed a hand to her heart.

"What's the matter?"

"It is nothing. It is only that you are so beautiful. It has made me quite fainting. I think it will be prudent for me to go away from Sirene."

"Why?"

"Because I must tell to you if I stay here how much I am loving you, and you will be shocked."

"No, I don't think I would be."

"I am in an eternal fever about you. This morning Dr Squillace was coming into the hotel, and I have turned as pale as the death, because I was afraid you were again ill."

"He's giving me injections."

"*Ah, ne dis pas ça,*" Rosalba cried out in horror.

"*Pourquoi?*"

"Because I will be altogether mad of jealousy. I cannot imagine that man to be making you injections. It is a *sacrilège*. I could kill him so easily."

"Poor Rosalba!"

"Yes, I *am* poor Rosalba. I am the most unhappiest woman in the world because I must suffer this torment of jealousy. Cléo is not unhappy like me. When I told to her about your injections she has laughed I am afraid she is altogether vulgar. But you are fond of her, so I must not say any things about her."

Rosalba spent more and more of her time with Janet Royle while Rory was hurrying on the completion of the Villa Leucadia in order to get her away from the hotel and while Cléo was thundering away at the grand piano which had been fetched over from Naples and put in the studio she had taken at the end of the Strada Nuova, just where the road begins to climb up to Anasirene. Rory striding past on the way to urge her workmen to greater speed used always to pause and listen for awhile to the furious music issuing from the big window, for she knew it was expressing Cléo's feelings about this friendship between Rosalba and Janet. Friendship ? Well, perhaps infatuation. Love ? No, surely not love. Rosalba could not be in love with that pale pretentious creature. But as the sound of Cléo's piano followed her up the road, until it seemed to turn into an echo of birds' voices in the gorges of Monte Ventoso, Rory began to feel less secure. That infernal music seemed to be the expression of a desolation that was her own desolation. What a perverse emotion love was ! Why couldn't she and Cléo have fallen in love with each other ? What a perfect background Cléo might have had in the Villa Leucadia ! She tried to imagine Cléo installed there instead of Rosalba. And the notion was ridiculous. She could as easily have installed one of those big statues in Rosalba's room. The thought of Cléo in the Villa Leucadia merely conveyed a sensation of something inanimate, something clumsy and cold and meaningless, something that the moment she had to fancy any closer relation with it became definitely ugly. That was one of the penalties of loving abnormally. She was deprived of all the feminine accommodation that seemed to come so easily to normal women, so easily indeed as to lay them open to the suspicion of insensitiveness. But suppose that Rosalba's attitude toward herself were an example of such accommodation and insensitiveness? Cléo always insisted she was a little fraud, always denied there was any temperamental need for her to behave as she did. Was she then no more than a combination of vanity and facile sensuality? Was her body so fair and the rest of her so worthless?

Tormenting herself thus with a thousand questions, Rory used to arrive at the villa, which always cast its spell of beauty anew, so that within a few minutes the only question she would be asking was when the workmen would be out of it. The echo of Cléo's disturbing music had faded from her mind. The image of Rosalba floated like an Ariel upon this crystalline serenity of sky and sea.

The exclusiveness of the Royles did not continue indefinitely. There came a moment when Rosalba longed to display the conquest she had made. Apart from any desire to enhance her own value in Rory's eyes she was genuinely proud of her latest triumph.

She had proved to Cléo the folly of hoping to compete with her. That was a satisfaction, but nothing beside the surrender of the cold and inaccessible Janet Royle, who in addition to being very intellectual, as Rosalba supposed, was also extremely *chic*; and this union of brains with a profile, an ivory complexion, a perfect figure, and a good dressmaker went as near to turning Rosalba's head as anything ever had. Janet's fastidiousness and eclectic taste filled her with reverence. Rosalba even began to fancy she had read Proust herself. It was useless for Rory to claim indignantly that she had read much more than Janet Royle or to point out that until she had rushed into this friendship with her the mere mention of a book had been enough to set Rosalba's eyes floating away like a couple of small balloons.

" Proust indeed ! " she spluttered.

" Perhaps you have read as much as Janet," Rosalba said doubtfully. " But I do not know why, yet I must tell to you that for me Janet is the most intelligent woman I have ever known. She makes me feel quite ignorant of everything."

" That wouldn't be very difficult," Rory said acidly.

Rosalba inclined her head in a bow of ironical thanks.

" *Grazie, signorina.*"

" No, but really, darling, you make me say catty things when you exaggerate like that."

Rosalba shrugged her shoulders.

" For you it is exaggeration, for me it is just the truth."

"I know the Janet type of woman," Rory spluttered. "Good Lord, don't I? She fairly mops up culture like a sponge, and it drips out of her just as quickly. The truth is, darling, English people are able to see through Americans more easily than Italians can."

"Oh, I understand so well that there is much jealousy between them," Rosalba said with a knowing little laugh.

"Darling, if I may say so, you really are making yourself a tiny bit idiotic. But don't let's argue about this quite unimportant matter. I've got such splendid news to-day. Maestro Supino promises to be out of our house by the end of this month."

But somehow Rosalba did not appear as much elated by the news as Rory meant her to be.

"I think it would not be prudent to go there at once," she said. "Janet finds I am delicate, and it is always imprudent to live too soon in a new house. We say in Italy '*casa* . . .'"

"I think most proverbs are nonsense," Rory interrupted quickly to fend off Rosalba's sententious wisdom. "Janet Royle only thinks you're delicate because she's mad on delicacy."

"I hope you will not be regretful one day of what you are saying. I do not want Janet for tell me that I am terribly delicate," Rosalba said huffily.

"Very well, darling, you *shall* be delicate, if you like. Only, please don't quote Janet as if she were a world-famous doctor."

And while Rory and Rosalba were exasperating each other on one floor of the Hotel Augusto, on another floor Cléo and Janet were drawing rapidly near to an open quarrel.

"I have no wish to tyrannize over you," Cléo was saying. "I have no interest in tyrannizing over anybody who does nothing but smell flowers when I tell her what a fool she is making of herself."

Janet drew in her breath painfully to mark her dislike of the loud way in which her sometime friend was talking.

"Perhaps I may be allowed to know what I am doing myself?" she asked with a languid contempt in her voice that made Cléo feel inclined to shake her.

"I find your pretence is despicable," said Cléo.

"I really don't care what you find it."

"And your manner of answering me affected and laughable."

Janet sighed elaborately and buried her face in the bouquet which Rosalba had sent up to her and on which Rosalba had scattered the scent she had chosen to be always associated with herself.

"*Elle te plaquera comme elle a plaqué tout le monde*," Cléo prophesied.

"You included," Janét smiled.

"Not at all. It was I who told her she was worse than a little *grue* who takes men for ten minutes."

Janet winced.

"I really cannot stand your vulgarity, Cléo."

Cléo spat in the empty fireplace.

"That is what I think of Rosalba," she declared. "If I am to be vulgar I will be really vulgar."

"I never had the least doubt of your ability in that

direction. It's a pity you cannot devote as much energy to your playing."

"*Assez!*" cried Cléo sharply. "I will not enrage myself by talking any longer with a woman who is as completely nothing as you. I believed that in spite of your pretentiousness you had something in you which was worthy of my love; but I do not wish to lower myself to behave like a dirty little schoolgirl, and that is what I must be to keep your admiration."

With this Cléo turned and strode out of the room.

A week later, on the afternoon of that June day when the first cicalas were singing in the garden of the Villa Leucadia and when the last pair of Maestro Supino's workmen were collecting their tools preparatory to the final evacuation, Mrs Royle and her daughter left Sirene; and Rosalba left with them.

The presence of Mrs Royle makes one hesitate to call it an elopement, though Janet and Rosalba regarded it as such. What began with crimson carnations had ended with orange blossoms. An hour after they had left Madame de Randan, who had been expected on Sirene every day for a couple of months, at last arrived.

There is perhaps something a little ludicrous in the sight of a woman with a monocle seated at the table of a café and confiding to another woman with a monocle the history of an unfortunate love affair. It becomes even more ludicrous when the monocle of one of the women is continually either being blown out like a pane of glass from the tempestuous emotion behind it or sliding down the wearer's cheek on a chute of tears. And it becomes most ludicrous of all when the other woman's monocle thanks to the comparative steadiness of a confidante's nerves magnifies an intensely fixed, slightly malicious, and completely cold eye.

"I am not at all surprised by what you tell me," the Countess was saying. "Ah, dear! dear! Attention, my dear, your monocle has now fallen into your grenadine."

Rory fished it out, wiped it, and fixed it in her eye again. This time, perhaps because some of the stickiness of the syrup had escaped her handkerchief, it remained where it was meant to remain.

"Not at all surprised," the Countess went on.

"But it makes me look such a fool," Rory moaned. "Here I am with this villa and nobody to live in it. The workmen go out to-day, and I thought we were going to have our housewarming party next week. And now . . . and now . . . you see, the worse of it is I'm not accustomed to making such a fool of myself, Hermina. It's a new experience for me."

"First of all Rosalba was trying to flirt, I think, with Lulu and Drenka?"

"Oh yes, but that was nothing. I was a little worried for a day or two, and Anastasia was most kind and sympathetic."

"She is always sympathetic," said the Countess sharply. "You know how fond I am of Anastasia. She has been my greatest friend. But I found her sympathy quite enervating sometimes. My own mind is so sharp that it does not like to be buried in a cushion.

I have quite enjoyed myself in Paris. It has been a little vulgar with so many of those strange people there to make the peace; but it was quite amusing. And I have seen such a wonderful ectoplasm. It was really marvellous. It appeared in floods, my dear."

"Did it really? I wouldn't mind so much about Rosalba's going off like that with Janet Royle if I could be certain she'd be happy. But will she be happy?"

"And I am so pleased to say that this woman who has such a splendid ectoplasm will come to me at the Villa Castalia. We will have many *séances* this winter."

"That ought to be very interesting, but I'm afraid I shan't be here."

"Why not?"

Rory shook her head sadly.

"My plans have changed since Rosalba went away."

"But, my dear, the stupid girl will be back in a week perhaps."

And with this possibility in view Rory stayed on in Sirene all the summer, though she could not bring herself to move into the Villa Leucadia.

In September a letter came from Switzerland to say that Rosalba was in a galloping consumption. The news ran round the island in a morning. Everybody was horrified. Rory was stopped by all sorts of people who asked her with tears how the Signorina was. Olga and Cléo, who had returned to Rome, received telegrams to warn them Rosalba was dying. Lulu and her Dalmatian baroness came and wept for an hour while Rory's trunks were being packed. Madame Sarbécoff walked down twice a day from her pastoral altitude to enquire. Even Madame de Randan was obviously moved.

Rory distracted by the slowness of the passport authorities, who were ignorant that peace had been signed and were indeed waging the war with an added ferocity, nearly went mad in Naples. At last, however, she obtained her visé for Switzerland and arrived there to find a note from Rosalba to say that she was much better and was now in Rome again. By the time the passport authorities had given Rory a visé for Italy Rosalba was cured.

"*Mon cher*, I am so glad to see you again," said the late moribund. "And now we will stay in Rome for the winter, and after we will go to Sirene to my house."

" Darling, did you suffer a great deal ? "

" No, not a great deal."

" I did," Rory groaned.

"*Pauvre vieux*," said Rosalba with her rogue's smile.

## CHAPTER TWELVE

ᾶς πάλαι ἀλλόμαν.
                    SAPPHO.

*Of her I had avoided too long.*

THAT winter in Rome was the old story over again of Rosalba's entanglements and disentanglements, with Rory in the background always ready to defend her against that world of which she was at once so deeply enamoured and recklessly defiant. Rory had at any rate the pleasure of paying Rosalba's debts, which by now had reached an impressive total. Somehow she managed to persuade herself that Rosalba's more demonstrative affection had nothing to do with this lightening of her burdens. That Rosalba should be grateful to her did not imply veniality. She flattered herself she had outlived her cynicism about other people's motives. The sentimentality to which she was now a complete slave appeared to her self-searching as a sign of maturity. The less kindly judgments of her youth were perceived in retrospect to be the result of an insufficient knowledge of life. She could not suppose she was wiser then than now. Reading through her old volumes of poetry she recognized their remoteness from truth. How shapeless and raw they showed now in the light of the real thing!

"The real thing does come later on," Rory assured herself. "And that's why I can understand dear

Rosalba's point of view about my paying her debts. And if superficial people do laugh at me and say that I have bought Rosalba's love, what do such people matter?"

And the way Rosalba so quickly saw through other people was most encouraging. She appreciated, dear child, the utter unimportance of people like the Royles. It had been natural, when the doctor in Switzerland frightened her in that abominable way about the state of her lungs, to cultivate an intimacy with another invalid. She had been in a morbid condition. But when the spectre of tuberculosis had vanished, how quick she had been to behold the Royles in their true light! What was it she had called Mrs Royle? A vulgar old clown. Yes, and how exactly that described her! Nobody had such a clear eye as Rosalba for the essential absurdity of a person. And she had not been merciful to Janet. When she had heard that Janet intended to spend the winter up in the sanatorium she had laughed contemptuously. Well, the Royles had gone their way. They had been a mere episode, for which she herself had been responsible. If the Villa Leucadia had been finished last spring as it was supposed to be and if she had not imported those wretched white peacocks, Rosalba and she would have been installed there by now. How mean it was of people to sneer because she had paid Rosalba's debts! Why, who else should pay them when it was partly her fault that they had mounted up as they had? It would have been perfectly easy for Rosalba to obtain the necessary money from her grandmother; but that would have meant spending several months in Switzerland. How could she be expected to do that after the shock about her health she had received in Switzerland? What more natural than that she should hurry back to Rome and trust a real friend to help her out of her difficulties?

"I am afraid that people are saying quite abominable things about me," Rosalba had burst out, tears brimming in her dear eyes.

"Darling, so long as you and I understand each other," Rory had answered, "what do people matter?"

"But they say I am being *mantenuta* by you," Rosalba had continued indignantly. "It makes me feel quite inclined to kill myself."

"Pay no attention, dearest, you can't expect not to rouse jealousy wherever you are."

"It is of course Cléo who is responsible for all this malice."

"In that case why bother? You know perfectly well Cléo has no reason to love you."

"I was not wanting to take away Janet Royle from her. It is Janet who has prayed to me that I must go with her. She could not at all suffer Cléo. I was always saying to her how sorry I am for Cléo, and this is the way *cette femme* is grateful for what I have said about her. It gives me a great deal of pain that people I thought are my friends should behave to me so. But I have told Bébé Buonagrazia what I think of Cléo, and Bébé has said that not for anything will she attend any more of her concerts. And then I have heard another abominable thing which somebody has said, and I think it was perhaps Cléo. Somebody has said that I do not know who was my father, because my mother was always making love with so many men at once."

"Darling, why pay attention? Even if you didn't know who your father was, it would be his loss not yours. It's you that counts, not your father."

"Yes, but I do not at all care to be called *bastarda*."

"Rosalba, don't let such paltriness worry you. In a few weeks we shall be back at Sirene, and you can snap your fingers at everybody."

"I am quite longing to be there," Rosalba had avowed in that voice of a young woman who has decided to renounce the world and could no longer contemplate anything except the celestial peace of a convent.

"It's worth all the storm and stress of these last months to hear you say that," Rory had cried from the depths of her being.

But when in March Rory suggested their leaving Rome Rosalba urged her friend to precede her and make ready the villa for her arrival.

"You're not going back to Janet?" Rory asked quickly.

Rosalba smiled sadly at her friend's mistrust.

"You are quite mad to think that I shall do such a thing. But I cannot leave Rome when people are saying these abominable things about me. I have a tremendous pride, and I would be too proud to run away. Besides, I want to stay and see what a terrible failure Cléo's concert will be. But you go, please Rory *mio*, because I know what a lot there is to do before my house is ready for me."

And Rory, who could never resist the delight of hearing the Villa Leucadia called her own by Rosalba, went.

There followed the usual business of announcing Rosalba's arrival for a certain date the following week only to receive a letter or, more usually, a telegram postponing it till the next week. This went on all through April and half May until at last Rory wrote to say that people in Sirene were evidently beginning to think she never would arrive and that the situation was becoming rather humiliating for herself.

However, Rosalba did arrive at last in the company of His Highness Duke Charles of Holberg-Dippe and his wife.

In spite of the danger that minor German royalties had seemed during the war, the world was now considered to be sufficiently safe for democracy not to allow them to suffer, at any rate in Sirene, such an eclipse after the war as no doubt they deserved. The fact was people could not quite bring themselves to lose an opportunity of hobnobbing with royalties on the more familiar footing that their misfortunes had brought about. This was particularly felt by the English guests at the Hotel Augusto. The male portion of them could not resist the temptation to display their knowledge of the way one talked to royalty, and the female portion could not manage to deny themselves the pleasure of curtseying to Duke Charles. After all, they *were* royalties. At any rate he was. They were not quite so sure about her, because on looking up the Hereditary Grand Duke of Holberg-Dippe in the Almanac de Gotha they could only find that she had been a Baroness somebody or other. It had all the appearance of a misalliance. Still, on the whole, perhaps it would be wise to err on the side of respect and curtsey to both. And there was no doubt at all about him. He was entitled to every 'Sir' and every curtsey he got.

Duke Charles made himself most agreeable to everybody in the hotel. This fair florid squire, for that was what he resembled, danced with energy if not with conspicuous grace and thrilled his English partners by describing to them how he had been in America when war was declared and how he had managed by disguising himself as a stoker to escape the cruisers that were after him. That he should have been so anxious to brave the obloquy of civilized mankind by deliberately contriving to fight for his country shed an entirely new light on German patriotism. He really seemed quite unaware of there being anything to be ashamed of in fighting for Germany.

It was obvious that the Duke and Duchess were much taken with Rosalba; indeed the way they put themselves in her hands to arrange all their amusements made people begin to wonder if the uncomfortable stories they had heard about her could be true.

Rory was disappointed by Rosalba's remaining in the Augusto when she had expected her to retire to the Villa Leucadia as soon as she arrived; but Rosalba had a sense of what was owing to royalty.

"*Mon cher*, you must please be reasonable. I cannot leave them alone in the hotel. They have come to Sirene for me, and I must not leave them alone. And I tell to you, Rory *mio*, they are both in love with me. It is very boring for me, I can assure you, but what can I do?"

"It's much more boring for me," Rory grumbled. "Are they going to stay here all the summer?"

"How can I tell? They find Sirene so amusing, and I am so sorry for them. But they are awfully anxious to visit my house, and I have arranged that you will give a party for them on Tuesday night."

"Thanks very much. How sweet of you!"

"I have combined with Bozzo to play till three o'clock, and then we shall all come back and drink a little champagne here and eat prawns."

"And who's coming to this party?"

"Oh, I have asked a lot of people. Perhaps fifty."

"Well, darling, I don't want to spoil your pleasure in any way; but I did rather want to have a house-warming with only our own friends."

"Ah, but this is an extra party. Because I am not yet living at the Villa Leucadia."

"I know you're not. I wish you were."

"Now please do not be disagreeable, *mon cher*. It is not my fault if the Duke and Duchess must always be running after me."

So on Tuesday the party took place; and it was an evening that Rory resented extremely. She had never meant the loggias and terraces of the Leucadia to echo with these tourist voices. She disliked parties at which the chief entertainment of the guests was the gratification of their curiosity. The pleasure of seeing Rosalba show off their moon-enchanted palace was continually being spoilt by the consciousness that everybody was asking who *she* was. In fact she did actually overhear one lank Englishwoman with a couple of out-stepping freckled daughters ask who was that queer ' new woman ' standing by the ices. To be called a ' new woman ' seemed to plunge her back a quarter of a century, and to have the Villa Leucadia of all places profaned by such a piece of suburban philistinism was hard.

"His Highness is quite pleased with where I am to live," said Rosalba, coming up with Duke Charles. "You are quite pleased, I think, sir?"

"Oh, it's delightful—delightful. I was saying to Signorina Rosalba that if ever you and she come over to the Argentine I shall be charmed to give you the freedom of the pampas."

"His Highness has bought a ranch in the Argentine," Rosalba explained. "And he is going to break a horse specially for me."

"All the horses you want," Duke Charles volunteered with an earnest smile. "Hullo! Isn't that your favourite tune? This dance is with me, eh?"

"*Con piacere*," said Rosalba, expelling the butt of her cigarette from its ivory holder into the middle of the biggest dish of strawberry ice where it fizzled and died.

"Oh, I am so sorry, my dear," she called back to Rory over the Duke's shoulder as he whirled her away in the moonlight.

"You have a very unique place up here, Miss Freemantle," one of the hotel bores came up at that moment to testify. "Very unique indeed. It reminds me a little of the house of a friend of mine in Algiers. In fact I was saying to the Duke—such a charming fellow—that we only wanted a few tom-toms, don't you know, and we might fancy ourselves in the gorgeous East."

"I don't want to fancy myself anywhere except where I am," said Rory frigidly.

"No. Quite. Quite. But you've no need to, because this is quite unique enough for anybody. Do you have any trouble with your water?"

"None."

"Because that is one of my little grievances against Sirene. I was saying to the Duke just now that if it weren't for the scarcity of water I might come and settle here myself. But I must have water. Of course, these natives don't mind; but you can't expect an Englishman to do without water."

The hotel bore found Rory's manner too discouraging, and he wandered off to be replaced by the Duchess. She was a thin pleasant little woman with a nose that in a few years would be permanently reddened by dyspepsia and with long narrow flat feet encased in shiny black silk shoes. Rory had decided that if she *was* in love with Rosalba hers was the innocent love a woman bestows on some bright flower in her garden. She looked older than her husband; but she was probably not yet forty.

"You have such a beautiful place, Miss Freemantle.

I think that Rosalba will be such a lucky girl to live here for always."

Rory flushed with pleasure, for the Duchess spoke simply and with obvious sincerity.

" It is wonderful, isn't it ? "

" Oh, it is altogether most beautiful. But there is, I think, something a little sad about Europe now. Naturally we in Germany feel that more than you. But I think everybody with imagination must be sad when they stand in your lovely loggia and look out across this wonderful bay and understand that everything we see is now in the past. You know, I would never have believed that I could ever be more happy in South America than in Europe ; but now I am only longing to be back on our ranch. One feels in a new world that perhaps one can make a new beauty."

" You are freer there anyway," Rory said, intensely conscious of the platitude, but unable to think of anything else to say.

" Yes, for we are not pitied there," the Duchess went on. " Here in Europe people like my husband and myself are just two dolls which the children have grown tired of playing with. We are luckier than others, because we have no regrets for when we were dolls. Indeed, we like much better to be people. And if one loves such things as horses one is happy. We ride and ride together all day. We are always riding in the Argentine. And next week we shall be going back again there from Naples."

" So soon ? "

" Yes, we are sailing to Buenos Ayres in the Italian

steamer. And I want to tell you how much I shall always look back to this evening."

"Oh, thank you!"

"No, no, the thanks are all for me to give. I shall always carry in my heart this moonlight of Europe that I see from your terrace; and it will become to me like a dream of when I was quite a small girl and came with my father to Italy such a long time ago."

"I am so glad you think it is the right background for Rosalba."

"It is a perfect background for her. In Rome she was always running too much here and there, and counting too much each moment as important. When one is as beautiful as that girl it is a duty to keep quiet sometimes and so become beautiful in repose. Do I express myself?"

"Perfectly."

"I am content, because I have been letting my English grow very stale during the war, though sometimes I have talked to English prisoners because I am really so fond of England," she sighed. "I have had so many good friends in England. Do you know the X——s?"

She mentioned some great family which Rory had to confess she didn't know, although, as one weakly does, she implied in the tone of her negative a slight astonishment at not knowing them.

"Lord X—— was such a charming man, and his son was killed. *Ach*, how terrible this war has been for us all! I feel so guilty to be standing here in this moonlight, which so many millions can never see again.

But I must not annoy you with my sad thoughts. We were talking about Rosalba. I was a little disturbed for her in Rome, and it will be a pleasure to leave her here. All the young people of the moment have such a claim upon us, I think, because we have set them such a bad example. We feel afraid to criticize them, because we are all like people who are walking about quite dazed by the stupid thing they have done. I asked myself to-night when I was standing on your terrace and looking at the bay in the moonlight how it was possible for us with such beauty to behave as we have behaved." She broke off with another sigh. "But now I am becoming moralistic, and all I have wanted to tell you is how happy I am to think of Rosalba in your keeping, Miss Freemantle."

All the while the Duchess was talking Rory was feeling acutely conscious of her superiority to the set of women she had allowed herself to make her only friends. She longed to give this simple and sincere little woman her confidence, to tell her all that Rosalba meant to her, to admit her many failings, but at the same time to obtain from her an endorsement of her fascination. And she might have managed to do so, if at this moment the hotel bore had not wandered back and asked whether she would not find the mosquitoes rather a problem later on. So, as it fell out, the opportunity passed; and Rory always regretted she had not been able to hear the point of view of a woman who appreciated Rosalba and yet who would have spoken of her unaffected by the distortion of a secret jealousy.

When Rosalba returned from seeing off the Duke

and Duchess in Naples she did not stay on at the Hotel Augusto as Rory had feared she might, but she came up at once to the Villa Leucadia with such a trail of luggage as lent her arrival a wonderful air of permanency.

That July was the happiest month of Rory's life. For one thing she had Rosalba completely to herself. Hermina de Randan, Lulu, the Dalmatian baroness, Cléo, Olga were none of them in Sirene, and Anastasia Sarbécoff might as well have not been there, so remote was she on her cliff at the other end of the island. Not that Anastasia's company would have been anything but welcome. Still, perhaps it was as well she was not in evidence, because Rosalba was capable of creating an intrigue even out of Anastasia despite her dislike of her and the prudence of Anastasia herself.

The Royles were still in Switzerland. Giulia Monforte had vanished completely from Rosalba's life. A threatened visit from the Princess Buonagrazia had been successfully staved off. The emotional horizon was as clear as the horizon of the Mediterranean between Nepenthe and the Parthenopean promontories.

Inside the villa everything was perfect. The cook was perfect. He had been the famous Alfonso of the Villa Amabile, in the legend of whose festivities Rory and Rosalba could hardly bring themselves to believe when they passed it on their way down to bathe at the Grande Marina. It had belonged to two American old ladies of apparently limitless hospitality, the younger of whom had died a year or two ago and the elder of whom had just returned to Sirene to find that her trusted household had robbed her of everything during her absence in America. Alfonso told the story, laying great emphasis on the fact that if he had been left in charge instead of Micheluccio and his family, such an outrage could never have happened. They saw old Miss Pepworth-Norton once—a tall hooky-beaked old woman in a trailing silk dress covered with lace leaning on the arm of her companion. She was just turning into the cemetery where it was said she used to sit for hours every day beside her sister's grave. She did not look like somebody who had been famous for her parties. Rory had heard about her from Count Marsac who came up several times to call with his secretary; and from him they gathered that it had been the younger sister who was the attractive character. He had formerly been great friends with them both, but when Miss Maimie—as he called the younger sister—died the older woman had turned on him in a most unaccountable way. They heard another side to the story from an extraordinary Englishwoman,—a Mrs Ambrogio, who was married to a local lawyer. According to her it was the Count who had behaved badly.

"Behaved abominably. One of those. Advise you not to have anything to do with him. Beastly man! Hate him! Hate him! Always speak my mind. Can't help it. English," Mrs Ambrogio had fizzed. And then she had gone striding off, dragging at her heels two horrible little coffee-coloured female dogs swathed in *cinture di castità*. "Must do it. Must do it," she had called back over her shoulder. "Dogs in

Sirene most immoral dogs in the world. Everybody immoral in Sirene. It's the air. Dogs. People. Can't help it, poor dears."

"I wasn't much impressed by Mrs Ambrogio, darling," said Rory afterwards. "She was so incoherent."

"I thought her awfully vulgar," Rosalba warmly declared. "I hope she will not talk to us again."

"And anyway these Sirene squabbles are all very absurd. One can't possibly take one side or the other. Everybody declares one cannot live here without having these absurd feuds, but I think *we* shall be able to avoid them."

"I am so sure we will," Rosalba agreed.

Rory and Rosalba were saying what so many newcomers to Sirene had said.

"And I find Count Marsac extremely intelligent," Rosalba proclaimed.

So Count Marsac was pressed to visit the Villa Leucadia as often as he could, while he in turn invited them to visit him at the Villa Hylas.

"We must certainly be allies," the Count proclaimed. "For I think we are both believers in the Greek ideal of love."

And while he was talking he was twitching his finely cut nose like a rabbit much to Rosalba's evident admiration, for she had tried cocaine herself.

"I find it excessively poetical," the Count continued as he paced the terrace in the shade of the cypress trees, "that our two villas should confront each other above this splendid scene. I must certainly felicit you, *mesdemoiselles*, on your superiority to this abominable epoch in which we are unfortunate to live. And if I may offer you my counsel it is that you will not permit these atrocious Sirene gardeners to prune your trees. I have created for myself a perfect refuge from the world—quite a palace *de la belle au bois dormant*—because I have not permitted one twig to be cut."

And when Rory and Rosalba visited the Villa Hylas they found it surrounded by a wilderness of mimosas and pines and casuarinas shutting out everything except the view of the peacock-blue water immediately below the terrace and the azure bay beyond. They did not say they preferred the view from the Villa Leucadia, because they had lived on Sirene long enough to know that one always admires one's neighbour's house even at the expense of one's own. Some of the greatest feuds in Sirene had begun over the merits of views and the comparative efficiency of sanitation.

"It is an extreme pleasure for me, *mesdemoiselles*," the Count vapoured, "to think of you propagating the Greek ideal in Anasirene. I can assure you that when I sit dreaming on my terrace the music of the Lesbian flutes will steal across the air to my ears with very great ravishment."

Rory noticed that while the Count was talking his dark handsome secretary was looking a little uncomfortable and self-conscious, and she wondered if the secretary was as much in sympathy with the Count's point of view as he supposed. She could not help congratulating herself on possessing in Rosalba somebody who was far nearer to the Hellenic ideal than anybody the Count had succeeded in finding.

"I regret very much that I can no longer offer you opium," the Count chattered on. "But I have not been able to refurnish myself since the war. However, I hope soon to be able to procure it again, and I must convert you both to its marvels."

"But you have cocaine, I think," said Rosalba quickly.

The Count laughed and tapped a small golden box he drew from his waistcoat pocket.

"Ah yes, but I am afraid that it is a little feebleness of mine which I cannot by any means recommend to young ladies."

"Don't talk nonsense, Rosalba. You don't want that beastly stuff," Rory exclaimed in alarm.

And Rosalba's sulkiness during the walk home over Rory's remark about cocaine was the only shadow on their intercourse throughout that perfect month.

Besides the perfect cook there were three perfect maids. At any rate they were perfect to look at, though admittedly their technical accomplishment was not yet on a level with their appearance. There were three of them—Fortunata, Caterina, and Francesca—slim as gazelles, with slanting Phœnician eyebrows and cheeks of dusky rose. And since nobody is more tolerant of the whims of rich foreigners than the Sirenesi they did not in the least mind being dressed in scanty draperies of lemon and orange stencilled with gold. They did not in the least mind showing a great deal of their slim legs nor binding their hair with fillets, provided they were allowed to dress themselves as hideously as they chose for Sunday mass. To be sure, some confusion was caused by the Count's first visit, when all three hurriedly pulled on white cotton stockings. This led to a remonstrance afterwards by Rory, who tried to explain that their modesty was completely secure with the Count. Fortunata, Caterina, and Francesca were firm on the subject of showing so much of their legs to a man. They explained that they did not mind. But it was the *parroco* of Anasirene. He had made it a strict rule that no member of his flock was to show any part of herself even to a painter. However, Rory raised their wages; and the next time the Count called the stockings were not called into action.

The weather was perfect. There was hardly any *scirocco*, and every afternoon about half-past-three the north-west *maestrale* flecked the deep blue waters of the bay with white flowers of foam. Sitting out in the loggia Rory and Rosalba felt that their house must seem to the rest of the world as airy and white as the dozens of little white boats scudding across the little white waves of the deep blue bay. There was not always a full moon, because even over Sirene the moon behaves normally. But in the evenings there was sometimes a crescent in the green western sky beyond the flat roofs of Anasirene, and sometimes in the east above the hill of Timberio hung a decrescent that faded slowly in the rose and lilac sky of dawn. And even when there was neither ivory crescent nor pearly decrescent nor gibbous yellow moon nor full staring silver moon, there were nights of starshine when the air was so tender that one seemed to be wrapped in petals and fanned perpetually by the wings of moths.

On such a night as this, when the glowing end of Rosalba's cigarette was like a small furnace in the heart of the smoky shadow that she was seeming, Rory put out a hand and touched that bare arm as if to reassure herself that her adoration was not a figment of the perfumed air.

"You *are* here, darling?" she murmured fondly.

"Oh yes, I am quite here, *mon cher*."

"And you are happy?"

"I am very content indeed."

"As happy as you thought you would be?"

"Oh yes, I think."

"Darling, only think?"

"Oh yes, I know."

"And you admit we are complete? Just we two?"

"Oh yes, I am quite sure we are."

But the next day Rosalba after opening a letter with a Swiss stamp exclaimed:

"Who do you think is coming to Sirene?"

"Not the Royles?"

"Ah, no, no," said Rosalba contemptuously. "That would not be much news. But this is a letter from Janet to say that Olimpia Leigh is coming to Sirene quite soon."

Rory's heart sank. Nothing that she could say or do would prevent Rosalba's trying to conquer that Himalayan peak.

## CHAPTER THIRTEEN

ῌλθες· κεὖ ἐποίησας· ἔγω δέ σε
μαόμαν ὂν δ' ἔφλαξας ἔμαν φρένα
κανομέναν πόθῳ.

SAPPHO.

*You have come. You have done well. I was longing for you, and now you have set my heart aflame with passion.*

RORY was not to be blamed for fearing Olimpia Leigh. She was indeed redoubtable. To be loved by Olimpia Leigh even for five minutes gave any young woman who cared about it a cachet not obtainable since the days when young women could boast of being loved by the mighty Sappho herself. There were plenty of people to maintain that here was the greatest female creative mind since Sappho, and there was none to deny her right to be called the greatest female composer the world had yet known. She was not one of the many female artists who hope by assuming the name of George to be judged as men. One pauses to ask why George should so often be chosen by women who wish to put their names into trousers. Olimpia would have regarded it as a kind of rape upon her Muse to call herself by such a patient plodding humdrum name. She would have scorned to hand over that creature of air and fire to the embraces of a husbandman. It was Olimpia's pride as a woman to contend with men in the art that above all they had made their own. She did not envy manhood enough to call herself George ; but she did not despise men, and she recognized that music had belonged to them hitherto as much as in the sciences, apart from Sophie Kovalevsky, mathematics had always belonged to them. She had no sympathy with the theory that men and women should be less differentiated. That seemed to her utterly retrogressive. She regarded women as an unexploited mine, with as limitless a capacity for development as man might have seemed to hold for some prehistoric dreamer in the cavernous deeps of Altamira. The idea of evolving a third sexless sex antagonized her. She would rather have put women back in the harem than admit the credibility of such a monster as the superfluous woman. She was not discouraged by the excess of women over men ; but she refused to allow that this was nature's provision for the preservation of humanity. She maintained that it was the margin of security for feminine evolution. Such women must keep in the present stage of human development a sexual life of their own. The notion of repressing it prematurely was horrible. Nor would she acknowledge contraception as a panacea for female woes. She believed that birth-control would degrade womanhood more effectively than prostitution to the level of machinery. She held that the average woman was intended to bear children as much as the average man was intended to beget them. Indeed, she considered that the average woman should bear more children in order to increase the number of physically sterile women ; and she would not have hesitated to restore polygamy if thereby she could have brought about a proportionate increase in homosexual men. She argued that art was slowly dying because the creative impulse in humanity was being increasingly exhausted by the procreative need. The struggle of human nature through æons to sublimate the sexual instinct was in danger of being finally defeated, and the only remedy she saw was homosexuality. She imagined a race of homosexual men and women who would in the course of time exhaust the physical expression of sexuality through atrophy caused by the repeated futility of a sterile act. The instinct of sublimation would thus be refreshed, and finally there would be achieved a race of creative minds which had completely mastered the body. She did not accept such a race as the equivalent of any third sex at present imagined. "Their sexual aloofness will have been achieved by a voluntary emptying out or κένωσις of human sexuality, not by an unnatural drying up or μάρανσις." Thus she argued.

Olimpia was the daughter of an American financier and of a Swedish mathematician who had also been a musician and a scholar of Greek. Olimpia was proud to have inherited her music from the maternal side, because, as she used to point out, although great men usually had remarkable mothers and often insignificant fathers great musicians almost always had musical fathers. It seemed a biological law that music should pass down through the males of a family. And that she should inherit music from her mother, though in her case it had been subordinated to mathematics, greatly encouraged a belief in herself and in her theories. From her mother, too, Olimpia inherited her Greek scholarship. She claimed to think in ancient Greek, and she was fond of pointing out that what made Sappho the supreme lyric writer of the world was that she had moved nearer than any poet toward a perfect fusion of poetry with music. If this contention were disputed, she would quote Dionysius of Halicarnassus on her side and end the argument by murmuring in that low thrilling voice of hers, " But after all, you only know Greek from the outside, do you ? " After which she might go to her harpsichord and chant to her own accompaniment as if she held in her arms a lyre :

> κὤττ' ἔμῳ μάλιστα θέλω γένεσθαι
> μαινόλᾳ θύμῳ · 'τίνα δηὖτε πείθω
> καὶ σ' ἄγην ἐς Fὰν φιλότατα; τίς τ', ὦ
> Ψάπφ', ἀδικήει;

And none had ever ventured to point out that with all her knowledge of Greek she could not be sure how these words were pronounced in Mytilene. But if any had been bold enough to challenge her on that, she would have shrunk back with her air of a crouching nightingale and said, " The only letter of which I am not convinced I have the very sound as it came from Sappho's mouth is the digamma. Yes, I do sometimes ask myself if my digamma is hers."

Somebody once asked why she did not write another setting for the *Chansons de Bilitis*. The wings of the crouching nightingale quivered : " Because I consider that the music of Debussy is as adequate for the *fausse antiquité* of Pierre Loüys as the words of Pierre Loüys are adequate for the music of Debussy."

The compositions by which Olimpia Leigh was best known were not those she cared for most. She herself preferred her music written for the *Lysistrata*, the *Thesmophoriazusæ*, and the *Ecclesiazusæ* of Aristophanes; the music she had written for almost every fragment of Sappho, were it only sometimes a single word; and an astonishing concerto for piano and antique instruments such as the tuba, the lituus, and the salpinx, the tibia both single and double, the syrinx, cithara, pectis, lyra, sambuca, and the tympanum. This work had never been performed because there were neither instruments nor players available.

There is always some suspicion attached to an unperformed or an unpublished work; but those who had been privileged to read the score of Olimpia Leigh's concerto declared it sublime, and she was constantly being entreated to surrender so far to modern limitations as to re-orchestrate it; but the composer was firm in her refusal to consider such a mutilation of her work. "I speak through the piano to the past, and the past answers me with its own instruments; and in that answer Sappho and I are one, Orpheus and Beethoven are one, Archimedes and Einstein are one." At that time Spengler's book had just appeared and was selling by the thousand among Germans who were finding in it an excuse for losing the war provided by the ineluctable laws of the tides. "What would Spengler say to your theory of art?" she was asked. "Spengler like every other

German is a Procrustean thinker, and whether my theory can be made to fit into his half-made bed is a matter of utter indifference to me."

From her Swedish mother Olimpia had inherited music and Greek; from her American father she had inherited money. She was indeed extremely rich. But unlike most rich people who indulge in art she had no need to suppose that her wealth was anything except a convenience. She never had a misgiving about the power of her genius and personality to compel recognition. She was not beautiful, being like Sappho small and dark, and as Lucian's scholiast says, καὶ τί γὰρ ἄλλο ἢ ἀηδὼν ἀμόρφοις τοῖς πτίλοις ἐπὶ σμικρῷ τῷ σώματι περιειλημένη. *Like a nightingale with shapeless wings wrapped round a little body.* That was exactly the effect of Olimpia in her draperies. But her body though little was not shapeless and her throat though tawny as the nightingale's was beautifully modelled, and her eyes as dark and bright, yet not like the bird's apprehensive. Olimpia seemed a big name for so small a person until one heard her speak, and then it could no longer be felt that she was overweighted by it.

This was the woman who was coming to Sirene, having rented the Villa Eolia for several months. Rory had never met her, though of course she had heard a great deal about her, and in other circumstances she would have been thrilled to meet her; but with Rosalba here she would be too formidable, for she was richer than Rory and beside her music Rory's verse was nothing. Nor was she ever known to have spared anybody's heart.

The Villa Eolia was not the right house for Olimpia Leigh ; but she preferred to savour a strange place in unsuitable surroundings. Only thus did she consider herself able to judge its effect upon her.

"'Ηχικὸς Αἰολίδης," she murmured to Olga Linati, who in the rapture of having for the first time in her life successfully let a friend's house regarded her client with a reverence that needed no Greek to enhance it.

"I mean that the name is appropriate," Olimpia explained. "Musical offspring of Æolus."

Olga frowned in perplexity because it seemed impolite not to understand what a client was talking about.

"Sappho belonged to the race of Æolus," Olimpia reminded her.

"Ah yes, how stupid I am," said Olga brightly, trying to respond with her own brightness to the brief illumination of Olimpia's intellectual match, which burned out much too quickly, however, to give her the least notion of her own mental whereabouts.

It was through Cléo, who had been playing some of Olimpia Leigh's compositions in Rome, that Olga had let the Villa Eolia. It had been built some thirty years before by an American painter of the narrative school who, after spending five years in an attempt to make up his mind whether he wanted a view of the bay of Naples or a view of the gulf of Salerno, had finally decided that he must have both. Not wishing to be perched on the top of Monte Ventoso, he had chosen the saddle of the island above the Strada Nuova, where he was directly exposed not merely to every wind that blew except one, but also to their concentrated force tearing between the precipices of Monte Ventoso and the Torrione. The west wind, which was the only one from which he had supposed he should be sheltered, was in fact the worst of the lot, because it rushed up the slopes of Monte Ventoso from the Anasirene side and charged down on the Villa Eolia from above. The owner lived for two years in the oriental confection he had invented. After that he only came for a few weeks in the summer, and only then when he had not succeeded in letting it, which seldom happened, for members of the Nordic race who take villas in the south of Italy have usually a beautiful climatic innocence. The painter, like so many painters, had supposed that architecture was merely a commercial tributary of his own art, and therefore he had made his own plans. These plans were excellent to look at. They told a story as clearly as one of his own pictures; but when the walls began to go up, every door and every window was in the wrong place. After a succession of improvised changes during the course of the building, while the outside of the villa resembled a miniature of the Alhambra, the inside was like—well, really it was not like anything except a number of very small square rooms and a maze of unusable staircases. There was only one large room, whose windows designed to have the most wonderful panorama in all Sirene ended in looking out on a dingy Moorish courtyard, extra corridors having been built round it on every other side in order to allow the inmates to get upstairs at all. However, the painter was not going to be cheated of his view, and built a tower under the impression that he was going to have a studio at the top of it. What he really had was just enough space to store the sentimental part of a household's rubbish and a rusty telescope. The view certainly was magnificent; but it was seldom enjoyed, savouring as it did too much of an expedition recommended by Baedeker. Tenants climbed up the spiral staircase to the top on the day they arrived, tried to work the telescope, failed to modify its permanently blurred vision of the world, slithered down the staircase again, dusted their hair at the bottom, said what a wonderful idea it had been to secure that marvellous view, and never looked at it again throughout their tenancy.

" Quite the most idiotic house I have ever seen," Olimpia declared to Olga, who was roaming round the Villa Eolia trying to gather its rooms into some coherent shape as a hen her chickens.

" You don't like it ? Oh, I am so sorry," said poor Olga much mortified.

" I don't blame you. All houses to let in places like Sirene are idiotic. This merely happens to be more idiotic than most."

" The last people who took it liked it very much," Olga urged.

" What were they ? Mohammedans ? "

" No, no. They were American."

" The most idiotic house I have ever seen," Olimpia repeated. She raised the lid of a piano and struck a chord.

"What is this?"

"I think it is a piano."

"It may have been. It may have been," Olimpia murmured in a voice remote and vague. "I think it would be happier out in the garden. It seems to want exercise. Or castor oil. Yes, give it some castor oil and put it outside."

"But will you not want a piano for yourself?"

"A what?"

"A piano."

"Yes, please have one sent over from Naples."

"This is not a good piano?"

"This is not a piano at all. I don't quite know what it is; but I cannot possibly spend the night here alone with it. Perhaps Cléo will go over to Naples to-morrow and choose me a piano?"

"I am sure she will be so glad to go."

Coming away from the Villa Eolia, Olga met Rosalba on the road down from Anasirene. They greeted one another warmly, not because either of them was glad to see the other again after some months, but because Rosalba was anxious to obtain all the news she could about Olimpia Leigh and because anybody would have been a relief to Olga after the critical tenant of the Villa Eolia.

"My dear, I am awfully pleased to see you," said Rosalba. "Has Cléo come too?"

"Yes, we are coming with the *vapore* yesterday."

"And she has had her concert in Rome?"

"Oh yes, but that was last month."

"And now perhaps she will rest a little, I think?"

Rosalba suggested rather anxiously, for she was not anxious that Cléo's renown should benefit from the visit of this great composer to Sirene. The less Cléo played, the better.

"Yes, she is resting now. She does not practise at all. And she is smoking too many cigarettes."

"She does everything too much," said Rosalba. "I think she will soon quite spoil herself."

There was a pause.

"And has the great Olimpia Leigh arrived?" Rosalba asked.

"Yes, we have left her in Naples yesterday, and she is here this morning."

"Did she say anything about me?"

"No, she has only asked about a piano. She finds the one at the Eolia very bad."

"Does she want another one?"

"Yes, she has asked for Cléo to go to Naples and choose for her a good one."

"I suppose Cléo is very offended against me?"

"No, no," said Olga, one of whose principles was never to admit that anybody was ever offended with anybody, because she hated to admit that anything was beyond repair. She was as fond of soldering up human relationships as remaking dresses. "She was wondering when she would be seeing you. Why don't you come back with me now to the Villa Rosamarina?"

"I will this evening perhaps. I must go back now to Anasirene."

"What pretty links!" said Olga, fingering the cuff of Rosalba's silk shirt.

The links were little chips of Roman tesseræ become iridescent with time and set in gold.

"I will give them to you," said Rosalba, unbuttoning her cuffs and pulling out the links.

"No, no, please, Rosalba, you must not rob yourself."

"My dear, I want you so much to have them. They will be very *chic* for you, I think."

And when Olga still demurred, she insisted:

"Please to take them, because I shall throw them away if you will not."

"I'd love to have them, but I don't like to rob you."

"Ah, my dear, please do not let us make a history of little nothings. You will think of me sometimes when you wear them."

Olga flushed with pleasure. She had reached an age, perhaps it would be truer to say an economical state, when presents bestowed without apparent patronage were grateful. She leaned forward to kiss Rosalba, who gave her a sun-warmed cheek as she turned to hail a passing carriage.

"*A rivederti, cara*," she called back over the hood, waving. "Zampone's at seven o'clock."

About two hours later Rory, who after waiting for Rosalba all the afternoon in Zampone's Café and walking back up the long dusty road in the glare of the westering sun because she could not get a carriage, arrived at the gates of the Villa Leucadia to find ten *facchini* struggling out of them with her Steinway grand piano.

"Che cosa è questo?" she demanded at once indignant and alarmed.

The grunting cursing band of porters did not reply, but came surging past her with their burden in a patter of naked dusty feet and reek of vinous sweat.

"Piano! Piano!" she cried, intending to convey an appeal to go carefully, but owing to the unfortunate ambiguity of the phrase stating what seemed to the loaded porters an all too obvious fact.

"*Si, signora!*" the hindermost called back contemptuously as the Steinway grand started to descend the road like a rollicking funeral.

Rory rushed into the villa.

"Fortunata! Caterina! Francesca!"

The roe-eyed maidens appeared in unperturbed beauty and unhurrying grace.

"Ma che cosa è questo?" Rory repeated angrily. "Perchè hanno rubata il pianoforte? È una cosa molto abominabile. Io sono molto rabbiato. Voi non dovete lasciare fare. Perchè? Perchè?"

The three roe-eyed maidens were relieved of the difficulty of trying to explain matters by the appearance of Rosalba.

"*È stata la signorina,*" they declared unanimously and vanished with suppressed giggles.

"Rosalba, darling, what does it all mean?" Rory gasped, sinking down on a seat of *verde antico* in the great entrance hall she had added to the old Villa Beer.

She looked a hot and flustered and rather ridiculous figure in that cool place beside the two marble flute girls and the clumps of bamboo rustling in the wind that played through the open arcade.

"*Mon cher*, it means that I have paid a little compliment to Olimpia Leigh who has not a piano at the Villa Eolia. So I have sent to her ours."

"Well, I think you might have told me first."

"*Mon cher*, I ask you please not to make yourself quite absurd. How can I tell you when you are not there?"

"No, I've been waiting for you at Zampone's," Rory said bitterly. "You might at any rate have sent me a message to say that you were spending the afternoon with Olimpia Leigh."

"But I have not been with her. So please do not put yourself in a rage for that. I have not yet seen Olimpia Leigh."

"Then why have you sent her the piano?"

"For a compliment, I tell to you."

"How do you know she hasn't got a piano of her own?"

"Because I have seen Olga Linati and she has told me."

"Oh, and I suppose this is your way of creating an impression on Olimpia Leigh. My name, I suppose, wasn't even mentioned?"

"I find it very sad that you have such a small mind, *mon cher*. I have not had time to think of a thousand little ceremonies. All I have wanted is to make a compliment to a great woman who has come to Sirene and is finding herself in a disgusting villa like the Eolia."

"I wonder you didn't offer to send her the Leucadia!"

"Please do not be stupid. How could I send to her the Leucadia?"

"If you'd got in a few more *facchini* they might have carried it down the hill."

"You do not know what you are saying. It would be altogether impossible with all the *facchini* in Sirene."

"Oh, good lord!" Rory groaned. "I was only trying to make a little joke."

"And I find your jokes awfully boring. To me they are not jokes at all."

With this Rosalba swung round on her heels in a huff and retired to her own room, where she remained until half-past six when she left the Leucadia to keep her appointment with Olga. Half-way down to Sirene she met the piano coming back up the hill again.

The porters put it down in the road and clustered round Rosalba in a state of indignant fatigue to explain that the signorina at the Villa Eolia had told them to take the piano back at once to where it came from.

"*E siamo morti, signorina. Signorina! Signorina! Non ci ha dato neanche un soldo!*"

Rosalba told them to take back the piano to the Leucadia at their leisure, consoled them with a hundred-lira note, and bade them tell Fortunata to give them each a bottle of wine.

The porters shouted their gratitude and grappled

with the piano again ; but Rosalba walked on with
a frown. So, Cléo meant to have her revenge for
Janet Royle. Well, Cléo should have another lesson.

Rosalba's heart began to beat fast when she reached
Zampone's and saw seated round a table on the
terrace not merely Olga and Cléo, but with them a
third woman—a little woman with burning eyes
wrapped in a cloak of what looked like white vicuña.
That must be Olimpia Leigh, and she could only be
seated at that table for the express purpose of meeting
herself. As Rosalba passed through the shadowy
inside of the café crowded with chattering people she
was saying to herself that Olimpia Leigh must find
before the summer was past that none of the women
she had known was worth Rosalba Donsante. And
as she reached the glass-fronted door which opened
on the terrace she paused for a few moments to
contemplate that white figure and ponder those
immeasurable eyes. Rosalba knew well that the most
prudent tactics to gain her ambition would be to look
through the door, call out a greeting to Cléo, and
immediately retreat. All her self-confidence was not
enough to make her perfectly certain of a victory over
Olimpia Leigh unless she could convince her adversary
that she was a match for her in aloofness and indifference. That white figure with the burning eyes
would have heard of her easy conquests and, being
able herself to conquer when she wished, would be
resolute not to be in her turn conquered. But it was
already too late to retreat, for she had already launched
her attack with the Steinway grand. Olimpia would

have told Cléo and Olga by now about the way she had sent back the piano. They would have been laughing at her discomfiture. She flung open the door and stepped from the shadowy interior into the light of the terrace and freshness of the evening air.

" *Eccomi !* " she cried defiantly.

And Rosalba was aware of the quick curious glance hardly a second in duration before Olimpia Leigh seemed to sink away from her into the folds of that white cloak. A diamond would have seemed to Rosalba a dull offering beside the brief flash of that first look. She was her debonair self again ; a fleck of deeper crimson staining her cheeks, a touch of swagger added to what was normally the perfection of easy grace, that was all there was to mark the heightening of her self-consciousness as she threaded her way among the tables to reach the one in the corner, a step up from the rest of the terrace, where the great woman was sitting.

"So you have come to Sirene at last," she said to Olimpia, who raised her black eyebrows.

"Have I been expected then ? "

"But naturally I have been hoping so much to meet you for many years."

"You are full of compliments, mademoiselle."

"Not at all. I say just what I am thinking. And please I must beg you not to call me ' mademoiselle '. I am Rosalba."

"I'm afraid I don't find it easy to call people by their intimate names the first time I meet them." Olimpia turned to Cléo who was staring before her more like a sightless statue than ever. " That is true, is it not, Cléo ? "

If Rosalba had been holding a hammer in her hand, she would have brought it down with a thump on top of Cléo's untidy head.

" I am quite snubbed," she said with a wry smile.

" *On peut dire ça, on peut dire ça,*" Olimpia murmured.

" But it is quite true," Rosalba went on. " I have just now seen my poor piano on his way home again."

" I am hiring a piano for myself from Naples."

" That is what I have understood. I regret so much that my enthusiasm has been *inconvenable*. It was an idea which has come to me that you would not care to sound——" Rosalba bit her lip in exasperation at the failure of her English—" to play, I must correct me, to play the pianoforte which our friend Olga has provided for you. I was afraid for your music."

" Thank you, but my music is not a disease," said Olimpia.

Rosalba, remembering the bottle of medicine she had sent to Janet Royle, found this a little difficult to laugh off with complete nonchalance, especially as Cléo let out a hoot which made all the other drinkers on Zampone's terrace look up from their glasses.

" I am so sorry that I have bored you with my piano," she said haughtily.

" Yes," Olimpia agreed, " it was an infernal nuisance." And in the same breath she added, " I rather like your hands."

Rosalba cheered up, and laying her hands on the

table regarded them, and the three signet rings on her boyish fingers.

"They are not so nice as other parts of me," she said at last.

"I didn't say they were nice hands," Olimpia responded. "I said 'I rather liked them.'"

"For me that makes them nice," Rosalba declared with a smile.

At this Olimpia rose abruptly from her chair and, wrapping her cloak round her head in the style of a Greek himation, walked away from the table without a word to her companions.

"*Tu sais, Olga,*" cried Cléo with one of her huge laughs as she banged her fist down on the table, "*elle est vraiment impayable. Eh, eh, tu auras à faire, ma poupée d'amour.*"

"I wish you would not use your beastly French cocotte language to me," said Rosalba furiously.

"Do not make any attention to her," Olga interposed pacifically. "*Non, mais tais-toi, Cléo.* It is not kind to laugh at Rosalba."

"I am quite indifferent," said Rosalba loftily. "Her vulgarity will not at all affect me. It is so easy for me to know that Cléo has said all that she has been able for setting Olimpia Leigh against me."

"*Eh, qu'est-ce que tu veux me ficher? Je n'ai dit rien. Seulement, écoute-moi quand je te jure que tu seras bigrement plaquée par la grande Olimpe. Elle aime les prémices, je t'avertis. Dès que je l'ai connu elle a cherché toujours les boutons de la rose. Elle n'aime pas les fleurs qui commencent à s'épanouir. Alors, garde à toi.*"

Rosalba rose from her chair, her eyes flashing.

"*Tu m'insultes, Cléo,*" she cried.

"*Ne fais pas la comédienne, ma petite.*"

"*Giù, giù, Rosalba,*" Olga begged. "*Tutti ci guardano. Fa attenzione, cara.*"

"*E che ci guardino!*" Rosalba snapped. "*Non mi importa. Sta contenta tu che non ho buttato un bicchiere di vermouth in faccia sua.*"

"*La donna è nobile,*" Cléo began to sing in derisive parody of Rosalba's airs.

With a not altogether ladylike expletive Rosalba rushed off the terrace before she gave Cléo the pleasure of seeing her cry.

"No, but really you were very unkind to her, Cléo," Olga protested. "Olimpia first was so rude, and then you were so rude. I was feeling so sorry for her."

"I have warned her for her good," Cléo insisted with a scowl.

"Yes, but what can it serve? She is only thinking that it is for jealousy."

"I am altogether and quite entirely sick of that little fool," said Cléo austerely. "Let us go home and eat."

Courtship in Mytilene is complicated by the fact that both the principals are women. There is often, to be sure, an assumption of masculinity by one or other or sometimes both, but it rarely survives such a searching test as courtship. Inevitably they both have to take turns at playing the maiden loth. They both have to struggle to escape. And they are both at any crisis of emotion apt to become as passive as ordinary women. Which is, if you come to think of it, a little humiliating.

The mighty Sappho herself must have been aware of the fact. She recommends in one of her loveliest songs an essentially feminine technique of courtship. We cannot therefore criticize Olimpia Leigh for playing the maiden loth with Rosalba, even though there was perhaps something a little ludicrous to the observer in the spectacle of a woman of European renown playing the maiden loth with a girl fifteen years younger than herself, especially when one considered that in turn the part would be enacted just as thoroughly by the late mad pursuer. In spite of Cléo's contemptuous warning to Rosalba there was no doubt it did interest Olimpia Leigh to suppose that Rosalba was wildly in love with her. There is no doubt it did afford her satisfaction, petty though this must sound in a woman of her genius, to know that Rory was fretting her heart out of herself up at the Villa Leucadia, expecting the worst. There was in fact when it came to it not a great deal of difference between her attitude and the attitude of Janet Royle the year before; and she was indeed obviously a little chagrined not to be receiving bouquets of carnations every day in order to have the pleasure of sending them back at once to the donor.

Rosalba, however, did not suppose that carnations were likely to succeed where a grand piano had failed. Moreover, she paid Olimpia the compliment, which perhaps in the circumstances she hardly deserved, of thinking her superior to such trifles as flowers. She did consider the idea of transporting one of the statues from the amphitheatre at the bottom of the Leucadia garden to the Moorish courtyard of the Villa Eolia. But luckily for the *facchini* an invitation to dine with Olimpia arrived in time to make such an offering superfluous.

The actual dinner-party was not a success, because Olimpia did not speak a word all through. So Rosalba for effect did not speak a word either, until poor Rory, after sustaining a monologue for half an hour, burst into tears and rushed from the table out of the house.

" Now will you please play to me ? " Rosalba asked, after assuring Olimpia that Rory often behaved like that when invited out to dinner.

" Why should I play to you ? "

" Because I do not want you to make love to me," said Rosalba.

" You will not get by impudence what you cannot get by charm," Olimpia warned her.

" But you are curious to know how I am making love," Rosalba pressed.

And since Olimpia really was rather curious she betrayed herself with a glittering eye.

Whereupon Rosalba jumped up and vowed that she must go and see what had happened to Rory.

And this kind of thing went on for a month and might have continued for much longer if Zoe Mitchell had not arrived.

## CHAPTER FOURTEEN

Εὐμορφοτέρα Μνασιδίκα τᾶς ἀπάλας Γυρίννως.
SAPPHO.

*Mnesidice more fair of form than the dainty Gyrinno.*

OLIMPIA and Cléo were sitting under the munificent August moon in one of the mismanaged courtyards of the Villa Eolia, and as usual the conversation turned upon Rosalba.

"The fact is," the composer proclaimed, "I don't really care for boyish girls. I like girls to be profoundly and ineluctably . . ."

"*Pardon?*" interrupted Cléo, who did not want to miss what might be an important word in such an enthralling confidence.

"Ineluctable means something that cannot be escaped."

"I understand. Please to go on with what you say."

"I like girls to be profoundly and ineluctably girls. It is the girlishness of them that I find attractive. Really in some ways I prefer a girlish boy to a boyish girl. You know how fond I am of you, Cléo. I think I've shown it by the way I've entrusted so much of my intimate work to your performance. But I cannot imagine myself being in love with you."

"I concur," said Cléo, who did not concur at all, because nobody yet has ever assented sincerely to the proposition that he or she cannot be fallen in love with.

"And therefore," Olimpia continued, "I cannot take any real interest in Rosalba. You were in love with her. . . ."

"For a minute," Cléo put in quickly. "But do not speak to me about her now. I find her quite impossible."

"I can understand the charm she must have for a woman like poor Freemantle. In her case Rosalba is a substitute. Poor Freemantle is obviously one of those over-sexed women who has had from earliest youth a fatally depressing effect on any male. She must always have been a great bundle of anaphrodisiac femininity. Her natural inclinations are, I am convinced, absolutely normal, but finding that men became studiously concave when they were dancing with her she forswore them."

"Please what means 'forswore'?" Cléo asked, hoping to add a word to her erotic vocabulary.

"Gave them up. Denied herself the pleasure of their company. And of course being as I say over-sexed she substituted women for men and instinctively sought in women what men had withheld. No woman with any real sense of what is beautiful in women would have devoted herself to the encouragement of female boxers."

Cléo nodded her agreement.

"It would be perfectly easy for me," Olimpia went on, "to whistle Rosalba away from poor Freemantle for ever. But I am not going to. Not because I have any pity for Freemantle! I have no pity for

Freemantle since reading her poetry. She appears to me to be almost as much of an exasperating muddle of mock antiquity as this deplorable house Olga has found for me. I should have no hesitation whatever in robbing her of Rosalba, did not Rosalba herself bore me to death."

"Ah, she does bore you, I think," Cléo exclaimed, inhaling a tremendous puff of smoke from her cigarette.

"My dear, it is exactly like having a nephew about the place, though I confess I never had a nephew of my own. But from what I hear of other people's nephews that is what Rosalba must resemble. And the only way I can think of to get rid of her importunity is to show her just what kind of a girlish girl I really like."

"Lulu de Randan is a pretty girl," Cléo suggested.

"Lulu de Randan is a very pretty girl, but she is not my type. Moreover, I regard her mother—why on earth she has come to Sirene I cannot understand; it has almost driven me away—I regard her mother as the most antipathetic woman in Europe. A woman who affects mediums is as bad as a man who affects choir boys. The medium's djibbeh and the choirboy's surplice are equally anti-Hellenic."

Cléo had by now very little idea of what Olimpia was talking about. So she lit another cigarette.

"And even if I could tolerate Hermina de Randan as a mother-in-law, I could not begin a love affair which might be interrupted at any moment of the day or night by Miss Chimbley's vox angelica piping, 'Are you there, Lulu?'"

It may be mentioned that Lulu's Dalmatian baroness had gone to the Riviera and that Miss Chimbley who had benefited greatly by her long rest was now back in the Randan household, exercising once more her shadowy authority as *dame de compagnie*.

"No, no, my dear, Lulu de Randan is quite out of the question," Olimpia decided.

"It would very much annoy Rosalba if you would be interested in Lulu," Cléo urged gravely.

"The girl I shall invite to come to Sirene will annoy her very much more. Have you heard of Zoe Mitchell?"

Cléo shook her head.

"Mrs Mitchell . . ."

"Mrs Mitchell? She is then married?"

"She is married, but not inconveniently married to Mitchell, the son of Mitchell et Cie in the Rue Castiglione."

"*Les bijoutiers?*"

"Yes, yes, the big American jewellers."

"And she is beautiful?"

"She is extremely beautiful."

Cléo's eyes sparkled grimly.

"*Bien*," she murmured, and lighting another cigarette she inhaled, it seemed, the half of it in one mighty intake of satisfied breath.

A week later Zoe Mitchell, accompanied by one of those mature and tyrannical French maids who never appear in the English drama, but are common everywhere else, landed in Sirene.

And Zoe Mitchell was beautiful. It was not just

a question of arguing that she was beautiful for the pleasure of mortifying Rosalba. Even Rory found it hard to deny her beauty, loyally though she criticized it. People who tried to give an impression of Zoe Mitchell alternated between calling her profile Egyptian and calling it Greek. They were both partially right, for she was Minoan—a votary of the Snake Goddess and as lithe and slender as the Snake Goddess herself must have seemed, but without those pointed prominent breasts, and without that Minoan corsetting. And then as soon as one had reduced her to a faience model of disturbing prehistoric womanhood she reminded one of the Psyche in the Naples Museum, perhaps because of the way her clouded golden hair was combed so smoothly back from her forehead of ivory. And then in her rose-dyed beauty she would look as if she had just been hatched from a tralucent hyacinthine egg like Helen of Troy, and one went back again to an earlier age of art for her prototype in Tiryns or Mycenæ. Actually she was American and she spoke English with a noticeable American accent; but she seemed entirely without any American past. One did not feel that she had ever been young or that she would ever be old. One accepted her as one accepted a statue. Although she carried about a volume of André Gide, one did not attribute to her any conscious intelligence. There was in the way she was managed by her maid a suggestion that if Victorine chose she could undress her mistress at night and shut her up in a drawer where she would lie immobile until she was re-wound and set on her feet to walk about again in this green world and there deceive people with the fancy that she was a sentient creature of flesh and blood. Nobody believed she was the wife of an ordinary man called Mitchell, a member of the great firm of jewellers ; and it might have been difficult to believe she was his mistress without those prodigious square sapphires and emeralds set in platinum, of which she apparently had an unlimited supply.

The long awaited filling up of Sirene with post-war travellers had happened a week before Zoe Mitchell arrived. The Hotel Augusto and all the other hotels were in a few hours full of visitors. The pale-blue porcelain tiles of the big terrace were hardly visible in the movement of dancers. And the guests belonged to a new world. They were the product of the war, and after reading memoirs of the years after Waterloo one realizes that such people are the inevitable product of a great war. These *nouveaux riches* on holiday were in the brightness of their hues, in the resemblance of each one to his neighbour, in their restless leaps and goggle eyes and gaping mouths like a shoal of stranded mackerel. So must their predecessors have been through the ages.

Here is Trimalchio nearly two thousand years later and hardly twenty-five miles as the crow flies from his native Cumæ. In 1914 he was porter to a firework-maker in Naples. In 1915 the *padrone* took him into partnership to help in the manufacture of munitions. In 1918 he was a millionaire advertising urgently in the *Mattino* for a palace, a secretary, an automobile, and a solitaire, each *urgentissimo*. Now he is seated at the head of a table in the Augusto surrounded by sycophants and parasites. They eat and drink at his expense, flattering him while he to call attention to the brilliant on his forefinger sits at the head of the table and picks his nose. Then a thought seizes him; he calls for pen and paper and bids his secretary pose. He draws what is intended to be a likeness, but what is not even a caricature. The sycophants belch forth praise and satiety in unison. They salute him as Mæcenas and Virgil in one. They proclaim a masterpiece this drawing which would disgrace a child scrabbling with a piece of chalk on a paling. The secretary takes the sketch round and exhibits it at the other tables in the big dining-room of the Augusto. While it is being looked at, he stands in the pose in which he has been drawn to show what a marvellous likeness his master has caught. Meanwhile, Trimalchio himself, as little Bozzo strikes up a fox-trot, leaves his place at the table and compels one of the waiters to dance with him. The sycophants and parasites applaud wildly. The head waiter draws near for a further order of wine. Trimalchio bids him offer champagne in his name to every table in the room. There is a popping of corks, a rush of servile waiters, the clink of glasses. Trimalchio vomits into an ice-box. Even this is applauded. Even the vomit of a man so rich as he has a value like ambergris. Trimalchio to show that he has recovered stands up and kicks his secretary's obsequious buttocks. More champagne. More shouting. At every table round the big terrace there are parties of people spending their money. Everybody is spending his money. Not merely profiteers, but soldiers home from the war, English people showing their daughters the continent now it is once more available, Neapolitans with pasty-faced, sweet-smeared children, Americans looking like the supernumeraries in a film, Germans swigging and guzzling and paying for it in Swiss francs, Russians who have decided to turn Bolshevik and so have money to spend, French artists who have won travelling scholarships, Dutch intellectuals, Scandinavian eccentrics, central Europeans flushed with self-determination, and of course pederasts and pathics of every nationality. This is the post-war Sirenian harvest, the thought of which had sustained the island through all those dreary winters when Sirenian life seemed to be dissolving utterly away.

And if a cynic on this August night, when Trimalchio sat eating and drinking and belching and vomiting with his sycophants and parasites, had doubted whether those famed Sirenian enchantments ever existed, he might have recovered his credulity when he saw Zoe Mitchell in her frock of ivory dancing with Rosalba in her frock of bronze. He might have followed them with his eyes as one follows a succession of exquisite figures along a frieze. 'These are the hours dancing,' he might have murmured to himself; and the clatter of the momentary scene would have been hushed in the immensity of time. It is even a temptation for the chronicler to lay down his pen at this point, and, content with having brought two such beautiful young women together in a Sirenian dance, to let them stay here for ever without trespassing any further upon their follies and fantastic emotions and obscure passions, to go and sit for ever with Olimpia Leigh in that dark corner under the ilex which thrusts forward a bough over the pale-blue porcelain tiles, to wonder for ever what music is being wrought behind those burning eyes of hers, and here to write Explicit, because that intertwining of bronze and ivory, that mingling of brown and golden hair, and those hands set palm to palm and tapering to a lily bud, might remain for ever thus and unfold as much of the mystery of life as any volume's end. But alas, the pen of the novelist lives by follies and fantastic emotions and obscure passions. For him, unlike the happy sculptor or painter the beauty of a physical act can only try to live in a parenthesis as a caged bird might try to sing. He cannot leave Zoe and Rosalba dancing here for ever as Botticelli left his Graces under the orange-trees or that unknown craftsman of Cnossos his three ladies in blue bright-eyed with the laughing secrets of how many thousand years ago.

> Κρῆσσαι νύ ποτ' ὧδ' ἐμμελέως πόδεσσιν
> ὤρχηντ' ἀπάλοισ' ἀμφ' ἐρόεντα βῶμον,
> πόας τέρεν ἄνθος μάλακον μάτεισαι.

*Thus did Cretan maids of yore dance harmoniously around some lovely altar, treading with delicate feet the tender bloom of the grass.*

" You will bathe with me ? " Rosalba was asking.

" Sure I'll bathe," Zoe was promising.

" You are not afraid to make yourself burnt by the sun ? "

" Why no, I adore to be burnt brown. I guess it

suits me to be brown. I don't burn red, you know, which is lucky with a skin as fair as mine."

"Yes, I am so sure it would suit you to be brown," Rosalba was approving eagerly.

She had heard Olimpia Leigh express several times her disapproval of the way girls let themselves get sunburnt. She knew that Zoe's roses were what Olimpia admired most about her, and she was determined that these roses should be blasted by the sun.

Among the intrigues of six years Rosalba could not remember anybody who had come within measurable distance of Zoe as a rival to herself. For the first time she felt insecure of victory. Olimpia had been difficult enough already. She had caused Rosalba many a sleepless night on her Venetian bed in the Villa Leucadia in searching for a key to unlock that heart. And then there had been no question of a rival. It was all very well for that stupid Rory to disparage Zoe's beauty and declare that any woman who could dream for an instant of preferring Zoe to Rosalba was not worth taking seriously. All she had effected by such injudicious flattery had been to drive Rosalba back to her room in the Hotel Augusto where three times a day notes were arriving from Anasirene begging her to return.

"I have come to stay here so that I can always be looking at your beauty, my dear," she told Zoe.

"You think I am beautiful?"

"My dear, you are quite marvellous. And I could not bear to hear Rory Freemantle say you were not at all so beautiful."

"Oh, her! I don't give a cent for *her* opinion," Zoe scoffed. "She's just a poor old hamfat. I heard lots about her in Paris. Nobody thinks much of *her*. Say, Rosalba, have you read any books by André Gide?"

"No, I think not."

"Oh, you ought to read André Gide. I'm mad about André Gide. I can't understand a word he says. Oh, I tell you, André Gide's some writer. You just *can't* understand him, Rosalba."

The situation was made more difficult for Rosalba by the consciousness of an audience watching her failure. She could not see Olga seated at one of the tables in Zampone's with Hermina de Randan and Cléo, nor Lulu walking up the road toward Timberio ten yards ahead of Miss to visit Anastasia Sarbécoff, without frowning at what she fancied was their eternal topic. Rory's laments exasperated her, because she could not see that Rory had anything to lament compared by herself. Rory should be used to failure by now. How often had she confided in her the disappointments of her intimate life! And how ridiculous to suppose that bed and board at the Villa Leucadia could compensate for a defeat at the hands of Zoe Mitchell!

Presently the Royles came back to Sirene. And not even yet was her cup full, for of all people Bébé Buonagrazia must take it into her head to try a *villegiatura* on the island—Bébé Buonagrazia with her small round head and long neck and sidelong malicious smile to concentrate into her own cruel wit the commentary

of the world upon the ridiculous figure her friend
Rosalba was making of herself. Nor was the dread of
being unhorsed in the lists of love under the eyes of so
many women she had despised the end of Rosalba's
apprehensions. A letter arrived from Baroness
Zaccardi in Switzerland to say that she was hearing
very bad accounts of her granddaughter's way of life.
Rosalba must be careful, or her allowance would be
reduced, and even her inheritance might be imperilled. By the same post came a letter from Françoise, her grandmother's maid, warning her that the
old lady was in worse health than she had ever seen
her, and urging that the sooner Rosalba came to
Switzerland, the better for everybody. *Madame la
baronne* had come very much under the influence of
an American woman who never lost an opportunity to
create prejudice against Mademoiselle. This American
woman was some kind of witch who claimed to cure
Madame by spells and diabolical heresies. She called
herself a ' Faith Healer,' and Françoise was convinced
that she was trying to persuade Madame to make a
new will in her favour. '*Venez, venez, tout de suite, chère
petite mademoiselle, je vous en prie. Je me méfie de cette
femme.*'

But Rosalba tore up both these letters and bade the
head waiter prepare another of those extravagant
dinners she was now giving every night. Queer
dinners they were too. The other guests of the Augusto
used to watch that gathering of extraordinary women
in the middle of the dining-room with a feeling that a
veil had been lifted from the debauchery of ancient

Rome. Like other ills and inconveniences of the moment they ascribed such female eccentricity to the war. They were shocked of course. Even the war had not made them quite immune to this kind of thing. But they comforted themselves by saying that after all it was the kind of thing which might happen on Sirene, but which could not possibly happen anywhere else.

These dinner-parties of Rosalba's had little in common with that form of entertainment as it is usually practised among civilized communities. They partook more of the nature of séances at which everybody is wrought up to a pitch of nervous tension and expectation. The mere passing of the salt or pepper involved as much expense of emotion as an elegy of Propertius. All life's fever was in the salad bowl. A heart bled when a glass was filled with wine. We know what an atmosphere can be created at a dinner-party by one jealous woman. At Rosalba's parties there were often eight women, the palpitations of whose hidden jealousies, baffled desires and wounded vanities was in its influence upon the ambient air as potent as the dreadful mustering of subterranean fires before an eruption.

Even when Olimpia Leigh was not present, because at the last moment without warning she had decided to make herself more desirable by withdrawal, her empty chair agonized the company. There were occasions too when she had definitely said she would not come, but when in the middle of dinner she would walk in, her brown legs bare except for the sandals on her feet, her small body wrapped round with a white cloak of fine wool, her jet-black hair bobbed long before such a style became the fashion. She would not seat herself at the table, but she would tell the waiter to put a chair beside it ; and what the company suffered under her burning gaze might be hard to make credible.

One evening Olimpia arrived like this at a dinner-party Rosalba was giving on the terrace of the Hotel Quisisana up at Anasirene. It had been a fairly cheerful gathering before she appeared, though Rory's tears had kept bubbling up into her eyes every time she thought how unkind it had been of Rosalba not to let her give the dinner-party on the terrace of the Villa Leucadia hardly a mile away. Rosalba had been in the best of spirits because everybody had commented on the depth of Zoe's sunburn. Her face was now as lifeless as that of a terra-cotta figurine, and this evening she was wearing a pale pink frock, which made the brownness more conspicuous. The tan seemed to take all the gold from her hair and to give it a dusty look. Her sky-blue eyes too it seemed to rob of their hot glow so that they might have been painted. And she really was not burnt so much to terra-cotta when one regarded her carefully. She was more like an image carved out of chestnut wood. She had a bleached shiny look. She had become more medieval than Hellenic. Bébé Buonagrazia had whispered to Rosalba that she had never seen the woodenness of a mind better expressed by the body that clothed it. " How naughty you are, *mon cher*," Rosalba had whispered back ; but she had squeezed with delight the hand of the slender and malicious princess under the table.

And then while the waiters came bustling out on the glowing terrace where the guests sat in cheerful talk under the great bunches of green grapes that hung down from the pergola above them, bustling out and holding high as if it were being offered to the Gods a dish of roast chickens, Olimpia Leigh slowly followed the waiters out of the hotel and stood in contemplation of the glittering table over the crook of her olive-wood stick.

"Ah, my dear, how glad I am that you have come," Rosalba cried as she leapt up to greet the imperturbable invader.

"Little beast," Rory groaned to Anastasia Sarbécoff who was sitting next her. "She knew Olimpia was coming all the time. I'm quite sick of all this pretence."

"*Vorrei vederla nuda,*" Bébé Buonagrazia murmured to Olga. "*Ha qualchecosa di zingara. Potrebbe essere spaventevole. Si figurerebbe rapita da un fauno, evvero?*"

"No, no, I don't want to eat anything," Olimpia was saying. "I'll just sit and watch you all eating."

Which was exactly what the assembled guests could not bear.

The dinner-party dissolved into pools of intense silences and thin trickles of passionate whispers, above which Olga talked excitably at the top of her voice about a plan she had for opening a shop in Paris next winter, which Madame Sarbécoff kept approving with a suave and serene flattery that only to her friend Madame de Randan appeared tinged with an infinitely faint derision.

"My plan is to take a small shop in Rue St Honoré,

because I have a friend who has found what I want," Olga was saying over and over again with variations.

"I am so glad for you, my dear. I am sure you will be so successful," Madame Sarbécoff was replying over and over again with variations.

"*I am so happy now that you have come,*" Rosalba whispered to Olimpia. She had moved her chair away from the head of the table, round which the waiters desperately circled in their endeavours to persuade somebody to help herself to chicken.

"*Oh dear, why will Rosalba have such bad manners always?*" Rory whispered to Cléo.

"*Because she is from the gutter,*" Cléo whispered back.

"*Please don't say horrid things like that about her,*" Rory whispered angrily.

"For I think if I open this shop I will have a friend who will perhaps give me twenty thousand francs."

"I am so glad for that, my dear Olga. Money is just what one wants."

"*You may be happy,*" Olimpia whispered to Rosalba. "*I am utterly bored.*"

"*Shall I make them to all go away and let us be here together?*" Rosalba whispered.

And for answer Olimpia beckoned Zoe to come and sit beside her. The waiters were shrugging their shoulders in their mortification over the unattractiveness of the chickens. Olimpia was studying Zoe's tan.

"You're getting very brown, aren't you?" she said distastefully.

"Why, I guess I'll be black before I leave here," Zoe declared.

At that instant Olimpia perceived the delight in Rosalba's face.

"I'm going to drive back to the Villa Eolia," she announced coldly. "Will you come with me, Zoe?"

"I do not think that we can have any more dinner," Rosalba exclaimed. "We shall all go down to Sirene."

"Why don't you all trot along to the Leucadia?" Rory suggested. "We can have our coffee there."

"Not at all, *mon cher*, it is most awfully dull for us to have our coffee there. *Pietro! Pietro!*" she shouted to one of the waiters. "*Chiamate, prego, le carrozze. Andiamo giù.*"

The head waiter came out to expostulate. The dinner was not half finished. He had prepared all sorts of delicacies that the Signorina liked.

"*Non fa niente,*" the Signorina declared. "*Non abbiamo più fame. Abbiamo mangiato bene. Allora grazie e buona sera!*" She pressed a hundred-lire note upon the mortified head waiter, and the wheels of the carriages crackled outside the festooned gates of the Quisisana.

"This is my vehicle," said Olimpia to Zoe. "You will drive down with me?"

"*Lulu, cara, tu scenderai con me?*" Rosalba asked, ignoring the entreaty in Rory's eyes. "*Avanti! Avanti!*" she cried to the driver, who was not keeping close enough on the heels of Olimpia and Zoe. Then turning to Lulu she kissed her passionately amid the cloud of dust in the wake of the *carrozza* they pursued. "*Ti adoro,*" she murmured feverishly. "*Sei un' angiolo.* No, but really, Lulu, I think you are the most beautiful of anybody. I do not understand how Olimpia can make this escape with Zoe when she might make with you an escape so much more beautiful. *Ti adoro, ti adoro! Baciami in bocca.*"

"*È pazza, quella signorina,*" the waiters decided when they were left regarding the uneaten chickens and the abandoned table under the stolid bunches of green grapes.

"We will make a little *mascherata* to-night," Rosalba said to her companion. "I am quite tired of everybody except you. *Tu resterai con me stanotte? Di, di, tu mi vuoi bene, Lulu?*"

"*Ma c' è sempre Mamma,*" Lulu murmured.

"*Mamma non ci entra. Baciami. Ti amo, ti adoro. In bocca, cuore mio, in bocca.*"

Then snatching herself from the kiss she cried to the driver of their carriage:

"*Avanti! Avanti! Non voglio che quella carrozza arrivi prima di noi.*"

But in spite of Rosalba's urgency the carriage with Olimpia and Zoe reached the Villa Eolia a couple of minutes ahead. When the pursuing carriage arrived the door at the bottom of the long flight of steps which led up through terraced vines to the main entrance was already closed.

An hour later, Rosalba wrapped in a Spanish cloak and supported by the presence of Lulu led four of the Sirene barbers to play a *mandolinata* beneath Olimpia's windows. The four barbers who practised their instruments whenever they were not attending to their professional duties played fervidly. The half moon on her way down to the sea shed a radiance on those Alhambrian courtyards. The precipices of Monte Ventosa looming ebony dark against the sapphirine sky made a fit background for the sombre figure of Rosalba posed in a Byronic attitude against a broken marble column. In spite of the romantic scene Lulu felt so much inclined to giggle that she had to bury her head in her knees as if the passion of the music had overwhelmed her. What amused Lulu so intensely was that when the *mandolinata* began all the windows of the villa were lighted up, but that one by one as the music continued all these windows were darkened, so that by the time the last chords of the third serenade had twanged there was not a glimmer anywhere visible. Even the moon had sunk behind the mountain, and Rosalba's attitude of brooding melancholy became only too appropriate.

" I don't think she wants to hear you," Lulu suggested.

" *Suonate ancora*," Rosalba commanded.

The barbers struck up another luscious Neapolitan serenade, which failed like its predecessors to elicit any response from the darkness and silence of the villa.

" We will go round to the other side," Rosalba announced, leading her orchestra through the mazes of the garden. Here two more serenades were performed without evoking the smallest sign of appreciation within.

" Why you laugh, Lulu ? " Rosalba asked indignantly.

" I cannot help laughing. It is so ridiculous."

"*Suonate ancora*," Rosalba commanded.

The barbers had exhausted their appropriate nocturnal repertory by now and were reduced to playing tunes like *Torna a Surriento* and *'O sole mio*.

"No, please, but listen to me, Rosalba," Lulu begged. "I shall die with laughing if we stay here any longer."

"I did not know that you were such a stupid girl," Rosalba said severely.

"*Non adirarti, Rosalba*," Lulu begged, tears of mirth running down her cheeks. "*Ma è tanto tanto ridicolo.*"

"Please to speak in English. I do not want these people to know how stupid you are, if you please. I am quite disgusted for your vulgarity."

But by now Lulu was nearly hysterical with mirth. She sat down on a parapet and rocked to and fro uncontrollably.

"*Basta, signorina?*" the leader of the orchestra asked. He was not sure what result his music was intended to produce; but he felt somehow that it was certainly not producing the result anticipated.

"*Suonate ancora*," Rosalba commanded.

So the four barbers twanged out *Il Balen del suo Sorriso* while Rosalba with folded arms stared at the unresponsive windows.

"*Allora, andiamo*," she snapped after a hopeful pause at the end to give Olimpia that one more chance had produced nothing.

They walked back to the Augusto in silence.

"I have learnt at least one lesson to-night," Rosalba said to Lulu in the lobby of the hotel. "I have learnt not to confide no more in stupid young girls who do not know when they must be serious. I advise to you, my dear, to find some boring and vulgar young boy with whom you can laugh as much as you wish."

And at that moment Lulu ceased to pay attention to Rosalba, for at the other end of the lobby she saw Carmine staring at her, and evidently waiting to be acknowledged before he came forward.

"Carmine!" she cried hurrying across the lobby to greet him. "*Che bella cosa! Come sono contenta!*"

"I speak English now very good," said Carmine, bending over ceremoniously to salute her hand.

## CHAPTER FIFTEEN

'Ηράμαν μὲν ἔγω σέθεν, Ἄτθι, πάλαι ποτά.
                                        SAPPHO.

*I was in love with you, Atthis, long ago.*

ROSALBA'S *mandolinata* became a good joke in Sirene, for which she blamed Lulu and made a resolution to pay her out at the first opportunity. As a matter of fact Lulu was not to blame at all, being too busily occupied in escaping from Miss in order to enjoy the company of Carmine. Miss had not had to run about so much for two and a half years. If Carmine had been delightful at eighteen Lulu found him twice as delightful now that he was well on in his twenty-second year. He had done splendidly during his two or three months of active service, having made friends with an influential member of that most powerful secret society in Europe —the society of people who have something to do with the management of big hotels. As soon as he was demobilised this friend had found him a job at some small hotel in London whence, as soon as he began to speak English fluently, he had moved on to the Carlton or some such place. Now he was back in Italy with the prospect of being made manager of a big new hotel that was being built in Rome, and he had every reason to suppose that his fortune was secure. He had already acquired that magnificent manner which distinguishes the management of big hotels. He was neatly dressed.

He danced well. He was tall and he was as good looking as a Southern Italian can be. Lulu had been afraid he might bear her a grudge for the way she had failed to answer his letters so soon after they had parted. But Carmine was as tactful as the man of the world he now claimed to be. He made no allusion to their boy and girl love-affair ; but he did show clearly how much he still admired her, and he managed to convey in his manner, formal and ceremonious though it was, a hope that possibly in the future his admiration might be returned. So, Lulu was too pleasantly occupied with finding opportunities for talking to Carmine and listening to his plans for the future to bother about Rosalba and her ridiculous *mandolinata*.

Rosalba forgot when she accused Lulu of being responsible for the joke against herself that the four barbers who made up the orchestra were not likely to cut their clients' hair without giving them the latest gossip. She chose to assume that Olimpia Leigh must have been asleep and therefore had not heard the strains of the mandolins outside her window ; and certainly Olimpia herself never alluded to the absurd episode. She did, however, complain to somebody of Zoe Mitchell's sunburn.

" A lovely rosy thing when I liked her in Paris. She arrives here and turns into the colour of an old flute."

This observation was repeated to Rory, who thinking to make Rosalba happier repeated it in turn to her. It did make Rosalba happy, but not to Rory's advantage, because it renewed her vision of a complete victory over Zoe, and she was farther away than ever from returning to the Villa Leucadia.

The next shock for Rory was the announcement that Olimpia Leigh intended to buy a villa in Sirene. It was true the information came from Olga Linati, which made it less reliable. Still Olga undoubtedly had let the Villa Eolia to her, and her success in the more elaborate transaction was not as much outside the bounds of possibility as once it would have seemed. Olga was rushing from one end of the island to the other, investigating discreditable stories about the sanitation of this villa, examining the claims put forward for the view from that one.

"You must forgive me because I cannot stay to talk just now," she would rush up pink-faced and gurgling to explain to friends on the Piazza, "but I must now go to see the Villa Capo di Monte which belongs to Major Natt. I must see for myself if it will fall down at any moment, because if it will not it will be an *occasione*. He is only asking 150,000 which is not at all too much, and I do not believe it will fall down as Mr Bookham says it will. And there is the Villa Zaffiro. But that would cost *un sacco di denaro*. And now, my dear, I must run. *Sono talmente occupata*."

Rory felt that her most dignified gesture would be to offer the Villa Leucadia to Olimpia Leigh. If the woman intended to live permanently in Sirene, it was idle to expect Rosalba would ever do anything except use the Leucadia as a convenience. Yes, it would be the most dignified thing to do, and also the most economical, for it was far too big for her alone. Let Olimpia Leigh have it. Let her live there surrounded by Atthis and Anactoria and Gongyla and Gyrinno and Mnesidice. With all her music and with all her fame she would not find herself capable of holding Rosalba, once she had surrendered to that supreme charm.

Rory drove back home one morning with the firm resolve to sit down at her desk and write an offer to sell the Villa Leucadia. But when the dusty road was behind her and she was in that cool and white seclusion, when she saw once again the azure sea through the colonnades and heard the bamboos whispering and walked past the cypresses to lean over the marble parapet and gaze upon the enamelled floor of the bay, she hesitated to forsake all this for another woman. Why *should* Olimpia have it? Why should she withdraw in favour of a woman who had already enjoyed all that life could give? She wandered sadly into Rosalba's bedroom. There was the window they had planned together, and there was the view they had so often gazed at together. There was the tall Venetian bed with scalloped valance of scarlet leather and counterpane of Rhodian embroidery. Why should that brown-faced dark-eyed gypsy enjoy the sight of Rosalba sleeping, as she was wont to sleep, with her face nestled in the crook of her slender arm and her bronze hair scattered in a glinting flood upon her shoulder?

" I have given up everything and everybody for this love," Rory groaned aloud. " Why should I break my heart merely to give two people an opportunity to satisfy their curiosity about each other? "

There passed before Rory standing alone in the luminous air of that room something like the fabled panorama which heralds the onrush of death for those who drown in deep waters or fall from great heights. It was as if all that had led up to the ultimate emotion with which through each month of building she had felt she was sealing each stone in its place more securely than the mason with his mortar began to reveal itself, so that she became aware how literally her life was bound up in this room.

She saw herself as a stocky little girl in a red and white tartan frock standing outside a grey house at Folkestone half covered with purple clematis, and holding in her hand a bag of sweets—crescents of lemon and orange which would not taste of either nowadays, but which for the unjaded palate of youth held the gardens of Damascus in their jelly. She was waiting outside that grey house for a fair-haired friend, and the sweets were for her. But instead of Phyllis there emerged a parlour-maid who said Miss Phyllis could not come out that afternoon. No more than that. No message of love. Nothing. And as she had crossed the road that smelt so strongly of summer Rory was looking up, and there in a third storey window above the cloud of purple clematis she was catching sight of Phyllis having her hair combed by that detestable family nurse who had once criticized a hole in Rory's stocking in front of Phyllis. There was going to be a party, then. Sick with the misery of her abandonment Rory tried to wave a greeting; but the bag of sweets shot from her limp fingers and fell into the road. Phyllis and her nurse were laughing. The grey houses wreathed in purple clematis swam in the tears of mortification that streamed into her eyes. She left

the bag where it lay and rushed forward toward the
sea through the hot perfume of asphalt and privet until
she found an obscure seat on the undercliff where she
had wept the afternoon away. This had happened over
thirty years ago. Phyllis if she were still alive was now
a faded blond. The errand boy who had found that
bag of sweets and eaten them was perhaps a shop-keeper
himself. But the tears of that fine summer afternoon
were not yet dry in the mortar of Rosalba's room.

And now Rory was on a platform of the Gare du
Nord in Paris, waiting for the boat train to arrive with
her friend Amy who was coming to stay with her in
the flat she had just furnished in the Quartier. She
had sat up all night writing an ode to Amy, glaring at
the moon while she wrestled with the sapphic metre
until the moon went early down behind the chimneys
and the smoky lilac dawn dreamed upon the house
tops. The thought that Amy would within another
hour be opening her grave eyes at the jolly things her
friend had gathered round her was nearly making Rory
dance a hornpipe on the platform. And then the adver-
tisements of apéritifs and the seemingly solid letters
of Chocolat Suchard receded and the incoming train
rushed toward her shouting, ' Here we are ! ' It was
difficult to resist the impulse to run madly along the
compartments, peering into each one for Amy's light
and lovely form. But Rory had managed to stand calm
like a sensible Englishwoman until she had caught
sight of her. Of Amy . . . Of Amy and a man !
' Dear old Rory ! I *am* so glad to see you. Isn't this
ripping ? Dick, this is Rory. Rory, this is my cousin

Dick. He's going to be in Paris for the next fortnight and he's longing to take us everywhere, aren't you, Dick?" And this well-groomed Dick had mumbled something under his moustache and called from far down in his throat, "Porteur! Porteur! Ici! Ici!"

It was the year of the Great Exhibition, and instead of visiting the galleries of art with Amy as she had planned and finding an excuse in each masterpiece to discuss Amy's light and lovely form from top to toe, Rory must put up with the company of Amy's cousin, the essence of dull gentlemanly Anglo-Saxondom. They had all gone on the moving-platform, and whether Amy and her cousin had contrived it or not, Rory had found herself rushing away from them both on the platform moving at eight kilometres an hour while they were walking fast in the opposite direction along the platform moving at two kilometres an hour. In the desperation of jealousy Rory had tried to leap after them, had fallen, and had been carried along for some distance in a sitting posture on the platform moving at four kilometres an hour. And for a whole wretched hour she had spent her time stepping from one to another of those diabolical platforms, trying to catch Amy and her cousin. It was like trying to catch Paolo and Francesca in the first circle of Hell. She would see them sweep past her walking at three miles an hour in the same direction as the platform moving at eight kilometres, while she herself would be half running in the opposite direction on the slowest platform of the three. The domes and cupolas and minarets of the Exhibition pavilions swayed below her nightmare of unnatural progress through giggling gaping crowds of passengers. Occasionally there would be murmurs of '*À bas les Anglais*,' or '*Vive les Boers*,' when in changing gears she cannoned into people. Finally a horrible little French boy in white socks, with a face like a pickled walnut, running along head down had butted her in the midriff and winded her completely. She had felt that Paris was a ghastly failure, that she should never write any poetry worth writing, and that she should like to become religious. In the mortar of Rosalba's room were enshrined those aspirations to lead a conventual life, the swirl of the moving platforms, that summer sun of twenty years ago which had shone from brazen skies upon her grief for the loss of Amy, who did not as a matter of fact marry her cousin, but who did marry somebody of the same type three months later and who always asked Rory to be godmother to her boys, not because she wished thereby to link Rory mystically with her normal female existence, but because Rory was rich and might leave them money. That moving platform had made a cynic of her, and for years afterwards she had led a cynical life, only trying to express in her poetry some of the profound sentimentality on which that cynicism was based.

Rory recalled the moment when she had decided that do what she might about it there would always be hairs on her chin, and she recalled what a brave gesture it had seemed to go in for breeding French bulldogs so that she could laugh about them and draw attention to the moles on her face that so much resembled theirs and the way her chin stuck out so much like theirs. She recalled the first *boxeuse* she had launched upon her career and the sensation it had caused in the drawing-rooms of Mytilene. And she recalled her pride when she had heard people comment in whispers upon her masculine appearance. The bowler hats she habitually wore for so many years had become so much a part of her that she had begun to think her head was just as hard. She had never stood any nonsense from her *boxeuses*. When one of them had been defeated in five rounds and had had hysterics like some actress Rory had been *effrayante*. She could see them now—those great hefty girls huddled in a corner of the private gymnasium frightened to death of their patron. *Effrayante*, yes, that was what she *had* been. They had all avowed it. Oh, it had been a well-ordered life after the first disillusionments of youth—a comfortable well-ordered life with poetry to express the secret hunger which had never been appeased. And then Rosalba had come on the scene. How well she remembered the very moment when she first saw Rosalba and knew instantly that she wanted nothing else from life!

It had been a billowy blue and white October day, and notwithstanding the gloom of mid-war that hung over Paris one was uplifted and rode majestically upon the great clouds above the grey city. She had walked for awhile in the early afternoon about the Parc Monceau, listening to the cheep of the sparrows and the thin cries of children at play and watching the first brown leaves swoop down to earth through the serene and glittering air. And after her walk she had gone to tea with Renée St Martin whose house was close by. She had not particularly wanted to go. She had thought it a pity to lose one breath of this benign autumnal day. She did not want to sit and listen to endless war talk, rumours of this or that minor success and to speculations when it would all finish. She did not want to hear where the butter came from or how it was that Renée managed to get hold of such delicious bread. But a cloud had passed across the sun and a chill had touched the afternoon, and she had thought a cup of tea would after all be rather pleasant. So she had gone to tea with Renée. The people she expected to find were all there. She had sat down, feeling a little sulky and remote in the farthest corner of Renée's oak-panelled room, and she had looked up indifferently when the maid entered and announced Mademoiselle Donsante. But Rosalba herself had been close behind ; and the indifference had turned to a fast beating heart as if a watch long wound up but never going had been suddenly shaken in the right way and started ticking. Rosalba was wearing a rifle green jacket and waistcoat, a black braided skirt, and a broad-brimmed felt hat. She had a white cambric collar and a black satin tie with an emerald pin. She had black silk stockings and patent leather shoes. There were jade links in her cuffs, an eau-de-nil handkerchief in the pocket of her coat, and she handed the maid an ebony cane with a knob of malachite. They had dined together that night. Rosalba had been enchanting.

They had had one of those tables for two *chez Prunier*, which more than any other tables for two in any other restaurant seem genuinely intended for two people. On one side of them had sat a fat Frenchman with three chins and the rosette of the Legion of Honour. On the other side there had been a panelled wall. And half-way through dinner, when the waiter had gone to fetch another half-bottle of champagne and when the Frenchman next door was brooding into his napkin and slowly twisting his glass of Bordeaux in departmental meditation, Rosalba had slid her boyish hand along the smooth wood of the wall and caught hers in its slim grasp, smiling her sidelong downward smile like one of Leonardo's pagan saints. That would be three years ago next month.

Rory groaned.

It was such a little way into the eternity of which she had dreamed.

She fell on her knees beside the bed and mingled her hispid cheeks with the rough Rhodian embroidery of Rosalba's counterpane.

"I will not let you go without a struggle," she sobbed.

Rory thought no more of offering the Villa Leucadia to her rival. That seemed too ignoble a surrender. She wrote instead invitations to all her friends, enemies, and acquaintances to come to what she declared was to be the real house-warming which had been put off for so long.

The night chosen was the night of the September full moon—the vintage moon, which we poor northerners call the harvest moon and worship with vegetable marrows.

It was intended to be a Sirenian night of nights.

And it was.

## CHAPTER SIXTEEN

κῆ δ' ἀμβροσίας μὲν κράτηρ ἐκέκρατο.
>                                    SAPPHO.

*There a bowl of ambrosia had been mixed.*

A REALLY great party should mark an epoch in the annals of pleasure. It should be a recognizable date for the beginning of new love-affairs, a reference for the end of old ones. It should be condemned as an orgy by people who were not invited. It should be the begetter of a dozen scandals, the inspiration of historical absurdities. It should appear in print as incredible as our own manners of the night before often appear to us at noon the following day. A really great party must be devoid of any conscious effort to put the guests in good fettle. Fancy dress parties may achieve classic fame; but a party which achieves classic fame by such elaborate preliminaries cannot rank with the greatest. Fame should rest on what the guests did, not on what they wore. A great party should be a world within a world, not a world temporarily outside it. It should effect a heightening and a concentration of ordinary life, so that in retrospect one may perceive the quintessential selves of the guests; and when those guests meet each other for the first time after such a party they should feel a kind of sacred elation such as we may suppose was felt by those who had been initiated into the Mysteries.

The party given by Rory Freemantle on the night of the vintage full moon will always rank in Sirenian tradition among the most productive of scandal and pleasure in the island's scandal-dogged and pleasure-haunted history.

It is a quarter-past nine. Two sun-ripened old Sirenian friends, two bachelors who compete with each other in the paraphrasing of an epigram from Martial or the Greek Anthology but in nothing else, have dined not at the Hotel Augusto nor at any other of the stereotyped expensive hotels which can be recognized from Calais to Palermo, from Lisbon to Constantinople by the flavour of their roast chickens and the dressing of their salads, but at a small *osteria* where the chickens and the salad taste unlike any others. They have drunk between them a bottle of genuine Sirene wine, not the slightly sweetened amber-tinted furniture polish which passes as such, but the authentic stuff, the colour of no matter what, which has a faintly sulphurous tang by no means displeasing. They have eaten several slices of raw ham and several discs of that well-flavoured sausage called *mortadella*, a dish of some variety of octopus which looks and tastes like a quantity of small tyres rescued from the sea, a crayfish with its cocoanut texture, and cutlets à la Milanaise which if they have removed the blanket woven of breadcrumbs will have been juicy enough. They have wound up by doing something between eating and drinking a *zabaione*, which they have followed with a cup of bitter coffee and a glass of that peridot-green liqueur known as Cento Erbe—stinging potent stuff which would make rejuvenating Voronof himself jealous. They have taken a second glass of Cento Erbe because they wanted to be sure that it was not exactly like the green Chartreuse they used to drink years ago. And they have taken a third glass for no reason, because no reason is required after drinking two. They reach the Piazza feeling as bland and as full and as golden as that great moon which by now will have climbed high enough up out of the sea to look down over the top of Monte Ventoso on the terraces of the Villa Leucadia, whither they and so many others are bound. A line of carriages seems to extend all the way along the zigzag loops of the road up to Anasirene, and others coming down hope to make the ascent a second time with guests who are now waiting for them among the noisy crowd of uninvited Neapolitans in Zampone's. Their carriage which they had the forethought to order yesterday is waiting for them, and as they get in several of the native loiterers in the Piazza wish them a merry evening. They feel it is going to be a good party. *Qualchecosa per aria* tells them so. The Sirenesi have good noses for an evening's pleasure. Pietro whips up his cob. In the old days before the war they would have been driven by a pair, and in spite of the Piazza optimism they are inclined to say that the parties nowadays cannot be as good as those of the old days. But this doubt is merely the short languor of incomplete digestion. Two hundred yards of rackety progress over the stones of the Strada Nuova soon shake the complacency out of their war-stiff bones;

by the time they reach the steeper slope of the road up, they are not sorry the little cob is walking. One's dinner adjusts itself better at such a pace. Before them and to left of them in a great sweep the precipices of Monte Ventoso tower against the warm bloom of the sky. The scent of the *macchia* on the foothills and in the gorges which here and there gash the perpendicular cliff above blows down upon them in warm gusts. Rosemary and myrtle, gum-cistus, thyme, juniper, and a hundred other aromatic shrubs and herbs shed their spices. To right of them the land tumbles in lemon orchards and terraces of already dishevelled vines to the purple waters of the bay, with the lights of Naples winking eighteen miles across and the dim ghosts of mountains in the farther background. There is a tawny stain upon the top of Vesuvius, which every few minutes brightens to orange as if a Titan were smoking an immense cigar. Behind them the town of Sirene lies like a scattered heap of mushrooms in the moonlight.

The two old Sirenians do not talk much. There is a *dolce dir niente* which marks a step nearer to the sun and the moon than the *dolce far niente* with which the siren worshipper is credited. They lean back in the carriage with their *napolitani* cigars going well, and listen indulgently to the laughter and chatter of some of their fellow guests who are not digesting their dinners as prudently as they should be if Piazza rumours about the quantity and quality of the hostess's drink this evening have not been exaggerated. It is pleasant to be driving up the Anasirene road to-night amid a fragment or two of the civilization that has survived the great war fought on its behalf.

Rory Freemantle had not set out to eclipse the brilliancy of bygone entertainments. She had merely invited everybody she knew on Sirene, ordered a variety of good drink, a quantity of rich food, engaged little Bozzo to play, and trusted to the Gods that her evening would go off well. She had welcomed the opportunity to extend a catholic hospitality and dispose of the notion that the Villa Leucadia was closed as rigidly to men as the officiating consul's house during the rites of the Bona Dea. While her guests were on the road Rory was turning off the electric light here, turning it on there, calculating which terrace would catch the moon's eye first, establishing Bozzo and his players on a dais, under which were stacked a dozen bottles of Sirene wine and as many glasses, calling Fortunata to draw back the curtains from this window, sending Caterina with extra cushions to the loggia, fetching Francesca from the front door and dispatching her there again a moment afterward to be ready for the early guest. She was in full evening dress, not unfortunately immaculate owing to having in the agitation of a waiting hostess squirted some peach juice on to her shirt front. She was not feeling as cheerful as she ought amid the bright evidence of hospitality, because Rosalba, after promising faithfully to dine with her alone beforehand and thus, as Rory hoped, convey an impression to the other guests that the party was a joint affair, had not turned up ; and Rory was now waiting in a condition of bitter eagerness to see with whom she *would* ultimately arrive. She heard the voice of Francesca in the *entrata* welcoming the first guest. Her ears fancied she heard ' *buona sera, signorina.*' The darling! She must have hurried on to be the first to arrive ; but it was not a signorina (if one may make a distinction without a great deal of difference) who entered. It was Daffodil. And Rory was glad to see this beautiful young man come coiling toward her over the Nile green porcelain tiles under the high vaulted roof of the big studio.

Amid the complicacy of feminine emotions which have occupied so much of our attention we have not yet had time to meet Daffodil, though he has been undulating up and down Sirene the whole summer. Daffodil was a young Norwegian whose real name was Krog—Hjalmar Krog ; but, as he did not look in the least like a person called Hjalmar Krog, we may as well forget that and with everybody else call him Daffodil. He had nothing of the modern girl about him ; he was as delicately feminine as a keepsake of fifty years ago. He was indeed a real womanly man, with his wide forget-me-not blue eyes, his silky yellow hair, and exquisite rose-leaf complexion, of which he took the greatest care, never going out without a parasol and always wearing a mask when he was bathing. He was a friendly happy creature who danced, and danced very well, with all the girls ; and he was never rude or boisterous. Rory was glad to welcome Daffodil as her first guest that night. Woman or man would have embarrassed her for different reasons, but this exquisite epicene with his benevolent neutrality soothed her anxiety. He was able to praise her flowers and the way she had arranged for the drinks to be served and the lighting effects as sensitively as a woman, but without that *arrière pensée* which women always suspect behind the most cordial admiration of their female friends. There was a genuine comfort in the way Daffodil bent as a willow to a lake over the great bowl of what was called cup, but which was in the fullest sense of the word punch, exclaiming with the rustle of leaves in his voice :

" How too delicious it smells ! "

Daffodil spoke English perfectly. He might have been educated at Lady Margaret's Hall.

" If I'd seen you this morning when I was down in Sirene I would have asked you to help me with the flowers," Rory told him.

" Oh, Miss Freemantle, I'd just have *loved* to help. I do *wish* I'd seen you, but I was lying down. I always lie down for two hours before a party. If I don't, my eyes get so *cernés*. And it makes me look *so* naughty, though I'm feeling as good as I can be all the time. Oh, Miss Freemantle, I *am* so misjudged."

" Silly boy ! "

" Yes, *aren't I ?* " he breathed, wide-eyed.

And in the way Rory patted Daffodil's shoulder there was the vaguest hint of a solicitous maternity.

" You'll help me to make things go to-night ? " she asked a little wistfully.

" Oh, I will," he promised effusively. " I'll do anything, Miss Freemantle."

"You needn't call me Miss Freemantle. I'm Rory to all my friends."

"And may *I* call you Rory?"

"I'd rather you did."

"Oh, but of course I will. I'd simply love to," he cried, arching his arm behind him like a fencer engaging and then launching into the air an unseen dart.

There was a sound of voices in the *entrata*. The stream of guests had begun to flow steadily.

"Shall I show the gentlemen where to put their hats?" Daffodil asked.

"Yes, will you. Do, there's a good boy."

He rushed toward the door, tittering in uncontrollable excitement at the prospect before him; and the big studio began to fill.

The pre-war Sirenian revisiting the glimpses of the moon would not have recognized many people present that night. Death or discord or whatever harsh deity banishes people from the sun's countenance had each done a hateful work. The two old Sirenians who had dined wisely and driven up together surveyed the gathering with critical eyes. They had not yet sampled Rory's cup, and the optimism they had felt in the Piazza about the future of the evening was again in abeyance.

"I don't see the Ambrogio anywhere," said the first old Sirenian.

"She won't be here to-night. Marsac has arrived with his Antinous," replied the other.

They gossiped for a minute or two about an old feud and returned to a consideration of the guests.

"Anyway, all Mytilene is here," said the first old Sirenian.

"And it looks as if the feathers would be flying presently," added the other.

The trouble was that Olimpia Leigh had withdrawn to a divan in a corner of the studio with Rosalba, who was talking to her with a passionate absorption that was evidently proving painful not merely for the hostess, but also for Zoe, Cléo, Janet Royle, Hermina de Randan, and Bébé Buonagrazia, so painful indeed that none of them could make the faintest pretence of being at a party. They were just creating in the crowded studio a little maelstrom of emotion into which one by one they all looked likely to disappear for the rest of the evening. In vain did Bozzo's violin throb upon the moonlit air of the terrace. Everybody hung about in the studio and talked. Rory did try several times to be hospitable, and in a distracted remote voice she did several times invite her guests to drink something; but though she stood beside the bowl with a large ladle in her hand it was obvious she was quite incapable of using it. She kept looking over her shoulder at Rosalba's lips moving incessantly while Olimpia's burning eyes gazed into hers; and every time she looked round, the ladle waved feebly in the air without entering the bowl. It was Daffodil who saved the situation.

"Oh, Rory," he cried from the door leading out on the terrace.

The ladies of Mytilene looked up. The agony of thwarted passion they may have been suffering was temporarily relieved by the madness of curiosity. Each one was asking herself how Daffodil had managed to get on such intimate terms with Rory as thus openly to salute her before the world.

"Oh, Rory," Daffodil repeated. "Mr Hewetson says he will dance for us if you'd like. *May* he have a bedroom to change in? He's brought his lovely Mexican dress. Such a dream!"

Hewetson was a visiting Englishman with very long legs and a very long face, who had already caused a certain amount of attention at the party by arriving in the white mess uniform of the Royal Naval Volunteer Reserve. He was willing to dance for the pleasure of the company, but insisted that he could only perform on the terrace.

"I must have atmosphere," he explained darkly.

"Oh, of course you must," the hostess agreed. "And it is getting frightfully hot in here. Oh, atmosphere, yes, of course. How stupid of me! Of course you want all the atmosphere you can get, don't you?"

"Why don't you give us a hornpipe in here before you change out of that steward's costume, Hewetson?" asked Captain Wheeler.

"Now, Wheeler, I want no sauce from you," said Hewetson as he hurried out with league-long strides toward the bedroom in which he was to change, preceded by Daffodil as the Ark was by David.

People thought that Mr Hewetson had done well to snub Captain Wheeler, though they did not feel sure that 'sauce' was quite the word they would have used themselves. But really considering that Captain Wheeler was himself wearing the uniform of the Legion of Frontiersmen this evening, spurs and all, he was the last man to take exception to Mr Hewetson's naval appearance. The genuine Sirenians resented Wheeler far more than Hewetson, because Hewetson was going back to England next month and Wheeler's rich maiden sister had bought a villa on the island. Wheeler was a dreadful permanency, and many people wished he had chosen a real frontier to live on instead of a small island. This uniform which he sometimes inflicted even on quiet dinner-parties was likely to be a menace for years. So was Wheeler himself. He was already talking about golf links, and he had actually begun to teach the youth of Sirene Association football, which was ridiculous because it only made them cry. He was going to be a bore, was Wheeler. His sister had bought him a small motor-boat, in which at any hour of the day or night he could be heard cruising round the island like a jumping cracker in a series of irregular reports. One might have a violinist of international renown playing to one in the moonlight after dinner and Wheeler's beastly motor-boat was not the accompaniment one wanted. Too many pseudo-Sirenians were coming to settle on the island nowadays. That was the general opinion of the senior residents. No doubt, Captain Wheeler was a he-man ; but it seemed unnecessary to lay such stress on his masculinity by attending an evening party in the uniform of a Frontiersman. No doubt, he had won his spurs in the war ; but that was no reason why he should wear them now. In fact, such was the prejudice he roused among the guests of the Villa Leucadia that they welcomed with warm applause the re-appearance of Hewetson dressed in an even tighter pair of trousers than before, a kind of Zouave jacket, and a basket hat of the same shape as Vesuvius, though a little smaller.

Hewetson's dance acted as a strong and rapid laxative on the pent-up spirits of the company. There was a sublime idiocy about the posturing of this long-legged long-faced Englishman which sent the company sitting round him in the moonlight into a rapture of suppressed laughter. Only one guest actually broke down before the dance came to an end—a fat jolly fellow-countrywoman who had to be led out by her two daughters in convulsions of irrepressible mirth, from which she had hardly recovered an hour later. And Mrs Wendle could not be blamed for her collapse, because it had been she who had had to bear the brunt of Hewetson's antic advances and retreats. It was she whom he had fixed with his prominent eyes every time he came stamping toward the audience, and it was still she on whom his eyes rolled as he wriggled away from the audience again, clicking his fingers as loudly as castanets, until Mrs Wendle began to wave her arms and had to be led off to an armchair in the loggia to prevent her choking. The rest of the onlookers simply shook internally until with what may have been a Mexican oath Hewetson leapt in the air, his back arched like a salmon, and brought the dance to a conclusion, after which everybody rushed away to get a drink.

"What a wonnderful dance," Madame Sarbécoff murmured enthusiastically. "I have never seen anything so wonnderful. I was altogether thrilled."

"It takes it out of one a bit," said Hewetson, puffing importantly and holding his sides.

"I am so sure it must. I was so glad your trousers were so tight. Where do you get such wonnderful material to stand such a terrible strain?"

"From Mexico," the artist replied casually. "All my costumes are genuine. I've always made a point of that. I hate anything in the nature of a fake."

"I am sure you do. But don't you find that beautiful hat a little heavy?"

"It is heavy, of course, though in one of my dances I fling it up from time to time, which is very effective."

"Yes, I am sure it must be very effective indeed. It would be quite easy, I think, to kill anybody if it was falling down on a person. And now I am quite sure you must be wanting to take a drink."

"Not if I'm going to dance again," said Hewetson, looking rather crossly at the way the audience was surging round the bowl of punch.

"Oh, I am sure Miss Freemantle will ask you to dance again. She quite adores dancing."

But before Madame Sarbécoff could attract Rory's attention and tell her that Mr Hewetson was anxious to give an encore, there was a wild shout and a tiny little man in a blue and yellow Russian costume sprang into the room and began one of the whirling dances of his native land.

"What the deuce is this?" Hewetson demanded indignantly.

"That is Kadáshoff. He was a professional dancer of the Imperial ballet. But poor fellow, since the revolution he cannot go back."

"A professional?" Hewetson repeated with a frown. "He doesn't dance very professionally."

Kadáshoff, who had a head rather like a thistle gone to seed, was whirling round and round on one leg so fast that one expected to see any hair he had left float away from it.

"But who on earth invited him to dance like this?" Hewetson expostulated.

"Oh, he has been very well taught," said Madame Sarbécoff, clapping her hands. "Bravo! Bravo, Kadáshoff!"

All the other guests began to clap and shout 'bravo,' because the dancing of the diminutive Russian did genuinely excite them apart from the exhilarating effect of Rory's punch. Then Kadáshoff began to yell, and everybody else began to yell, everybody, that is, except Hewetson, who folded his arms and regarded the scene morosely. At one moment when he lifted his conical hat and took a stride forward, people near him thought he was going to clap it over his rival and extinguish him; but he contented himself with a sneer that gave him the look of a vicious horse, and during the applause that followed Kadáshoff's defiant final pose on one leg he retired to don his naval uniform again. As for little Kadáshoff, he went back to the task which had been perplexing him considerably since the triumph of Bolshevism had deprived him of his job with the Russian mission in Rome. That task was to find some person or institution or government to support him. He was ready to become a Bolshevik himself; but the Bolsheviks did not want him. So he had decided that the permanent support of his disorganized life would have to be, as it so often is, a woman.

The dancing was now general. The evening was really beginning to go. Bozzo was playing in an ecstasy. The bowl of punch had been twice refilled. The hostess was happy at last, because she was dancing with Rosalba; and although Rosalba kept telling her how badly she was dancing she was too happy to be clasping that slim form in her arms to mind what she was doing. And then suddenly Rosalba stopped and took the man's position. Rory did not care. She was content to hold or be held. That a woman of her bulk in an adaption of masculine evening dress should be steered by an exquisite girl did not strike her as ridiculous. She leaned her head against Rosalba's shoulder and lived to the uttermost this delicious moment. It was only gradually she began to be aware how often she was bumping into other couples. She looked up to make a laughing protest and saw that Rosalba's gaze was fixed on Olimpia and Zoe dancing together just ahead. She realized that she was being bruised merely to enable Rosalba to keep up with *them*.

"Darling, must you bump me into everybody?" she asked plaintively.

"*Mon cher*, you are so awfully clumsy that I cannot at all help it."

"Perhaps I shouldn't seem quite so clumsy if Olimpia Leigh and Zoe Mitchell weren't dancing together."

"You are an impossible woman," Rosalba snarled, and loosing her grip of Rory she turned aside to invite the first disengaged person she saw to dance with her. This happened to be Captain Wheeler, who was delighted to be her cavalier. He had been arguing all the summer that these poor women only ran after one another because there was a deficiency of men. This was the moment to prove his theory, and what more charming creature for the experiment than Rosalba?

"I say, you have got a topping figure," he opened. "You'd make old Venus look like a Sunday-school teacher. What? Topping! Now this is what *I* call dancing."

Rosalba smiled at him. She had just observed that Olimpia's burning eyes were upon her. Here was a new idea for arousing jealousy. It had not struck her before. She smiled again at Wheeler, whose tail was now wagging very fast.

"Oncora! Oncora!" he shouted as they passed Bozzo.

"*Si, signor capitano*," the little fiddler acknowledged.

"These natives will do anything for me," said Captain Wheeler with simple faith. "I suppose it's because I've been out in India and know just how to handle 'em."

Meanwhile Rory when abruptly relinquished by Rosalba had shot into the arms of Kadáshoff, who in his blue and yellow costume with baggy breeches and high boots and fur trimmings had been leaning against the parapet and twirling his little fair moustache waiting for the female glance that would respond to his languishing and hungry gaze. That a rich woman like his hostess should fling herself into his arms encouraged Kadáshoff so much that he pinched her leg before they had danced five yards. Rory was too miserably oblivious of everything except her desertion by Rosalba to notice what he was doing, and Kadáshoff encouraged by this complaisance tapped her hip in time to the rhythm. Nor did such a comparatively light assault alarm her after the way she had been bumped into people by Rosalba. She did not notice it, her eyes following Rosalba in the khaki arms of Captain Wheeler. Kadáshoff was convinced that at last he had found the material support for which he had been looking since 1917. He squeezed Rory so close that her shirt front began to crepitate.

"Je vous adore," he muttered thickly.

"Pardon?" she asked, and leant down to catch what he said.

Kadáshoff had no longer the slightest doubt of her amorous surrender.

"Je vous adore à la folie," he panted, and bit her ear.

"Oh, you loathsome little brute! How dare you do that?" she screamed.

Kadáshoff, imagining this to be the conventional protest of virginity, winked lubriciously and snapped at her ear again. Rory shook him from her as if he were a brightly coloured poisonous insect. Kadáshoff sprang after her, and she was on the point of screaming really loudly and creating a scene when she found her waist encircled by Daffodil's discreet arm.

"Oh, Daffodil," she half sobbed, "he bit me, and he was going to bite me again."

Daffodil rose to his full height and looking over Rory's shoulder (whom he was handling as tenderly as a soap-bubble) he opened his forget-me-not blue eyes very wide and ejaculated:

"Go away, you horrid little Tartar!" Then turning to his partner, he said, "I think you'd better come and have an ice. Oh, Rory, you are in a fluster. Please take my arm. A nice ice will steady you."

She took his proffered arm gratefully and allowed him to escort her to the ices.

"You really are a dear boy," she sighed. "Is my ear red?"

Daffodil arched his neck to examine it.

"No," he decided, "but your cheeks are. And I think when you've had an ice you ought to go and put on a teeny-weeny speck of powder."

Rory gazed at him with an almost tender admiration.

"How marvellously you speak English! *No* one would think you were a foreigner."

"Oh, but I went to school in England and lived there entirely till I was seventeen. I *love* England."

And Rory who had been despising her own country for years and congratulating herself on her Latin emancipation began to feel a little sentimental about England.

She was almost inclined to imagine herself settled in a little thatched cottage in the leafy depths of Dorset. The tingling of her ear from Kadáshoff's bite turned to the distant chiming of Sabbath bells. She felt a sudden incapacity to deal with the excitable life she had created for herself. But after the ice she felt stronger.

"Luckily I'm a very cold person really," she assured Daffodil, under its influence.

And with exquisite tact he reminded her about the need for that touch of powder.

"The tiniest little spickle-speckle, that's all. And while you're powdering your cheeks I'll go and powder mine. *Won't* that be fun?"

"You think the party's a success?" Rory asked pathetically.

"Oh, my dear, it's perfectly divine. They're all enjoying themselves too deliciously."

And this was true even of the guests whose underworld of emotions was beginning to assert itself at the expense of the *beau monde* of polite behaviour. Rory's punch and Bozzo's violin had between them keyed the company up to the pitch of the natural scene. There are only two ways of enjoying supreme beauty. One is to remain in silent contemplation of it; the other is to celebrate it with as much noise as possible. Phrenzy is not induced by the prospect of midland elms and the drinking of tea. Do not let us suppose that Rory really wanted to live in England and talk about herbaceous borders. It was but a brief weakness induced by the shock of having her ear bitten by

Kadáshoff.  She did not really want to abandon that moon rolling lazily south along the line of Monte Ventoso and watch no more those stars coruscate into the sea to quench their prismatic fires.  She did not really want to lose this aromatic air.  The voices and laughter of her guests, the twanging of the mandolins, Bozzo's mad violin, the chink of glasses, the shuffle of dancing feet, and all about those wild shadows of people the incredible serenity of sky and sea did combine to convince Rory that her first big party at the Villa Leucadia was turning into a big success.

## CHAPTER SEVENTEEN

Ἀλλα, μὴ κάμπτε στέραν φρένα.
SAPPHO.

*Crazy girl, do not try to bend a stubborn heart.*

WHEN Rory went into her own room and saw in the mirror the crumpled state of her shirt front, she felt that the party was going well enough to give her time to rest her emotions by a change of linen. She spent half an hour in improving her appearance with a fresh shirt, a new white waistcoat, a glossy collar, and after four unsuccessful attempts a perfect tie. Then with re-powdered cheeks and monocle fixed firmly in undimmed eye she emerged from her room, a figure of almost ducal severity and haughty calm. As she crossed the loggia to join her guests she saw the door of Rosalba's room opposite being gently closed. And when she cautiously tried the handle she found that it was locked. All the confidence her change had given her vanished. She seemed to feel the starch oozing out of her shirt front as her heart swelled with indignant emotion. She stood in the loggia hearing infinitely far away the music and the laughter. The monocle fell from her eye and tinkled against one of her pearl studs. Then her chin shot out;

"I'll not stand this," she muttered.

But as she was on the verge of hammering loudly on the locked door the figure of a tall man with apparently nothing on at all came prancing round the corner of her own room and vanished round the corner of Rosalba's room in the direction of the music.

" My god," Rory gasped, passing a hand across her dazed eyes. " Am I going mad then ? "

As she demanded this Daffodil appeared from the same direction as what she was imagining had been a figment of her overwrought mind.

" Oh, Rory," he cried. " Do come ! Mr Hewetson simply insists on doing a classical dance, and he's got nothing on but a pink silk handkerchief and a paper rose."

It was true. Hewetson had been brooding all the evening over the eclipse of his Mexican dance by Kadáshoff's Russian dance and then over the conspicuousness of Wheeler's appearance as a Frontiersman compared with his as an ex-sub-lieutenant in the Royal Naval Volunteer Reserve. Brooding and drinking punch, drinking punch and brooding, he had gradually come to the conclusion that somehow or other this evening must in the future of Sirene be definitely associated with his name.

" At least I have a figure," he had argued, when Daffodil had entreated him not to rely entirely upon the pink silk handkerchief and the sham flower. " Anybody can dress up. But not everybody, I flatter myself, can undress."

With this he had broken away from Daffodil's restraining arm, and, uttering loud cries of ' Evoe ! Evoe ! ' had leapt into the middle of the terrace.

" *Mamma mia !* " Bozzo gasped, standing with violin and bow in a paralysis of astonishment.

"I don't *want* any music! I don't *want* any music!" Hewetson shouted, as he raised both arms in that conventional gesture of shocked amazement which all classical dancers affect, and which so many audiences must long to imitate.

Most of the onlookers were laughing, and Mrs Wendle who had never really recovered from Hewetson's Mexican dance of a couple of hours ago was again seized with helpless mirth when he stood fluttering his hands above his head and murmuring in an inconceivably ridiculous tone of voice:

"Now the dew is falling."

"You ought to be ashamed of yourself," Wheeler shouted from the audience.

"Rats to you!" Hewetson retorted, as he sank down into a profound obeisance before the rising sun. Since the sun was still several hours from rising most of the audience failed to grasp what he was doing.

"What's he sitting down for?" somebody whispered.

"Hush, I think his handkerchief has slipped."

But no, it was still there when Hewetson leapt to his feet and went bounding off in a circle round the audience, clapping his hands above his head.

"Bacchic phrenzy," he panted in explanation.

Rory gripped Daffodil's wrist in sudden apprehension.

"Where's Kadáshoff?" she asked. "He hasn't gone away to undress too, has he?"

"No, I've locked him up."

"Locked him up?"

"Yes, he was making himself such a nuisance to all

the ladies. So, I asked him to come and have a drink and I've locked him up in the *cantina*."

"Oh, Daffodil, you really are a dear boy," she sighed gratefully.

Hewetson's dance was over, and he was hurrying off to put on his mess kit again. As he passed Rory he gushed with a display of big teeth:

"Such a lovely party, Miss Freemantle."

At any rate, he was evidently beginning to enjoy himself, and she heard him yodelling as he vanished round the corner, ' Tra-la-la-la-ity ! '

But Rory's mind had gone back to that locked room, and finding herself next to Zoe Mitchell she asked where Olimpia was.

"Oh, don't ask me. Olimpia makes me tired."

Zoe spoke crossly. She had had enough drink by now to feel she did not want to waste the evening, and though Rory supposed she was jealous at being pushed aside by Olimpia, that had not annoyed her as much as the evidence of Wheeler's interest in her rival. She could not understand why he should prefer Rosalba to herself. Olimpia who was not an easy person to deceive had been quick to notice her mortification.

"If you've come down to Sirene to play the cocotte," she had said to her, "don't expect me to take any more interest in you."

"I don't give a darn if you take any more interest in me or not. I'm tired of being fooled around the way you're fooling me around over Rosalba."

"In other words you don't appreciate my friendship?"

"Oh, hell to your friendship! I don't call it friendship to have a girl come all the way down from Paris to this bum little island just to pep up another girl. I wouldn't care to say what I do call that, but it's not friendship."

"You shouldn't have let yourself get sunburnt."

"Well, aren't you the . . ." Zoe had gasped. "Why, you're nearly as black as a buck nigger yourself and you talk about me being sunburnt. Say, Olimpia, you make me tired. And don't you glare at me like that, lady, or I will be real sunburnt."

Then it was that Olimpia had beckoned Rosalba away from Wheeler and that Zoe had been mortified by not at once finding herself as much the object of Wheeler's attention as her rival. She had gone indoors and drunk three glasses of punch right off, and now she was looking round for somebody to keep pace with her own rapidly ascending temperature. She fixed on Carmine.

Lulu had been having a splendid time with Carmine. Her mother's cold monocle had not once been fixed on her while she was dancing every dance with him, because the Countess early in the evening had developed an interest in Janet Royle with whom she had retired to talk about the spiritual side of life on one of the lower terraces remote from the interruptions of a material existence. Hermina de Randan's fresh vision of Janet Royle must not be ascribed to Rory's punch.

"It is curious," she said, gazing intensely into Janet's languid face. "It is very curious, like a revelation. It seems that I see you to-night for the first time."

"Music and moonlight perhaps," Janet murmured.

"No, no, my dear, it is a revelation of beauty which has taken from me my blindness."

"But you've seen me so often before without noticing anything particular in me," Janet argued.

"I have been horribly blind," Hermina insisted.

And the courtship proceeded on the lines of a million others.

Lulu free of her mother's cold and critical eye abandoned herself to the delight of dancing with Carmine. She was more in love with him than ever, and she threw her arms round Madame Sarbécoff's neck when Madame Sarbécoff drew her aside to whisper her admiration of the young man.

"It is quite wonnderful, my dear, to see him so distinguished and such a beautiful dancer. I am sure you must be very much in love. I am so glad for you, my dear Lulu. It is quite a delight for me to see how charming you both look."

"But do you think I'll ever be allowed to marry him?" Lulu asked.

"I am sure you will. The world is quite upside down now. Oh yes, I am so sure you will be able to marry him."

At that moment Carmine had come up to claim another dance, and Madame Sarbécoff had told him how beautifully he spoke English and French and how well he carried himself and how sure she was that he had a great future before him. And the style with which Carmine had bent over and kissed her hand and murmured '*troppo gentile, signora*' could not have been improved upon by the count or marquis that Lulu had always been led to suppose she must one day marry.

"Say, Lulu, you'll let me take your beau for one dance?" Zoe asked.

Poor Lulu would have liked to smack Zoe's Minoan face; but she only dissolved into self-consciousness and turned away.

"You should not let her take him from you like that," Olga Linati said fussily. "It is quite a shame."

Zoe was a much better dancer than Lulu. Zoe could do the shimmy shake. Lulu could not. Carmine apparently could do the shimmy shake too. And he was doing it.

"She is making him dance quite disgustingly," said Olga Linati in an access of indignant puritanism. "I think it is perfectly horrible to wriggle like that. Cléo, do you not think it is horrible the way Zoe is trying to make that poor boy lose his head?"

Cléo had come up chewing a cigarette. She had drunk a good deal of punch. She was in the mood to play, or at any rate she was in the mood to be asked to play whether she decided to accept or not. She felt like making somebody else dissatisfied with life and decided to upset Rory. Lulu's misery over the shimmy shake was too insignificant. Olga's spinster-like jealousy was a little too petty and obvious.

"I just went past Rosalba's room," she said to Rory. "She and Olimpia are in there—sitting on the bed."

"I know they are."

Rory spoke in what she hoped was a voice as stiff as

her shirt front. Cléo looked at her and with a shrug of her wide shoulders turned away.

"It's a pity Cléo cannot learn to dress herself suitably for a party," Rory observed severely. "I do think white canvas shoes with rope soles are really just a little bit too casual."

"It is because she wants to be asked to play," Olga bubbled.

The seeming irrelevance of this explanation puzzled Rory for a moment.

"She doesn't play with her feet," she said sharply.

"No, but if she is playing people do not see her feet," Olga amplified.

"Well, I shall be delighted for her to play. The only objection is people may not keep quiet, and you know how angry that always makes her."

"I think perhaps they will," said Olga who was always optimistic.

Rory looked at the swirl of the dance. People had reached the stage of dancing because they could not help it. If she did succeed in herding them into the studio to listen to Cléo, they were capable, in the mood of elation they had reached, of dancing just as rowdily to her music as to Bozzo's.

"Well, I'll try," she said doubtfully, and beckoned to Daffodil. He was dragging round the terrace an elderly woman who after several glasses of Rory's punch had decided to make a trial of these new-fangled dances. Had he been trying to teach her to swim she could not have clutched him more desperately; and every time he attempted to display his own grace she uttered a muffled scream as if he were taking her out of her depth.

"Thank you so much," he said to the novice, relinquishing her at Rory's signal. "I think you'll soon be a marvellous dancer. You have such heaps of different steps."

"My first attempt at a fox-trot," the elderly woman explained, looking round complacently for applause. She might not have appeared more proud of her prowess, had the Master of the Quorn just handed her the brush.

"Hard work," Rory observed to Daffodil as the elderly woman, evidently trying to remember what she had been told about keeping her legs together, slid off in a semi-rhythmical condition to have another drink.

"My dear," he said. "I felt like a mahout trying to guide a paralysed elephant. It was too awful. I'm all wibbly-wobbly."

Rory told him what his next task was to be.

"How lovely!" he exhaled, and coiling round and round the guests he gently urged them into the studio. What a comfort he was, Rory thought.

Cléo chose for her performance some of the fragments of Sappho which Olimpia had set to music. Considering that they were written in an unfamiliar antique scale and that there was nothing which remotely resembled even the beginning of a tune the audience kept laudably quiet. Part of this attitude was secured by Cléo's own personality, which quelled those nearest to her; but the chief credit belonged to the dim lighting of the remoter corners of the studio and the opportunity it gave people to hold hands. It is true that some of the hands thus held were not the hands that were intended to be held. The brothers Isléneff sat clasped in a rapture on each side of Madame Sarbécoff, each supposing that his brother's hand was hers. Kadáshoff, who had been released from the store-cupboard, was softly stroking Mrs Royle's shin under the impression that it was a much more recent shin. But what did it matter? Kadáshoff was not an archæologist. Whether he were caressing a Neanderthal or a Neolithic shin lacked importance provided it was strong enough to support him.

Not everybody was making these mistakes. Carmine for instance was perfectly clear whose waist his arm encircled. So was poor Lulu. And it was no consolation to be assured by Olga in an austere whisper that Carmine's behaviour made it plain how far Zoe Mitchell was ready to go. It was the extent of *his* stamina which worried Lulu. Indeed, it tormented her as she sat trying hard to pretend she was listening to the music. However, happily for Lulu's self-consciousness many other people besides herself were looking rather wretched.

" When's she going to stop strumming and begin ? " asked the elderly lady who had been learning to dance with Daffodil. Her neighbour, who happened to be a young man with a contempt for the obvious, turned his horn-rimmed spectacles on her as a battleship might turn its searchlights on a bumboat.

" This is *rather* wonderful music," he whispered with

a crushing but still exquisite Oxonianism. "I don't think we ought to talk. She's playing Olimpia Leigh's *Æolian Graces*."

The elderly woman might have been tempted to defy such an objectionable young man by telling him that she liked music to be music and even by humming an example of her own taste, if from the entrance of the studio had not sounded a cold voice that made everybody feel horribly embarrassed.

"Cléo," it said, "I wish that if you *must* play my Αἰολίδες Χάριτες you would take the trouble to play them properly."

The elderly woman nudged the spectacled young man triumphantly and turned to nod and smile at the composer standing so ominously in the doorway, as if to assure her that one of the audience had realized from the start that something had gone seriously wrong.

Cléo's answer was to slam down the lid of the piano, jump up from her stool, and rush out of the room.

"I'll go after her and fetch her back," Olga told Rory. But though she hurried fast Cléo had fled faster. She was not seen again that night.

"Daffodil," Rory entreated. "Do get them all out to dance again. The whole evening is on the verge of collapse."

Daffodil made a tremendous signal to Bozzo who had come in to hear Cléo play. The little violinist at once struck up a fox-trot and with him for a bell-wether Daffodil shepherded the flock out into the moonlight again.

"Look here," said Rory angrily when she and Olimpia were left alone, "this is my house, you know."

"It may be your house, but it was my music," the composer retorted as she pulled her white cloak close and flung herself down on one of the divans.

"I'm not talking about music," Rory said, for though she had intended to make Olimpia's interruption of Cléo the theme of her attack, she was not anxious to be defeated in an argument over music, and annoyed by the insolent way Olimpia was lying full-length on one of her divans she resolved to attack her over what much more than the interruption was the cause of her rage against this woman.

"I'm not talking about music," Rory repeated. "I'm talking about manners. Personally I don't think it good manners to snub anybody in front of a lot of people like that. But then I'm not a great composer. Nor am I an American."

Olimpia without moving otherwise turned her eyes from the contemplation of the domed ceiling to the contemplation of Rory, who, though she rather wished she had left out anything about being an American, held her ground.

"What I'm talking about is locking yourself up with Rosalba in her room," Rory insisted.

"In Rosalba's room?"

"Yes."

"It is Rosalba's room?"

"You know it is."

"Isn't Rosalba allowed to lock herself in her own

room ? " she asked coldly and scornfully. " My poor dear lady, if you want to make a slave of a girl, you will have to learn to conceal the threat of your possession and the evidence of your infatuation."

"Look here," said Rory, fixing her monocle and thanking heaven that it stuck fast, " I'm not going to be talked to like that by you or by anybody else. If you want Rosalba, you can have her. But you're not going to use my house for your intrigues."

"You bore me," said Olimpia, turning away from Rory and covering her face with the cloak.

Rory looked at the white form stretched contemptuously on one of her own divans. She looked at the bowl of punch. The only answer to Olimpia's insolence seemed to be to pick up the bowl of punch and empty it over her. She took a firm step toward it ; and then, either because her monocle fell out or because from the past came a memory of being sent to bed by her governess for rubbing a little friend's head with a lump of sugar, she hesitated. Olimpia was her guest. She must neither rub her head with a lump of sugar nor empty over her the contents of a punchbowl. She hurried from the room to tell Rosalba what she thought of *her*.

It was some time, however, before Rory could get hold of Rosalba. Rosalba, finding that Zoe was enjoying herself with Carmine, had determined to annoy her and revenge herself at the same time on Lulu over the serenade by taking Carmine herself. And curiously enough by doing this she rendered Lulu the greatest service she could have rendered, because she added much to the young man's self-confidence. To find himself pursued first by Zoe and then by Rosalba gave him a high opinion of his attractiveness. Zoe and Rosalba were, Lulu aside, unquestionably the two prettiest women in Sirene. Moreover, from what he had heard about them they were both entirely indifferent to other men. Carmine expanded. He had evidently been too modest. Why should he not aspire to marry Lulu? That's what he was saying to himself when Rosalba led him down the steps to the amphitheatre at the end of the garden where the great statues of nymphs and emperors and gods stood round in a circle, their shadows lying in long black islands on the withered grass.

Rosalba flung her arms round him.

"*Baciami in bocca*," she murmured hotly.

It must be admitted, for this does not claim to be a tale of true love, that Carmine did kiss her on the lips. Hermina de Randan and Janet Royle who were sitting on a sarcophagus out of the moonlight saw them kiss, and whatever they had both thought of Rosalba it gave them a shock.

"Hadn't we better cough?" Janet whispered a few minutes later.

"What a Puritan you are," Hermina gently chuckled. She clasped Janet's hand in a state of delicious anticipation; but the amorous scene was interrupted by Lulu.

"I only wanted to see if you really were down here with Rosalba," Lulu said to the abashed Carmine in Italian. "Now I'm going home."

"No, Lulu, *prego*, do not to go," he stammered. "*Senta! senta!*"

"I won't listen and I will go."

"Pay no attention to that stupid girl," Rosalba commanded.

But Carmine was hurrying after his lost love up the long flight of steps, at the top of which she turned and faced him.

"You may like to know," she said, "that before Rosalba made love to you she has made love to me."

She turned round again and ran on toward the next terrace, her green silk dress shimmering in the moonlight. Carmine followed her with his appeals and Rosalba was left with the statues. The Countess with a light and malicious chuckle made her presence known.

"I really think poor Lulu deserves to have that very ordinary young man if she will want him now," she said. "Janet and I have been so much amused, my dear."

Rosalba was incapable of carrying off the situation bonnily. In this hollow which Rory had supposed would more than any other make the perfect background for her she was for the first time in her life completely extinguished.

"I hope that you and Janet have been enjoying yourselves," was the only retort she could think of as she turned to walk back up the steps of the garden alone. It was indeed a blunt arrow, and it only provoked once more that light malicious chuckle from the Countess.

Rosalba was not sorry to find Rory waiting for her

on one of the upper terraces. At any rate *she* was vulnerable.

"Look here, Rosalba," Rory began at once, "I'm sick of the way you're behaving."

"Please do not speak to me in that haughty tone. I am not at all accustomed to being spoken so."

"I'm sick of it," Rory continued. "I don't intend to be made a fool of any longer. What do you mean by locking yourself in your room with Olimpia Leigh for hours?"

"And so that is, I suppose, why you have sent Cléo to climb up and spy upon us through the window."

"I didn't send Cléo to spy upon you."

"*Ma chère* Rory, I think you are being quite a liar. You know that you have sent Cléo to climb up and make her hideous smorfs at us through the window."

"I didn't, I tell you. If she made a smorf, by which I suppose you mean a grimace, she did it on her own account."

Rosalba paused a moment before she delivered what she felt would be a master wound.

"If you would like to sell the Villa Leucadia to Olimpia I am so sure that she will buy it from you. She finds my room so very beautiful for me."

"So that's what you were plotting!" Rory blazed.

She felt that the long drama of her relation to Rosalba was drawing to its close. She was on the point of summing up in one tremendous speech the history of their life together preparatory to announcing that such a life together was now for ever finished when Captain Wheeler appeared.

"Ah, there you are, little lady. I've been looking for you all over the place."

Rosalba was not sorry to re-enter publicity under the escort of Captain Wheeler. He would serve admirably to cover the brief triumph Lulu had secured at her expense.

Rory walked down in the direction whence Rosalba had come. On her way she met Hermina de Randan and Janet Royle emerging from their spiritual seclusion.

"It has been a most wonderful evening," Hermina declared with what for her was enthusiasm.

"Too exquisite," Janet sighed.

"You're not going?" Rory asked, trying to jerk herself back into the rôle of hostess.

"We must go very soon, I think," said Hermina. "Have you seen Lulu?"

Rory remembered with a start that Lulu had called out to her something about having to go home when she had hurried past her just now. But she did not feel she could begin a discussion of Lulu's whereabouts. All she wanted was to get as far away as possible from this party of hers.

"I'll be back presently. Don't go yet," she mumbled and plunged off down the steps to reach that hollow at the end of the garden.

An hour later Daffodil found her sitting with her back against the pedestal of the Emperor Caligula and staring at the moon.

"It's three o'clock," he said, "and they're all beginning to talk about going home."

"Have I only been here an hour?" she asked wearily. "I thought I had been sitting here for a century."

He came gambolling towards her with outstretched arms.

"Upsi-daisy!" he cried as he pulled her to her feet.

"I *am* getting stiff and old," she confessed.

"Oh, Rory, don't be so naughty!" he exclaimed, tapping her shoulder and wriggling with benevolent reproach.

Feeling as she did so greatly aged by the last few hours Rory derived an hygenic pleasure from being treated by Daffodil as a child. She took his arm and came dutifully back to receive the farewells of her guests.

"Has Olimpia Leigh gone yet?" she asked.

"Yes, she went with the Principessa. They've gone to look at a property at the other end of Anasirene near the lighthouse."

"Oh, so she understands that I don't intend to sell the Leucadia?"

"Does *she* want the Leucadia?"

"So I've been kindly informed."

"Oh, my dear, but a wigwam is quite good enough for *her*. *Such* a rude woman. I can't *bear* her."

Rory pressed his arm gratefully.

Bozzo was still playing when they reached the top terrace; but there was no longer a swirl of dancers. The guests were sitting about star-scattered, and wherever one looked empty glasses were winking in the moonlight.

"It has been such a wonnderful evening, my dear Rory," said Madame Sarbécoff. "I don't think I have ever enjoyed an evening so much. It has all been so charming. Mr Hewetson was so charming. I liked his dancing so much. It was so fresh and beautiful. I have been thinking myself quite a Greek. I shall go down to my little shop to-morrow feeling so hopeful about everything."

"To your little shop?" Rory repeated.

"Yes, I am to open a little shop. And I have one room behind it where I am going to live so comfortably, I think."

And when Rory glanced at Madame Sarbécoff's hand she saw that she had come to the end of her rings at last.

"What are you going to sell?"

"Oh, just old things. You have seen what kind of things I discover in my little house on Timberio which I am so sorry to lose. That is really quite sad for me."

"I shall come and buy all your things," Rory promised warmly.

"Yes, please do. That will be so charming. You did not know I was opening my little shop?"

"No, I seem to have been living in a dream these last weeks."

"Thank you again a thousand times for your wonnderful party. And now the two Mr Isléneffs are so kindly seeing me home."

The Isléneff brothers—a pair of beaming impoverished Russians—saluted Rory; and in groups, one after another, the rest of the company bade her farewell.

"Whom did Rosalba go with?" she asked Daffodil when he alone of the company remained among the winking glasses and empty moonlit whiteness of the Villa Leucadia, and the last carriage had rattled away into silence.

"She and Zoe Mitchell went off with Captain Wheeler and Contessina Lulu's young man. It was really rather uncomfortable, because Miss Wheeler had hysterics and rushed away like a mad cow when her brother told her he was going to send her home with Mrs Brown-Hammond."

"Oh, heavens," Rory groaned, sinking exhausted by emotion and anxious hospitality into an armchair. "What a ghastly failure my party has been."

"Don't be so abysmal, Rory! Everybody said it was the best Sirene party since the war."

She laughed bitterly.

"I'm glad other people enjoyed themselves." Then suddenly the thought of Rosalba was once again too much for her. "Oh, Daffodil," she cried. "Do you think Rosalba will be safe with Captain Wheeler?"

"Oh, yes, it was such an elaborate uniform, wasn't it?" he exhaled.

"Daffodil, I wonder if you'd do me a great kindness?"

"I'd do anything for you, Rory."

"Would you—could you—*could* you find out at the Augusto if Rosalba got safely back to her room? I daresay it's silly of me to worry; but Captain Wheeler seemed so very excited, and you know what men are."

"Oh, don't I?" Daffodil enthusiastically admitted, opening wide his blue eyes.

"And you will hurry, won't you?" she begged.

"I'll run all the way," he assured her.

"Daffodil, you really are a dear."

He kissed her hand and skipped out of the Villa Leucadia like a willing child upon an errand.

The two old Sirenians had just reached the Piazza when Daffodil bounded up to them to ask if they had seen anything of Signorina Donsante and Captain Wheeler.

"That punch of the Freemantle's must have been very strong," said the first old Sirenian, when Daffodil, dashing into every nook and cranny as he went, had hurried on.

"It was. Very strong!"

"With Daffodil after the ladies and Donsante after the men," chuckled the first old Sirenian, "can we still say with Alcaeus, οἶνος γὰρ ἀνθρώποισι δίοπτρον?"

"I don't know," said the other meditatively. "I fancy that wine still remains a fairly reliable peep-hole upon men. Is that the grey of dawn over Timberio?"

"Yes, another Sirene night has waned. And we shall sleep soundly after that punch. There is something to be said for middle age," the first old Sirenian chuckled, after which these friends of many years took each his road for home.

## CHAPTER EIGHTEEN

ᾇ
πολυρέμβαστον φιλίαν μέμειξαι
καὶ κάλον δόκεισαν τὸ δαμόσιον.
                              SAPPHO.

*With whom you have mixed yourself up in a vagabond friendship which thinks beautiful what any man can have.*

ROSALBA had returned with Captain Wheeler to the moony terrace of the Villa Leucadia after that stab which sent Rory reeling down her marble steps to collapse at the base of Caligula's statue. She had given him the end of the dance in progress, and then she had broken away to tell Olimpia Leigh of her successful cruelty. Olimpia, who was sitting talking in a corner of the studio to Bébé Buonagrazia, received her with obvious hostility.

" I am afraid poor Rory is a little upset because we have been so much together in my room, *mon cher*," Rosalba began.

" Are you suggesting that I am one of your scalps ? " Olimpia asked with a cold scowl.

The phrase was beyond Rosalba's English. She looked puzzled.

" What an extraordinarily stupid face you have got," said Olimpia, slowly shaking her head at the realization of something, the full force of which had never before struck her.

" Please do not be rude. It is not at all amusing," said Rosalba.

The Princess put up her fan to hide a smile.

"It is not at all amusing for me," Olimpia replied, "after giving you so much of my company to hear your behaviour a few minutes later made the subject of a public argument between Lulu de Randan and her idealized waiter."

"Where is Lulu?" Rosalba demanded dramatically. "I will not permit her to use my name in public."

"The child has gone home after an attractive display of girlish temper. But she has left the idealized waiter behind. He is consoling himself at present with the Mitchell young woman."

Olimpia drew her white cloak round her and rose to the full height of her five feet.

"Do not come and serenade me to-night. I am going with Bébé to look at a house."

Fortunata came in at this moment to announce:

"*Gli asini sono arrivati, signora.*"

And presently Rosalba had the mortification of seeing Olimpia and Bébé Buonagrazia on the backs of two white donkeys disappear into the moonlight over Anasirene. She was on the verge of weeping. She was sure that one of the donkeys had been intended for her. And to be supplanted by Bébé Buonagrazia with her ruthless serpent's tongue! It took all Rosalba's strength of mind to appear again on the terrace as if she were enjoying herself. There she found Carmine dancing with Zoe, and Captain Wheeler waiting for herself. She did not want Captain Wheeler. She only wanted to take Carmine from Zoe, not because she cared any more for Carmine than for Wheeler, but because she wanted to score a triumph over Lulu, Zoe, Rory, Olimpia, and Bébé Buonagrazia, for that was what the fascination of Carmine presented itself to her fancy as likely to effect. However, she danced for awhile with Captain Wheeler who by this time had had enough to drink to make him reckless of his sister's reproachful glances and who was holding Rosalba in the way a man does hold a woman when he has convinced himself that before sunrise she will be his.

"It's time we went home, Harry," Miss Wheeler said every time her brother with Rosalba in his arms came within ten yards of her. He paid no attention. He was feeling thanks to his uniform and to Rory's punch as invincible as Solomon.

"My gad, with you beside me," he muttered, "I could be another Napoleon."

"Yes, but please do not squeeze me so close," Rosalba protested.

Rory's stiffest shirt front in her most passionate moments was a blancmange compared with these belts and buttons and medals against which she was being crushed.

"You intoxicate me," the Frontiersman muttered. "Do you know what we say in England? All for love and the world well lost. By Jove, I never realized the truth of that until I held you in my arms. Look here, I can't lose you now."

"You will lose me very quickly if you hold me so tight. Please, now the music has stopped, do not continue to hold me."

"Back to earth with a jolt," Captain Wheeler sighed. "I'm not a particularly religious man, but by Jove, it's heaven to dance with you; and look here, don't think me disloyal to my poor sister, but it's simply hell to be dependent on relations for all one's little luxuries."

"Now will you dance with my friend Mrs Mitchell," said Rosalba primly, and catching hold of Zoe she pushed her into Captain Wheeler's arms, herself into Carmine's.

"*Di nuovo! di nuovo!*" she called imperiously to Bozzo, who struck up the dance again.

To Carmine while they danced so exquisitely together she confided in softest Italian her horror of Captain Wheeler and a hope that he would escort her home to-night. Carmine had never heard of the delightful embarrassment of Paris. If he had, he might have compared himself to the young Trojan. As it was, he merely asked himself what other young man had in one evening been invited to decide between three such lovely young women as Lulu, Zoe, and Rosalba. To be sure, one of them had fled offended from the scene. But it would be no disadvantage to his serious aspirations in that direction if his desirableness were made apparent. For a moment he had been abashed by Lulu's anger, but the surest way to win her back would be to show her that not by flouncing away from him into a carriage and bidding him go back to Rosalba's kisses could she prevent his going back to them. He pressed Rosalba closer, and she yielding her supple form deliciously to his ardour made him feel more than ever inclined to give Lulu a lesson. And then as he held Rosalba the memory of Zoe's equally supple form recurred to him. Could he in the few hours of darkness that remained of this night contrive to make love to both of them? It was just a question of being able to get rid of the two young women in turn. He was not troubled by any fears on his own account or theirs. Still, he had already promised to escort Zoe home, and he should have to be skilful. It would not do to lose the pair by promising too much to one.

Zoe had grasped at once that Rosalba intended to take Carmine away from her if she could. And it annoyed Zoe. She wanted this handsome youth not to spite somebody else, but for her own amusement. The emotional surf in which she had been struggling to swim on Sirene was beginning to get on Zoe's nerves. She could not stay away from Paris much longer, and her reunion with the junior member of Mitchell et Cie was not what she wanted to look forward to at summer's end. There had been during these last weeks too much talk and not enough action. Zoe, under the encouragement of Rory's punch, felt that she needed something more substantial than a volume of André Gide beside her bed. She was, as anybody could tell from her jewellery, a very practical young woman.

"Say, why don't you and Rosalba make up a party with Carmine and me and drive back right now to the Augusto?"

"That's a jolly good idea, by Jove," said Captain

Wheeler. "Look here, we will. I'll just see if my sister wants to go home."

"Oh, you have a sister, have you?"

"Yes, but that's all right. She's bound to be feeling a bit tired."

Captain Wheeler relinquished his partner and approached his sister.

"Hullo, I was wondering where you'd got to," he said. "I thought you must have gone home. Feeling tired, old lady?"

"Very," said Miss Wheeler with a resentful sigh. "Is Carlino outside?"

Carlino was the Wheelers' pet driver.

"Sure to be. I told him sharp at two. I'll go and find Mrs Brown-Hammond."

"Mrs Brown-Hammond?"

"Yes, I thought you and she would like to go back together. I'm going to walk down."

"Who with?"

"Well, I've rather let myself in for seeing Miss Donsante and Mrs Mitchell home. I couldn't very well get out of it."

It was probably nervousness more than a musical temperament that made Wheeler begin to whistle *All Souls' Day* under his breath.

"Harry," said his sister, "if you don't come back with me I'll bolt every door and window in the house, and you shan't come in at all to-night."

This was precisely the course of action Captain Wheeler had outlined for himself, and he had some difficulty in looking suitably dismayed by the threat.

"Now, look here, old girl, don't be unreasonable."

"Don't call me 'old girl'! Are you coming back with me now?"

Captain Wheeler looked down at his spurs.

"No, I'm not," he declared firmly. "I'm not going to make a public fool of myself by telling those girls my sister won't let me see them home. You don't seem to grasp the fact that I'm ten years younger than you. I don't want to say anything that's likely to hurt your feelings, but really, Ethel, you'll make me wish in a minute I hadn't set up house with you. What would you do if I got married?"

At this Miss Wheeler fled sobbing into the house to put on her cloak.

"She's a bit overwrought. The fact is one glass upsets her," the brother explained, when sobbing she had been packed into a carriage with Mrs Brown-Hammond who was just Mrs Brown-Hammond and the sort of woman one always used for crises like this as people use embrocations for sprains.

Of course even on Sirene, if all the other guests had been absolutely sober, a domestic scene of this kind would have been extremely painful; but most of them by now had reached the stage of taking everything for granted as in a dream. The emotional exit of Miss Wheeler was hardly an incident in that evening of absorbing emotions. Bozzo was playing as well as ever; a fresh bowl of punch had just been brought in; the moon was not yet setting.

Rosalba recognized that Zoe had scored by saddling her with Captain Wheeler and his leather accoutrements. She saw it would require address to take Carmine away from Zoe. Lulu would of course be acutely mortified to hear of Carmine's surrender to Zoe; but she would be much more acutely mortified to hear he had surrendered to herself, and that would mortify Zoe as well. The first step was obvious, Rosalba decided. All four of them must drive down in the same carriage. The elimination of Captain Wheeler must be managed later on.

"You will sit up there, please," she told him, pointing to the box. "And you will sit here between Zoe and me," she told Carmine.

Carmine had a paradisial drive down wedged between the two girls; nor was a final sweetness withheld, for when they reached the Piazza Rosalba insisted the drive was to be charged to her.

"*No, prego, Signorina Rosalba!*" Carmine protested.

But she scoffed at the notion of his paying, and the three ten-lira notes, which he had been calculating all the way down between ardent simultaneous hand-clasps and alternate sighing forth of fond words to right and left of him, ought to be enough to avoid an undignified argument with the driver, went back into his pocket. They did not stay there long, because when they were passing down the narrow street by Zampone's Wheeler drew him back to ask if he had any money with him.

"I've come out without a blessed centisimo," he said. "You can't carry money about with you in uniform."

Carmine thought that Wheeler had enough pockets

in his khaki to carry a fortune; but though he had learnt a good deal during these last two and a half years he had not yet learnt how to refuse to lend anybody money without feeling awkward and ashamed.

"I want to tip the night porter," Wheeler explained. "Fifty liras will do the trick."

But on reaching the hotel the Frontiersman, evidently much to Rosalba's relief, bade them good night. Carmine in desperation conquered his embarrassment so far as to lead up to the fifty liras with which he had parted so meekly by gulping out, 'Capitain!' But Wheeler saluted and with a 'cheerio' turned on his heels. The doors of the hotel were closed behind him. Rosalba after bidding Peppino the night porter to go and wake the barman, led the way downstairs to the bar.

Only somebody who owed as much as Rosalba owed the Hotel Augusto would have dared to arrive back at half-past three in the morning and have the barman woken. Not that Adolfo was anything but delighted to be woken. The drinks could go down on the bill, or one might say up, attached to it like one more insignificant scrap of paper to the tail of a huge kite. That was the management's look out. His own was brighter. His tip for willing service at such an hour would be paid in cash.

"Say, Rosalba," Zoe observed irritably. "I don't see why you side-stepped Wheeler like that. I asked him to come right in."

Rosalba laughed and murmured something in Italian to Carmine, whereupon Zoe faced her angrily.

"Now listen, Rosalba, I'm not going to stand for you talking in Italian to this kid. Hear what I am telling her, Carmine? If you want to keep friends with Zoe, ring down on your native land, honey-bunch, and talk English."

"I wish always to make practice for my English, signora," said Carmine firmly. "From that I am being at London I am appassionated for English."

While Rosalba and Zoe were seated on high chairs in the bar waiting with Carmine between them for the arrival of Adolfo, Captain Wheeler returned to the hotel, in the lobby of which he at once presented Peppino the night porter with Carmine's five ten-lira notes. Then he proceeded to walk upstairs.

"*Signor capitano*, where you go?" Peppino asked.

For answer the Frontiersman stopped and, putting the finger of his right hand to his nose, winked three times. Now, in the classical language of gesture the apposition of the forefinger to the nose merely expresses acute pensiveness. It is no indication of an amorous resolve. So Peppino failed to gather from Captain Wheeler's signal that he was on his way up to Rosalba's room. He supposed that Captain Wheeler after laudably returning to present him with fifty liras was under the impression that the way out of the hotel again was upstairs.

"From here one sorts, *signor capitano*," he emphasized, pointing to the front door.

"I know the way out," said Captain Wheeler scornfully. "Only, I happen to be staying here to-night."

"But you have not combined with the manager for a room," Peppino protested.

"No, not with the manager," it was admitted. "But I know where my room is, thanks very much and all that."

Wheeler turned round to continue his ascent. Hannibal and Napoleon did not scale the Alps more confidently.

"I cannot permit you to ascend the stairs, if you please, sir," Peppino insisted.

"Now look here, my good chap, you don't want to annoy the Signorina Donsante, do you? Right. Well, my advice to you is to look after your front door and let the stairs look after themselves."

Peppino hesitated. He certainly was not anxious to offend the Signorina Donsante. He was too dependent upon her for whatever small luxuries brightened a night porter's obscure employment. Captain Wheeler, quick to perceive the effect of his last allusion, continued to ascend.

Peppino shook his head. If the Signorina desired to give this brigand the freedom of her room she must be allowed to do so, whatever the regulations of the hotel. He shook his head again and returning to his hooded chair he lulled his perplexed conscience by poring over the feuilleton in the *Mattino*.

Downstairs, Adolfo blinking with interrupted sleep was mixing stingers to Rosalba's order. Being in a hurry to know whether she or Zoe should conquer and perhaps having a few scruples about keeping Adolfo out of bed indefinitely, Rosalba had bidden him mix a dozen so that he could retire and leave them to renew what might become a too personal argument for a barman's ears.

"*Bastano, signorina?*" Adolfo enquired when the twelve glasses of silvery green liquid were set out in a row along the marble counter.

Rosalba was loth to admit that there could be enough of anything in this world. The moment she was invited to give a decision involving the least prudence she was perplexed.

"*Ancora quattro*," she decided.

Four more glasses were added to the line. Adolfo wiped his hands of ice and minty stickiness, took Rosalba's fifty-lira note with a smile of thanks, and paused a moment in the doorway to look back at his handiwork.

"*Carini assai, tutti quei bicchierini*," he commented with the Southern Italian's childlike pleasure in the prettiness even of a little row of green-filled glasses. "*Allora, buona notte, signorina. Buona notte, signora. Buona notte, signorino. E buon riposo!*" With a friendly smile all round he retired to bed.

"Let us now drink a little," said Rosalba.

With every glass of the mixed brandy and crême de menthe they drank on top of so many glasses of Rory's punch it became more and more imperative for Rosalba and Zoe to tell Carmine what each thought of the other. When either of them fancied she had made a particularly good point at her rival's expense she would climb down from her tall chair and embrace Carmine, who, having no prejudice in favour of either, but a strong hope to achieve both before sunrise, sat perched on his chair with a judicial calm, which only the lustre of his brown eyes and the flush on his velvet cheeks prevented appearing unnatural when he accepted their kisses.

Carmine became that night the recipient of feminine secrets which would have made a Lucian blush for his ignorance. Under the influence of the stingers these revelations made no more apparent impression on him than copy-book maxims; but readers unfortified by Rory's punch and Rosalba's stingers might be less stoical.

At last, tired of statement and counter-statement, Rosalba declared she had something to tell Carmine about Zoe which she could not tell him in front of her, but which would make him understand once for all what kind of woman Zoe really was.

"Tell him, tell him," Zoe challenged. There was some excuse for her defiance, because it was impossible to suppose that Rosalba could go beyond the frankness she had already achieved. She had accused Zoe of being the slave of morphia and cocaine. She had gone into details about her amorous technique, which the most earnest psycho-analyst would have hesitated to publish in a book under three guineas net. "Tell him anything you like, Rosalba," she repeated. "You're too drunk and I'm too drunk and he's too drunk for it to matter."

"Ah, no, signora," Carmine protested. "I am not at all too much drunk. I can to do big loves. I am quite strong all over myself."

Rosalba was pulling him out of the bar toward the dark ballroom when he leaned back thus to reassure Zoe about the future. After they disappeared behind one of the columns Zoe rushed out on the terrace, and perhaps with the notion of demonstrating her own sudden sobriety she began a solitary dance, in the course of which her clouded golden hair came down and turned her thoughts to hairpins, so that she went crawling over the porcelain tiles in search of them.

"Do not to go with that awful woman," Rosalba begged, hugging Carmine passionately and kissing him as fast as the needle of a sewing-machine hems its busy course. "I will tell to you now a secret about her which everybody knows. I think you will be quite disgusted. *Non è signora. Non è sposata. È una donna mantenuta.* She is not at all the wife of Mitchell."

This after what Rosalba had accused Zoe of already was to end the indictment with a truly Ciceronian diminuendo of guilt. The murder of one of her female friends was all that Carmine might have supposed outstanding in Rosalba's account against Zoe. He replied a little lamely, considering how much she evidently relied upon the effect on him of such a revelation, that he was not at all surprised. He was in fact making up his mind that a bird in the hand was worth two in the bush. He was on the point of discarding Zoe and urging breathlessly on Rosalba '*andiamo sopra*' when the voice of Peppino was heard:

"*Signorina, signorina! Ci sono due signori nella Sua camera.*"

"*Due signori nella mia camera?*" Rosalba echoed.

Peppino explained that first of all the English *capitano* had gone up to her room apparently with her permission, but that another *signore* had without his permission rushed upstairs and that they were at this moment arguing together inside her room.

"*È un oltraggio,*" Rosalba declared angrily.

"*Si, si. Evvero, signorina. Ha detto bene. È un oltraggio. Mi ha fatto un gran dispiacere.*"

"*Verrò subito,*" Rosalba proclaimed grandly.

"*Si, si! Venga. Venga,*" he entreated.

When Rosalba reached her bedroom door with Peppino, the voice of Daffodil was heard within saying:

"I'm not going to leave you alone in here, Captain Wheeler. So now!"

"You wait till I get you outside. I'll jolly well punch your head," the deeper voice of Captain Wheeler rejoined.

Then Daffodil was heard again:

"The less you say about punch the better, Captain Wheeler."

"*Badi, signorina, badi,*" Peppino implored when Rosalba grasped the handle of her door; but she brushed him aside and entered.

"Here I am, my darling," Captain Wheeler just had time to mutter before he collapsed on the floor in a stupor produced by drink, emotion, and fatigue.

"We'll put him in an empty room for to-night, porter, and lock him up till the morning," said

Daffodil practically. "You take his head and I'll take his feet. Good-night, Miss Donsante."

Leaving Peppino and Daffodil to dispose of her admirer's body, Rosalba hurried back to the bar. There was no sign of Carmine or Zoe. She ran out on the terrace and searched the garden. There was no sign of them there either. She went back upstairs and along the corridor to Zoe's room. It was empty. She went down into the hall again where she found Daffodil puffing delicately after his exertions. He told her that Zoe and Carmine had gone out of the front door five minutes ago, and when Rosalba started off in pursuit he announced that he should escort her.

"Rory told me to see you were safe."

"I am entirely safe, thank you so much," said Rosalba haughtily. "I am only worried about Zoe. She is quite drunk; and I do not know what may happen to her if she is with a boy."

"*Anything*," Daffodil earnestly declared, his eyes like saucers in the grey dawn that was flowing into the lobby of the hotel.

"If I permit you to come," Rosalba continued, "it is because I feel I must take care of her. She is such a terrible drinker, and she has no respect of herself at all when she is like that. She will undress all her clothes. She will do all the things she must not. It is terrible. We must somehow find her, my friend."

In the fresh twilight of dawn they stood listening outside the hotel.

"Hark, I think I have heard a scream," Rosalba said in a hushed voice.

"No, no, that was the morning boat hooting," Daffodil reassured her. "Such a nasty noise!"

"I wish I knew which way they are going. Look what is in the road."

Daffodil swooped down and picked up a hairpin.

"All her hairs are coming down," Rosalba cried excitedly. "They must be going this way."

A quarter of a mile further along the Via Caprera four more hairpins glittered wanly in the roadway by the lamplight paling beneath the lavender sky. A hundred yards beyond a handkerchief lay in the dust. Rosalba picked it up and looked at the monogram.

"That stupid girl has begun to undress herself," she announced solemnly. "It is terrible."

"Oh, isn't it awful?" Daffodil echoed. "I feel quite dithered."

And had he but known the word that was the one Carmine might have chosen to express what he was feeling at that moment. He had set out in the grey of dawn with what he had every reason to suppose was an exquisitely beautiful, deliciously yielding young woman, the thought of whose caresses when they should lie deep hidden in the dewy *macchia* somewhere on the lonely cliffs beyond the Punta Caprera compensated him for the less romantic but more practical comfort of her room in the hotel, to which she had denied him access on the plea that she wanted to be sure Rosalba was out of the way.

Carmine had acknowledged her prudence. Moreover, by leaving the Augusto he should escape the difficulty of attempting to square the conscience of the night porter with that one grubby cobweb-thin two-lira note, which was all that Wheeler had left him. Love beneath the dawn-dimmed stars would be all the sweeter for being divested of any financial responsibility. Before the sun rose he should be escorting her back to the hotel; he should part with her on the doorstep; and before the sun set again he should have made his peace with Lulu.

They wandered slowly along the Via Caprera past the shuttered villas among their palms. Zoe's hair came down twice; and the second time she had a good deal of difficulty in putting it up again while she held on first to a lamp-post and then to the railings of the Villa Florida as passionately as a moment before she had been clinging to Carmine. It did occur to him that she was not quite so steady upon her feet as she ought to be if they were to walk along the narrow cliff path beyond the Punta Caprera; but he elbowed prudence out of the way and urged Zoe to let her hair hang down.

"You can make your hair when we are sitting," he pointed out. "We must now progress."

She had let go of the railings and was trying to climb over a wall to look for a hairpin which she said had dropped into the garden on the other side. It took all Carmine's persuasion to prevent her making a drop down twelve feet into a thicket of prickly pears to rescue it.

"Haven't you got any hairpins?" she asked.

"No, I have not," he replied solemnly.

"Well, why haven't you, cuckoo?"

"Because I does not carry such things."

"How do you keep your hair up then?"

"I have not the need of hairpins."

"Yes, you have."

"No, madame, I have not. My hair keeps himself up."

At this Zoe sat down in the road with her back to the wall and laughed very loudly. Then close at hand a cock crowed, upon which she became inordinately grave.

"Because I've been laughing at you, you can't laugh at me," she said crossly.

"I does not laugh for you."

"Why, I heard you. You were laughing like a rooster. I never heard anybody laugh so much like a rooster in my life. Cock-a-doodle-doo! Don't you call that a darned fool way to laugh?"

"But he is a chicken who makes that rumour, madame," Carmine protested.

"A roast chicken or a broiled chicken?" she asked. "You know, I don't believe I ever felt so naughty in my life as I feel now. If you sit right down here by me, I'll give you such a thrill."

"But this is not the place for sits."

"Oh, very well, if you don't want to be thrilled, don't be. I don't care. I'll stay right here where I am. Run away and leave me alone, and put that lamp-post out before you go. The darned thing keeps jumping about and gets on my nerves. No wonder I can't find my hairpins. In America we

have lamp-posts you can see by. If I was in America
I'd have found all my hairpins by now."

Carmine was on the point of turning round and
leaving her to talk to herself about hairpins when she
called him to give her a hand up. Hope returned,
and they reached the Punta Caprera without her
trying once to put up her hair. This famous belvedere was scattered with seats for the benefit of tourists
who wished to contemplate the view. On one of
these Zoe stretched herself at full length and announced
she was going to spend the rest of the night there.

"Come on, Carmine, you can lie down beside me,"
she told him.

"But there is not the place for me," he objected.

"Oh well, I guess I'll have to make room," she said,
and turning over alluringly she rolled off through the
gap between the back and the seat on to the ground.

"Now, listen to me, honey, that would never have
happened in America," she avowed solemnly. "Never.
You see, we know how to build seats in America."

"Have you hurted yourself, madame?"

She examined her knee and pointed to a rent in
her stocking.

"That's a Paris stocking. Well now, you hear a
lot about Paris clothes, but they don't last. Not that
I want them to last. Why no, I'd be mad if they did
last, because I'm just crazy about change. A friend
of mine took me to be psychoed last spring. Know
what that is? Well, I don't believe I do either. But
it's the latest thing since the war. And he asked me
a lot of questions. Well, I wouldn't ask such questions

in a cloak-room. He had a nerve. But I answered him because I thought it was something to do with telling fortunes, and I'm crazy about fortune-telling. Why, I could sit all day having my fortune told. Why, I think it's so interesting. But this was a doctor. And it seemed all he cared about was to find out about my inhibitions. Say, do you know what an inhibition is?"

"No, madame, I does not know. Please to say what is."

"Oh, I couldn't tell you, because, you see, we aren't married. But believe me, kiddo, that doctor couldn't find any inhibitions on me. No, sir! I just hadn't *one*. It put his back up at first. He said he'd been psychoing around since before the war and he'd never met anybody like me with *no* inhibitions. And then he gave it up and said all I wanted was change. So, I told Mr Mitchell he could look on my dressmaker's bills as doctor's bills in future."

"Please do not speak now of Mr Mitchell," said Carmine. "It makes me too much jealous."

He was not really in the least jealous of Mr Mitchell; but he was anxious to put the conversation on a practical basis. These irrelevant reminiscences were as bad as hairpins for wasting time. However, when Zoe began to laugh again he wished he had not mentioned Mr Mitchell. Her laughter seemed to have the effect of hastening the sun, so rapidly much lighter was it growing every moment.

"Please let us now walk where it is more seclusive, madame," he pleaded.

"I'll do just whatever you want," she offered expansively. " Why, Carmine, I think you're so cute, though why you have such a darned silly name I don't know. Who called you Carmine anyway? Why, it's no name at all for a nice kid like you. You're not a Cissie. You don't want a name that sounds like a face-cream."

" Madame, please let us march. I am so excitated. You must please have some misericord for my ardent spasms."

" Say, did you learn English in a fire-insurance office? "

" No, madame, I have learnt him in the linguage school. I no speak well, yes? "

" Dry those tears, my angel child. I was only jollying you. Come, give me a batcho—you know— a kiss."

*"Ah, signora!"*

He folded her in his embrace and greatly encouraged by her sudden ability to concentrate once more he led her to the steps cut in the rock that descended from the belvedere to the narrow path along the cliff.

" *Piano, piano,*" he called out apprehensively as Zoe started to run down them.

It was too late. She took fifteen steps in one slide and might have taken another thirty and rolled on two or three hundred feet into the sea if she had not managed to grasp the stem of a wild olive and save herself.

" Well, here I am now," she said, " till you can fetch my maid."

"Why you want your maid?"

"Why do I want my maid? Why, because I've ripped up all my clothes and myself too. Oh, isn't this grass good and cool?"

Carmine was bending over her solicitously. But she pushed him away.

"No more loving to-night. I've sprained my affections. Oh gee, my head's going around!"

"You will break my heart," the young man declared.

"Kid, if you knew what I've broken, believe me you wouldn't worry."

"Are you so terribly damaged?"

"Damaged? I guess I look like one of last year's models after the Fat Lady's worn it. Go and fetch Victorine, there's a good boy. Tell her to bring my blanket coat, and plenty of hairpins. Oh gee, my poor head!"

"I am not pleased to leave you here, madame," he protested.

"Don't argue, there's a good boy. My head's going around and around and around. Go and fetch my maid."

Carmine sighed. This was a wretched end to the triumphant night he had promised himself. At this moment two sportsmen came down the steps, out early in search of quails. One of their lean red dogs turned aside to sniff Zoe.

"Oh god," she groaned. "This dog thinks I'm something his master's shot."

"*Chiama il cane!*" cried Carmine angrily. "*Via! Via!*"

The sportsmen called off the dog and passed on with profuse good mornings. Carmine unwillingly left Zoe to go and fetch Victorine. At the head of the steps he met Rosalba and Daffodil, to whom in Italian he explained what had happened.

"Of course, she is terribly drunk," said Rosalba loftily to Daffodil. "What was I saying to you? It is quite disgusting."

She ran to the railings of the belvedere and called down over them:

"Zoe, you are quite drunk!"

"Yes!" Zoe shouted back.

"I will not come down to make myself a figure beside you!"

"Don't!" Zoe shouted.

"You have made a disgrace for all of us. I am furiated!" Rosalba called down. "I will go back now to the Augusto with Carmine and send Victorine for you. Daffodil can stay here."

"I shall be safe!" Zoe shouted back.

Rosalba fancied that it was not too late even now to secure her quintuple triumph; but by this time Carmine was only anxious to go home and sleep. When he reached the turning that led up to Via Timberio where he was staying, he bade Rosalba an abrupt good-night and left her to deal with the problem of Victorine. In the future this night would doubtless come to figure in his memory as a temptation successfully overcome.

Victorine was very severe with her mistress in the yellow sunlight. She scolded her all the way along the Via Caprera, and it was only Daffodil's magnificent insouciance as he half led, half carried Zoe to the lobby of the hotel, where the chairs were standing upside-down for the morning brooms, which quelled the inquisitive glances of the passers by.

"You're a Cissie, aren't you?" Zoe murmured when he bade her good-bye and wished her deep and sweet repose.

He shook his finger at her and skipped away.

"Give me a Cissie when a poor girl's in trouble," Zoe murmured when Victorine, still grumbling about her duty to Mr Mitchell, was tucking her up in bed.

## CHAPTER NINETEEN

ὄττινας γὰρ
εὖ θέω, κῆνοί με μάλιστα σίννονται.
SAPPHO.

*For those whom I have treated well are the very ones to turn against me.*

THE return of Zoé to her hotel at half-past five in the morning so obviously battered by her night's amusement provided the Piazza with minor gossip for exactly a quarter of an hour. Piazza gossip serves in Sirene as the chocolate to take away the taste of the day's housekeeping expenses. The larger the account the richer must be the gossip. Whatever chance Zoe's behaviour had of carrying off an extra couple of liras in the household book was destroyed by the news that the Villa Eolia had been burgled during the night. This did cause a sensation. All the cooks bought extravagantly. A burglary! The household books of every family jumped up to the dimensions of a religious festival. The provision shops were without attractions by half-past nine. A burglary on Sirene! '*Sarebbero questi maladetti socialisti.*' That was the unanimous opinion of the Piazza.

The chatter died down to an awed silence when the *maresciallo* preceded by two *carabinieri* passed solemnly along on his way to investigate this affair. The *maresciallo* showed that tendency to obesity which in all countries seems to accompany seniority in the police;

but that very obesity heaped an extra grandeur upon his progress toward the scene of the crime. He and his *carabinieri* gave the effect of some mighty natural upheaval, by the majesty of which the commonplace of life was temporarily suspended. The cooks did not linger to gossip any more. They set out home in a hush of meditation, their *facchini* loaded with provisions, themselves with news.

When the *maresciallo* reached the Villa Eolia he found Bébé Buonagrazia with Olimpia Leigh. She was to recount to him in Italian what had happened.

" *Io sono la principessa Buonagrazia,*" she explained.

The *maresciallo* was suitably impressed. He did not arrest her. But the Princess had hardly begun her tale when Olga Linati swooped down upon it. The *maresciallo* frowned. He looked very much inclined to arrest Olga. Her mother was a Russian. That in these disordered times was almost a criminal offence. He asked if the Signorina Linati was a friend of the Signora.

" *Della Signorina Leigh, si, si,*" said the Princess.

The *maresciallo* shook his head. The law took no cognizance of friendship. He must request the immediate withdrawal of the Signorina Linati. Although he suspected nobody, it would be equally true to say he suspected everybody. It was his duty, he added with a bow of martyred officialdom. Olga was indignant. She felt as if the *maresciallo* were trying to deprive her of a commission. To be excluded from anything shook Olga's confidence in her ability one day to become rich. She protested. The *maresciallo* grasped the hilt of his sword. He did not intend to convey that he should be compelled to draw upon Olga if she did not retire. It was only a gesture to plead an authority stronger than himself. It was, one might say, a denial of his humanity. He added politely that it displeased him to ask the Signorina Linati to retire, but that the law of which he was the representative could not tolerate her presence at the critical moment of preliminary investigation. Olga withdrew expressing in rapid French, Italian, and English her feminine horror of the Law's unreality.

When she was gone the *maresciallo* held up the narrative by asking first of all what was the Signorina Leigh's name, nationality, the name of her father, the place and date of her birth, and the length of her sojourn in Italy. Such details were the necessary preliminaries to any kind of *perquisizione* he might have to make. He had already mistaken her for a signora. That had been the result of scamping the preliminaries. He took out a note-book.

"Olimpia Leigh."

"*Come si scrive Li?*"

"L-E-I-G-H."

The *maresciallo* sat back and wiped his brow with a red silk handkerchief.

"*L-E-I-G-H?*" he repeated.

"*Si.*"

"*E si pronunziano quelle cinque lettere 'Li'?*"

"*Proprio così.*"

The *maresciallo* shook his head. This burglary looked

like being a long, involved, and obscure affair before anybody's guilt was established.

"*Nome di padre?*"

"Chester Urquhart."

Chester did not offer great difficulties; but Urquhart visibly aged the *maresciallo*. Between Olimpia's pronunciation of the letters of the alphabet, the Princess's attempt to translate that into their Italian pronunciation, and the unnatural juxtaposition of the letters themselves, the result in the note-book of the *maresciallo* read *Urququhuhuquhuart*. He regarded this concatenation of letters with a disgusted perplexity. Then he remembered the origin of many Americans, and smiled with relief.

"*Sarebbe un nome indiano?*" he suggested.

"Yes, yes, an old Choctaw family," said Olimpia impatiently, for by this time she was not perfectly sure herself how Urquhart was spelt.

The *maresciallo* read out the details he had obtained up to date.

"*Olimpia Li, americana, figlia di Kaystair Oorquorquoourt. Giusto così?*"

"*Giustissimo,*" he was assured.

"*Nata?*"

"Schenectady."

"*Dio mio!*" the *maresciallo* groaned.

"I'll write it for you," Olimpia volunteered, making a snatch for his note-book.

The *maresciallo* recoiled in horror.

"*No, no,*" he cried, and begged the Princess to impress on the Signora that the Law was already in motion, and that she really must be serious. Then, after mopping his forehead again, he tackled Schenectady.

"*S-H-C-I-N-I-S-T-E-D-I-Y. Giusto così?*"

"*Giustissimo.*"

"*Allora, anno di nascita?*"

Olimpia rang the bell.

"Fetch my passport," she told her maid. "Oh, yes," she said when she had perused it. "1881. January 23."

This was not difficult when translated by the Princess.

"*Professione?*"

"Composer," said Olimpia.

"*Composatrice*," the Princess translated.

"*Di musica?*"

"*Si, si.*"

"*Bello!*" the *maresciallo* sighed. Such a calling seemed to add a touch of romance to the grim prose of those official secrets in his note-book.

"*Arrivata in Italia?*"

That date was easily supplied and recorded.

The *maresciallo* grunted with satisfaction. Whatever the result of his *perquisizione*, he should not have to reproach himself with having omitted anything that might help to solve the mystery. He sat back to listen to the Princess's account of what had happened.

The Signorina and herself had left a party at the Villa Leucadia.

"*Sarebbe la villa Beer?*"

The Princess turned to Olimpia.

"I believe it used to be called that," said Olimpia. "I really don't know why the name was changed."

They had left this party about half-past two to ride on donkeys to that part of Anasirene which is called Limbo. There was a cottage there in the middle of an old olive-grove which the Signorina Leigh had wished to look at with a possibility of buying.

"*La conosco. Bella proprietà! Bella! Bella!*" the *maresciallo* declared, wheezing with enthusiasm.

The Signorina Leigh had wished to see what it looked like by moonlight. That was the reason for visiting it at such an hour.

The *maresciallo* interposed to say that he appreciated the Signorina's impulse. It was, he might explain, an artistic impulse. It came from being a composer of music. Artists were unlike other people. An ordinary person would have examined such a property by daylight. But artists had their own methods for finding out what they wanted. There was nothing suspicious in that. Nothing at all. He had a brother-in-law whose cousin had become a famous tenor. It was perhaps easier for him therefore to regard sympathetically the mental processes of the artist.

The Princess resumed.

She and the Signorina had sat talking in the olive-grove for a long time—until dawn in fact. The donkey-woman had gone to sleep under a bush, and one of the donkeys had wandered off into the *macchia* to feed. It had been nearly seven o'clock before they reached the Villa Eolia. There was nothing unusual noticed at first. It was the habit of the servants when they left in the evening after the Signorina had gone out to deposit the key of the front door under a flower-pot in the garden. Nobody slept in the house at night. Even the Signorina's maid slept at the Hotel Sirene. They had found the key under the flower-pot as usual, had gone indoors, and had noticed nothing, until they saw that the *vaso di notte* was standing upside down in the middle of the Signorina's bed.

The *maresciallo* clicked his tongue.

But even that had only struck the Signorina at first as a piece of carelessness by the housemaid.

"*Spiacevole però*," the *maresciallo* muttered.

Presently the Signorina had gone to one of the drawers in her toilet-table, in which she kept little pieces of jewellery of more sentimental than real value. These had all vanished. The Signorina had written out a list of these articles, with a full description of each, the Princess added hastily when she saw the note-book appear again. The odd thing about the theft was that in the same drawer as the jewellery there was paper money both French and Italian to upward of two thousand francs. This had not been touched. On the Signorina's table was a large photograph of herself, and the thief had pencilled on this a moustache and beard. She would show him this photograph presently. On returning to the *salone* they had noticed that all the photographs of the Signorina's friends had been turned upside down, and finally that over a bust of the Signorina, which a Russian sculptor had recently finished, had been fixed a pair of antlers, the property of the owner of the villa and intended by him to be used for hats.

"*Uno scultore russo?*" the *maresciallo* repeated gravely.

Then he clicked his tongue again. The whole affair reeked of Bolshevism.

Naturally, the Princess resumed, they had made a search of the house, but had found nothing else touched. They had discovered, however, that the back-door had been kicked in, which showed the way the thief had entered.

"*Sicuro*," the *maresciallo* agreed, glad to have one fairly obvious fact at last in this dark affair.

Presently he asked if the Russian sculptor had a wife. Olimpia thought not. The *maresciallo* with many excuses went on to ask whether he did not have at any rate some woman who was interested in him. That she did not know. What was the point of such a question? The point of the question was this. The impression on him, though he admitted first impressions were not always to be relied upon, was that this *brutto affare* was the act of a woman. It did not seem to him to be simple case of theft. It seemed rather an exhibition of *dispetto*. Had the Signorina any female enemies?

"Hundreds," said Olimpia.

"*Sarebbe una nemica*," he declared portentously.

The Princess and Olimpia looked at one another. They had already decided as much.

Of course, the *maresciallo* went on, he should examine the servants severely. In cases of theft the first people to examine were the servants. The theft at the Villa Amabile had as the ladies might have heard been conclusively traced to the servants. Still . . . the *maresciallo* shook his head. This could not be a simple case of theft. Darker emotions were involved. Malice, revenge, jealousy. Where had the Signorina Linati been last night? At the party. But she had left before the Signorina Li. No doubt the ladies would have noticed her eagerness just now. Might not one say her nervous anxiety? And she had that Russian mother. A Russian mother. A Russian sculptor. One was treating of something in which there were undoubted elements of Bolshevism. La Linati was in debt. That was common knowledge in Sirene. Did the Signorina Li know of any cause why La Linati should bear a grudge against her, the gratification of which might be combined with sordid gain?

"Why, no, she can't have any grudge against me," said Olimpia, "though I might have a grudge against her for letting me this villa."

"But she is a great friend of Cléo Gazay," put in the Princess. "And Cléo was very angry with you. She left the party in a rage, and Olga Linati went with her."

Who was Cléo Gazay? A French pianist? French? The *maresciallo* clicked his tongue. The French were a violent and haughty nation. Their treatment of Italy both during and after the war was evidence of that. A Frenchwoman was capable of anything. Ah, there had been a disagreement between this French pianist and the Signorina. A disagreement over music? That was important. As a connection of the famous tenor he could appreciate the importance of that. There had been an occasion when the cousin of his brother-in-law had thrown a plateful of *spaghetti* over a *basso profondo* who had insinuated in a Naples restaurant that the tenor had sung flat on the top note in *Di Quella Pira*. The Signorina would appreciate what bitter feelings such an accusation might rouse. She was no doubt an admirer of the immortal Verdi. She would readily forgive his brother-in-law's cousin for resorting to *spaghetti*. But that had been a manly expression of resentment. The *spaghetti* had been flung over the *basso profondo* in public. Here one treated of a feminine revenge. There were signs too of a French hand at work. That *vaso di notte* for example placed upside down on the Signorina's bed. He did not hesitate to say that such a use of a *vaso di notte* was pre-eminently a French conception. It was stamped with Gallic indelicacy. And then the horns? *Le corna*. Was not that a characteristic piece of French vulgarity? To be sure the implication in the Signorina's case was rather hard to unfold. But that pointed more particularly to a French mind. It was the kind of spontaneously indecent gesture that one expected from over the Alps. It might be that while La Linati was occupying herself with the jewellery this French woman had exercised her debased ingenuity with the *vaso di notte* and the horns. Yes, the whole ugly business wore a distinctly transalpine air.

"Tell that fat fool," said Olimpia to the Princess, "I don't believe for one moment it was Olga or Cléo. Tell him I would a hundred times sooner suspect that little bitch Rosalba."

The Princess could not have translated this quite accurately, because it evoked from the *maresciallo* a pæan of praise for Rosalba.

"*Una signorina così graziosa, così fine, così gentile!*"

The Signorina Li was indeed right. Nobody could possibly suspect her. The notion was risible. There indeed was a *creatura innocente*. He could not recall in his life any young woman whose charm had been so instantly impressed upon him. Always gay, always a hand or a smile. No false pride. Generous, some might say extravagant. But was she not the heiress of millions ? Who had a better right to be extravagant ? There were, it was true, a certain number of envious nobodies who accused her of vices which he after a lifelong experience of human wickedness simply did not believe existed except in the vile imagination of her accusers.

In the middle of this testimonial to her charms and virtue Rosalba herself came into the room, looking not at all as if she had scarcely had a couple of hours' sleep.

"*Buon giorno, signorina*," exclaimed the *maresciallo*, rising from his chair to salute her and, when she grasped his pudgy hand, giggling in delighted diffidence at the honour paid him. "*Proprio benarrivata*," he gurgled. "*Perchè noi stavamo parlando proprio di Lei.*"

"*Mon cher*," said Rosalba to Olimpia, who was regarding her from the corner of the room in a huddle of cold dislike. "I am so sorry to hear what has happened. They say you have been terribly robbed ? I hope it has been so much exaggerated."

*La Signorina Rosalba* could help them, the *maresciallo* suggested fatuously ; and before either of the others could stop him he was launched upon a voluble account of the burglary together with his premature theories about the guilty persons.

Rosalba expressed her horror at the suggestion that either Cléo or Olga was capable of such behaviour. No, no, it was a hundred times impossible.

"*Lei è troppo buona*," the *maresciallo* sighed, shaking his head in melancholy admiration of Rosalba's radiant scepticism.

"Cléo and Olga are not the only people who have gone away angry from the Villa Leucadia last night," she said. "Lulu was very angry and Miss Wheeler was very angry and Anastasia Sarbécoff is opening her shop to-day."

"*Una Russa?*" queried the *maresciallo*; and when he learned that Madame Sarbécoff had started a shop for the sale of curios his first theory was evidently shaken.

"It was not Zoe Mitchell," said Rosalba in a tone that implied a certain regret in having to admit as much so confidently. "I have had quite a terrible night with her. She is now in bed. She was so much drunk, my dears. It was quite disgusting."

Olimpia had not uttered a word since Rosalba came in. She just sat gazing at her from those burning eyes until even Rosalba could stand it no longer.

"I am afraid that I bore you," she suggested.

"Very much," Olimpia agreed.

On this Rosalba left the villa in a cloud of cigarette smoke, and immediately afterwards the *maresciallo* armed with a description of the missing jewellery and a number of facts more or less relevant set out on the time-honoured task of examining the servants.

The problem of the burglary, as soon as the facts

were generally known and the certainty of its having been the work of no ordinary thief was practically established, occupied Sirene to the exclusion of any other topic for quite three days. To be sure, as one would expect, some of these facts were distorted during the various arguments over the guilty person. To begin with, the condition of the villa when the victim returned was much exaggerated, so much exaggerated indeed that the owner of it telegraphed from Rome, where the rumour of the outrage had arrived by the morning after, to find out how much of his house had been left standing.

The travels and feats of the *vaso di notte* would have provided material for another Odyssey. It was stated —and all these statements were made with a positive authority which brooked no contradiction—that whenever the tenant of the Villa Eolia went out the key of the front door was hidden in a *vaso di notte*, which was placed with a candle burning inside it under one of the garden seats. It was stated that when Olimpia arrived home she had been stunned by a blow with a *vaso di notte* and that during her subsequent unconsciousness the thief had escaped. It was stated that all the *vasi di notte* in the villa had been heaped up in a trembling column against the front door and that when the front door was opened this column had toppled down on to the terrace. Two people who vouched for the truth of this version claimed to have actually heard the noise of the crash. Even those who agreed that the *vaso di notte* had been found in Olimpia Leigh's bed were by no means unanimous about its position.

Some said that a nightgown of Olimpia's had been stuffed with a pillow and that the base of the *vaso di notte* had been painted in a gross caricature of the great woman to serve as the head of this dummy. Others declared that the *vaso di notte* had been placed inside the bed and that Olimpia Leigh had not been aware of its presence until she got inside and touched its cold surface with her feet, upon which she had rushed screaming to the *maresciallo* that there was a corpse in her bed and would he come at once with the *carabinieri* and take it away. In the more remote parts of the island this variant led to the complete supercession of the *vaso di notte* by a corpse, and several Anasirenesi came down to stare at the villa in which the murder had been committed. Then there was extensive support for the story which eliminated the antlers and gave the *vaso di notte* as headgear for Olimpia's marble bust. Everybody talked about this *vaso di notte*. It will be idle to accuse the chronicler of bad taste in dwelling on the subject. The English visitors, some of whom will be reading this story, talked about it just as much as everybody else, and though with nice Anglo-Saxon pudicity they referred to it as 'a certain article of china' or a 'certain domestic utensil' the fact remains that they did talk about it. To be sure, one old maid tried to turn it into a tea-cup; but she knew, and all her listeners knew, that it was not a tea-cup. And on her fell a nemesis, because one day when she found herself *senza vaso* she asked the chambermaid for a *tazzo di notte* and was brought a cup of camomile tea.

But the stories about what had been taken and what had been done at the Villa Eolia could not compare in interest with the debate over the author of the outrage. Here it really seemed as if everybody had a different theory, and the championing of these theories by their authors led to a lot of bad feeling on the island. Nobody likes to go into a room and hear somebody confidently maintaining over a cigarette or a piece of bread and butter that an intimate friend is unquestionably a thief. Don Pruno, the *parroco*, escaped calumny; but several of his assistant priests were mentioned in connection with the affair. Nobody ventured to put forward the Bishop as a candidate for guilt; but Monsignore's private chaplain was suspected by at least two people and one of the canons by half a dozen. There was strong support for the guilt of Miss Wheeler, who was said to have rushed shrieking from the Villa Leucadia on hearing that her brother had galloped down to the Villa Eolia on a mule with Olimpia Leigh riding pillion behind him. Nobody of course suggested that Miss Wheeler was a thief. The disappearance of the trinkets was attributed to her anxiety to secure a locket belonging to her mother which Captain Wheeler was alleged to have given to Miss Leigh. Several people who had caught sight of Lulu's green silk dress and her pale distracted face as she drove down through the moonlight were convinced that she was the culprit, and of course there was a strong party against Olga and Cléo, and one only a little less strong against Madame Sarbécoff. Kadáshoff did not escape suspicion, while Hewetson in respectable cliques was stated with absolute conviction to be the criminal. Numerous residents and visitors who have not made even a brief appearance in this story and therefore whose guilt or innocence cannot at this stage be discussed came up in turn for condemnation. Entirely mythical figures were accused, as for instance a Russian ballerina who was said to be living somewhere down on the Grande Marina. The case against her was particularly strong because, since she did not exist, several people claimed to have seen her crawling stealthily up to the villa—a swarthy sinister gaunt woman, knife in hand. The evidence against her was so overwhelming that the *maresciallo* would undoubtedly have arrested her, could he have found her. But he could neither find her nor anybody who had seen her by daylight.

It was left to Rosalba to throw suspicion on a person whom nobody had suspected. The only excuse for her is that she was distracted by the sight of her failures on every side since that party at the Villa Leucadia. It is true that Zoe Mitchell had been eliminated. She had spent a couple of days in bed with a bad jag, and Victorine had telegraphed to Mr Mitchell suggesting he should summon her mistress home at once.

"So we're going by the afternoon boat," Zoe had told Rosalba. "I felt like death after mixing my drinks like that. And Victorine was so darned unpleasant. Well, I pitched a bottle of *Mes Délices* at her in the end, and she smells like the Café de la Paix. I guess we'll be followed all the way back to Paris."

"You have not seen Olimpia?" Rosalba asked.

" No, and I don't want to see her."

Rosalba had smiled.

" It is better not to want what one cannot have," she had said. Zoe's defeat was so complete that she had begun to feel quite well disposed towards her. " Perhaps we shall meet together in Paris."

" Sure we will," Zoe had assented cordially. " Oh, and Rosalba, here's my book of André Gide you might like to read. I haven't finished it yet, but that doesn't matter. It's the kind of book you don't have to finish. It's too clever to be finished like you would a novel."

And leaving behind her the slim volume which had waited by her bedside all through this summer jaunt Zoe left Sirene for good. Whatever Rosalba might find to say about her behaviour on the night of the party was waste of breath. Zoe burnt brown as dry chestnut wood was gone to recover her roses in Paris. Whether she was or was not married to Mr Mitchell had no importance any longer. She was gone. And by going she had deprived Rosalba of triumphing over her either with Olimpia or with Carmine or with anybody else. There was no point in telling people how much she had drunk, how much her frock was torn, what bad language she had used, what open improprieties she had committed, because none of these tales could be repeated to her. She was gone.

Lulu had forgiven Carmine, and what was worse her mother seemed disposed to accept his suit seriously. Infatuated herself more completely by Janet Royle than she had ever been infatuated by anybody the Countess could not bother any longer about arranging a good match for Lulu. Besides, the war had changed things. If Lulu was set on marrying a chemist's son, what did it matter provided such a young man had prospects? And Carmine had prospects. He left Sirene to take up his post as assistant-manager of that new hotel in Rome with every reason to suppose that it now rested with him and with him alone to win Lulu. It was most irritating to see how happy Lulu was.

Nor was Janet Royle's preoccupation with Hermina de Randan anything except an annoyance. Rosalba was bored to death with Janet herself; but that was no reason why Janet should be so obviously contented with somebody else. It was all against precedent in her emotional life.

The sight of Madame Sarbécoff making the best of her paltry shop was displeasing. She had never had any satisfaction out of Anastasia Sarbécoff, not even the satisfaction of feeling that she was more hurt by Hermina's infatuation with Janet than herself.

And Cléo? It had been amusing to see Cléo's wrath when she had sympathized with her over the suspicion under which she like so many others lay of the theft at the Villa Eolia. It had been amusing to see her face when she had assured her that, whatever anybody else might think or say, she at any rate should never believe in her friend's guilt. But Cléo had told her she was not her friend, and Olga amid bubbles of ridiculous indignation had slammed the door of that poverty-stricken villa in her face.

But the greatest failure of all was Olimpia. The gate of the Eolia had been closed against her. No letter that she wrote was answered. And Bébé Buonagrazia who was supposed to have come to Sirene for the pleasure of her company had openly advised her in Zampone's not to bother Olimpia any more, because she had quite made up her mind not to see her again.

"Does she then perhaps think that I made the thief in her house?" Rosalba demanded.

"*Je ne sais pas. Peut-être*," Bébé had replied with that laugh of hers which tinkled and pricked like broken glass.

There was indeed only one person left with whom she had not failed. That was Rory. To be sure, they had quarrelled on the night of the party, and Rory had not sent any word begging for a reconciliation. But she had only to go up and be charming for five minutes. Rory would succumb at once. She was only sulking in her own undignified clumsy fashion. But she did not intend yet awhile to give Rory the satisfaction of condoling with her over her other failures. On the contrary, Rory must be punished severely before she was, if ultimately more convenient, forgiven.

The summer visitors were all gone. The big dining-room of the Hotel Augusto had recovered most of its stateliness and tranquillity. Even Rosalba under the pressure of that noisy horde which had thronged the place for the last eight weeks had received less attention from the head waiter. He had done his best to hover round her lightest wish; but the insistent wealth of the profiteers, the demands of the Neapolitans and

Germans, the jam of tables, the din of orders and clatter of plates, the hurry and confusion had prevented his being always at her service. And now peace had come back to Sirene in this rolling rain-washed blue and white October weather.

The canvas of the clouds was full set; all day long with easeful majesty they breasted their azure main. Mellow the sun, ripe the air, bright green the budding spurge on the cliffs; at twilight the sharp scents of earth again. Richest of months October everywhere, but nowhere so rich as in the South when age is dying in golden dignity and at the same hour verdant youth is being born. And people in October seem to have a plenitude of leisure no other month can allow them. It is then that we apprehend what Horace meant by his praise of *aurea mediocritas*, in this well-balanced month when nights are not too short, nor days too long.

And it was at lunch on one of these benign and just October days, at a special lunch which the Augusto cook had so much enjoyed preparing and which the head waiter was getting so much pleasure from serving, that Rosalba announced her belief in Rory's guilt. In the clamour of August or mid-September such an accusation would have seemed inspired by the garish and fidgety moment. It would have been contested, supported, argued over in the same excited way that eating, drinking, sleeping, bathing, driving, and swimming were being carried on. It would probably have seemed unreal and certainly trivial. But in this atmosphere of blessed calm such an accusation had a horrible weight. It was impossible to suppose that anybody would thus affront a friend unless from her heart she believed her guilty and resented the suspicion which had been cast so lightly all around. Yet Bébé Buonagrazia, heiress of too long a civilization to be ingenuous where human emotions were concerned, inheritress of too ancient an urbanity to be affected by atmosphere, protested immediately.

"You say that, Rosalba, because you want to keep Olimpia in Sirene. *Mais elle n'est pas une verre que tu sauras épater, ma petite*. She thinks no more to remain in Sirene. Whatever you can say or do, she will go from here to-morrow."

"I speak what I speak because it is true," Rosalba declared.

"From when have you commenced that pretty habit?" the Princess asked. Then she turned to her fellow guests—Olga Linati, Cléo Gazay, Hermina de Randan, and Janet Royle. "Olimpia has quite forgotten what has happened on the night of the party. And she is a woman great enough to wish that it may remain for ever a mystery. *Dunque basta, cara Rosalba*."

"Because you are Principessa Buonagrazia I do not permit that you speak to me with such impudence."

The head waiter seeing Rosalba's flushed face feared for the merit of the last dish.

"*Non Le piacciono le melanzane?*" he enquired anxiously, offering to remove the dish of egg-plants fried with cheese which none of the guests had tasted.

"*Si, si, sono buone*," said Rosalba, dismissing his solicitude impatiently.

"*Pardon, signorina.*"

"It is not because I am Principessa Buonagrazia, but because I am a woman that I speak so to you, Rosalba."

"*Archifemme d'ailleurs*," Rosalba sneered.

The other guests watched the duel in silence.

"I would like more to be *archifemme* than to be *mezzosignore*," the Princess stabbed.

"I can insult as well as you," Rosalba cried. "Be careful, *ma chère*."

"I am so sure that you can, *ma petite*, for I have just now heard you insult what was for you a good friendship."

"I must be sincere even if it is against my friends."

The Princess raised her eyebrows.

"What you must suffer, my poor Rosalba, for I am sure that sincerity is terribly painful for you."

"I believe that it was Rory who has gone to the Villa Eolia that night. Why does she not show herself at all no more in Sirene? You have not heard what she has said to me that night because she was jealous of Olimpia. I cannot blame her. Poor woman, she was of course entirely out of her mind. It is terrible for me to make her a criminal, but it is better for me to do so than to hear Cléo accused, or Olga, or Anastasia Sarbécoff."

"I tell to you, Rosalba," said the Princess, "that you are just a little fool to speak as you speak now. You will never take Olimpia for yourself. She does not even find you at all beautiful. If we are to be sincere it is better that I am sincere with you. You could never have taken Olimpia for yourself. You have done all you could, if that is at all a consolation. But you are not her style. *Ti consiglio come un'amica.* Forget about Olimpia as she has already forgotten you and about what happened on the night of the party and as to-morrow she will forget about Sirene. A small flea can perhaps disturb a beautiful dream, but it is the flea who is forgotten."

"*Allora tu mi chiami pulce?*" demanded Rosalba in a rage.

"*No, cara,*" the Princess drawled. "*Pulcinella piuttosto. Allora mangiamo.* I must be quick because Olimpia and I shall go with the boat to-morrow afternoon, and there are always my trunks to pack."

Rosalba stood up in her place at the head of the table.

"Principessa Buonagrazia," she said grandly. "I have made a sacrifice of myself to find the truth. But I cannot be insulted. I will not lower myself to eat no more with you because I would choke myself with disgust for your vulgarity."

With this she walked out of the dining-room.

"And I thought the comedy was quite finished," laughed the Princess.

"I find that Rosalba becomes very insignificant when she blows herself out to be big," said Hermina de Randan.

"Yet she *had* a great deal of charm, a really quite extraordinary charm," Janet Royle commented. "But this year she seems to have coarsened somehow. You know, I don't think she has any sense of values," she added, relapsing languidly into one of the easy phrases of current intellectual cant.

"*Elle finira mal*," Cléo growled. "*Pourquoi tu pleures, Olga?*"

"*Je ne sais pas.* I just am crying *senza ragione. Ou peut-être c'est pour la vie qui passe. Non so. Povera Rory*, it is terrible for her; and it is also a little terrible for Rosalba I think."

A silence fell upon the table, and, it seemed, over all the big dining-room, for there were very few other guests, and they talked only in fragmentary murmurs hardly as insistently as the two or three flies buzzing against the panes that were warmed by the mellow October sun, hardly as loudly as Olga's occasional sobs that she stifled in her napkin.

CHAPTER TWENTY

"Ατθιδ' οὔποτ' ἄρ' ὄψομαι
>> J. M. EDMONDS from a '$\psi$' of Sappho.

*For I shall never see Atthis again.*

IT had not been easy for Rory to allow a fortnight to go by without sending a message to Rosalba. There had been moments when the impulse to fling herself headlong from her own Leucadian promontory had been nearly too much for her. She had leaned right over the parapet of the terrace and studied the sheer face of the cliff as carefully as if she were proposing to scale it from below. And then one afternoon she walked out by herself to see how the white peacocks were getting on and found a pair of grubby bedraggled birds in the cage she had provided for them. The peasant put in charge had not been neglectful. It was just that they evidently could not endure being shut up together behind wire. Their snowy plumage was smutched, and the radiance of their pride was turned to the stale white of an old dust-sheet. The decline of their beauty had been gradual through months of captivity ; and Rory looking back at the wreck of her friendship perceived that it too had gradually been falling to pieces a little more irremediably every day.

The only person Rory saw during this fortnight was Daffodil. She had been alarmed by the first news of the outrage at the Villa Eolia, for until Daffodil was able to assure her positively of Rosalba's complete innocence, it had been seeming just the kind of reckless folly she might commit. The relief she felt made her more kindly disposed than ever toward the absurd young man.

On the afternoon before she was to leave the island Olimpia, much to Rory's surprise, was announced as a visitor.

" May I use your piano for a few minutes ? " she asked.

Rory, thinking vaguely that it was rather an odd visit, made haste to raise the great harp-shaped lid. Olimpia threw back her white cloak and crashed out a series of such terrific discords that Rory wondered whether the musician had been driven mad by the problem of her secret enemy or whether it was that she herself had already been living too long away from Paris in this lucid southern air to appreciate any more the cerebral convulsions of modern art. Then the discords gave way to a little austere melody, the kind of little austere melody that one might hear in the music of César Franck. It was brief. The discords crashed again, after which Olimpia turned round on the stool and said to Rory :

" Did you ever read all the fragments of Sappho ? "

" I've read them in a French translation, I think."

" You don't know Greek ? "

There was nothing hybristic in the way Olimpia asked this, and Rory answered with a simple and humble negative without feeling she was being put in her place.

"The fragment I had in mind only consists of four words, μάλα δὴ κεκορημένοις Γόργως. Some grammarian preserved it to illustrate that particular genitive form. It means 'being quite fed up with Gorgo.' The colloquialism translates the Greek perfectly. I have set most of Sappho to music, but it had never occurred to me to bother with those four words. What I played you is the music I have had in my mind driving up this afternoon and which I have just played for the first time."

"I appreciate the compliment," said Rory rather fatuously.

"Gorgo was, as far as we can make out, some kind of rival poetess, but there is no reason to suppose that this crumb—it hardly deserves to be called a fragment—has any reference to her verses. I feel myself she must have been in Mytilene very much what Rosalba has been here."

Whatever Rory might have suffered herself from Rosalba she was not going to sit quietly under another's criticism of her. In a flush of indignation she began a hasty defence.

But Olimpia turned round to the piano again and began to crash out those discords above which her voice rang out chanting strangely, "μάλα δὴ κεκορημένοις Γόργως." Having silenced Rory, she faced her again:

"At lunch in the Hotel Augusto an hour or two ago Rosalba announced her conviction that it was you who made the rather feeble mess of my room on the night of your party."

"Me?" Rory gasped.

"And as I am going away to-morrow afternoon I wanted to assure you that I am as positive as I am of sitting here that you did not go near the Villa Eolia that night. I have not told you this with any idea of hurting your feelings. It was inevitable that somebody would tell you sooner or later what Rosalba had said, and I should not care to have you think I believed such a stupid calumny. I wished to make that perfectly clear before I went away. I think you are a very stupid woman. I think all women are stupid who imagine themselves artists when they are all the while nothing more than sexually starved. I think that your poetry would be just as good if you sat at a desk and screamed at the top of your voice. I do not think that in essentials your poetry differs from a screaming fit. At the same time I do believe that you are genuinely abnormal, and though I look in vain for any single masculine quality in your mind I do not believe that your ridiculous style of dressing is adopted for effect." Olimpia left the piano-stool and pulling her cloak round her again she intently surveyed Rory, who fingered her monocle and longed to be sure that it would remain in her eye if she put it up to rebut this uncomfortable stare. "Stay," said the little woman with the burning glance. "I do recognize one masculine quality in your mind. I recognize that your infatuation for Rosalba approximates to the self-deception of the foolish middle-aged man. I recognize in you the symptoms of the buffer. You probably suppose I have tried to take Rosalba away from you. I cannot be bothered to argue about that. You should have enough intelligence to grasp the state of affairs more clearly. Perhaps after what Rosalba said at lunch you will. I do not propose to provide you with a character of that intolerable young woman. Nor am I in the least anxious to give you the impression that I am trying to defend or to justify my own behaviour. I merely wanted to give you an opportunity of numbering yourself among those κεκορημένοις Γόργως. Good-bye. Such a delightful party. I enjoyed it as much as anything in Sirene."

"Who *do* you think broke into your villa?" Rory found herself asking as she escorted Olimpia Leigh to the door.

"I haven't the slightest idea. That is why I am not going to buy a property here. The classic perfection I seek can never be achieved in the squalor of an unsolved mystery. If Mytilene had not been defiled by a Genoese castle and the detestable excesses of Turkish architecture I might live *there*. And I have thought sometimes that perhaps in Epidauros . . ."

She broke off to step into her carriage and without looking round she departed from Rory's ken.

When she was back in the studio Rory allowed the lid of the Steinway to fall from its full height, thereby achieving a noise beyond the power of any of Olimpia's discords.

"The idea of my being so soft as to ask that damned woman who she thought broke into her beastly villa! Why, she must have thought I believed . . . my God, but perhaps Rosalba did accuse me! Perhaps she really did! Or have I been mesmerized?"

377

"*La signorina Linati*," Francesca announced.

Olga came babbling in hotfoot.

"Oh my dear, I am so sorry that I have not been to see you before, and now Cléo and I are going to-morrow. She will come also in a moment, but she has waited to speak a moment with Olimpia Leigh."

"Do you know what she has just told me?" Rory asked solemnly.

"About what Rosalba said? Oh, I am so glad she has told you, because all the way up I have been saying now to myself yes to tell and now yes not to tell, and I have been in such a bother. You can feel how red I am. I have been so upset. I was crying when Rosalba said it for you. They have said it for me and Cléo, *ma noi ce ne infischiamo*. But for Rosalba to say it for you, *che schifo!* I tell you really that I am so glad to be going back to Rome. And I am really very happy, because with the commission I have taken for letting the Villa Eolia I have bought some quite beautiful material, and I think I will make a very good profit with my work this winter. Everything now is so expensive. It is so difficult to find the money to buy the material. I have so many orders, but I am always using what I make for one dress to buy the material for another. It is really quite difficult."

"You support your whole family, don't you?" Rory asked.

"Well, I must, because my father cannot make money and my mother does not see very well now, and my grandmother is quite in bed. She is now quite in bed for all the summer. So it has been a little difficult for me. Ah, here is Cléo, and please we must not stay, but say only good-bye and how sorry we are. *Cléo, Olimpia avait déjà rapporté. . . .*"

"*Elle m'a dit*," Cléo interrupted brusquely. "I want please now to walk once more upon your terrace," she muttered, turning to Rory.

And in the golden-lighted afternoon she looked out in a long silence across the bay, still herself in the transuming air as a form carved from honey-coloured travertine.

"I speak nothing please about Rosalba," she said. "And now we go."

But in the entrance, when Olga had hurried away first, Rory called Cléo back.

"Tell me something, please," she begged. "Is it true Olga cried when Rosalba said that about me?"

"Yes, yes, she was crying at lunch."

"And she is finding it difficult, isn't she, to get hold of a little money to buy her stuffs?"

"She is poor like a rat," said Cléo.

"Well, would you . . . could you, without offending her at all, persuade her to borrow . . . it can be a loan which she can pay back when she likes . . . I thought that two thousand francs might be useful."

Cléo took the notes, scowled heavily at Rory for a moment, then shook her hand.

"This money is very good for her," she growled.

"Well, but don't give her the notes till you get to Naples. I am in such a silly state of nerves that I really couldn't be thanked or even know that anybody wanted to thank me."

"You are sad for Rosalba?"

"Well, it has been rather a shock."

Cléo nodded, scowled again, shook Rory's hand again, and strode after Olga.

As for Rory she retired to bed. A grand passion had turned into a bad headache.

Olimpia Leigh and Bébé Buonagrazia left Sirene by the early morning boat at half-past four. So did Cléo Gazay and Olga Linati. So did Madame de Randan, Lulu, and the Royles, who were going to stay at the Villa Castalia until Mrs Royle went to America on business and left Janet to spend the winter at Stabia.

When Rosalba awoke she found a note from Rory:

*Even after what you said at lunch yesterday about me, if you want to be friends again I will be friends. But this really is the last time I shall make an effort to preserve this friendship of ours. Come to lunch.*

*Rory.*

Rosalba read the note through twice before she dropped it over the side of the bed. With her hands enlaced under her bronze hair she lay back on the pillow to watch a small prism of reflected sunlight slowly quiver across the ceiling. When she had made the accusation yesterday she had not really believed at all in the justice of it, but after Rory's note she felt perfectly sure that she had been right; and in a short while she was lying back in a state of amazement at her own acuteness. To her the note sounded like a frightened admission of guilt. She jumped out of bed in a happy conviction that at last she had something to compel Olimpia's interest. What a triumph she should have over Bébé Buonagrazia when it was proved that she was right after all! In her black and white pyjamas she stood before a mirror to receive from the image of herself within the felicitations she deserved. And to make the critical visit that was to keep Olimpia in Sirene or ensure her leaving it in her company she hesitated between navy blue and dark brown tailor-made. In the end she chose the blue. It was the severest turn-out she possessed. Before going out of the hotel she sat down in the lobby and scrawled a hasty ink-speckled answer to Rory's note:

*I cannot come to lunch because I must see Olimpia so that she will not do anything about that terrible business. I shall try to make her do nothing, but I hope that you will write to her and say that you are sorry. I shall certainly go with her in the boat to Naples this afternoon and perhaps afterwards where she wants me to go. I think Paris might be very nice in October.*     *Rosalba Donsante.*

As she was on her way to give this note to the head porter for prompt despatch to the Villa Leucadia she was intercepted by the postman with a telegram. It was from Françoise, her grandmother's maid:

*Venez mademoiselle est très necessaire vous venez aussitot possible madame est gravement malade*

Rosalba paused. Here was an obvious escape from further humiliations. Should she not be prudent to cross to Naples by the same boat as Olimpia, bid her a dignified farewell, and hurry to Lucerne? But Rosalba all her life had invented so many urgent reasons for going and coming and staying that a real reason no longer presented itself to her mind as credible. Everybody would think this illness of her grandmother was another excuse. Besides, why should she fail to conquer Olimpia now that she was so well armed? She tore up the telegram, and, lighting a cigarette in a long holder of satiny blue enamel, set out to the Villa Eolia.

"*La signorina Leigh?*" she cried buoyantly to the *colono* who was tidying the vines on the upper terrace.

"*È partita stamattina.*"

"*Col vapore?*"

"*Sissignorina.*"

There was a moment when Rosalba nearly turned to the left as she came out of the gate of the empty villa—a moment when she was on the verge of going directly up to Rory and asking her to come with her to Lucerne. But the belief in her own invincibleness was still too strong. She could not bring herself to surrender so feebly. Françoise had always been an alarmist. This absurd faith-healer woman whose influence over her grandmother she so much feared was only an American crank. Anyway, she could not go to Switzerland until she had made one more effort to see Olimpia. Why should she not persuade Olimpia to come with her to Switzerland? Optimism flooded all her being with the radiance of a victory already won. And if she had had any doubts about the wisdom of her course she had none when she got back to the hotel and learnt that she was practically alone in Sirene except for Rory and Anastasia Sarbécoff in her wretched little shop. She was filled with rage at the idea that all these women whom she had fed and feasted, loved and left, should have plotted among themselves this public humiliation of her. Did they think to lunch together in Naples this afternoon and laugh over her discomfiture? Did they perhaps count on her following in the afternoon boat only to find that she was alone in Naples and they already on their way to Rome?

Pursuit yes, but it should be a pursuit in the grand style, and she gave orders to charter a large motor boat which would reach Naples long before the afternoon express left for the north. A valise would be enough. Nor was she sorry to leave her luggage behind, because her bill at the Augusto was now many thousands of liras and she should require all the ready money she had left from her grandmother's last cheque to scatter in the whirlwind of her departure. Yet, she had a feeling that it would be long before she came back to Sirene; and in the same spirit with which she gave fifty-lira notes to people who had been able to do nothing more for her than smile when she wished them 'good day' she felt that she must leave something behind her for Rory.

"Poor old Rory," she said to herself, and turned aside from the farewells in the Piazza to visit the office of the *maresciallo*. To him after a cordial handshake she confided that it was not Rory who had committed the outrage in the Villa Eolia. The *maresciallo*, who had never supposed it was, looked a little puzzled. Then she pulled him close and whispered that it had been the Signorina Leigh herself who had done it.

"*Davvero?*"

"*Sicuro,*" she declared. "*Allora, a rivederci e mille ringraziamenti.*"

"*Sempre a Suo servizio,*" he gurgled as he wrung her slim boyish hand in his pudgy fist. She vanished from the musty office in butterflies of waved farewells, and the *maresciallo* sitting down again at his desk muttered to himself with a shrug of his fat shoulders:

"*Delle donne non si capisce mai niente.*"

So in the end Olimpia was credited with having committed the outrage upon herself. Yet she was as innocent as Rory. Who did it? Nobody ever solved the mystery. And its solution has no importance nowadays, because that kind of outrage could not possibly occur on a Sirene that wears the clean pinafore of the new régime.

The letter from Rosalba announcing that she should leave with Olimpia on the afternoon boat was brought up to Rory before noon.

"*La signorina non sera ici per collazione,*" she told Fortunata dully. And five minutes afterwards she rang the bell.

"*Moi aussi non sero qui per collazione. Date fromaggio, pane. Mangio fuori.*"

"*Ma dove mangierà?*" Fortunata enquired with a touch of contempt in her voice.

"*Sopra a Monte Ventoso.*"

Rory was feeling that unless she planted herself on the highest point of the island she should never have the will to remain inactive at home while Rosalba went away. She should find herself hurrying down into Sirene to beg Rosalba not to go; she should squander in an instant all the dignity she had been amassing during a fortnight of silent withdrawal up at the Villa Leucadia. Not that she would have minded sacrificing her dignity if by doing so she could have won Rosalba back. But this scrawled note in answer to her last desperate appeal, in acknowledgment of a forgiveness that surely few women could have brought themselves to offer, was too final. Besides, if already it had been blazed over Sirene that she had made hay of Olimpia Leigh's room after receiving her as a guest in her own house, it would look as if she were afraid, as if in begging Rosalba not to go away she was really trying to propitiate her.

"After all, damn it, I am English," said Rory aloud, stretching out her hispid chin at this wash of golden southern air and defying its fragrance by lighting up the strongest cigar she had.

And it was with a profound consciousness of being English that Rory strode up the long rocky diagonal that gradually mounted the flank of Monte Ventoso, grasping an alpenstock with one hand, a packet of bread and cheese with the other. She was pestered for some of the way by various bands of very ragged and very dirty children who wanted to guide her to the summit, and who when she refused them this gratification wanted her to accept the limp bunches of crimson cyclamens they had been gathering in the copses. And their pestering fed her Anglo-Saxon consciousness. Those whining reiterated cries for *soldi* and cigarettes sustained her. She derived a genuine pride from her unmistakably English appearance, though yesterday she would have felt hurt at being mistaken for a tourist. When she came to the end of the diagonal and followed the steeper path that climbed in a spiral among the boulders of limestone she flung behind her a dozen coppers and was left in peace. The boulders gave way to a tract of heather and cistus, out of which here and there rose a stunted pine-tree, leading in a gradual ascent to the summit two thousand feet high. Here still clinging fast to her English origin Rory sat down with her back to the wall of what was left of a small circular fort, which had been erected by the French when in the days of Napoleon they had driven the English out of Sirene. But that did not disturb Rory's national conscience. The view before her spanned too much of history, offered too much of beauty. Trojan and Goth, Roman and Greek, Oscan, Norman, Spaniard, Angevin, Saracen, each in his turn had left a sign and a legend of his passage. One could no longer be English. One could not even be a citizen of the world. Time alone was here one's country, where the windless gold of this October day diffused a richer peace than Rome's. The mountains and the sea, the temples of Pæstum, the snowy cloud above Vesuvius, the goddess and the hero who gave their renown to promontories and received from them a long commemoration, the shimmer of famous towns round all that coast, the white villas of to-day, the brown ruins of yesterday, the old plainsong of the husbandman chanting at his toil upon the stony hillside, the tinkle of goat-bells, the chatter of Sirene reaching this stark height like the thin voice of the air itself and mingling with the deeper murmur of late industrious bees—all were fused up here in an eternal now : time and space, the works of man, the might of nature. Pompeii was not more dead, Naples not more alive.

While Rory sat munching her bread and cheese the importance of Rosalba's elopement began slowly to diminish. The ache of disappointed love was assuaged. *All are at one now, roses and lovers.* She repeated over and over again Swinburne's line. She was old enough to be affected by his music. *All are at one now, roses and lovers.* And as she munched and munched she followed with her eyes the course of a small boat speeding over the bay. She was thinking how in another two or three hours the steamer would be carrying Rosalba away from Sirene. She did not know that in the very boat she was watching Rosalba was seated far up in the bows, her gaze fixed on Naples, nor that Rosalba was turning continually to ask how long before they would make the port. The course of the boat that Rory watched had for her no more significance than the flight of an insect or vagrant wafting of a dandelion's plumy seed. Yet while she watched this boat her mind turned toward the problem of Rosalba's future. What would become of her?

Sitting up here and munching her bread and cheese with her back against the warm stones of that old French fort, Rory was aware acutely enough of the finality of the parting to imagine the life of petty emotional adventure which lay before Rosalba. The girl she loved was already a woman in whom she would perhaps at last not even be interested. She was quickly apprehending the painlessness of separation once it is effected. The last fibre of Rosalba's being had been plucked from her heart, and she was still here, breathing in the benign sun of this great blue and white October day. Her memory travelled back to that October day in the Parc Monceau three years ago. She had changed the whole appearance of her outward life for Rosalba's sake. She had suffered the pangs of jealousy, the torments of unrequited love, the bitter and fugitive content of requited passion. To the world she had presented herself as a figure too ridiculous to be tragic, too prosperous to be pathetic. But had not that been the effect she must always have had for the world? She was not likely to seem more foolish now than she had seemed before. That was the curse of abnormality, its dependency upon success. Nobody laughed at Olimpia Leigh, because she was successful. Yet what did success ultimately matter? *All are at one now, roses and lovers.* Foolish she might be, but not so foolish that she could not let her folly rest for ever at peace with the follies of two thousand years.

How complete one felt, and how secure once the separation was made, as if a stream flowed round one, forbidding access and cooling the fevered air and creating a small comfortable world in which one sat and munched bread and cheese with such a heightened relish. She had climbed up here to fly from the temptation of a last appeal to Rosalba's decency. Only an hour ago she had still been terribly vulnerable;

and now she had no more pity for herself. Away over there from Africa the tears and moans of Dido had reproached Aeneas all the way across that same silver-sheeted sea, and over there across that same azure gulf Aeneas had cried vainly for his lost helmsman. She had no pity for Aeneas or Dido or the drowned Misenus, no pity for Agrippina struggling in the waters of Baiæ, no pity for any of the figures infamous or splendid or obscure whose pains and griefs and thwarted hopes for centuries were all at one now with the rosemary and the thyme. How could she still pity herself? A lizard came close and paused to regard her, his throat palpitating. She threw him some crumbs, and he darted off. That's what she had been doing to Rosalba, Rory thought. She had been trying to feed a lizard with bread-crumbs.

A drowsiness came over her. The sun up here was strong as wine, and she had in fact drunk half a bottle of amber Sirenian. She slept; and she woke to hear the steamer hooting the signal of departure. She did not know that Rosalba had arrived in Naples an hour since, and that she was receiving at this very moment a message in the lobby of the Grand Hotel Eruzione to say that Olimpia could not see her. She did not know that she would receive the same message again in Rome and again in Florence and again in Paris. She did not know that old Baroness Zaccardi would die, without seeing her granddaughter again and that Rosalba would be disinherited in favour of a woman whose parvenu creed had brought consolation to a dying cynic as illogically as a philosopher made bald by thought might be granted faith in a new hair-restorer. She would hear nothing more about Rosalba for a long time, and then only vague rumours of her in cities far from Sirene. She did not know that Rosalba would cease to be a precursor and that her boyishness would presently be blurred by myriads of post-war girls affecting boyishness. And, most mercifully of all, she did not know that within a year or two Rosalba would shingle that bronze hair and by doing so become in appearance a perfectly ordinary young woman. All this not to spoil the drama of the moment was hidden from Rory. She could thrust forward her chin, and clench her fists, and listen to those hoots as if they were veritable muted trumpets sounding for love's funeral.

"There she goes out of my heart," Rory informed the golden-pale October afternoon, unaware that there was not a single human being on board the steamer whom she knew even by sight. "Thank goodness I had the strength of mind not to make an ass of myself in the end!"

So long as Rory remained on the summit of Monte Ventoso she was able to recognize her own wisdom. It was only when she came back to the snowy loggia and sat staring at the closed door of Rosalba's room that the sense of completeness and security she had gained from the knowledge that all was finally at an end between Rosalba and herself began to desert her. So much of this house had been an attempt to express and become and provide for Rosalba's personality. This loggia had been built for them both as one builds